Caroline Seebohm is the author of *The Man Who Was Vogue* (1982). She lives in Princeton, New Jersey.

By the same author

The Man Who Was Vogue

CAROLINE SEEBOHM

The Last Romantics

GRAFTON BOOKS
A Division of the Collins Publishing Group

LONDON GLASGOW
TORONTO SYDNEY AUCKLAND

Grafton Books
A Division of the Collins Publishing Group
8 Grafton Street, London W1X 3LA

Published by Grafton Books 1988

First published in Great Britain by
George Weidenfeld & Nicolson Ltd 1987

Copyright © Caroline Seebohm 1986

ISBN 0-586-20004-5

Grateful acknowledgment is made for permission to reprint
excerpts from previously published material:

'Sea Fever' by John Masefield, from *Poems* by John Masefield.
Reprinted by permission of The Society of Authors as the
literary representative to the Estate of John Masefield.

'Coole Park and Ballylee, 1931' from *The Poems of W. B. Yeats*,
edited by Richard Finneran. Reprinted by permission of A. P.
Watt, Ltd on behalf of Michael B. Yeats and Macmillan
London Limited.

'We'll Meet Again' by Ross Parker/Hugh Charles. Reproduced
by kind permission of Dash Music Co. Ltd. Used by permission.
All rights reserved.

Printed and bound in Great Britain by
Collins, Glasgow

Set in Times

To my mother and father

Prologue

ALICE

I went back to Oxford recently. I had not been
back since we all left, almost twenty years ago.
That's too long to leave a place that matters to
you, unless you are a sucker for punishment. I
was surprised how little, geographically, the city
had changed. Of course I was not a child when I
went up (at least not physically), so did not
encounter the experience, so often described in
literary memoirs, of everything looking so much
smaller than remembered from childhood's van-
tage point. But although there were new buildings everywhere, and the main crossroads at
Carfax had been widened into a shopping centre,
the landmarks of St John's (where I once fell off
my bicycle), the Randolph Hotel, and the Ash-
molean remained in place. I walked past the
Taylorian, now fitted with chic storm windows,
past the Randolph, where one of Oxford's more
exotic postwar products, a young theatre critic
named Kenneth Tynan, once admired my friend
Penny Coverdale's legs. I looked back to the

corner of Pusey Street, where there had once been a Wimpy Bar, unpromising first trysting spot of our most passionate, if ill-matched, couple, Daphne Fanthorpe and Alan Moss. The Wimpy was gone, and in its place stood a Burger and Pizza Parlour, its name written in ornate Elizabethan script. Alan would no doubt have found that politically significant.

I turned left down the Broad, passing a woman who looked uncannily like my old tutor – only frighteningly aged and in a wheelchair. On the wall of Balliol College hung a plaque I had never noticed before: 'Opposite this point,' it read, 'in the middle of Broad Street, Hugh Latimer, one-time bishop of Worcester, Nicholas Ridley, bishop of London, and Thomas Cranmer, archbishop of Canterbury, were burnt for their faith in 1555 and 1556.'

For the first time I thought of Edmund. He might have liked a plaque: 'In this place Edmund Wales, most promising man of his generation, drowned for his faith in 1977.'

He didn't drown in the middle of the Broad, of course. He drowned in the Irish Sea. And I was not quite sure how to define his faith. Unless you called his obsession with Louisa Better a faith. A secular faith perhaps, but more respectable and consistent than anything the rest of us could come up with. And, like most faiths, totally out of step with the rest of the world, which is why, I suppose, like those poor bishops, Edmund had to die for it.

I walked on past Blackwell's, where Alan Moss and his leftist friends stole books about once a week (as a political statement, you understand). Then on towards the Bodleian Library, whose Roman emperors on their huge columns had been restored since my time; the endearingly chipped noses now sported proud Roman nostrils. (Which reminds me of a memorable conversation I once had with Daphne's mother, during which Her Ladyship told me that her least favourite word was *nostril*. 'And *tube*,' she added after a moment's thought. I could only come up with *menstruation*, but it did not seem quite suitable to mention.)

On I went, past the Radcliffe Camera and across the High into Merton Street, whose cobbled surface had been invoked for generations to restore unmarried maidens' peace of mind. Penny, our most active representative in this department, was far too efficient ever to have taken this bumpy road to salvation, but Daphne, after her deflowering at the hands of the leftist Moss, insisted one January that I keep her company while she bicycled madly up and down in the freezing cold. I suggested that gin would be a more agreeable remedy, but luckily by

February things had returned to their normal cycle. Whether Merton Street was responsible for the miracle we were never sure.

I was now approaching Oriel Square, and the back entrance to Christ Church. Oriel, whose undergraduates were considered of inferior quality during our three years there (such were the hierarchies within the confines of Oxford itself), now struck me as one of the most elegant of all the colleges. 'Regnanto Carolo,' I read over the architectural jewel of a gate, recalling its historic origins. But I turned my back as I had so many times before and walked through Canterbury Gate into Peckwater, the eighteenth-century quadrangle whose beauty went almost entirely unheeded by those of us who tromped through it on our way to various cocktail and other assignations. I stood in the middle of the square, hearing old voices, remembering old scenes. Was it on that staircase the mysterious Indian Maharajah, who played such brilliant cricket, had his rooms? Was that where Sykes and Sweeney gave a party with only water to drink, and everyone got paralytic anyway? Looking round now at the graceful proportions of the buildings, so ordered and peaceful, I had difficulty imagining the wildness, the barbaric nature of those parties, those years. Here, after all, some of the greatest minds in history had lived and worked. Here Edmund studied, read, and talked to Gerald, and here, at the Christ Church Commemoration Ball, he fell in love with Louisa.

I read in the newspaper recently that female mud wrestlers were the high point of last year's Oxford Commem. A full-sized ring had been erected in the quad and covered with eight barrels of mud from a nearby building site. Two Apache princesses (that is, two large women wrestlers from Liverpool) fought three rounds for the amusement of some nine hundred black-tie undergraduates and their friends, who then danced till dawn. There were protests afterwards from outraged women's liberation groups.

'Do you think we would have been outraged?' I asked Gerald.

'Of course not. You weren't liberated.'

Lack of liberation was not our problem, however, I thought as I made my way through Tom Quad, past the statue of Mercury where undergraduates got ducked from time to time, and out through the main gate. Not in the literal sense, anyway. We were hardly kept behind bars, except for our first year, when we all had to live in college and obey a curfew. That was the astonishing good luck meted out to the four of us, the chosen ones. Paradoxically, our ungated quarters were perhaps the single most important factor in the cementing of our friendship.

I had not particularly looked forward to revisiting Somerville. First-year memories did not flood my heart with warmth. But as I arrived at the Woodstock Road, I was suddenly overcome by an urgent call of nature. Where better to answer it than in my old college, where at least I knew exactly where to find a WC? Charmed by the symbolic aspects of this unexpected turn of events, I went through the gate, now free of eagle-eyed keepers, and walked purposefully through the grounds.

There were some new buildings in the Garden Quad, but no mistaking the gloomy Victorian façade of Penrose, to which I smartly repaired. Remembering the bathrooms on the second floor as vividly as ever, I put my hand on the distinctive oval-shaped wooden handle with perfect confidence. On the inside of the door hung a sign which read, *Please use the other loo between 10:30 P.M. and 8:00 A.M.. Or do not flush!* This last exhortation had inspired another anonymous stanza, *Quelle horreur!* The college belles-lettristes had clearly not improved much since our day. As I pulled the chain (I was safe, it being two o'clock in the afternoon), a metallic din rang out, as though Alberich had suddenly jolted the Nibelungs into a frenzy of hammering. It would have woken Brünnhilde from her magic sleep, let alone the poor undergraduates in Penrose. I did not recollect such problems with the waterworks, but then the plumbing had been considerably younger then.

I made a short detour to look at my old room, and Daphne's next to it. The names of the present occupants were in their slots on the doors, and I felt a momentary pang of recognition as I remembered those first odd months before the four of us aligned ourselves as a unit. There is no stranger experience than living through the first days of school. The only way to bear it, as I tell my son, is to remind oneself that it cannot last. The newness becomes old – until the next time. Perhaps never having to go through a first day on the job ever again is another way of saying life is over.

I walked back to the main gate and stepped through the arch out into the world again, just as the four of us had when we moved into Bardwell Road for our last two years. I don't think then we had the faintest thought that we would remain friends forever. Such notions of eternity were as alien to us as monogamy to Bluebeard. Sentimental claptrap, Penny would have called it. She was always the realist among us. Perhaps that is why, after her unlikely marriage, she is now, while still a devoted mother, determinedly single. And, as sometimes happens with unmarried women of a certain age who have enough money to buy beautiful things, her sexual life, which once far outstripped ours, has been sublimated into auctions, dealers, the hunt for treasures.

I suppose much of life is a question of sublimation. At least for many people. Louisa would not agree with that. She spends her life refusing to sublimate anything, which is both exhausting and ultimately unsatisfying. Even Edmund's death, which so wrenchingly involved us all, made no impression on her. By which I mean that in all her subsequent romances and affairs, Edmund was right there, intrusive, reproachful, mocking. Even after all these years, she can't let him go.

'It's all your fault, Alice,' she accused me once, 'for marrying Edmund's best friend.' I refrained from pointing out that at least my marriage endured. I say that not with pride exactly, for I do not believe that a lasting marriage is so much a triumph of the personality as a calculated hypocrisy. Gerald and I were lucky enough to stumble on a solution to the usual boring marital difficulties, the recipe being if you enjoy eating together, almost all is forgiven. The shared enthusiasm for a pot of Beluga caviar, a steak au poivre, a chocolate soufflé – these bind a relationship more strongly than sex (fickle at the best of times), intellect (apt to provoke competitiveness), or family obligations (obligatory). The most hostile person becomes benign over a Château Talbot; the most politically conservative turns liberal over a fettucine Alfredo; the most emotionally unstable is serenity itself over a tarte aux pommes. Is this sublimation, my dear Louisa, or is it wisdom?

Penny, Louisa, Daphne, and I were recently invited to a Somerville gaudy, one of the big ones occurring every ten years or so. My feeling was that we should go. Daphne was in America, trying to get pregnant with her tennis-playing millionaire, Parker Ferris. (She assured us that things picked up considerably after she started seeing a fertility doctor. Parker was apparently enchanted by their new regime of lovemaking by the clock, his 'invasions' timed to the second just like Field Marshal Montgomery's campaigns.) Louisa was in New York, living for love (a pursuit somewhat slowed down, one suspected, by encroaching age), while her children, as Edmund would have wished, continued their boarding-school education in England. Both Penny and I were in London. (Gerald and I had decided to move back when Bert's best class at PS 186 in New York turned out to be a crash course in mugging.) All of us could have made the trip easily enough.

They were apprehensive about the idea. They feared reminders of Edmund, and of even worse things – their lost innocence, unfulfilled dreams. But this is your life, as Eamonn Andrews would say. It's crammed in a book and you can't change the story. It's all you've got, I told them. It's more than we had when we started out at Somerville. In spite of everything, at least there is a story. And what's more, I argued, even if our careers have taken a slightly different form from those envisioned by our tutors, we can at least claim we have finally received an education.

LOUISA

Somebody once said that seventy-five per cent of all Englishmen are homosexual until they are twenty-five. In Edmund's case, it was probably longer. The trouble is, I was married to him. For some women, it might not have mattered. Alice, for instance, must have a very low (or is it high) sex threshold, being married all these years to Gerald, who was Edmund's old school chum and bred in the same mould. And since one presumes that public-school boys make up most of that percentage, we should, after all, have expected it.

I just wanted something different, that's all. I wasn't going to have one of those bloodless marriages with everyone having affairs on the side without rocking the boat. I know a man who has been in love for years with the wife of the man he plays golf with every weekend. She cooks his meals every Saturday night after the game. Yet these two lovers go on enduring it, week after week, with no more emotional fulfilment than is contained in 'pass the salt, please.' What on earth is the point of such a life?

'Few people realize the tomblike silence in which most Englishmen spend their lives. Their education trains them to silence, their marriage system encourages it, their belief in physical exercise makes intellectual silence easy.' Hugh Walpole said that, a man who must have known. Perhaps he went to Oxford. Go back to that place again, which started me on my hopeless road with Edmund? Alice must be bonkers.

DAPHNE

I have an old photograph of the four of us, taken by Edmund at a cricket match. He gave it to me, much later, in New York. Funnily enough, at that time – it must have been our last year at Oxford – we all looked very alike. Blurred, unformed faces, featureless, no identities. Just four young women, squinting self-consciously against the sun. The camera never lies. Looking closer, one can see beneath the cotton dress a clue to the voluptuous bosoms for which the old Penny was famous, and which Freddy Weathering made his own. They were roughly the same shape that Louisa had made-to-measure for herself in America a decade or so later. No breast on me; not much of a spine either, then. Mind you, women who complain about breastlessness are often disingenuous. I have never wanted breasts that jiggled and wiggled and got in the way of a good game of tennis, particularly now when I am really working on my game with Parker. Nor would I want to end up with them

19

looking like the ones so brilliantly described in a novel I once read, sagging down 'like empty hot-water bottles.' It certainly never stopped men making passes. Not even Alan, who regarded my body as essentially bourgeois.

Louisa did not find this to be true, I suppose. Hence her self-improvement. She would look very different now if we had another photograph taken. But then, so would we all. It might be worth going back to Oxford just to see. To take our measurements. Only who could we ever find instead of Edmund to record the results for posterity?

PENNY

Running one's own business is immensely satisfying. I suppose I have always run things, but
until now my own name has never been on the
top of the letterhead. I ran our lives at Oxford, I
ran Freddy, I ran my children, but only now do I
get the credit – loved for myself alone and not
my yellow hair (brown, actually, with threads of
grey). Penelope Coverdale, finally in control.
How awful it sounds. Some dyke-lady in a tie,
pulling strings to make people jump. I wonder if
they all think that of me now.

Louisa has become so remote from me, living
as she does on her permanent emotional roller
coaster, and yet once our lives were inseparable.
Daphne is in her latest incarnation as a Long
Island Virginia Wade, and Alice – well, Alice
was always more preoccupied with her irregular
bowel movements than our various psychological states. She was good for us all the same.
Otherwise we would all have dissolved in oceans
of sentimental claptrap. It's ironic that she is

21

the one now who wants us all to go back to Somerville.

Edmund is the one who would have loved the idea. He was the one who insisted on our friendship, courted it, encouraged it, held it together. We were all the same to him, with Louisa as the figurehead, the Loved One, embalmed in a kind of Oxford Forest Lawn. The trouble is, we fell for it. For a lot of the time, anyway. If we hadn't, the end might have been quite different.

Part One

1

ALICE

We called the Bardwell Road Four, not for any
political affiliation – in those days, a sit-in
meant you were taking too long in the bathroom
– but because there were four of us, and unlike
most of the other female undergraduates who
lived out their nine university terms inside the
formidable keep of the college building, for our
second two years, owing to lack of space in
college, we lived in unorthodox freedom in a
house in Bardwell Road, a thoroughfare whose
only claim to immortality was that one passed it
on one's way to Blenheim Palace.

We had met during our first term at Somerville over dinner in Hall, where, until we knew
better, newcomers gathered together to eat stew
and soggy vegetables under the eagle eyes of our
tutors seated at High Table. I don't think this
was to assess our table manners, but rather to
impress upon us that passing the entrance
examination into this august institution should
in no way give us ideas above our station.

I noticed Penny Coverdale first. It was impossible not to notice her, given the surroundings.
She had brown eyes, a peachlike skin, and an
aura of luxury that made her stick out like an
azalea in a cabbage patch. She had obviously not
spent most of her adolescence studying for
exams in tiny back rooms over shilling-in-the-
slot gas fires and flickering light bulbs, the lot of
most women who succeeded in getting into
Oxford. The word was that Penny had already
had a passionate affair with some kind of Ruri-
tanian Prince. Since his name was Rupert, he
lived in St Moritz, and he wrote her letters (we
all checked each other's pigeonholes) in a florid
purple hand on coronet-studded stationary,
there was little room for doubt. In those days,
such an authentic past aroused the most feverish
admiration.

Penny had another advantage; she came up to
Oxford with a friend and thus was not subjected
to new-girl-itis. The friend was Louisa, whose
father was the famous George Better, coach of
the English football squad. Louisa had enormous
grey eyes and reddish brown hair and was very
skinny, a condition she regarded as terminal (no
one had yet said, You can never be too rich or
too thin), but which gave her an intriguing
quality of frailty, particularly when she was
with her awesome father. The Coverdales had

moved from West Hartlepool to Weybridge on
the proceeds of a new fortune in tractors, where
they became neighbours of the Betters; Penny
and Louisa had gone to school together. During
dinner in Hall, they would sit together and
loudly discuss the new undergraduate arrivals
who came in alone and palely loitering, thus
causing some attention and a great deal of
hostility.

After a few weeks of this, Penny invited
Daphne Fanthorpe to join them for meals. This
meant having me along, since Daphne and I had
joined forces since our arrival for the simple
reason that our surnames began with the same
letter (Daphne Fanthorpe, Alice Fugate), hence
our rooms in Penrose were next door to each
other – this accident of alphabetical geography
pairing us, so to speak, for life. It turned out
that we also shared boarding-school experiences
and debutante seasons. Daphne's, however, was
on the grand scale, since her father was a lord
and her mother a determined hostess. She had
her own dance at the Dorchester, parties every
night, a hundred long dresses, and photograph
in the *Tatler* by Lenare.

My family, untitled and impecunious, could
not stretch to such extravagances, but felt I
should learn the trappings of my class. So they
mustered up a few country-house weekends for

me, which I spent huddled in my room wondering when I should go down to dinner, and then enduring a few dances with chinless wonders who trod on my toes and dripped sweat into my ear. After a few months of this, my father went into his long decline (too many impractical inventions such as self-cleaning Wellington boots and cork wasp-crushers), and we had to retire to Warwickshire where if you didn't ride a horse you might as well have leprosy. So that was the end of my social debut.

Later, I realized why Penny selected Daphne to join them. Daphne had the class credentials that might interest a tractor-heiress from West Hartlepool. Most of Penny's Oxford career, after all, was concerned with upward mobility. At the time, her choice seemed merely aesthetic. Daphne was far and away the most beautiful girl of our year. She had that type of transparent skin people claim is English, with blue eyes, huge lashes, a straight nose, and a soft, cushiony mouth. She also had 'it', as our mothers used nervously to call it, and was the state of the art in flirtatiousness. Owing, however, to her convent-school education and strictly no-nonsense series of Nannies, this powerful impact was entirely without follow-through, a fact hard for the opposite sex to grasp. A friend from New College once told me a Daphne story that perfectly typified her frustrating qualities. He took her out several times, during which, encouraged by her alluring looks and inviting mouth, he made discreet attempts to embrace her, all of which were sharply rejected. He continued to pursue her until, after a final, desperately aroused lunge on his part, she turned to him and said crossly, 'Really, Geoffrey, you're only doing it to annoy me.'

What a 'stiffie' meant to Daphne was a wonderfully thick invitation card, heavily embossed, suggesting cocktails, lunch, or dinner in someone's rooms in Christ Church, Magdalen, Univ, and so forth, their architectural glories taking second place to the scintillating company. At the end of Daphne's first year, when most people were grateful to have a few invitations to sherry with one's tutor, the pile of stiffies on Daphne's mantelpiece must have denuded several Canadian forests.

The sex ratio at Oxford at the time was five males to one female – a heady statistic. The irony was that in those days most of us were unable to take advantage of it. As far as the women went, if they did not come from upper-class protectionism such as Daphne and myself, or middle-class puritanism like Louisa (Penny being a splendid exception), they came from determinedly working-class families and had

clawed their way into England's most presti-
gious university (we never considered Cambridge as anything but distinctly second-rate) by
dint of hard work and exceptional brainpower.
To waste such an opportunity going to cocktail
parties or mooning over the Worcester punters
was tantamount to treason. For most female
undergraduates, in short, enlightenment
remained limited to the eighteenth century.

Penny, Louisa, Daphne, and I were not excessively burdened by any moral or scholarly
responsibilities. What made the bond between us
stronger than mere recognition that we were
perhaps the most 'visible' Somervillians of our
year was attributable to our different enthusi-
asms. Penny was the only sexually liberated one
and therefore an instant magnet to virginal ex-
public-school boys who wanted to practise. Louisa
was politically sophisticated, perhaps owing to
living with a father who survived by reason of his
negotiating skills, and her verbal dexterity
inspired late-night conversations with the Union
debating society hopefuls, as well as admirers of
soccer, a game played by proles but acceptable to
intellectuals. Daphne was the darling of the
social and theatrical crowd. I collected poets, biol-
ogists, and hypochondriacs. This meant that the
competition between us was virtually non-

existent, a considerable advantage in female relationships.

For our first year we drank a lot of tea and rode bicycles to our various lectures and parties. Lectures were amusing at first, since they provided a good opportunity to see a large number of one's fellow students from all the different colleges assembled in one room. But the novelty soon waned, and we limited our lecture appearances to those requiring obligatory attendance, or those which were fashionable that term, regardless of subject matter. I remember one term I suddenly started learning about the motifs in Wagner's operas because the lecturing professor was currently modish. I had clevely decided to read Law, a discipline not known for its intellectual demands, and an agressively male preserve (only two women took Law my year), so the brilliantly staged entrance of yours truly into the Bodleian Library on Tuesdays and Thursdays had an invigorating effect on the male students huddled over their books. Notes were passed in an endless stream ('How about coffee at the Cadena?' 'What are you doing at lunchtime?' Do you want to come to a party at St John's tonight?'), and one's lids positively drooped with exhaustion after so much eye contact with the various suitors.

Penny and Louisa had similar experiences in

their libraries (Penny was reading English and Louisa Politics, Philosophy, and Economics), and we would compare notes (literally) over tea and crumpets. Daphne very rarely went to the library. She was reading Geography, the bottom of the intellectual barrel, and her studies were approximate. The effort of carrying books hither and thither failed to ignite her enthusiasm, and anyway there was no need. Her name had already spread far and wide in the various taverns frequented by the other sex.

'Who is this?' Penny would say, waving a card around as we all opened our mail in clouds of anticipation.

'Jock MacDonald? He's the Earl of McBaine,' Penny said, already a walking *Burke's Peerage* from her encounters with Old Etonians. Louisa groaned.

'Really, Penny, you *are* getting disgusting. She used to be all right, you know,' she explained to Daphne and me.

'I didn't get the invitation,' Penny pointed out.

'I did,' Daphne said. 'And the point is, should I go?'

'What's it for?'

'Dinner at the Bullingdon.'

Nobody turned down invitations to the Bullingdon. 'But he's bound to be boring,' she complained. 'Those Scottish types always are. I bet he's got red veins in his nose.'

'But they have wonderful castles,' Penny said.

'You wouldn't really like them,' I assured her. 'Freezing cold, only one bathroom that's about a ten-hour walk from your bedroom, no hot water when you finally do get there. I'm sure I got my fibrositis from staying up there once. And it's always pheasant for dinner and conversation.'

'I like pheasant,' Penny said.

'All right, Penny,' I said. 'Let's send you instead.'

So we did.

While Penny pursued Scottish aristocrats, Daphne met her first Americans, a nationality that was to play an important part in all our lives. There were always Americans at Oxford, or Yanks as they were called by people who called England Blighty. The Americans at Oxford were usually Rhodes Scholars, who in our day spent most of their time rowing, earning the title, needless to say, of Rowed Scholars. Their rowing, rather than their scholastic contributions, made them legendary. During our first year, American oarsmen caused a revolution in the Oxford Boat by introducing a new way of handling the oars. This was the kind of thing Americans were expected to do, of course.

But it did not make their suggestions any more palatable to the English crews, who had been trained under the sterling, if conservative, leadership of Bodger McCloud, a man whose taste for the new did not extend beyond potatoes. Oxford watering holes buzzed with the crisis, for rowing, something you would never do again, was typically Oxford's major sport. There was the inevitable confrontation, a putsch took place, Bodger was removed to the Yacht Club for some consoling Tall Ones, and everyone thought the whole thing amazingly bad form. It did, however, have the effect of making Oxford win the Boat Race that spring for the first time in living memory, thus muting everyone's disapproval.

Daphne was thrown into this excitement bow first, so to speak, by meeting a Rowing Blue from this famous winning eight during our first summer term. We were all frightfully jealous, except for Louisa, who had had a surfeit of exposure to muscular specimens owing to Life with Father. The Blue was huge, rich, and very confident, and his name was Cliff Honeywell.

'Cliff,' we said as we watched her put on a kind of pink knitted stocking to go out to dinner with him. 'It could have been Hank, perhaps. Or Chuck. Or Steak.'

'He's got a car,' Daphne said.

It was difficult to find undergraduates with

cars. In fact, the only ones with wheels were Americans, who could afford it, or cripples. The advantage to both these minority groups was that with them you could be taken to eat somewhere other than the usual dreary local joints.

'I wonder what he's reading,' Louisa said.

'Rhodes scholars don't read,' I said.

Daphne sighed. 'I hope it won't be boring,' she said.

'Americans are never boring,' I told her. 'They are so incredibly healthy. Just look at his teeth.'

Daphne failed to take my advice. She performed her usual Mata Hari number, rousing Cliff to the highest pitch of carnal lust with her pink knitted dress and her pink knitted mind.

'What are your fantasies?' he asked her over vichyssoise at the Bear in Woodstock where he had taken her in his shiny Jaguar.

'What?'

'What do you fantasize about in bed?'

Daphne drew a blank.

'Don't kid me. Everyone has fantasies. Don't be inhibited. Tell me.'

'Everyone does?' She looked at him doubtfully. 'Oh, dear,' she said at last, trying to be conciliatory. 'I'm terribly sorry. All I can think of is Alice snoring next door.' (This was a wicked lie. I do not snore. I sometimes have slight respiratory difficulty if I lie on my back, but the doctor told me it was hardly audible.)

Honeywell began to get annoyed. 'Look,' he said, 'I'm only trying to get you a little more relaxed. I really think you're great, you know. What do you say we just forget the meal and go back to the car.' He put his great hand on her small one.

'Don't be silly, Cliff,' she said in her best Nanny voice. 'I haven't had dinner yet.'

'You know what?' he snarled. 'I think you're just like all the other English girls I've come across in this goddamn town. You're just a little pricktease.'

Daphne stood up, threw down her napkin, walked out of the restaurant, and hitchhiked back to Bardwell Road.

'He was right, of course,' we said, feeding her biscuits since she had made her exit before the Dover sole.

'He had an incredible neck,' I added. 'It went straight up into his chin. All cartilaginous fibre.'

'Well, what on earth was I supposed to say?' demanded Daphne. 'What sort of fantasies do you have?'

We looked at each other and then expectantly at Penny.

'Each to her own,' she said irritatingly. 'Read *Lady Chatterley's Lover*.'

'Flowers and John Thomas?' Daphne asked. 'Is that what he meant?'

'At least,' Louisa said, 'you might have made up something to last you through the Dover sole.'

'Grilled to perfection,' I murmured ecstatically, 'with oceans of butter and lemon.'

Everyone groaned.

Imagine. There we were, the most educationally advanced representatives of our sex, surrounded by the greatest resources Oxford could provide, and all we could get excited about was fish.

DAPHNE

It was easier to talk about fish than sex, and frankly, compared to all those Oxford blokes, I found fish warmer-blooded. It wasn't that I didn't try. I wanted Penny's looks, for starters, and I attributed her looks entirely to sex. In books one read about ripened fruit and all those gardening metaphors; well, when one looked at Penny one knew at once Life was once more imitating Art. Rubens in particular. She seemed to radiate a kind of warmth that made

37

the rest of us look like uncooked shrimp, all blue and veined. We all envied her her Knowledge. Well, we were eighteen, which in Shakespeare's time would have taken us long past motherhood, and here we were, rambling on about John Thomas.

It was not, of course, quite so innocent. Exposure of one sort or another had indeed taken place. My first was the unnerving sight of the largest, reddish sausage I had ever seen, protruding from a sort of black casing between the legs of the local horse on the farm where we sometimes spent our summer holidays. I stared at it, knowing it was somehow Important, but revolted by its lurid colour and crude shape. This did not augur well. Nor was I reassured by a very different sight, many years later, of the scrawny chicken-neck produced from the trousers of a dinner-jacketed escort at a deb dance, after we had sunk on to a chintz-covered sofa in the library for a bit of a rest. I was so disgusted by his pale purplish part that I hardy had to feign sickness to be excused from the chintz, returning, outraged, to the safety of the slow, slow, quick quick slow.

These organic extremes seemed to me to have no connection with the only other contribution I can offer towards my sex education, which occurred in the sixth form at my boarding school.

During the summer term (I must have been sixteen), I developed a crush on the gardener, whom I watched with devoted languor as, stripped to the waist, he dug the flower beds and mowed the lawn. When by chance I thought he caught my glance, I dissolved in a fluster of heated delight.

Armed with these inauspicious experiences I arrived at Oxford, where the game began in earnest. Compared to most of the bookworm types who had worked hard enough to gain entrance to that most exclusive of institutions, my looks were in my favour – just as Penny's, Alice's, and Louisa's were. Do not suppose it was just me. But I spent most of my first year fending off tense undergraduates whose lips and knees pressed against mine as I attempted to escape through the gate at Somerville before curfew. Most of them at the beginning seemed as deeply suspicious of these exchanges as I was, and I would watch them tank up on whisky or wine at dinner in order to pluck up courage to go through this consistently embarrassing performance of storming the citadel, while I tanked up too in order to muster the strength to remain unstormed. It always puzzled me that in spite of my defensive successes they continually wished to try again – the triumph of optimism over experience, like a gardener planting agapanthus in Alaska.

Penny would have been the person to talk to about this, for although it was often funny it was also rather mysterious. But I was afraid she would laugh at me or think there was something wrong with me. She had this power over me at the beginning. I often wonder what would have happened to us all if Penny hadn't chosen us, the way she did, that night in Hall when she picked us off with the precision of a fairground rifle shooter, and down we went, ping, ping, ping, like tin rabbits. Gosh, she was powerful then. In the ghostly procession of chilled females, carrying plates of fish cakes to their places, Penny, her eyes big and brown like Marmite jars, watched us with a sort of mocking amusement as we went through the ritual of sitting down as far away as possible from High Table, avoiding everyone except those of our own year, hoping against hope that a body, anybody, would sit next to us and not leave us back in the old nightmare of being the most unpopular girl in the Upper Third.

I was afraid of her even after we became friends. She was so competent. I always admired people who could do things well, like play the piano or sew quilts. My best friend at school could read in three languages and sing in four. I was brought up to do nothing well. That was the point. Doing nothing well was an art, my mother used to tell me, as she dressed for dinner. Anyone can buy a Balenciaga, she said. But wearing it well, that's an art. That's why she sent me to Oxford. 'Then you'll be just a teeny bit different, Daphne darling,' she explained. 'And as you go through life, you'll see how useful that is.' My mother was different all right, and so was Daddy. I think she was afraid that deep down, I was a mouse. Well, I was, really – like one of Daddy's field mice, scrabbling about in a box in his study, trying to get out. My mother was not a thinker, but I desperately admired her certainties about life. Like Penny, you see. Ping, ping, ping.

2

ALICE

At the end of our first year, having somehow
scrambled through prelims, we were fortunate
enough to be assigned rooms outside college. (By
this time, even the administration knew we
were a movable feast.) It was no great wrench to
say goodbye to Somerville, an architectural dud
of a building situated on the fringe of town, as
though symbolizing women's apologetic appearence in the all-male groves of academe in 1879.
Somerville's main advantage was that at least it
was within earshot of gaudy nights; the other
women's colleges were mile off in the suburbs –
a devastating bicycle ride for late-night carous-
ers anxious to beat the clock home, and a daunt-
ing journey for weary escorts trailing back at
midnight to Merton or Queen's. Somerville had
the reputation of attracting the most intellectual
women (our inclusion doubtless being the exception proving the rule), while Lady Margaret
Hall, like its name, was the most social. St
Hilda's, St Anne's, and St Hugh's, three obscure

saints, were shrouded in spinster-like anonymity. How we loved to exploit these artificial hierarchies, strutting in our class superiority, a microcosm of the country outside. 'What college,' one would be asked. 'Somerville,' we would drawl, watching arrogantly for that twitch of suppressed surprise, quickly followed by respectful recognition, that would cross our interlocutor's face.

Each of us had her own room in the Bardwell Road house, which was a Victorian pile with eaves and peeling drainpipes, depressingly familiar to those who had spent much of their adolescence in boarding institutions. Louisa's and my rooms were on the first floor, furnished in parental eclectic: cast-off sofas, the odd cushion with horses on it, a table with a typewriter, and the other necessities of a student's life. My mother drove me up from London to settle me in my new lodgings, crying a lot (I was an only child), carrying some of my old books (including the indispensable *Black's Medical Dictionary*) and stuffed animals that she had always longed for me to love but which I had always hated. 'Your father,' she told me wetly (he was in Holland at the time, investigating an artificial tulip), 'wanted you to have this.' She handed me a silver cigarette lighter. Knowing my father, I flicked it open with trepidation, and sure enough, there was a fist with a boxing glove where the flame should be. 'Never forget your uncle and your great-aunt both died of cancer,' she said. The fact that one was leukaemia and the other ovarian did not diminish the parental anxiety at my potential demise via the lungs. Still, I shared their interest in my health, and was grateful.

Daphne's room was the most eccentric. On the attic floor, it had been draped in strips of damask stolen from the Fanthorpe linen cupboards, and a few Fanthorpe heirlooms such as a moose head and a badger trap decorated the narrow walls. Lord Fanthorpe, whose career was devoted to the study of the natural world, in particular burrowing animals and birds with acute sensory powers, wanted her to take a tame bat up with her, but Daphne had told him she would forget to feed it. Her mother apparently put a stop to it in the end, telling her she would have to find insects and worms for its meals.

Louisa's room was the prettiest, decorated with provincial prints and lace, mostly chosen by her mother, Mary Better, the poet. George had given his daughter an extravagantly framed photograph of himself surrounded by the 1956 English World Cup Team, full of signatures and footballs. 'How can you bear to look at all those knobbly knees and baggy shorts all day?' Daphne demanded, peering at it. Louisa, as usual, took this to be an attack on her father. 'Better than unloved stuffed animals,' she said furiously.

Penny's room was our best receiving room. She had real pictures by real artists on the wall, a record player, and on the bed a wonderful antique quilt found by her mother on some fund-raising trip to America. We watched in impressed silence as the Coverdales drove up in their Rolls Royce to distribute their daughter's equipment. Noticing she had nothing on the mantelpiece, they rushed out to some shop and bought her a sweet little Ming vase. 'Blue and white is so cheerful, isn't it?' Mrs Coverdale said in a broad northern accent. The Coverdales also stocked her up with real grown-up drinks like whisky and gin, instead of the half-bottles of sickly Spanish sherry we kept for appearances. In those days, undergraduate entertainment in one's room depended heavily on tea and crumpets.

Our afternoon salons at 55 Bardwell Road became famous. Part of their charm depended on the erotic promise offered by Daphne, and the erotic satisfaction offered by Penny. Louisa and I were merely wallpaper. But our desirability lay also in the novelty of visiting four under-graduettes in almost total freedom from procto-rial jurisdiction. Our landlady was only a little older than her tenants, and suffered from a permanent cold (not surprisingly in view of the amusingly named heating system). She had two children under two, a husband doing research in Central America, and a faulty boiler. She had made her house available to Somerville purely for commercial gain, so concern about four extra women in the place did not come high on her list of priorities. Sinking into an exhausted, rheumy sleep as soon as the elder toddler had ceased his nightly crying jag, she was hardly likely to care at which time we, or our visitors, came or left the house. So our guests, liberated from their own historic chambers, could forget their responsibility to thousands of generations of scholars, and behave like normal cads and rapists.

It was Penny who first brought Edmund Wales to 55 Bardwell Road. As a collector of persons (Daphne and I being only the first in a long line of Coverdale acquisitions), it was inevitable that sooner or later she would lure Wales into her parlour. He was as famous in his way as Daphne was in hers. Edmund Wales was that sacramental combination, Eton and Christ Church. Eton and Christ Church still summoned up the same sort of emotions in the English breast as, say, 'God Save the Queen,' or 'Is there honey still for tea?' Those melodious names, joined in a marriage as elegant as Fortnum & Mason, as stylish as Gilbert and Sullivan, and as historically sound as Victoria and Albert, purveyed the aroma of breeding more strongly than the fox's scent, which I have heard can send properly trained hounds into a perfect frenzy of ecstasy. ('The nice thing about going to Eton,' Edmund's school chum, Gerald, told me once, 'is that one knows people afterwards who live in the most splendid houses.')

Edmund Wales was not the only undergraduate with Eton and Christ Church after his name. But he was the only one who was expected not only to get a double first, but also to become a member, nolo contendere, of All Souls. His cleverness was what originally made his reputation. Awards, prizes, contributions to the various publications and Union debates confirmed the rumour that he was the cleverest undergraduate, not only of his year, but possibly of all years. Add to this his looks – tall, pale, willowy, with strange green eyes and a long mouth that curled at the edges – and you have someone worthy of Penny's attention. Yet I have still not finished his list of virtues. He was also a sportman, could play a fiendish game of tennis, run a mile in just over four minutes, and keenly proselytized the game of baseball, a sport of such theoretical opaqueness to most Englishmen that his support of it only compounded his impact upon his contemporaries. He had learned baseball while spending the summer with some Americans abroad, and his enthusiasm for the sport baffled those who knew, deep in their hearts, that the only game worth even considering for more than two minutes was, of course, cricket.

Penny invited this paragon of academic and physical perfection to tea, along with his friend and inseparable companion, Gerald Glynn, another Etonian, towards the end of the spring of our second year. This may sound late, but Edmund was in his third year as a Greats scholar, and Oxford etiquette was such that one did not mix with other years until well established as a second-year student oneself. We almost collapsed at the news of his imminent arrival; intellectual brilliance was not our strong suit, and we hoped Louisa would be on her best form to keep things moving. She and I lurked in our first-floor rooms until we heard the familiar clumping of feet signifiying the arrival of guests in Penny's suite, then hastened up after them.

'As a hypothesis, I would like to present this possible evaluation,' Edmund was saying, a teacup poised on top of his knee, which was clad in white flannels, showing a little Old-Etonian-blue sock. He was wearing a beige linen jacket; a beige cashmere scarf was slung loosely round his neck. Nothing remarkable in any of that, you may say. But this was long before the 'English look' became a designer's trademark. Edmund was the real thing. (I never saw him look in a mirror, but some people simply don't have to.)

'In the past,' he went on, nodding briefly at us, 'parents looked to their extended family of grandparents, aunts, uncles, and lifelong friends for assistance in child-rearing. Parents turned to these trusted persons for advice on how to handle particular child problems, and how to organize family life to run smoothly. More importantly perhaps, the extended family rendered valuable feedback and advice on standards of acceptability for children's social behaviour.'

'Now that's all gone down the drain,' Penny said inelegantly, holding a crumpet to the electric fire with a silver toasting fork.

'The modern family finds itself separated from friends and relatives. Our society is becoming more mobile, and more families are living among neighbours with whom no adequate support has been established.'

'The Fanthorpes haven't moved for generations, and I haven't a clue who our neighbours are,' Daphne piped up.

'Rural areas do not comply with these findings in such detail,' Edmund answered with a tinge

The Last Romantics

of impatience. 'What we have to do is canvas the relevant population to determine the extent of the dilemma and degree of interest in obtaining a solution.'

A silence fell. We all watched Penny spread the hot crumpets with butter.

'There's a debate at the Union,' Gerald explained kindly. 'That parents are unqualified child-rearers, or something like that. Edmund is speaking against the motion.'

'Against?'

'Inadequacy does not necessarily imply lack of qualification,' Edmund said, again with that edge of irritation. 'We have to approach the subject systematically. A priori psychology is little less futile than a priori philosophy.'

Most of the tea went like that. Edmund talked like Isaiah Berlin, Gerald occasionally interpreted, Penny, Daphne, and I uttered inane noises. Louisa did not talk at all, to our fury. When everyone had had two cups of tea, and all the crumpets had gone, Edmund and Gerald said they had to go to a discussion on the Place of Pessimism in Nineteenth-Century Thought in All Souls Library and did we want to come?

After they had gone, we had some more tea (I sometimes saw my poor stomach as a teapot, stained brown, with tea leaves at the bottom arranged in patterns of direst doom) and held a

50

postmortem. The overall impression was favourable, in spite of his tendency to arrogance.

'I didn't understand a word he said,' Daphne volunteered. 'It was madly exciting.'

"He's very beautiful,' Penny said.

'Did you think so?' Louisa asked. 'He was – cold, somehow.'

Penny piled up the Meissen tea plates and put them on her Georgian silver tray. Penny always had things you could identify by name – Wedgwood, Chippendale, Picasso . . .

'Well, he's obviously a virgin,' Penny observed. 'He didn't exactly radiate sex appeal.'

'Oh, didn't you think so?' Daphne asked. 'With that mind? I think minds are incredibly erotic. Look at Bertrand Russell. People like that are so wonderfully sure of themselves. I'd just like to listen to them all day.'

'Bertrand Russell had lots of women,' Louisa agreed. 'Do you suppose they all fell for his mind?'

'He dropped them, too,' Penny reminded us. 'Woman as Distraction, like Venus for Tannhäuser.'

Penny had been going to the trendy Wagner lectures, too.

'Well, do you want him, Penny?' Louisa asked.

'Daphne does,' Penny said.

51

'Only his mind,' Daphne said dreamily. 'You can have him from the neck down.'

'What strange priorities,' Penny said, shaking her head. 'Let's go to the flicks. I think *À Bout de Souffle* is still on.'

'What about Gerald?' I asked. But nobody had noticed Gerald except me.

LOUISA

It was me, dumb, too-thin Louisa, whom Edmund started to invite to dinner. Lunch, then dinner, then other dinners, then, to top it all, the Christ Church Commem.

Why did Edmund pick me? I have gone over and over it, starting with that first tea in Bardwell Road. Why single me out then? Penny was sexier. Daphne was more beautiful. Alice was funnier. And I didn't even open my mouth. None of it made sense. I didn't even really find him attractive. Not then. I thought he must be vain, wearing such elegant clothes. Undergraduates didn't look like that. And he talked too fast. Never let anyone get a word in. And if you analysed what he said, a lot of it was absolute rubbish. Oh, he could talk well, of course. He had the knack of forming perfect sentences with

perfect dependent clauses and perfect parenthe-
ses, and placing them in perfectly formed paragraphs with perfectly formed endings, so that
the competition was left speechless. It was his
grasp of logic that made him able to do this. He
was a brilliant logician. So his arguments
always sounded foolproof even it logic was not
what the subject required. I think even at that
early date I was suspicious. But he was so
confident, so damn arrogant.

And he was wonderful-looking. I suppose I had
grown up with the kind of course, stocky male
type that played football, and that is what I was
used to. This fluid, etiolated figure was truly
fascinating to me. You could almost see through
his skin to his long, Giacometti-like bones. But
that was about it, as far as I was concerned.

The truth was, I was interested in someone
else, someone quite different, someone I never
mentioned to the girls, because it sounded so
juvenile. I knew the silliest people fell for their
tutors, and there were all sorts of psychological
reasons for it, God knows. But I was secretly in
love with my senior tutor – Professor Borianov,
the great political scientist, who was at least
thirty years older than me, and anyway was
happily married to the perfect wife, Lady Diana
Blackwood.

I could imagine Penny's scornful laugh. She

knew me so well. We had almost grown up
together. She was sure I had the most terrible
father complex. Just because Dad and my
brother always went to games together, leaving
me at home with Mum, she thought I felt
neglected and unloved. She thought I was
always trying to get his approval, by doing well
in exams, getting in to Oxford, all that. Things
my stupid brother couldn't do. But he could play
soccer, of course. That's what really counted to
my Dad. I don't deny it. But that had nothing to
do with my falling for Boris Borianov. I'm sure
of that.

So when Edmund invited me to the Christ
Church Commem that summer, I couldn't have
cared less. I wish I had. Everyone wanted to go
to that dance. It was the ultimate party that
year. One would have really felt a failure not to
have been there that night. People went to
inordinate lengths to be invited. Girls were
imported from London, twittering with excitement to be among the academic elite of the
country, while we looked down on them with the
supreme superiority Oxford fostered so successfully. Christ Church, beautiful under any circumstances, was transformed with lights, bands,
and the subtle aura of pent-up romance. Men in
dinner jackets and girls in fabulous dresses
floated through the glorious cloisters; the

ancient panelled rooms rang with champagne glasses and laughter; the indulgent sky unveiled a thousand stars over the dreaming spires. People were sick in a thousand flower beds.

And I was there with Edmund. Lucky you, I could hear people think as we wandered through people's rooms sampling champagne and oysters. He knew everybody, he was greeted like a king, and I was treated with the respect due the royal companion. I liked that. Who wouldn't? Edmund too treated me with respect, rushing about getting me champagne, anxiously enquiring if I was enjoying myself, discoursing on the phenomenon of an all-night party. I struggled to keep up with his brilliant references, his quotations of poetry, his literary allusions. At one point, I looked at his broad, pale brow as though to penetrate its encyclopedic memory, and noticed a small pulse beating just below the hairline. For an awful moment I imagined that there was a machine inside, turning over and over, marshalling relevant facts and spewing them out like the teletypewriters I used to watch as a child when I stayed with my mother at the Lansdowne Club. Tick, tick, tick, tick, went the tiny pulse. The weather tonight will be cold with rainy spells, tapering off towards morning . . .

Lucky Louisa, everybody thought. Lucky Louisa to be with fabulous Edmund. How many girls would have loved to be in my place. And what on earth does he see in her? Oh, I knew that is what they were all saying. And all I wanted was to be with Borianov. I saw my beloved professor once that night, looking divine in a dinner jacket, discussing something about the statue of Mercury in Tom Quad with his wife and laughing. I have hated that statue ever since.

3

ALICE

Oxford looked beautiful in the spring, when the walls of the colleges glowed with a kind of Tuscan radiance (Florence, as opposed to Cambridge's Rome), but it was autumn that evoked the memories that were to last. The smell of smoke from burning leaves, the twilight mist hanging over the grim Victorian houses along Bardwell Road, the dampness in the air that seeped into one's bones as one did the rounds of wine-warmed college parties, all permeated our souls with the atmosphere of a period, our third year at Oxford, when we were young and there were no wars and Edmund loved Louisa.

It was the talk of Oxford. Edmund was now president of the Union and a Tennis Blue, as well as being the only person in the history of the university who had been the *Isis* idol twice. He was always the central figure in the rooms of dons and students where his precocious outpourings stunned and stimulated a generation of intellectual has-beens. His radiant good looks counteracted his arrogance; his passionate expression enlivened his dialectical discourse. Contemporaries were aware that they were associated with someone destined for greatness. And all this talent was now focused on our Louisa.

Louisa's father, though a hero to the working classes, was not a great figure in Oxford eyes, so she had escaped the relentless spotlight of the gossip columns of *Cherwell* or *Parson's Pleasure*. It was not surprising that she did not feature in *Isis*, since that magazine, the most serious of the three, was currently in the throes of a coup organized by 'Red' Kittredge and his revolutionary cronies. Red, a riot-loving and demagogic third-year political scientist from Corpus Christi, had kidnapped the rather orotund Old Harrovian editor, Mungo Twistleton-Smith (whose only claim to fame was that his father had been a distinguished fly-fisherman), and swept him into the publisher's office, declaring him unfit, politically a disgrace, and a capitalist tool. This kind of confrontation took place when, approximately every three years, a new generation of Lefties appeared at the University. So the publisher, a retired businessman named Grainger, was unmoved.

'Let Mungo go,' he said to Red and his men. 'Acts of violence do no good in the long run, you know. You are stifling free speech here. Mungo may be a little to the right of Genghis Khan, but as long as I own this magazine, it is my prerogative to choose its editor.'

Since Grainger's position was precisely the point on which Marxist theory hinged, this was regarded as a call to arms, and Red and his Lefties rushed out muttering about controlling the means of production and finding a buyer for *Isis* who would be sympathetic to their cause. As Grainger knew, this would be fruitless. Every three years, the local left-wing millionaires, most of whom lived in comfortable mansions on Boar's Hill, were approached by groups of radicals about buying *Isis*. After these encounters, the millionaires would telephone Grainger and relate the details, which varied little from year to year, and then they would all meet for a gin and tonic at the Randolph and have a good laugh.

But while Mungo was *ex cathedra*, so to speak, it was difficult for *Isis* contributors to activate much material – even *Isis* idols languished – so we had to turn to the others for our scandal. *Cherwell* charted the comings and goings of the Bardwell Road Four with diligence, and Louisa's public appearances with Edmund were carefully relayed to a bored public. *Parson's Pleasure*, the most satirical of them all, had more fun. Having already pilloried Penny, dubbing her the Plum

Pudding (after Little Jack Horner), and Daphne the Meringue ('when you take a bite, it vanishes'), Louisa's love match was grist for their mill. 'The Prince of Wales,' they reported, 'has deserted the lecture halls of Isaiah Berlin to attempt rape upon the loftily bluestocking offspring of England's premier football dynasty. Is this the ultimate union of brain and brawn?'

Louisa took all this very hard, which was silly of her. You would have thought her irritating sense of inferiority would have been banished by Edmund's suit. Instead, it seemed to make it worse. The rest of us, of course, would have been over the moon with triumph. We were jealous, I'll admit it. I think it was connected with the fact that we were all getting a little nervy. It was our third year; we knew most of the people worth knowing, and many more knew us. Stretching ahead was more of the same, and frankly, how many more parties in Peckwater could one really face? There were more sinister entrails which we examined over tea and crumpets late into the night. For instance, we were aware of a new set of Somervillians, not only the year behind us but the year behind that – younger, fresher, prettier. We felt old and used. And at the heart of the matter was, of course, the looming shadow of finals. We all wanted to go down with respectable degrees. A poor third or less was simply too lowering. Sooner or later we would have to come to terms with lectures, classes, books, and thought.

It was Penny, our high priestess, who seemed the most affected by Louisa's romance. They had been the closest of friends, while Daphne and I were relative newcomers. But as is often the case when a man enters the scene, Louisa had become remote and absent, vanishing off with Edmund at every spare moment. We lost the intimacy of our teas, the four of us together sifting through our Oxford days to find the gold. Everyone had expected that it would be Penny who would first discover the treasure. Each term she came back with a new wardrobe of long dresses which she wore to the hunt balls and various dress-up affairs beloved of Oxford's upper-class hearties. Each term she collected a new batch of old Salopians or old Marlburians, their skin still stinging from Matron's harsh dormitory rituals, their minds inflamed with their brief prefectorial power over blushing boy-slaves, their souls anxious to reconcile their Greek ideals of sexual passion with conventional mores. Each term they made the pilgrimage up the stairs of 55 Bardwell Road to Penny's lair, where she made them Earl Gray tea laced with brandy, played Wagner, and drove them to an ecstasy of acceptable pleasure. At breakfast she would look as glowing as ever, but her usual deprecating remarks about the night before were missing. She would ask about Louisa, who was never there, and give a little sigh. Breakfasts became even more depressing than usual, and we would vanish upstairs to our rooms with a mixture of reluctance and relief.

She continued to attend banquets and be taken out to grand social events by titled escorts. But we began to notice a disturbing pattern. Lord Toby or Viscount Haven would squire her around happily for one or two terms, spending time with the Earl Grey and Wagner and carrying her off in vacations to Scottish hideaways, with or without bathrooms. But when it came time for her suitors to leave Oxford and enter the real world, to a man they dropped her for more suitable mates. The upper classes stick to their own, don't you know, when it comes to pleasing Mama or continuing the line. Penny Coverdale was a delectable little morsel to pleasure backstairs, but she was not marriage material for these characters. Tractors and Yorkshire accents made that quite certain. Even at Oxford, harsh reality was beginning to creep in.

PENNY

I suppose I played around more than most
during those three years. I think I was one of
the few women up there who actually liked sex.
I once told Louisa I could get an orgasm just
watching a film at the cinema. She never got
over that. 'A French film, I suppose,' she said
sarcastically. It was true though. I didn't realize
till later that it was quite unusual. Most girls I
knew seemed to have no sexual knowledge what-
soever. I can't imagine what their mothers did
to them when they were fourteen or whatever.
Tied up their hands? Daphne told me that when
she complained of 'tickling' as she put it, 'down
there,' her mother would slather zinc and castor-
oil cream all over it, telling her not to touch and
the cream would make it better. Poor Daphne.
What fun she missed. From then on, I expect
any feelings she had 'down there' were regarded
as nasty infections, to be cured by zinc and
castor-oil cream. No wonder she was frigid.

The trouble at Oxford was that the men were
so weedy. Most of them had no clue about what
might please the opposite sex, if indeed it
occurred to them to think about pleasing us at

all. The thing was to get their rocks off at all
costs, so that they knew they could do it. A few
of them had been abroad before coming up,
which vastly improved matters. An experience
with a foreigner (or, failing that, a local chambermaid) was definitely liberating. The occasional prince of a lover had actually been farther
afield – to Cairo, for instance, the finest education in the world for keen Etonians. How grateful I have been in my time for those unknown
Egyptian sirens who taught their secrets so
thoroughly and so well!

But the girls thought I was looking for a
husband. They saw my constant association with
all these posh blokes as an attempt to marry
myself into a title. Well, I wasn't thinking of
marriage at all, but I did love turning them on.
I remember Gordon St Claire (the future Twelfth
Lord Brackenbury) downing quantities of Bollinger in order to quench his nerves at having to
face me between the sheets, gloomily confessing
that he only liked it 'doggy style.' By the time I
had finished with him he was whooping like a
crane with excitement, promising me Brackenbury Hall and all its contents in return for my
continued services. Power was my aphrodisiac,
to be sure. I never wanted Brackenbury Hall. I
pitied the poor deb who ended up there. (I used
to think how grateful some of them should be to

me, the unknown mistress, for doing their work for them.) But I loved to see these boys respond to my whistle. Florence Nightingale without her uniform, going from bed to bed tirelessly dispensing her cures. But if I'd tried to explain that to Daphne or Louisa, they would simply have thought I was nympho, an accusation worse than death in those days when girls still had Reputations. As for Alice, that Victorian throwback, she would have diagnosed a glandular disorder and recommended barley-water.

4

ALICE

While Louisa and Edmund walked off into the
sunset together, and Penny threw herself at
various unsuitable beaux, Daphne, jaded by
ceaseless exposure to pawing males for whom
she cared nothing, decided to fall in love herself.
And she decided, not surprisingly in view of past
conversations, on a Mind. The Mind she picked
was not your run-of-the-mill collection of brain
cells; it belonged to Alan Moss.

Everyone at Oxford knew about Alan Moss. If
Edmund was the golden retriever of our girlish
dreams, Alan was the lean black Alsatian. Dark,
moody, he had the looks all convent girls
swooned over from reading Georgette Heyer
under the sheets – hooded eyes, cruel mouth,
brooding expression, and so forth. He was reading English at Magdalen, and specialized in
acting, which added to his appeal; I remember a
brilliant Mercutio, a tragic Trigorin. He wrote
witty poems with an undercurrent of exhilarat-
ing cynicism for a new left-wing magazine

founded by Red Kittredge. He was militantly
political, making speeches at Labour Club meet-
ings that were openly subversive. He was our
Byron, prepared to die at Missolonghi.

But it was rather more complicated for
Daphne than that. One of the reasons Alan Moss
was such a cult figure in the posher sections of
Oxford's women's colleges was that he was working-class, a fact that acted like a powerful pher-
omone on the senses of girls brought up in the
cloistered groves of those upper-class institutions located mostly in the southwest of England. Not that he was vulgar, brutish, had dirty
fingernails, or spoke with a cockney accent.
Perish the thought. The Moss parents, in their
wisdom, had sent their adored offspring to elocution classes almost from birth, to better his
chances in life, so that he now spoke in the
mellifluous tones of a Laurence Oliver. Encoun-
tering Alan Moss was like drinking Black
Velvet, that paradoxical union of Guinness and
champagne. The girls nearly went off their
heads with rapture.

And Daphne, our Daphne, saw Alan Moss at
the Playhouse in *Romeo and Juliet* and decided,
rather as she might pick out a blouse at Ellis-
ton's, that she must have him. Her infatuation
and its repercussions dominated our last year in

that sweet city which needed not June for beauty's heightening.

'He's too political for you,' Penny told her over tea one day. 'Political people like other political people – on the same side, of course. You, Daphne, are not political, and even if you were, you would not be on the same side as Alan Moss.'

'Political?' Daphne said vaguely. 'Well, my father makes speeches in the House of Lords. I've often heard him. There's a special place in the House where peers' daughters are allowed to sit. And besides, my mother is always opening fetes.'

'That's precisely what Penny means,' I said. 'You're the wrong colour.'

'You don't mean he fancies West Indians?'

'I think we'll just have to leave her to her fate,' Penny said. I hummed the appropriate Wagner motif. 'Or fete,' I added with my usual quicksilver wit.

The only obstacle to True Love, in Daphne's view, was that Alan Moss was conducting a discreet but well-publicized liaison with an upper-class Lady Margaret Hall undergraduate called Serena de Courcy. I used to see Serena at deb dances before my ignominious retirement to Warwickshire.

'She's not only pretty,' I told the group over crumpets, 'but bright.'

'So?' Daphne demanded, glaring at me.

'She's not that bright,' Louisa said kindly. 'She sometimes comes to my tutorials. But she's very keen. A quick learner, I would say. She talks very fast too, which gives the impression of knowing a lot, like Edmund.'

'I used to talk quite fast,' Daphne said. 'But in those days it was called gabbling.'

'We'll have to engineer a meeting,' said Penny, in her element as always when manipulating people. 'We have the utmost faith in you, Daphne love, to eliminate this pretty gabbler.'

'I think Moss is going to give a talk on producing Shakespeare at the OUDS meeting next week,' Louisa volunteered. 'Edmund wants to go. Perhaps Daphne could engender an interest in theatre production by next Friday.'

'I didn't know Edmund was interested in the theatre,' Penny said.

'He's interested in everything,' Louisa said, with a faint note of gloom.

'I'll go too,' I said. 'Then I can flush out Serena and leave Daphne the field.' Actually, I thought I might see Gerald there if Edmund were going. Gerald and I had come together at the Christ Church Commem, after my escort had run off with a waiter, and Gerald's girl had fainted in a punt and had to be put to bed. We found we shared a passion for *Black's Medical Dictionary*.

When I told him that since my upbringing had been based on a series of failed inventions and that I could only confront reality by studying my own body, he responded that since his mother, an alcoholic flower-arranger, had refused to allow him to admit to any physical disability or illness throughout his childhood, he now freely indulged in every little ache and pain with the greatest pleasure.

'My sister and I used to write each other letters at school,' he said, as we sat by the statue of Mercury and gazed at the silhouette of Tom Tower rising to the moon, 'describing in filthy detail every ailment we could possibly drum up. I would say things like, "my turds are greenish butter pats," and she would come back with, "I have a suppurating sore on my inner ear . . ."'

'How marvellous,' I breathed. 'Tell me more.'

So he did.

Overwhelmed by these revelations, he must have taken fright after that, and gone into hiding. I was quite anxious to renew our dialogue. But of course Daphne was our first concern. So there was quite a turnout for Friday's meeting. In a smoke-filled room at Worcester, we listened respectfully while Alan Moss explained the problems of producing a play like *Romeo and Juliet* unless the full sociopolitical implications of the drama were extracted. Without this, he suggested, no producer had the right to come to any conclusions or bore us with what could only emerge as flippancy. Edmund and Louisa stood in a corner, looking like examples of a superrace. Gerald was nowhere to be seen. I later found out he had been sure I would not go to such a left-wing affair and had repaired to 55 Bardwell Road with a new issue of *The Lancet* for me to read.

'You have to see the characters in their social context,' Alan Moss said, his piercing eyes lacerating the cowed audience, his finger pointing like some Pentecostal preacher at the unoffending text. 'There is an essential dialectic between the aristocracy and the bourgeoisie in Shakespeare's Verona.' Serena de Courcy, wearing a fair isle sweater and tweed skirt, and Daphne Fanthorpe, wearing a fair isle sweater and flannel trousers, gazed at him with the same expression of doglike devotion and mental bafflement. It was enough to turn anyone to Marxism.

I played my role as planned.

'Hello, Serena,' I said when the talk was over. 'Haven't seen you for ages.'

Serena was reluctantly diverted from her progress to Alan's side. 'Hello, Alice,' she said. 'I can't remember what dance it was, can you?'

I could, of course, having only been to three.

'Lord, no. By the way, what is it you're reading?'

'English.'

'Is that why you're here?'

Serena blushed. 'I think Alan is so interesting,' she said. 'He is really helping me with my work.'

'How nice. Reading the *Communist Manifesto* together, are you?'

She looked at me sharply, but my smile was all innocence. She tried to find Alan again, who was surrounded by Shakespearian dialecticians. Daphne, I was gratified to note, was up there in the front row, looking intriguingly remote.

'Why don't we have coffee,' I persisted. 'I long to know what happened to your season and all that.'

'Well . . .' The season was obviously not in the forefront of her mind when in Alan's presence, but she was too well-brought-up to be rude, a fact I had banked on. One more check of Alan revealed him deep in argument with a group of well-know Lefties, including Red, who had come in late and missed most of the crucial points.

We went to the Wimpy Bar opposite St John's and ate slimy slabs of meat inserted in stale buns. I silently admired my sacrifice.

'How did you meet Alan?' I asked. 'I can't

imagine him being part of the circle you came
up with.'

'Lord, no,' she laughed. 'It was at a party. He
came up to me and asked if I was the girl he had
seen in the library reading Sartre.'

'Were you?'

'Well, no, as a matter of fact. But we began
seeing each other after that. He lent me his copy
of *Being and Nothingness*.'

'Nice of him. It's the kind of thing you can dip
into when you go to bed. What are you going to
do when you go down?'

'Heavens, I haven't thought about it. I have
enough on my mind trying to get through
Schools. Mummy thinks I should get married.'

'Don't all Mummies.' I paused. 'Well, what
about Alan?' I added with studied casualness.

'Marry him? Gosh, no. I'd never even consider
it. My parents would have a fit if they met him.
Anyway, he's not the marrying kind. He thinks
it's incredibly bourgeois.'

I wondered what he thought affairs with
upper-class girls were.

'You must come and have tea with us sometime,' I said, generous now after these satisfactory revelations.

'I've heard all about your fabulous setup,'
Serena said with a twinge of annoyance. 'A

73

house to yourselves, no landlady, no curfew, and your own keys.'

'Well, we do have a landlady,' I explained. 'But she's too preoccupied with her children and her nasal passages to care much what we do. The only time she gets cross is if we wake her up coming in at three in the morning. On those occasions she refuses to cook our breakfast. There's a creaking board right outside the baby's door and the frightful kid's got ears like a bat. But Penny has isolated the board and drawn chalk around it, like a corpse, so we avoid it and the bacon and eggs are produced as usual.'

Serena and I got on our bicycles for the journey back to our digs. Her legs were beginning to look a little overdeveloped from those long rides back to Lady Margaret Hall. Daphne's would surely benefit from the comparison.

'What about Louisa, then?' Serena said as we said goodbye. 'Hasn't she made the catch of the century? A friend of mine at LMH went out with him once and said she was so scared she never dared open her mouth. We couldn't believe it when we heard he'd gone for Louisa.'

'Louisa's probably the only girl around who isn't scared of him,' I said, moving off. 'In fact, I don't think she even likes him.'

I only said it for effect, and it was worth it. Serena looked gratifyingly shocked. But as someone once said, many a true word is said in jest.

DAPHNE

That hurtling sensation through the blood-stream, that liquidizing of the limbs, the way the heart flips over and over like a pancake – I had felt those heady rushes for my gardener while studying for my A levels. I had felt them briefly for an Australian I met in a London coffee-bar the summer before I went up to Oxford. The Australian talked in rather a provocative accent, and he drank milk straight out of the bottle, rendering me breathless with excitement. He was rather in awe of me because of my titled parents and kept giving me the kid-glove treat-ment, as he called it, which meant not sleeping with me. I think he was scared of deflowering this pure example of English breeding. I was terribly disappointed, as my heady rushes by that time were reducing me to a puddle of unfulfilled desire. (Not that I knew it at the time – I don't think I knew what desire was, except as a literary word for 'want.').

With Alan, it all happened again. The gar-dener had been Irish, with dark blue eyes and a

mass of black curls. I suspect he was my model
for all future crushes. I used to gaze at him out
of the window while I was learning my Latin. I
certainly beat Virgil for thrills. Alan's dark hair,
deep-set eyes, and glowering expression set me
frantically off again, like a fuse to a grenade.

Alan later told me all this was simply a
symptom of my class, the falling for a servant,
a serf, so common in English literature. I swore
that class had never entered into it. 'I didn't
even know the expression "working class" until
I met you,' I would earnestly explain. 'You have
put the whole thing into my mind. I was
brought up un-class-conscious. I just fancied the
gardener, that's all. It's probably because he
was the first man I saw without his shirt on.'

Alan would cackle mirthlessly at my protests.
'Everyone is a product of his class,' he would
argue. 'You more than most, with your privi-
leged, protected, imperialist background. It was
simply not necessary to talk to you about class
because you were never exposed to any but your
own. It amazes me that such stratification still
prevails. Jesus. Wait till the revolution comes.' I
would always apologize for my stupid upbringing, but the more I apologized, the more he
imprisoned me in it. 'Yours is a case of inversion,
that's all. You think the working classes are
stronger and sexier than Old Etonians, and

that's why, like so many females of your class,
you are attracted to us.'

The explanation hit me like a ton of bricks.
Wasn't it true that I had never felt so much as a
quiver of interest in all those public-school types
I had gone out with? Even Edmund, whose
beauty and elegance were the stuff of poetry,
aroused my intellectual admiration only. My
body remained impervious to his charms. Alan
was brilliantly, shatteringly right. How perverse. How much easier life would have been if
there had been the slightest touch of eroticism
in my social equals. I was lucky, as it happened,
that my tastes had emerged during a social
upheaval in England, when working-class
acents were becoming not only acceptable, but
commercially profitable, and people like the
Beatles, Michael Caine, and Terry Stamp were
representing the idols of a new, deracinated
generation. I was simply in the vanguard with
my gardener and Alan.

Anyway, that first night at Worcester, while
Alice took care of Serena, I attached myself like
a limpet to my working-class paragon, little
knowing the implications of my un-thought-out
infatuation. I am ashamed now to think of it.
Whatever Alan may have thought, all my
upbringing prepared me for was to get what I
wanted, and certainly so far there had been no

failures. My wants as a child were hardly excessively imaginative – a doll, a bigger doll, a doll that talked, a doll that walked, finally a pony – wants, rather than desires, satisfied without too much difficulty. Wanting Alan, however, was not like wanting a doll that cried *ma-ma*. My mother might have told me that. But then she would probably have told me, as so many mothers have told their daughters, to close my eyes and think of England.

When all the other faithful Lefties had finally peeled off, leaving us alone, Alan Moss took me to a disgusting meal at the Wimpy. Disgusting? It was working-class, luv, wasn't it? I wouldn't have cared if I had eaten cat's piss, I was so pleased to have got him to myself. And he was going to take me back to his digs, to his inner sanctum, to his lair. I was humming with triumph. I had waited through all the boring argy-bargy about dialectics and Trotsky and materialism and I was finally alone with the newest object of my passion.

His room had green linoeum on the floor and smelled of kerosene oil. His bed, a slim pallet, was covered with a dingy green candlewick bedspread that I carefully described to the girls as eau-de-nil. For me, you understand, surrounded since infancy by cabbage-rose chintz and silk-fringed lamps, Alan's decor held more promise than Valentino's tent.

I was gratified to see that unlike so many boys who finally got me alone, Alan did not appear the slightest bit nervous. He picked up a guitar and began to sing a Chaucer poem, read it really, while strumming. It was the one with all the bawdy bits in it. As it was mostly in Middle English or whatever, I had some trouble understanding it, but I could see Alan was getting a lot of pleasure out of it. As for me, I was transported by the scene. Nobody had ever serenaded me before, and the fact that the words were Chaucer's only enhanced the romance of it all. I was one of those deprived people who were never read to as children, after my father found the incumbent Nanny reading me *Great Expectations* with such emissions of spit through her brown and gaping teeth that she was dismissed on the spot and *Great Expectorations*, as Daddy amusingly dubbed it, was banished to the downstairs library along with the ten-volume *Mice of South America* and five-volume *Bats of Java*.

So Alan played and I listened, and waited. I knew this was going to be my finest hour.

'All right,' he said finally. 'Knickers off.'

Honestly. That's what he said. I obeyed at once, of course.

5

ALICE

Thus was Daphne launched upon the course that was to see her through her last year at Oxford. She was strangely reticent about her first night in his arms, with the kerosene and the eau-de-nil, but we put that down to breeding. All she said when she came home was that she was seeing him again next week. 'He's giving a speech to the Labour Club. Something about Trotsky and the Welfare State. I'd better find out who he is.'

'Was,' said Louisa. 'He's dead.'

We watched Daphne with the greatest interest as she attached herself to this new organism. She began to wear different clothes. Gone were the fair isle sweaters, fur coats, and stiletto heels. In their place were peajackets, jeans, boots, and of course a newspaper under her arm. Newspapers were an essential ticket to working-class authenticity. Alan and his henchmen, Mick and Fred, Red Kittredge's heirs, always carried left-wing newspapers and journals under their arms and made furious statements like, 'Have you seen what the arsehole has done to the miners?' or 'What's in that arsehole's manifesto speech?' or 'There's a new demo in Birmingham.' Then they would open their newspapers and fold them into squares in order to point to some tiny paragraph that had caused their ire, thus provoking much stamping and swearing and lighting of cigarettes.

Daphne was too refined to go that far, but when the stiffies continued to roll in, she would throw them away and refuse all parties, saying, 'Oh, those awful hearties, braying pigs,' and occasionally, tentatively, 'arseholes.'

Alan, we felt sure, said much worse things about these upholders of the English class system. But Daphne was not quite ready to use the words 'reactionary' or 'capitalist tool' in Bardwell Road. All she knew was that Bucks Fizz, the Bullingdon, and fair isle sweaters were very bad form indeed.

'The most important issue is not suicide,' she would announce over breakfast. 'It's nationalization.'

We would groan, accustomed now to bearing the brunt of Daphne's conversion. Penny was the main target for Daphne to practise her new ideology on, Penny with her devotion to the Old School Tie, country-house weekends, her paint-

ings, her record player, her Persian rugs, and
the other symbols of capitalist oppression with
which she surrounded herself. Daphne would
not listen to Mozart any more. 'Music is antire-
volutionary,' she said. 'It dulls the mind, lulling
the people into passivity.'

'What about the "Internationale"?' Penny
asked.

'That's not music. That's . . .'

'Propaganda,' Louisa finished.

Daphne never won these little exchanges. She
was like Olympia in the *Tales of Hoffman*,
singing impeccably for a moment and then wind-
ing down, unable to complete the routine without assistance. Penny and Louisa were far more
familiar than she with the jargon of Moss's
circle. Daphne had never heard of the *Communist Manifesto*, let alone the withering away of
the state.

Moreover Alan was not a pushover, as most of
Daphne's suitors had been. If he had planned
the capture of Daphne's heart, he could not have
executed it better. For a while he continued to
prefer Serena's brand of fair isle perfection,
giving her the Chaucer treatment too while
Daphne smouldered with jealousy, reduced to
gazing hour after hour at the photograph of Moss
which had accompanied his *Isis* idol feature. But
our heroine persevered, and it was this persev-

erance, gained, she claimed darkly, from an
experience in childhood (it turned out to be a
parentally enforced stay at Pony Club Camp),
that finally won her her trophy. Serena told me
later that she foresaw the absurdity of wasting
her valuable time with someone dedicated to the
destruction of the class which she so triumphantly represented, and scratched from the
match. She later married a chinless wonder, had
stacks of children and ponies and drawers-ful of
fair isle sweaters, and moved to Worcestershire.

With Daphne as sole ruler of the Chaucerian
paradise, it was left to Louisa and myself, the
only ones yet to be deflowered, to complain about
our lovers' lovelessness. Gerald, now permanently in my corner, kissed me about twice a
week after a full bottle of Bollinger. One night,
after a particularly abandoned session, we found
out that it was after midnight and decided I
should stay in his rooms rather than risk capture returning over the wall to Somerville.
While I took my shoes off and eyed his narrow
bed with blood pressure escalating, Gerald
removed his pyjamas from under the pillow and
proceeded to the bathroom. When he returned,
he was suitably clad in his nightwear – but with
the bottoms back to front.

What tact! What delicacy! What a bore! Needless to say, we both slept rather well, a portent of things to come.

As I said to Louisa afterwards, it was not as though I was panting with lust, but I really wanted to get the damn thing over with. She agreed. Apparently Edmund had told her that he had no intention of defiling her body until they were married. She had mixed feelings about this grand gesture. First, she was rather put off by his assumption that they would get married, and second, she was not sure she would not like a little experimentation to take place first. But Edmund was always so sure of everything. To resist would have appeared churlish, if not wanton.

It was at such times we saw the advantages of an Alan Moss, whose thoroughly proletarian upbringing had included the opportunity to tickle the local girls all the way to Kingdom Come behind the bushes on the village common – places where our Nannies always most scrupulously refused to take us. The fact that Daphne had relatively little to say about all this excitement we put down to the bourgeois nature of the language of love.

LOUISA

My dad used sometimes to joke about his daughter, the soccer coach. He'd do that when he was angry with my brother about something. For of course it was my brother who would one day be the soccer coach, not me. What could girls be? During my last year, recruiters came to Oxford all the time to search out the most employable graduating males, but they never came to us.

Edmund used to hate my saying this. He would argue that my talents were equal to his, that there was no reason I could not have a brilliant career, etc., etc. But I got a dismal second in prelims. I would be lucky if I got a dismal second for my degree. Edmund, a double first, was in another sphere. How could he believe what he was saying when he spewed out all this rubbish? How could I believe him? He wanted to please me, of course, but he did not. His stupid encouragement only made things worse. He wanted me to be his equal, but I was not, nor could I ever be. His assurances were ultimately condescending and cruel. I saw that later. It was telling a terminally ill patient she would be cured.

Boris Borianov understood. That's why he was so important to me. He always took me seriously, and treated me as a grown-up, not as a child. He told me the truth. I used to talk to him about what I should do afterwards. We were all getting pretty preoccupied about it. Long gone were the lingering tea parties, the crumpled crumpet packets, the noise of Old Harrovian feet clumping up the stairs to Penny's room, the discussions of which stiffies to answer, who was the latest *Isis* idol, what hat to wear at the Provost's garden party. We sat listlessly over the Royal Doulton in Penny's room and listened to Elvis Presley singing 'Lovin' You' and wondered where were the snows of yesteryear.

Boris used to feed me sherry and tell me I must not give in to pressure. 'You must live your own life, not someone else's,' he would say. 'Women are at a crossroads. You are not equal to men, of course not. Your opportunities are minimal. Your ambitions will be frustrated. But this does not mean you must not try, if not for your own sake, for those who come after. You will win the game, and your father will be proud of you. By the way, is he thinking of putting Joe Bankside into goal this year? He did such a good job against Wales when he substituted for Wiggins.'

Boris knew I adored him, I think. I could feel

a kind of soppy look creep over my face when I was with him, however much I tried to disguise it. Most people can pick up on the symptoms of unrequited love, particularly professors, who must be used to it. I was always writing little notes to him with thoughts, or even poems, I am ashamed to admit. Having lived around my mother, it was hard not to. My poems were no better than hers, either. Stuff about autumn and faded leaves and dying on the vine. Boris never mentioned them, but I expected he kept them, along with all the other love letters he received from his female students over the years, and read them when he needed a rush.

In my worst moments, I blame him for my marriage to Edmund. We never talked directly about Edmund, of course. It would have been out-of-bounds to mention anything personal. But towards the end of the summer term, when I was beginning to get desperate, and he could see I was really falling apart, he sat me down and said that I was too romantic for my own good. I remember to this day his dark, jowly face as he bent over his pipe, his eyes avoiding mine, his Russian accent heavier than usual. 'Louisa, you are fighting life instead of welcoming it,' he said. 'There is nothing amusing about suffering. Suffering depresses, fatigues, diminishes the personality, except in very rare cases. You are not a rare case.

Not yet.' He said this kindly, and smiled. He walked to the window and stared out over the quad, which looked particularly beautiful with its brilliant green lawn and climbing roses over the archway opposite. 'I think you must choose a peopled path,' he said. 'Only artists should choose the lonely one. You must do what you can within certain boundaries, or you will be a very unhappy woman, Louisa. And remember what Erich Fromm said, that the Western notion of the "pursuit of happiness" does not produce well-being.' He turned back into the room and tapped his ash out into an ashtray which had the college arms engraved on it.

'Fred Wheeler will make a good striker for the England squad,' he added, gazing at the tobacco he was restuffing into his pipe. 'If your father saw him last season with Manchester United, he'll know what I mean.'

Was I fighting life? What was the peopled path? Who was I to turn my back on the greatest chance for a fulfilled relationship anyone could hope for, with a man so talented, so gifted, so full of potential – and so obviously in love? Who could be sure enough about anything to say no to all that?

One week later, I told Edmund I would marry him. I invited Boris to the wedding, but he was going to an international soccer match at Wembley.

6

ALICE

Elvis Presley's throbbing tones echoed through
the Bardwell Road house as we settled down for
the final summer term of Oxford life. Presley's
rubbery eroticism was a healthy antidote to the
desiccated flesh of most of our friends, who were
also deep in the death throes of final examina-
tions. Madly we pursued the elusive Oxford
degree, presumably under the impression that,
while it had not trained us for anything, it would
surely help us in our applications to be waitresses or charladies.

Louisa had taken us rather by surprise by
announcing that she was going to marry
Edmund as soon as they went down. We were
nibbling on cheese sticks and sipping sherry in
Penny's room to the strains of 'Blue Suede Shoes'
when she rather gloomily told us. (Tea and
crumpets had rather lost their potency; something a little more substantial was required
these days.) We stared at her reproachfully,
stung by feelings of betrayal.

The Last Romantics

'Marriage is so bourgeois,' Daphne said. 'I think we should all be a little more existential about it.'

'What do you mean by that?' I asked. Daphne was such fun in her new role.

'Well, um, we ought to take responsibility for our actions and um, not act in bad faith.'

'Why is getting married acting in bad faith?' Penny asked.

'Oh, why can't you leave me alone,' Daphne said. This was her usual response when she ran out of Alan Moss's steam.

'I suppose Sartre is at the top of Alan's reading list for you at the moment,' I suggested.

'There's no need to be sarcastic,' Daphne said.

Louisa sighed. 'Well, I must say, it's nice to see how pleased you all are for me.'

Penny laughed. 'Sorry, love. It just seems a bit – well, precipitate.'

'And you don't seem exactly overjoyed yourself,' I pointed out.

'Well, what else am I going to do?' she demanded. 'I can't pretend my vocation is summoning me to duties elsewhere.'

'You mean, to the African veld or the Red Cross?'

'Or a nunnery, like Audrey Hepburn?'

We all sighed, yearning for a wimple.

'I know somebody who actually wants to be a

psychiatrist,' I said. 'Mary Wishart, at St Hilda's. Isn't she lucky?'

'Well, I suppose marrying Edmund is a sort of vocation,' Penny said. 'You could always look at it that way.'

We all rather liked this idea; looked at in that light, our male companions took on a slightly more useful cast. Whatever the reason, Louisa's wedding plans rapidly stepped up everyone else's ideas about the future. Edmund, flushed with his prize, urged Gerald to claim his own. He did this embarrassingly in my presence, telling Gerald that I was the perfect woman for him and so forth, something Edmund was hardly capable of judging, but which did the trick. It now became imperative that all four of us should have at least a reality to look forward to, even if it was in the form of human bondage, as well as that spiritually uplifting but elusive ectoplasm, a career.

Thus Gerald and I, without much fanfare, agreed that when we went down we would get married and live in London. (I was grateful to Edmund for his forwardness in proposing his friend. Gerald would never have done it on his own, he told me later. That, he said, was what friends were for.) Daphne's plans with Alan were less clear-cut, largely owing to Alan's inevitable resistance to anything smacking of bourgeois

respectability. But at least Daphne felt that Life
after Oxford would include a joint campaign
with Alan against the crumbling façade of capi-
talism (i.e. she thought they would live
together).

As for Penny, our siren, our leader, she waited
till we were all safely tamped down, so to speak,
before producing her triumphant bloom from the
increasingly barren Oxford soil. Her victory took
the form of the unlikeliest candidate we could
have imagined – The Honourable Freddy
Weathering, an Old Wykehamist with drooping
eyelids, drooping back, and a gloriously languid
manner. He smoked cigarettes constantly, holding them delicately between his second and third
fingers as though they were orchids. He always
wore a handkerchief in his breast pocket which
drooped like the rest of him. When he laughed,
he never made any sound, but his shoulders
shook, just as they do in novels. He used to gaze
at Penny admiringly, as though she were a
strange vision, while she whisked about with
brandy and Camembert (Freddy hated things
like cheese biscuits). He called her Penelope. I
suppose she was strange to him; her Yorkshire
energy and rude health must have contrasted
greatly with the etiolated earls and countesses
who had populated his childhood.

'Penelope, Penelope,' he used to say, waving

his wilted orchid of a cigarette in the air, 'you
are the spirit of youth. I am exhausted just
looking at you.' And she would blush and pat
him briskly, pouring more brandy. It was quite
a puzzle to guess how she had snared him. Not
that he was such a catch – only the second son,
after all, and a notoriously tighfisted father –
but he probably wanted a Nanny figure. Those
sorts of inbred family members generally do.
'It's her blood,' he said to me once. 'We Weatherings are clean out of it, my dear. We need that
Coverdale red-cell count. Dracula's instincts
were perfectly sound, you know.' And his shoulders shook with silent laughter.

He was not very interested in Louisa, whom
he found sulky. He was amused by Daphne's
leftist spoutings, and was always provoking her
to say more, and then mutely laughing. He
found me interesting because he thought I was
cynical, which I took as a compliment. My name
inspired him to furious bursts of Latin verse.
'Fugate? Fugate?' he said when he first heard it.
'Sed fugit interea, fugit inreparabile tempus.'
After that, he always quoted that line when he
saw me, sighing deeply. Sometimes it was
Horace: 'Eheu, fugaces, Postume, Postume,
Labuntur anni,' to the wave of a crooked finger.
His melancholy (symptom, Daphne said, of his
decadent class) infected us all during our last

term, and what with Presley's wails and Postume, Postume, we spent a lot of time brooding over time slipping by. It was then that I spotted my first wrinkle – a line, really, between my eyebrows, but as sharp as any thorn.

The Christ Church Commem seemed a distant dream when we donned our gowns for the first week of Schools. A new generation of undergraduates was thinking about invitations, ball dresses, May Morning, and punts at dawn. We were already passées, gone down, reunion fodder. Gibbon said that his Oxford years were the most idle and unprofitable of his life. I would not go so far as to say that. After all, we all got seconds, to our surprise. But more important, although we were not aware of it then, the four of us had become friends.

DAPHNE

Lord and Lady Fanthorpe
At Home
8 Cadogan Gardens SW1
January 6, 1964
For Daphne and Alan

Nobody thought I'd get married to Alan at all, let alone before anybody else did. It came as just as much of a surprise to me. Alan went abroad immediately after the announcement of his rather embarrassing third (a gesture against the Establishment was how he explained it), first to Paris, where I heard he had a French girlfriend called Solange who introduced him to the Algerian struggle for independence, and then to Ireland, where he studied the tactics of the IRA. I expect there was a colleen there too. Meanwhile, I sobbed my heart out every night in the bath, while my mother flapped her hands and told me no man was ever worth it. If she had met the man in question, she would, I'm sure, have been even more vocal.

When Alan returned to his parents' home somewhere in South London, I telephoned him. I couldn't help it. Of course in those days it was not done, but I was desperate and anyway Alan had taught me not to be bound by convention. I was terrified and my voice was trembling and I knew he couldn't hear because he kept shouting to his mother to turn the fucking hoover off. I couldn't imagine talking to my mother like that. That was the kind of thing that made Alan so exciting. He was so direct about everything. I told him I wanted to see him and he said he'd think about it and then I knew, clear as a bell, what I had to do.

I announced it to my parents over the Potage

St Germain, just before Christmas, when families are full of goodwill, ha ha. My mother was
in a particularly expansive mood, not because of
the season, but because she had just opened a
new wing of St Edward's Hospital in Greenwich.

'It was such fun,' she told us as we sat down in
front of the bowls of thick grey liquid that passed
for soup. 'There were some cadets there from the
Naval College, looking quite adorable in their
uniforms. Uniforms do so much for a man. I wish
you had come with me, Daphne, don't you think
the navy attracts the best types of all?'

'I am going to live with Alan Moss,' I said.

As one, the heavy soup spoons clattered down
on to the Crown Derby.

'What?'

I continued to penetrate my soup.

'I'm going to live with him,' I said. 'He's come
back from Ireland. I can't live here any more.
Mummy's seen how ghastly it's been. I'm going
to live with him.'

Daddy wiped his mouth with one of our sheet-
sized damask napkins.

'Live with him? Live with who? You're too
young to mate.' A blob of soup quivered on his
moustache.

'Darling, you can't,' Mummy said. 'What
would we tell everyone? Oh, do stop being so
silly. You haven't been eating the right things,

obviously. You'd better go and see Dr Spinoza. He completely cured me of my constipation.'

'I'm sorry, Mummy. I'm perfectly well and I've decided. I'm grown-up now. You can't stop me.'

'Live with him?' my father sputtered again. 'Well, if you're going to live with him, you'd better marry the fella.'

This, I must confess, was an unexpected parry.

'Well,' I said cautiously. 'All right.'

Of course I knew by then that people like Daddy were an anachronism, and would have to be overthrown. But I preferred to think of the destruction of the whole class, rather than individuals. To be quite honest, I was ecstatic with my old man's solution, which was the one I secretly longed for myself, even though I knew it was out of the question, considering Alan's views about bourgeois institutions and historical materialism.

But there was some life in the ancien regime yet. I did not mention our decision to Alan, fearing reprisals, but when he next came to the house to pick me up, my father opened the door and invited him in.

'Oh, hello sir,' Alan said furiously. Daddy, indeed any titled personage, made him nervous, a fact that annoyed him greatly and provided another strike against the bloody imperialists.

'I believe you've come to see my daughter,'

Daddy said, brushing some animal hairs off his coat. 'Damn badgers,' he added, 'they shed, you know, even in winter, when you'd think they'd want to keep their coats on, what?' And he gave a barking laugh that I could see unnerved Alan even further.

'Uh – badgers, sir?'

'Well, that's not what we're here to talk about, is it? Come into my study for a minute.' He waved me off, while Alan cast me a furious glance. I placed myself carefully by the door and listened to the following exchange:

'Now, young man,' Daddy said, pouring something from a bottle. Sherry, probably. 'When are you going to marry her?'

'What?' Alan's voice was a sort of strangled gurgle.

'When are you going to marry my daughter?'

There was a short pause. I could feel my cheeks flaming.

'Oh, er, well, sir in a month.'

I could hardly refrain from a discreet shriek.

'Fine, fine,' my father said. 'Her mother won't like it, but she'll get over it quickly, that's my view. Put the animal out of its misery. Some members of the natural world are quite peculiar that way, you know. Mating seems the most unpleasant aspect of their lives. Most odd. You've heards cats at it, I suppose.'

98

'Well, er . . .'

Daddy strode to the door where I attempted to show I was just crouching to do up my shoe.

'You can come in now,' he said. 'I think we've settled everything, haven't we, Mr – er – Fern?'

'Moss, Daddy, Moss,' I said, sending a grateful look to Alan, who was jigging his leg up and down in that well-known sign of impending breakdown.

'Perhaps you'd like a drink?' I hastily added.

'Thanks, old girl, but I have one. Oh, you mean your chap here,' he added, seing my expression. 'Of course. What about that French stuff some twerp sent me after I identified a rare bat he had found in Java? Far too sweet for me, but I believe young people like it.'

He held out a bottle of Grand Marnier to Alan, who rapidly poured himself a tumbler of it.

'Ha, ha, that's the way,' said my father. 'I've never understood why they drink it out of those idiotic thimble glasses.'

Alan said later that my father had intentionally humiliated him. I could not make him believe that Daddy was not remotely clever enough for such a ruse. But I could see how totally ideological conviction coloured one's view of the world.

I poured myself a glass of sherry and we all drank deeply.

'Alan,' I started to say, but he moved abruptly to the window and looked stonily down at the Rolls Royces and Jaguars parked in the street.

'Well, I'll leave you two lovebirds together,' Daddy said heartily. 'I'd better prepare your mother. She's not going to like it, you know.'

'Of course she will,' I said, glaring at my father and indicating the back of Alan's head.

'Nothing personal, old chap,' Daddy hastily went on. 'You'll find Daphne's mother is a plucky old bird deep down. Just don't get her on to the colour problem. She can be damned tricky about that.'

'Come on, Alan,' I said. 'Let's get out of here and find Mick and Fred.'

'Are they going to be ushers?' my father said as we fled for the door. 'And what about your drinks? There's still half a bottle of this foul frog's piss here. Damn shame.'

I held my breath, but Alan did not go back on the agreement. I never understood why. Alice said that the British working classes were all basically reactionary and that he secretly loved marrying an earl's daughter. Penny said he probably found the idea sexy. Louisa said it was the perfect solution for a Marxist sadist. They were all, in a way, right.

7

ALICE

So Daphne won her Red Byron. The marriage
was of the 'least said, soonest mended' variety,
since an engagement had no other meaning to
Alan than military, and Daphne was petrified
that if she delayed, her beloved would realize
the traitorous path upon which he had embarked
and call the whole thing off. So a month almost
to the day after Lord Fanthorpe popped the
question, Gerald and I were summoned to meet
the bride and groom as witnesses at the Chelsea
Registry Office at 4:30 P.M – when most sane
people would be sitting down to a cup of Lapsang
and a watercress sandwich. It was agreed that
Louisa and Penny should hold the fort at the
Fanthorpes', where the reception was to take
place, in case guests of the wrong stripe arrived
early, or the bride's parents collapsed. Lord and
Lady Fanthorpe had wisely decided to finesse
the legal part of the marriage ceremony. Lady
Fanthorpe was too distressed at her daughter's
forfeiture of a white wedding to countenance

101

such a gesture, and Lord Fanthorpe was driving
back from Norfolk where he had been visiting
some unconventional breeding sites for badgers.
Alan's parents were going to show up, and we
all thought that a confrontation between the in-
laws should be postponed as long as possible –
preferably until both parties had been plied with
several glasses of numbing bubbly.

We set off down the King's Road in plenty of
time, my own plans including several diversions
into the flashy boutiques that had changed the
face of the genteel old neighbourhood of Chelsea
in the years since we had been at Oxford. Gone
were the little greengrocers, the bakery, and the
modest bookshop. In their place were garish
clothes shops plastered with silver foil and
sequins and little coloured balls. The weather
was unseasonably cold and the clothes looked
more than usually like Christmas wrapping
paper.

'Aren't they hideous?' Gerald said.

'Wouldn't you like me in that?' I pointed to a
red leather minidress with an orange ostrich
feather wound round the neck. He looked at my
sensible Jaegar camel coat and skirt and
squeezed my hand with something approaching
affection. How lucky I was to have Gerald, I
thought, instead of the mad revolutionary poor
Daphne was throwing her life away on.

Entering the gloom of the Chelsea Registry Office after our walk soon lowered our spirits. We climbed the imposing stone steps with an increasing sense of depression, past peeling walls and dusty banisters, Outside the wedding office were several shabby chairs where the happy couple and their witnesses were supposed to wait. A tooth extraction came more easily to mind. It was there we first saw Alan with his mother and father, two small people in brown, who beamed with pride. We shook hands and nodded to Alan, who grunted and then started to read the newspaper he had presciently tucked under his arm.

'Where's Daphne?' he asked, staring at the *Daily Herald*'s editorial page. 'The sooner we are out of here the better.'

Gerald and I stared at each other in momentary panic. Were we supposed to have picked her up? Luckily at that moment she sailed up the stairs, wrapped in her mother's raccoon coat.

'I'm sorry I'm so late,' she said breathlessly. 'But no hairdresser would stay open on a Saturday afternoon, so I found this weird place in Earl's Court. What do you think?'

Her hair had been coiled up like a kangaroo's pouch, with a metallic flower stuck in the middle of it.

'They're obviously accustomed to Australians,'

I said. Daphne looked crushed. 'But the coat looks great,' I added. She giggled slightly and flashed it open for me. She had nothing on underneath. 'No time,' she whispered.

'For Chrissake, Daphne, let's get the bloody thing over with.'

Alan's mother sighed and his father began a coughing fit. At that moment the bureaucracy stepped in, in the form of a female registrar who was probably a military adviser to South American dictatorships in her spare time. Poking her head round the door, she barked at us to sit down quietly until she called us. We humbly obeyed.

'Mummy's completely hysterical,' Daphne whispered to me. 'I hope she hasn't put arsenic in the champagne or anything.' She smiled sweetly at Mr and Mrs Moss, who were looking at her coat with undisguised admiration. Finally we were called into the inner sanctum, where the military adviser stood behind a large desk heaped with papers and folders.

'Come up here,' she said sternly to Alan and Daphne, as though they had played truant from school. 'And your witnesses.' We stepped up beside them. 'You sit down,' she commanded the Mosses, who found chairs at the back of the room. 'Room' was perhaps a euphemism for this dingy cell assigned to marriages. The walls were acrid green, enlivened by dark cracks. To the right of the registrar's desk hung her certificate of authorization from the London County Council to perform her happy duty. I wondered what kind of test one had to take to be awarded such an honour. Behind her head was Salvador Dali's picture of the Queen in her regalia, our symbol of the secular nature of the occasion.

'You may take your coat off,' the woman said, glaring at Daphne, whose complexion was taking on the hue of the walls. She shook her head violently. 'I hope you realize the seriousness of this ceremony,' the registrar went on. 'It retains the weight of law in our unwritten constitution, and in the sight of God, although it is a civil rite. If therefore there is any reason you think this marriage should not proceed, you must now declare it.'

A thousand reasons flooded my mind. It is surely the most compulsively answerable question in the history of interrogation. We held our tongues, however, and our celebrant read some paragraphs from a little black book before pronouncing Alan and Daphne man and wife. We all looked at each other in depressed silence, then Alan took Daphne by the arm and said, 'Let's go and get a drink.'

We all piled into the Markham Arms, a pub whose claim to fame was not its fine glass

panelling, but that it was frequented by the
Chelsea set (everyone of our age who didn't go
to Oxford or Cambridge) in large droves. The
pub had only just opened, so it was still empty,
but a few typical King's Road types were already
ensconced at the tables – miniskirted birds with
white lipstick and mascara-black eyes, and mop-
haired boys who looked like Terence Stamp and
sounded like factory workers from Liverpool.
Everyone in those days wanted to sound like
factory workers from Liverpool – I had even
started modifying my vowel sounds myself –
which must have annoyed Alan Moss's parents,
who had spent all that money on Alan's elocution lessons.

Everybody chose beer, to be democratic.

'Cheers,' I said to Alan and Daphne. Alan
grinned demonically. 'So far, so good,' he said.
'Nothing to it, is there, love?' He kissed Daphne
loudly on the ear.

'Isn't he awful,' his mother said lovingly. 'He's
always been difficult, even as a child. Always
ungrateful. I went on breastfeeding him until he
was two as he never could get enough of it, and
the screaming if I tried to pull him off! Do you
remember, Dad? He never thanked me for it,
though, oh, no, not our Alan. It nearly killed me
too, I can tell you.' She laughed and gave him an
affectionate nudge.

106

'What, thank you for the bitter aloes you put on your tits to wean me, eh?' Alan said in mock horror. 'Should I have been grateful for that, then? It's made me a pervert for life.'

'Oooh, don't you say such things, Alan Moss, and in front of your new bride, too.'

'Now you leave your Mum alone,' Mr Moss agreed, lighting a cigarette. 'She's done everything for you, and don't you forget it.' The rest of his words were lost in an explosion of coughing.

'He won't give up smoking,' Mrs Moss confided to me over the paroxysms. 'It'll be the death of him, but he's stubborn. Like Alan.' She looked at them both with unabashed pride.

'Do belt up, Mum,' Alan said. 'I can't take you out even for five minutes before you start.'

'You know, they scream at each other all the time,' Daphne explained to Gerald. 'Alan and his mother. You'd think they were deadly enemies.'

'We are,' Alan said. 'My mother will be the death of me.'

'It's good for you to have words from time to time,' Mrs Moss said. 'Gets all the poison out. I always feel ever so much better after a real set-to with Alan or his father. Oh, I say, isn't that Terry Stamp?'

Alan looked disgusted. 'Is that all you can do?'

107

he demanded. 'Look round for nonexistent film
stars?'

'Well, you see stars all over the place these
days,' she said. 'Do you know, I was in the local
shop one day last week, and who do you think
walked in? Ted, stop that coughing. You'll bring
up your dinner.'

'I think we'd better be going,' I said, seeing
Gerald's face. 'The Fanthorpes are probably
waiting for us, and Daphne hasn't got anything
on under that coat.'

At least that put a stop to the coughing.

Lady Fanthorpe greeted us at the door of
Number 8, Cadogan Gardens, with shrieks of
relief. Lord Fanthrope had only just returned,
and she was not sure if she had enough glasses.
'You may just have to run out for me, Gerald
dear.'

She was decked out in fuchsia pink, with a
blue fox stole and blue feathery hat. (We must
keep cheerful,' she explained to me.) Lord Fanthorpe, unaware of the importance of his role,
wore some sort of shooting outfit that had seen
better days on the Yorkshire moors, or perhaps
that was what he had worn to investigate the
badger breedery. At some point in the afternoon
I had the distinct impression there was some
small furry animal kicking around in his pocket,
but it could have been simply a nervous hand.

We were all nervous. Louisa and Penny arrived
after we did (Edmund was helicopter-skiing in
Alaska, and Freddy was attending the funeral
of his grandmother, the dowager countess of
Hammock). We agreed that it was going to be a
rough couple of hours. Daphne looked beige and
pinched, Alan was getting drunk, and Lady
Fanthorpe flitted about like a tropical bird protecting its nest from hostile predators.

'Thank goodness you are here to stand by
Daphne in her hour of need,' she said to us as we
helped ourselves to the Bollinger. 'Did you see
Moss's frightful red nylon socks? I have hidden
the silver, you know.' She threw a significant
glance over at Mick and Fred, Alan's ever-
present henchmen, who, having worked to over-
throw most of Oxford's institutions as a preparation for overthrowing the British Government,
were now huddled by the bar, pamphlets and
journals secured firmly under their arms, eyeing
the Old Master over the fireplace and refilling
their glasses with Chivas Regal. Even if they
thought Alan the worst kind of turncoat for
marrying Daphne, their disapproval of his bourgeois act did not, needless to say, prevent them
from enjoying his bride's hospitality. When it
came time to cut the cake (Lady Fanthorpe had
chosen a simple Fuller's layer cake as being the
most appropriate), they made a lot of snorting

noises, while eating it in great handfuls, dropping crumbs on the Persian carpet and grinding them in with their boots.

'Never mind,' Penny said to Lady Fanthorpe, whose pained expression had begun to turn to anguish. 'It's only crumbs.'

'Let them eat cake,' I added brilliantly. Nobody laughed.

'It could have been a lot worse, Lady Fanthorpe,' Louisa said. 'At least they haven't broken anything. You should see our house after a soccer match.'

'But those socks!' Lady Fanthorpe said despairingly. We had not realized how socks made the man.

Alan's parents looked on with serenity. Their son had done the very thing they had most often dreamed of – married into the class to which he was not born but to which he rightly belonged. Now those costly elocution lessons could be justified; now those expensive clothes, the guitar, the posters, the kerosene, the patience with which they listened to him read incomprehensible poems in what he swore was English, were all triumphantly accounted for. Of course they would never be close friends with the new in-laws, as Mrs Moss had hoped. She saw now that the Fanthorpes would never come to tea at 2 North Villas, Peckham. But they had a nice chat about Alan's career as a playwright. ('Such an amusing profession,' Lady Fanthorpe had said. 'Terence Rattigan is such a charming man and Noel Coward often pops in when he's over from Switzerland. I'm sure your son' – here she wavered for just the fraction of a second – 'will be just like them one day.') In return, Lady Fanthorpe had confided that Daphne's talents in the kitchen left something to be desired. ('She can't cook at all, you know, Mrs Moss,' Her Ladyship had said. 'We've always had McCloud, ever since Daphne was a baby. So she's been brought up to enjoy the very best Scottish cooking.') If Mrs Moss felt a few tremors about this in view of her son's impossibly demanding tastes, she did not let on. 'Such a nice woman,' she whispered to Mr Moss, who was in the middle of a coughing fit and failed to respond. 'She said something about Alan being like Terence Stamp. Now isn't that grand?'

'Where are they going on their honeymoon?' one of Daphne's dippy aunts asked me at one point.

'A weekend at the Savoy, I think.'

'Really?' She looked shocked. 'Is that all?'

'It's quite enough, Mrs Egerton-Twistle. They are both working, you see. It's difficult for Alan to take any time off. He's rehearsing his new play, you know.'

111

I refrained from mentioning that Alan's new play was about battered babies, crippled earls, and the Welfare State, to be performed during an antinuclear march scheduled for the following week. Nor did I add that it was only through Lady Fanthorpe's insistence and Lord Fanthorpe's chequebook that the newlyweds were going anywhere. I think the honeymoon was where Alan had drawn the line. Ideology had to take a stand somewhere.

Daphne kissed everybody goodbye, looking slightly less beige, her Australian hairstyle now unpinned, greatly improving her appearance. Alan stood beside her, smiling satanically, a cigarette hanging out of his mouth. Lady Fanthorpe briefly covered her eyes. As they left, his collection of publications slipped from under his arm and lay forlornly on the floor – *New Society*, the *New Left Review*, and the *Daily Herald* as the bridal bouquet.

The Savoy was, needless to say, a disaster. Alan had never stayed in a deluxe hotel, and did not know he was not expected to carry the suitcases himself. Nor did he know you had to tip the person who was engaged to carry them. The sight of Alan fumbling in pockets, his face dark with fury, was one of Daphne's more lasting memories. As soon as they got upstairs into their white and gold suite, Alan fell into a complete decline and lay groaning on the bed, complaining of stomach pains. Daphne had to ring for room service and ask for Alka-Seltzer, a lowering request in view of the circumstances. She spent most of the honeymoon weekend holding Alan's hand and ringing for room service, while Alan groaned and made speeches about the economic apartheid inherent in the institution of tipping. If one were a nasty person, one might suspect a little revenge had been played by the Fanthorpes in suggesting this form of marital consummation. Personally, I don't think they were devious enough for such a gambit. Alan, naturally, was convinced otherwise.

Penny, Louisa, and I left the wedding party together, feeling as though it were the end of an era. 'I know I'll never get used to those frightful socks,' was Lady Fanthorpe's final cry as we said goodbye. 'If only she'd married someone like Edmund Wales.' Fortunately, I was unable to see Louisa's face at this last, sad farewell.

LOUISA

Mr and Mrs George Better request the pleasure of
your company at the marriage of their daughter,
Louisa May, to Edmund James Wales at St Mary's
Church, Weybridge, Surrey, May 14, 1964

It was a stitch about Daphne's father having
arranged their marriage. I suppose he was born
to that kind of authority. Did it naturally. Like
my father. Not that Dad was born to it, of course.
He was a farmer's son, and proud of it. He
always said that the best thing about football
was that it was played on a green field. You can
imagine what he thought of the American invention of Astroturf. 'You can't even piss on it,' he
said. 'It pisses right back at you.'

My father thought my marriage to Edmund
Wales was 'better than a win at Wembley.' He
meant it, too. He never thought I had much in
the looks department. He used to tease me about
my bony nose and bony knees and the lack of
curves where it mattered. 'I could fry an egg on
your chest,' he used to say. 'And sharpen a knife
on your knees.' There's nothing worse than
being an ugly child. You are too young to know

how to compensate. You only know you are singled out, punished, rejected for the way your face is put together. I once asked my mother, 'Which is better, to be pretty and nasty, or ugly and good?' 'Ugly and good,' my mother said. I knew she would say that, and I knew she was lying.

Edmund seemed totally calm about our impending nuptials. No doubts, no anxieties. Sometimes I felt he was so sure about everything that I must be wrong. If he was so happy, perhaps there was something about me after all. Yet he knew nothing about women. He'd never met any at school. All he had done was take early morning runs and cold baths to destroy desire and build character, along with Gerald Glynn and his other chums. His schoolmasters meant more to him than his mother.

That, perhaps, I could understand. Emmeline Wales, the dreaded gnomette, was a diminutive woman with velvety eyes and a whispery voice who was then called 'active' in conservative politics. She was against homosexuality, abortion, wine, and working mothers, and believed that childbirth was a sacred calling. This was consistent with the views of Edmund's father, an avant-garde vicar of a public-relations-conscious parish in East London. The Reverend Wales, who with the dreaded gnomette managed

115

to produce only one son (a deeply felt inadequacy), believed that religion was essentially sexual, thus making him the favourite of radio talk programmes and newspaper reporters short of a story.

Edmund seemed to be completely free of these odd parents. He talked about them with detached amusement, admitting quite openly that he preferred the company of his housemaster at Eton and the man who gave him sailing lessons at Cowes. Since the idea of religion had no place in his makeup, the father's notions took no root in the son's soul. Better, perhaps, if they had. Such total alienation from one's genetic origins must exact a price.

So must such emotional distance. It may sound silly, but when he went on about his school friends and the sailing holidays and the camaraderie and the lifelong friendships forged in his younger days, and his extraordinary loyalty to them, I was desperately, furiously jealous. For those were the people and places he really felt something for. They had touched something in him, something accessible when he was still very young, before it all went underground.

I had no part of that. I represented all women to him. A woman was someone you loved and admired and worshipped and married. When he kissed me, it wasn't *me* he was kissing, not plain old Louisa with her flat chest and bony knees. It was the Perfect Woman, the Favoured One, the One He Had Chosen to Marry. Therefore I was perfect. For Edmund would not have chosen someone less than perfect. I could, in fact, have been anyone. Alice, Penny, Daphne. I was like Wallis Simpson, the King's Choice. Nobody would ever look at her again except as 'The Woman I Love.' The difference between us was that Mrs Simpson didn't mind, because she wanted to be Queen. I only wanted to be Louisa.

But on 14 May 1964 I became, till death us did part, Mrs Edmund Wales.

8

ALICE

Edmund and Louisa got married in May in
Weybridge's local church, Edmund's father co-
officiating with the highly excited vicar of St
Mary's. There had not been a wedding like it in
some time. Both Edmund's and Louisa's fathers
were public figures and the press was out in
force, as well as hundreds of locals hoping to get
a glimpse of such celebrities as the country's
current heart-throb, England's goalkeeper Joe
Bankside.

To be quite honest, I can't remember much
about the wedding. I had had some mild stomach
virus all week that made me extremely tired
and at times nauseated. I also felt that the event
was one of the less happy celebrations of our
lives since Oxford. Ever since this glamorous
marriage had been announced, Louisa seemed
to be heaving one big sigh.

'If you don't love him, don't marry him,' I told
her on more than one occasion.

'Of course I love him,' she asserted. 'I'm very

lucky to have him. It's just rather nerve-racking, that's all. I don't know how you can be so calm about marrying Gerald.'

I laughed. 'Marrying Gerald is like having dinner at Boulestin's – guaranteed quality without frills.'

'How boring,' Louisa said.

'It's just how I like it.'

I remembered that exchange as Gerald and I stood in our pew and listened to the Reverend Wales give a ludicrous sermon about young love and coupling and the new form of marriage that required equal positions for both sexes and other clunking innuendoes that had the old folk squirming in their pews and the young ones giggling in embarrassment. One of the many bad things about Louisa's marriage was her frightful father-in-law, a man of the cloth who gave vestments a bad name. He was the new kind of Anglican vicar – relentlessly modern, *au courant*, candid – who was supposed to blow away the cobwebs of irrelevant ritualism and bring in a new, with-it clientele. Gerald said these theories smacked of Gladstone and his prostitutes, which seemed to me closer to the mark than a simple case of religious revivalism.

Louisa looked thin to the point of disappearance in a white silk dress with pink rosebuds at the waist. Edmund looked extraordinarily ele-

119

gant in his tails, with a white gardenia in his buttonhole. I remember an idiotic exchange in the tent the Betters had erected for the reception, during which Edmund told Louisa how wonderful she looked, and she told him not to be so silly. 'What am I to do?' I remember him saying, turning to me. 'She won't believe me. You tell her, Alice.' This unlikely appeal rendered me momentarily silent, an uncharacteristic condition for me that Gerald put down to my lingering germs. Louisa ignored me anyway, saying something like, 'I just wish you wouldn't go on so. How can anyone believe such ludicrous blandishments?' in the voice of controlled irritation that was so often to accompany their marital exchanges.

Luckily at this point Louisa's mother appeared. She was a small woman with one of those faded faces about which people say, 'She must have been pretty once.' She was fumbling in her pocket. 'I have something for you all,' she said. 'It's so exciting to see you all here together.' She pulled out a knitting pattern from her handbag.

'She won't accept the fact that I worship her, adore her, and am the happiest man in the world today,' Edmund went on.

'Why don't you go down on your knees and kiss her feet?' Gerald suggested.

'No, how funny, that's not it,' Mary Better said, gazing in puzzlement at a picture of a baby's matinee jacket. 'I wrote a poem for Edmund and Louisa . . .' She again attacked her bag. Mrs Better had published poems in women's magazines. She had also been known to read them aloud on the occasion of her husband's greatest triumphs on the football field.

'I think we should all be quiet, Mother dear,' Louisa said. 'Dad's going to make his speech.'

With flashbulbs popping, George Better called for silence in the authoritative way of one used to bellowing commands to recalcitrant midfielders. He was very big and broad, like a boxer, with the same dark blue eyes as his daughter, and I'm sure Mary Better was not the only woman with whom he shared his person. He seemed pleased enough at Louisa's choice of husband, though doubtless would have preferred a world-class placekicker. He had never shown much interest in his daughter, in spite of her pathetic crush on him. If your whole life is dedicated to a sport involving only males, the odd female here or there is hardly going to make much difference. I remember once when Mr Better came to Oxford for some soccer game, scouting probably, he didn't even call in to see her. Louisa made some idiotic excuse to cover up

for him, but the episode was exceedingly painful
for all.

Louisa's mother had made her way to her
husband's side, her yellow straw hat slightly
askew, her hand clutching a piece of paper. As
Better resonantly declared his interest in his
daughter's going over to a rival team and his
hope that Edmund would play the game and
other jovial remarks, she unfolded the paper
with some difficulty, balancing in her other hand
a full glass of cherry-coloured liquid. When she
opened her mouth to read what was on the
paper, George Better calmly turned to her and
said, 'My wife, as you all know, writes poems.
This one she has here will be passed round to all
of you and no doubt copies can be obtained if you
make the request in writing. Now let's toast the
bride and groom.'

'Thank goodness,' Louisa said as I drank her
health. 'Mother's been at the Lancer's Rosé again.
She brings it with her in a silver flask. Wasn't
Dad marvellous?'

I made appreciative noises, privately regret-
ting that Mrs Better had been deflected from her
course, since her versifying talent had never
failed to please when Louisa read us the latest
efforts over tea in Penny's room at Oxford. I
remember one that began, ''Twixt day and night,
He dribbled right, And to the goal, Betook his

might.' I'm sure the Lancer's Rosé was never far from reach as George Better paced up and down the field all winter and his wife stayed home by the TV set, summoning up the immortal muse.

Edmund and Louisa were going to Venice for their honeymoon. We stood around the happy couple, envying them their journey.

'Bellinis at Harry's bar,' I sighed, suddenly revived.

'Tizianos in October,' Gerald groaned.

'Carpaccio,' I murmured.

'Ravioli Guardi,' Gerald uttered.

'Fegato alla Veneziana,' I cooed. Everyone laughed, even Louisa, who began to brighten for the first time that day. 'It's impossible not to be romantic in Venice,' she said hopefully. 'Even if one isn't food-mad like you two.'

'Embodied enchantment, delineated magic,' said Edmund, putting his arm around her bony silk shoulder. 'One of Ruskin's three great thrones of man's dominion over the ocean.'

'Edmund, you're so disgustingly encyclopedic,' said Daphne, who had been spending most of the afternoon talking to a hirsute waiter. Alan had let her out for the day, naturally disdaining to attend this Establishment ritual. He was rehearsing a play about a battered viscount, crippled babies, and the Welfare State, to be performed before a group of picketers in Cardiff.

123

'Who was your hairy employee?' I asked. Daphne blushed.

'We were just discussing the miners' strike,' she said. 'A little more relevant than Ruskin,' she added defiantly.

'Particularly at weddings,' I agreed. 'Considering what happened to Ruskin on his wedding night.'

'What did happen?' Daphne asked in spite of herself.

'He had never seen a naked woman,' I told her. 'The sight so disagreed with him that he never went to bed with poor Effie again.'

'Well, that didn't exactly bear on his scholarship,' Edmund said dismissively.

'And that's the only thing that mattered, of course,' Louisa retorted.

'Have some more champagne, Louisa,' I said. 'It's your Day, remember.'

'I wrote quite a nice little verse about Italy,' Mrs Better piped up. 'Not about Venice particularly, but about the grace, the nibble footwork, the wiry legs, the tight . . .'

'All right, Mum,' Louisa interrupted. 'Here is Edmund's mother to tell us we should be going, I expect.'

The dreaded gnomette was wearing a cascade of ruffles round her neck and a pink and white

hat on which some spectacles were perched. She
looked like the Easter Bunny.

'Now, Louisa,' she said, in a tiny voice that
made us all lean closer to hear her. 'You look
pale, and you have a long way to go' – here she
paused and looked meaningfully at the group –
'so I suggest you go in now and change. I'll see
that Edmund does the same.'

Mrs Better gave a muffled exclamation as she
pulled out another knitting pattern from her
bag. 'I must have brought the wrong bag,' she
said. 'Mrs Wales, I thought your speech on that
TV program about pornography was quite
delightful. I had no idea people did such things
... Knit one, purl one,' she murmured doubtfully, reading the paper in her hand.

'That is a fine start to a poem,' Gerald said
kindly. 'It's something Emily Dickinson might
have thought of. Domestic literature has a power
all its own.'

'Do you really think so?' Mrs Better beamed.

'"Parting is all we know of heaven, And all we
need of hell." And I must be parted from Louisa
so soon?' Edmund kissed his bride's hand and
the dreaded gnomette steered her off.

Edmund's poetic ardour was in full flight that
day. Even I began to feel my heart beat as I
watched him and Gerald discuss Ruskin's other
two thrones of man's dominion over the ocean. If

Gerald was Boulestin's, Edmund was ... the Caprice? Romantic and expensive. I decided my beating heart was a sympton of increased blood pressure. It was time to go home.

'I'm going to say goodbye to Penny,' I told Gerald.

But Penny was deep in conversation with the Reverend Wales and I was reluctant to intrude. As the vicar talked, his hand was going up and down her suntanned back.

'Do you want to come with us?' I asked Daphne.

'Not yet,' she said. 'I think I'll go and ask Ted some more things.'

'Ted?'

'You know, the waiter. Alan would really be interested in his point of view. He told me he actually voted Tory. It's outrageous.'

I nodded. I wasn't sure which conversation would be worse, Ted's or Pastor Wales's. Turning back, I saw Mrs Better stuffing knitting patterns back into her bag. She gave me a sad little smile. I remember very little else, as the Wales leave-taking was conducted at the other end of the tent and the crowds of well-wishers concealed my view. Gerald took my hand as we slipped out through a side door and drove home. He was always most sympathetic when it came to a crisis of a circulatory nature.

The photograph in the press the next day showed the happy pair smiling radiantly as they came out of the church. 'A couple to watch,' said the *Sunday Express*. 'Products of an Oxford romance, Mr and Mrs Edmund Wales will be delightful new additions to the London scene. Making their home in Chelsea, they promise to enliven the capital's social life and give the old-timers a run for their money. Watch this space.'

The only part that made me hoot was a photograph in the *Daily Mirror* of Mary Better staring at one of her matinee jacket patterns with a bemused look on her face. 'Grandmother-to-be???' ran the insinuating caption. The reporter had obviously not got the measure of the virgin bride.

PENNY

Jim and Betty Coverdale
invite you to a rave-up
to celebrate the marriage of their daughter, Penelope
to The Hon. Frederick Arthur Weathering
on July 27, 1964 at Raymond's Revue Bar

Freddy hadn't been to Cairo, but he had known Doris, which came to almost the same thing. Doris was the resident tart of Lower Snodbury, in Norfolk, where the Weatherings had their stately home. Doris also worked as a downstairs maid at Weathering Hall, and during her stints there serviced all of the Weathering boys as well as, one assumes, the father. I loved listening to Freddy's descriptions of her. 'Big tits,' he would say. 'Big, but not pendulous. One's hand fit round them as though holding one of your Wedgwood teacups. Papa, I think, preferred beer mugs. Touch Doris anywhere and she giggled. And when she giggled, one could see her tiny little teeth, gleaming like the horns of a Sidonian heifer. All passion and nothing upstairs. Dido as opposed to Cleopatra. Pyres rather than asps were her thing – she had to make up fires in all the rooms in the house every morning, poor love. One used to watch her on her hands and knees, her little rump bobbing up and down as she swept the ashes out, her little voice piping out some frightful tune by those Beatles. Ahh, Doris.' At which point he would turn to me, randy as a hoot owl, and that would be the end of conversation.

Ahh, Freddy. He was different from the others, in that sex, for him, was more than just a tumble in the hay in between the real amusements of life like racing or cricket. Freddy really needed it. That's why he wanted to marry me. He had never met a girl to whom he could both

talk intelligently and make love successfully.
My education far surpassed that of most of his
debby girlfriends, and my Yorkshire background
excluded me from their sisterhood of total sex-
lessness. This combination carried an almost
mystical weight with him, and he couldn't get
over his luck. 'You should have seen me with
Fiona Coomb-Downing, or Sarah Drummond-
Bond, or Lady Alice Bywater,' he said. 'You
wouldn't have thought it was the same man.'
And he would burrow his head in my belly,
muttering 'Penelope' in that slow, lingering was
of his. I felt like a Virgilian heroine.

His family, needless to say, was less enthusiastic. The earl and countess of Weathering
were appalled at Freddy's choice of mate, regarding me as little better than Doris, in spite of
Oxford and the tractor fortune. It turned out
that they had only just managed to dissuade
Freddy's eldest brother (and heir to the title),
Viscount Bromley, from marriage to a blonde
American title-hunter from Orlando, Florida.
Exhausted from this battle with the flawless
teeth and suntanned limbs of the New World,
they found Freddy's insistence on bringing a
Yorkshire lass into the Weathering dynasty in
the poorest possible taste. My Oxford degree
only made me more alarming – I would be
cleverer at sticking to my suit than the poor

American claimant, who fled in tears from the Weatherings' withering disapproval and hastily hitched herself, so we learned, to a showbusiness lawyer from Anaheim, somewhere near Disneyland. I thought it unfair that everyone should make such a fuss about me, since Freddy, being the second son, counted for nothing in the family hierarchy, and had no say in the family future.

Their real objection, to be candid, was of our sex life. They could sniff it out a mile off, with Freddy constantly gazing at my body and grinning like a Cheshire cat. You could almost hear him purring whenever we showed up together after a certain absence. Not only did they think it unseemly to reek so of lust, but deep down they were madly jealous. Lord Weathering was always putting his hand on my bottom and squeezing it just that much too hard to be friendly, and Lady Weathering, whose skin was puckered like seersucker, was never able to iron out her lips sufficiently to show me even the faintest of smiles.

Their hostility welded us even more firmly together. Freddy was deeply offended by their snobbishness and felt like protecting me even more. He enjoyed the role, a new one for him, and frankly I enjoyed my part in it. I had spent so much of my life organizing other people that this respite was very pleasant, and I allowed

him to mastermind the marriage on his own. My
parents, of course, were thoroughly on his side,
and egged him on, longing to see their daughter
married to an aristocrat, just as Alan's parents
had cheered for their son when he married
Daphne.

We decided to get the marriage done secretly
(with the financial help of Mum and Dad), and
the night before the appointment at the Registry
Office, we drove up to dine at Weathering Hall.
It was as though we were saying goodbye.
Freddy drank a lot of claret, and I had second
helpings of the perfect roast beef. Nobody talked
much, since my presence seemed to put a stopper
on general conversation. I suppose they were
pained by my accent. Afterwards, Lady Weathering, whose mouth seemed more shrivelled
than usual, took me aside and, pouring me a
demitasse, murmured, 'Of course you know it's
only an infatuation. You are much too clever,
Penny, not to see that. Freddy is infatuated with
you, and the reason is sex. I know my son. I
know how he feels. He is like his father. He has
always had difficulties, you know, that way.
When that wears off . . .' She shrugged. 'It isn't
much fun then,' she said, looking down into her
coffee cup. 'Do you really want to throw away
your life for that?'

I watched her as she fitted her lips round the

coffee cup. For what, I wanted to ask. I wasn't getting the title, the house, the inheritance. I was getting a splendid workout, and a loving companion.

'You're wrong, Lady Weathering,' I said. 'You've got me wrong, and you've got Freddy wrong. Thank you all the same.'

Brave words, Penny me lass. When I told Freddy this, he chortled with his shoulders shaking in that characteristic way and said his mother had once been madly in love with a French count and his father refused to let her spend summers with him. 'Wouldn't look right, my dear,' Lord Weathering would say, vanishing into his bedroom with Doris.

I have sometimes thought of Lady Weathering's frustrated existence with a twinge of pity. Perhaps she really wanted to save me from something. Lacking the gift of prophecy, her efforts were in vain.

9

ALICE

So Penny got her title, but a pretty watered-
down one. I suppose any man who married
Penny would appear watered down, her own
personality was so dominating. I would have
preferred to see her with someone of more spunk
and energy. At least Freddy showed enough
enthusiasm to run off with her to some Registry
Office in Ipswich to escape the wrath of his awful
parents, who obviously thought Penny far
beneath him. When faced with the *fait accompli*,
the Weatherings, acting in the long tradition of
British aristocrats, responded pragmatically.
There was talk of sending Freddy off to Australia like a remittance man, but I think even
old Lord Weathering saw that Freddy would
quickly sink into a decline when exposed to
surfboards, billabongs, and Australian beer. So
the couple was allowed to stay in England, as
long as they remained outside a hundred-mile
radius of Weathering Hall. His Lordship even
sent them a map, framed in baroque gilt (an Old

Master no doubt having been removed for the purpose), showing the geographical limits to their freedom. The history of the English, after all, is largely territorial.

Jim and Betty Coverdale ignored these trumpetings from the further reaches of Norfolk, and sponsored a large party at Raymond's Revue Bar to celebrate the happy pair's union. The venue could hardly have been better chosen, either to enrage the in-laws or delight the groom, whose taste for vulgarity was insatiable. 'My dear, isn't it all glorious,' he murmured, waving a cigarette at the peeling French-Empire interior decor, shuddering in ecstasy when one of the topless waitresses chucked him under the chin. The wedding party mixed jovially with the local tourists, who included a spangled crowd of dolly birds and Beatle-haired youths who looked like Terence Stamp.

'Isn't it nice that he married her,' Oxford types murmured, remembering other aristocrats who dumped their mistresses rather than marry out of their class.

'Isn't it nice that he married her here,' other Oxford types murmured, who had assumed the values of the vulgar proletariat in order to fit in with the topsy-turvy times.

'Can't Buy Me Love,' we sang along with the Fab Four, adding a working-class twang to our

accents and hitching up our groin-length skirts.
Louisa and Edmund were there, looking remote
and unhappy, obviously in the middle of a row. I
suspected Edmund disliked the noisy, smelly
atmosphere, and Louisa was angry that Penny
had deserted her for a weedy Honourable. Marriage definitely changed the emphasis of one's
alliances.

These were not precisely my thoughts at Raymond's Revue Bar that night. I was busy coping
with my own unusually aroused feelings in the
company of Gerald. It was not Gerald who had
aroused them. Perish the thought. No, it was
Alan Moss, rather drunk, who was having this
odd effect. Alan had agreed to accompany
Daphne to this particular event, since Raymond's Revue Bar did not offend his own political opinions and anyway, he never hid his
appreciation of sexy young females with no
clothes on. He had attempted to teach Daphne
to dance the way the kids from the local dance
halls were dancing, and to watch them together,
Alan all intent on swivelling his hips and bending his knees, a cigarette hanging precariously
out of the side of his mouth, opposite Daphne,
who was tensely biting her lip in her efforts to
sway empathetically with her energetic husband, was like witnessing some ritual execution.
One felt sure that one wrong move from poor

Daphne would have Alan yelping in triumph and slicing her breasts off with some concealed machete.

At one point in the evening, Alan deserted his exhausted wife and asked me to dance. He was unshaven, and his hairline was beaded with sweat. I could smell his singeing armpits. I said no, but refusal was irrelevant. He dragged me on to the floor and swayed about in front of me, raising his arms and snapping his fingers, howling occasionally, while I jigged and jogged in an effort to be unnoticeable. For this kind of dancing, distaste was also irrelevant. After a while he took my shoulders and leered at me with his Limpopo eyes and said, and I quote, 'You're such a tight-arse, Alice. You must be dynamite to fuck.' And with that he looked so hard at my mouth that I thought he was going to bite it. Then he laughed and led me back to Gerald. 'Take her, she's yours,' he said, and with a flick of his fingers against my cheek he was gone.

My heart was pounding. My blood pressure must have shot up, and there were spots before my eyes. My lower abdomen was churning and my legs had lost all control. I could feel my cheek stinging where he had touched me. I had to sit down. Gerald rushed to get me a glass of water, thinking I was going to faint. I wasn't, of course. I have never fainted. I was simply stunned by what I felt, which was something I had never remotely felt before. It was the overwhelming desire for Alan to rape me. Yes, rape me, right then and there on the floor of Raymond's Revue Bar. I could feel my legs stretched apart, my back against the dance floor, and his rough, sweating body ramming into me. The tune of 'Love Me Do' rang in my head.

'Here, Alice, drink this,' Gerald said, his voice filled with consternation. 'You look quite done up.'

I drank the water and thanked him. His voice and presence calmed me. He began to talk about the temperature in the room, and hyperventilation, and other reassuring nonsense, and my extraordinary dream began to fade. And as it faded, I realized how wild it was, how reprehensible, how inconsistent with my nature, and how close to losing control I had been. I asked Gerald to take me home, and when he gave me his usual hygienic goodnight kiss I told him we should get married as soon as possible.

'Good show,' he said. 'I wasn't sure when to ask you. These things are difficult for a chap, you know. Wasn't sure if you really wanted to quite yet. You're a dark horse, Alice.'

'Not really,' I said hastily. 'I just don't want to wait any more.'

So Gerald and I slid quietly into matrimony

in a country village near Colchester, without
friends or relatives in attendance. I didn't really
want to see anyone, even Penny. Gerald's retired
admiral father pronounced us shipshape, his
mother gave me a vase that was a good shape
for flower arrangements, and my parents provided the champagne. My father, preoccupied by
his current project, which was inventing a plastic pourer for milk bottles, unfortunately broke
a fine antique bottle with a ship inside it in the
admiral's drawing room while demonstrating
the efficacy of his latest idea. Otherwise the day
went off smoothly, apart from a momentary
twinge of diarrhoea on Gerald's part that we put
down to the local oysters eaten the night before,
and an inexplicable sharp pain in my abdomen
that afflicted me when I heard the strains of
'Love Me Do' coming from the radio in the next-
door garden.

'How lucky we decided that you should not go
though with that silly season,' my mother said
as we left for our honeymoon in the Lake District. 'I always thought Gerald a far better sort
than Edmund Wales, whatever everybody said.'

'He'll go far, that Edmund Wales,' my father
said. 'He has an inventor's mind. You can see
that a mile off. Intelligence like that is hard to
come by in these days of bureaucratic domina-
tion. Perhaps we should go into business

together.' My mother and I exchanged glances. Father always became erratic after champagne.

Our marriage was of the English kind so baffling to foreigners – no billing, no cooing, no hand-holding or touching (except for the occasional affectionate pat on the bottom); merely a shared acceptance of functional intimacy. Gerald was not very interested in what he called sexualism. I think he saw sex in exclusively biological terms, rather, I imagined, like an artist painting a nude. This, of course, was exactly what I needed to keep my own darker instincts under control. It was a mutually gratifying relationship. About once a month, after a particularly good claret or champagne, we would turn to each other and match up organs as nature had so whimsically prescribed.

'Satisfactory conveying of semen through the vaginal orifice,' he would murmur, or something to that effect, after which he would fall instantly asleep. My body, calibrated to his rhythm, subsided just as rapidly and I would fall asleep too, Quality, and no frills.

PENNY

Is there anything more gloriously satisfying than that final push of childbirth? After those relentless, spirit-breaking wrenches of the body, those metal rods encasing your belly and then being squeezed tighter, tighter, tighter until you would bite through your own flesh to be relieved? Push, you hear those white-masked gods and goddesses urge, push, harder, *push*. And you strain, and your veins burst and your head spins and then suddenly, like the final releasing surge of orgasm, the baby's head bursts through and you can breathe again.

Oh, dreadful is the check, intense the agony, when the ear begins to hear and the eye begins to see . . . Emily Brontë never had children but she knew pain and there is no pain like the pain of childbirth. But they told me I would forget it, and indeed I did. I tried not to; for months after I would rehearse the labour, replaying the contractions, reliving the torture. But after a while it became simply history being rewritten, a description rather than an experience. How oddly nature works.

Freddy was ecstatic. He loved the whole thing,

the blood, the cord, the squiggy squirmy animal being extruded from my thighs. Freddy often shocked even unshockable old me with his earthiness. For someone so otherworldly in appearance and background, his fascination with ordure was most peculiar. Men never came into the delivery room in those days, but Freddy was insistent, and nobody could refuse the Honourable Frederick Weathering, so he was ushered in with due respect for his position, and he grunted and sighed and moaned just as much as I did.

'My darling Penelope,' he said after Caspar was born. 'That was magnificent. Homer himself could not have risen to such heights. One must give you Virgil: "Labor omnia vicit Improbus et duris urgens in rebus egestas."'

I never understood Freddy's Latin remarks, and he never translated them. The only one I knew was 'Eheu, fugaces, Postume, Postume, labuntur anni,' which he wrote on postcards to Louisa, Alice, and Daphne after Caspar's birth. The next generation, as he said, was waiting in the wings.

Capon House, bequeathed to us by Freddy's frightful old man, turned out to be a Georgian gem, somewhat dilapidated but still in form a real beauty of line, proportion, and space. The reason he gave away such a splendid architectural specimen was because the previous inhabitant, one of His Lordship's furthest-flung tenant farmers, had taken an axe to his wife while she was feeding the pigs and buried her in the vegetable garden in a plastic bag. This was local lore, anyway, and it rather put a curse on the place for any prospective buyer. Freddy, naturally, was thrilled with this detail of our property and spent hours speculating on what the decomposed body might look like wrapped in polythene – 'perhaps one of those awful plastic dolls with detachable limbs you can buy in America.' He asked our gardener to do some discreet digging, but the man laughed and told him that if the body was indeed mouldering away under the cabbages, he would not be the one to transplant it. 'Fine fertilizer,' he said, 'don't you disturb it, milord.'

I had never really lived in the country. My parents were unreconstructed suburbanites, my father's tractors notwithstanding. I had been brought up to ignore the muddy side of Dad's business and think only of the gleaming red and yellow machines that we saw in his catalogues. Earthiness, it seems, is only permissible if you have long departed from the soil. The Coverdales, in any case, were close enough still to feel pained about it, and our house in Weybridge had a lawn, a box hedge, some stone statues, and a lot of gravel driveway.

Capon House, on the Norfolk-Suffolk border, was in deep country. No other house could be seen for ten miles, and our village of Little Dexton had two shops, the newspaper and sweet shop, and the post office. Food had to be picked up at Dexton, another village twelve miles down the road, which had three shops, a grocery, a newspaper and sweet shop, and the post office. People in the country wrote a lot of letters and ate a lot of chocolate.

I thought I would do that too, but children put an end to that idea. Well, I ate the chocolate. But I didn't write anything for about four years while I had Caspar, Chloe, Camilla, and Postumus. (He wasn't christened Postumus, of course. His real name was Crispin. But by this time the Postume joke really required some conclusion, so to speak.) I know the rest of the Bardwell Road Four thought I was completely mad, breeding like that. But once you've started, it becomes addictive, and as I said, you forgot the pain. Freddy was equally enthusiastic, in a sort of clinical way. He was fascinated by how different the results of our always-identical physical effort could be. The pregnancies and births took the place, for him, of sex, a development causing immense relief to me. Yes, relief.

People did not write articles back then about the effect of children on one's sex life. It was yet

143

another of those Dirty Little Secrets kept hidden in the basement. That a mother of four, after a full day's feeding, washing, nappy-changing, consoling, disciplining, feeding again, nappy-changing again, and so on and so on, could then turn over in bed with a voluptuous smile of enthusiasm to her spouse was strictly in the realm of True Romances, those romances women knew, deep in their hearts, were false. If Freddy's interest ultimately began to wane, it was received with no discouragement on my part. I fell asleep as soon as my head hit the pillow, several fibres in my body remaining alert to the mewling sounds of a bad dream from one of the next-door bedrooms. To inspire my husband to nocturnal rapture under these circumstances was about as remote a possibility as springing up at dawn with a song on my lips. The babies had my body; they possessed it more totally than a man ever would. It was a development I had not bargained for.

This may have been my undoing.

10

ALICE

Since friendship feeds on proximity, the Bardwell Road Four began to divide and reassemble
in a new configuration under the changed geographical alignments of our marriages. For the
first years, struggling feebly against the idea of
'settling down' – a concept invariably rejected
during late-night sessions at Oxford as being a
fate worse than death – we found ourselves
sucked into the daily round of tube to work, bus
home, Sainsbury's for chops, launderette for
washing, weekends shopping for the latest Rolling Stones' single or Biba's newest clothing
outrage, and the duty visit to one's parents for
dinner once a month.

I say 'we,' but this excluded Penny, who was
firmly ensconced in the Weathering patrimony
in Suffolk having babies. Being the only one of
us living outside London, she was frequently the
victim of friendly escapees from the city. Gerald
and I were the most reliable guests, partly
because I belonged to that unfortunate group of

people who had been brought up to believe that
country air was therapeutic, and partly because
of its impressive vegetable garden. (The notorious axe-man's wife's doing, no doubt.) The house
was more than a Georgian gem, as Penny so
casually decribed it. It was an Adam masterpiece, with something like twelve bedrooms, the
usual lack of bathrooms, and a long central
corridor-gallery upstairs hung with the second
string of Weathering family portraits and Old
Masters winkled out of the paternal stately
home by Freddy's ancient Nanny, who still
resided in a cell on the top floor, rather like at
Brideshead.

Nanny was not allowed to move out and come
to Capon House to look after the new generation
of junior Weatherings, in spite of the fact that
her expertise at the Big House had long fallen
into disuse, but another old retainer was sent in
compensation. This was the old boy who greeted
one at the peeling but still splendid Palladian
entrance. I say 'greeted' advisedly, since he had
a severe case of the shakes and was too debilitated to carry anyone's luggage inside the door,
let alone up the grand staircase to one's distant
bedroom. Lupin, known inevitably as Loopy, had
been demoted from his position as handyman at
the Norfolk castle because of his physical infirmities, but he still carried himself with the hau-

teur expected of his position, dressed himself
impeccably, and added an air of strange gran-
deur to the proceedings. Freddy also employed
him as one of the gardeners, a job to which he
was not suited, judging from the total wilderness
that passed for grounds one glimpsed through
the drawing-room windows. The vegetable
garden was looked after by another man, who
charged Freddy an arm and a leg for his efforts,
but who also produced the prize marrows and
cucumbers at the local fetes, occasions which
invariably gave rise to disgusting jokes about
polythene bags and rotting limbs.

Loopy's major contribution to the household
was his wife, Mrs Lupin, a rotund soul who
cooked, cleaned, and fed the rapidly increasing
Weathering family with inexhaustible energy.
We used to speculate on the Lupin marriage,
since Mrs Lupin was so obviously a cut above
her husband, whose charisma, even at the
height of his powers, must have been about as
powerful as a wet Kleenex. Penny insisted that
his organ was responsible for her devotion.
'Weedy, small men often have huge ones,' she
told us, speaking, as we knew, from experience.
Freddy said Mrs Lupin wanted someone to
mother, not having children of her own. 'Don't
all women,' he added, gazing at his endlessly
pregnant wife. Gerald said that for any woman,

147

the marriage state was more socially acceptable than spinsterhood, and perhaps she had been jilted by some former lover and took Loopy as a last resort. I found this point of view condescending to women, but irritatingly plausible. Louisa's typically Mahlerian suggestion was that Loopy had once been a talented artist, but conditions forced him to reject his vocation and marry Mrs Lupin as an alternative career.

I remember staying at Capon House once when a Rowed Scholar from our Oxford days showed up, having heard that the architecture was something out of the ordinary. Imagine his shock on seeing the shabbiness of the place. Ants had eaten into the original eighteenth-century four-poster beds; vermin had nibbled away at the French tapestries in the hall; Penny's ever-accumulating offspring had put toys in the fireplaces and food particles in the statuary. The fine Persian carpets were threadbare, the damask curtains motheaten.

'Jesus,' the American kept muttering as he watched the children finger painting on the Louis Quatorze dining table, or realized that on the cracked and shadowy wall behind the dog-hairy chintz sofa hung an authentic Van Dyke. How he must have yearned for the brilliant lime-greens and acid yellows of Southampton,

Long Island, where Quality meant newness and Art had special lighting.

'Jesus,' he murmured, as he sat down to dine with us and faced a roast beef as rare and thinly sliced as smoked salmon, handed casually to him on a priceless piece of Sèvres china.

'Jesus,' he gasped as he watched Loopy's trembling hands desperately wave a bottle of vintage claret in the direction of the huge Georgian goblets.

'Jesus,' he moaned as he tried not to hear the Honourable Freddy Weathering belch and burp his way through the meal, napkin tied round his neck like a two-year old, picking his teeth noisily between courses and slugging back the wine as though it were water.

'Don't mind Freddy,' Penny told her guest as he looked desperately around for help. 'You should see how the duke of Ellsworth eats.'

This was not the kind of reassurance our poor Rowed Scholar needed. His whole conception of the British upper classes in disarray, he retreated back to town, no doubt telling his friends that at last he understood why Britain was going to the dogs.

Penny's pregnancies put a slight damper on things, as far as Gerald and I were concerned. Both of us regarded babies rather as Nancy Mitford described them – bawling oranges in

black wigs – so Penny's unbridled enthusiasm
for motherhood fell on rather barren soil, and
the sight of those revolting rubber teats and
pailfuls of nappies put us off our appetites.
Freddy, who at first had thrown himself with
passion into his role as father, seemed as time
passed to be less and less interested. Occasionally one saw an expression of pain flit across his
face as a distant child bawled for his mother in
the middle of a Mrs Lupin soufflé and Penny
would shuffle up from the table, apologetic but
single-minded in her duty to the nursery set.
(On asking why she didn't get help with the
children, I was treated to such a lecture about
responsibility and early development and other
pediatric claptrap that I never raised the matter
again.)

Of course Freddy was a special case. Gerald
and I often used to talk about the Trouble with
Freddy, a trouble that afflicts many of those who
are not driven by economic necessity: what to do
with oneself all day. Every time we saw him he
was involved with a new 'project,' as he called it.

'One must have a project, Alice,' he would say
over a typically claret-laden dinner. 'One must
always get up in the morning with a project.
Otherwise, frankly, one might not get up at all.'
His shoulders shook, but there was something
unsettling about his remarks, which Penny

shrugged off as mere indulgence. Anyway, she was too busy thrusting nipples into hungry orifices to identify with his particular complaint.

Freddy's projects ranged from complicated efforts to solve the problem of Northern Ireland (this involved writing long letters to his Irish relations who never answered), to backing Art in Public Places, which generally meant Freddy forking out large sums of money to con artists who wanted to set up hammocks at bus stops or wrap benches in silver foil or read poetry in pubs. So it was all the more astonishing when one of Freddy's projects turned out to make history.

The years of swinging London are now, surely, entrenched in the reader's mind as a time when the British flag became the symbol of the biggest party the nation had even known. I think I can safely say that the Honourable Freddy Weathering was the first person to come up with the idea of putting the Union Jack on something other than a flagpole. His workroom in the attic was full of them – big Union Jacks, little Union Jacks, long Union Jacks, all being pasted on matchboxes, wastepaper baskets, shooting bags, ashtrays, jugs, even chamber pots; in short, the usual detritus one find in an English country house. In a year, all those things (and many more as the commercial imagination began to soar) were to be seen in souvenir shops and tourist centres all over the land.

Freddy was modest about his idea when we found him working on all this. 'One was just larking about,' he said, 'and it occurred to one that the Union Jack has a very appealing design. It's distinctive, it's colourful, it's known to everybody. And since there's nowhere to wave it much any more, one thought one might do one's bit to uphold the flag right here at home.'

I must confess we failed to see its potential, as we cautiously turned over some of the items he had rather clumsily decorated. 'There's nothing wrong with red, white, and blue,' I admitted. 'But it's a bit limited.'

'I think you should use a better glue, Freddy, old chap,' Gerald said. 'A lot of this is peeling.'

'Have a glass of this Pomerol,' Freddy said. 'You're perfectly right, of course. One doesn't seem to have the knack of getting anything quite right.' He leaned back and surveyed his handiwork. 'But there is something there, isn't there?'

'It beats fighting for it,' I said.

Penny had her doubts. 'I'll admit that it's cheaper than some of his projects,' she conceded, veinous breast under attack by bewigged orange as usual. 'But I keep losing things like the teapot, or the baby's potty. I've also begun noticing some of the Chinese Export is missing, let alone the set of Greek vases Freddy's mother smuggled out of Weathering Hall last year for his birthday.' She shoved the milky tit more firmly into lucky diddums's beak. Gerald turned away, wincing, though I was longing to have just the teeniest taste of the meal myself. ('Think of it, Gerald,' I said later. 'It looks like condensed milk, it tastes like condensed milk, and you make it yourself. Free.' Gerald, a pedant, pointed out that Penny would no longer be producing colostrum at this point. 'Still, I wouldn't mind trying it myself,' I murmured, knowing it would alarm him. It did.)

Penny's objections finally forced Freddy to look elsewhere for objects on which to paste Union Jacks. The local junk dealer in the village responded enthusiastically to Freddy's appeal, indulging his Lordship's whim while saying to his wife within Penny's earshot, 'I think there's something wrong with the young fella upstairs. Too much inbreeding.'

To everyone's surprise, the objects, when placed in the junk shop window, sold immediately. Thus from such modest beginnings are revolutions made. Alan Moss would have been amused at the irony. Freddy, needless to say, never got a penny for his idea. It was not the kind of thing you could patent. Nor has he received any credit until now, but his shoulders used to shake when he saw dolly birds walking about with Union Jacks pasted on their shopping bags and later, more saucily, on their bottoms.

I think I can place it at around this time that life at Capon House began to change. I thought it might simply be the exhaustion from all those children, combined with Freddy's lessening interest in his family as he gained confidence from his little decorating success. He used to come to London much more, calling us up to see if we could have lunch. It was always lunch, never dinner, for reasons which naturally intrigued me. Gerald was generally too busy at his magazine (he had begun writing about health and food for *Herself Magazine*, a glossy publication for educated, middle-class women such as myself, that enjoyed a brief flowering in the sixties, when everything, it seems, flowered for a season). But I often lunched with Freddy, who always chose splendid restaurants and ordered splendid wines and amused me in a slight, frivolous sort of way. He was proud of his children, and obviously still adored Penny. 'Imagine, four children,' he would say. 'Beyond one's wildest dreams.' Yet he was terribly moody and distracted at the same time, as though he were struggling against something. But that, of course, was a feeling most of us had at one time or another.

PENNY

Alice was a bitch. I knew what she was doing. I was stuck in Suffolk, trying to look after four wayward children, a loony handyman, and a relentlessly cheerful cook, plus managing Freddy's money from his family and trying to stop him spending it so profligately all the time, which made me into the villain of the piece – while Alice was lunching at Boulestin's with Freddy and egging him on as he complained what a bore I was.

There's nothing worse than getting up in the morning, knowing that the whole day ahead will be filled with nothing except Marmite sandwiches, crumby floors, snotty noses, and the endless 'Mummy, Mummy, Mummy' of petulant children who want attention. Christ, how the thrills of childbirth wore off! I could still look in a pram and feel floods of the old warmth and desire, but in that bloody draughty house with spiderwebs everywhere and a cold, empty bed to climb upstairs to after finally persuading the last yowler to belt up, only to be faced with a pile of bills, mostly from your husband's idiotic 'projects,' the magic was well and truly gone.

You know what it was? I'd run things before. I knew about managing things alone. I had always had prefectorial tendencies, if you like. That wasn't the problem. But this was the first time in my life I had assumed control and found I could not keep it. I had always known how to run my life and had had no trouble in executing my plans. I had known what I wanted, who I wanted, and when I wanted it. But here, I had lost control. My days no longer belonged to me. My emotions were permanently on the surface, ready to burst like a balloon at the slightest pinprick. Spilled milk, a clogged drain, a lost bottle, an unanswered phone, and I would be engulfed in uncontrollable rage. I suppose some might say that this was a highly beneficial experience, a learning experience as Americans say, a discovery of my anger, etc. etc. I found it simply disgusting and humiliating. My sleeping habits, my physical appearance, my mental attitude, always slaves to my requirements, now rose up against me and fought me, in a bitter battle for my spirit. I looked at my face in the morning, saw the sallow skin, the unplucked eyebrows, the diminished, bleached eyes, and felt not even the slightest urge to pick up a hairbrush, to make the slightest adjustment.

Body and mind had lost their way. I wore the same clothes day after day, pulled on trousers and a smock without even looking. I moved like a giant boiler, huge, hot, taut, ready to explode.

And Alice lunched at Boulestin's with Freddy, filling his ears with poison. How she hated children, and how she must have passed on that hate. How she must have ridiculed me, stuck, trapped, fat, boring, beyond the pale, a Yorkshire cow. I thought of her, free, irresponsible, amusing, amused, filled with days of wonderful choices. Should it be a trip to Harrods today? The Victoria and Albert maybe? Let's have lunch at Wilton's instead, for a change. Why not? I can do whatever I want.

I can do whatever I want. Six words that alter forever a person's attitude to life, to living. Would I ever be able to say them again?

DAPHNE

How do you prevent a marriage from being bourgeois? The struggle nearly killed us. We moved into a two-room flat in Kilburn that belonged to one of Alan's left-wing friends and so was politically All Right. But wedding pre-

sents of china, glass, silver, and linen appeared
with alarming regularity from my parents' conventional friends, who did not know the full
political story, presents that, since they represented the ultimate in bourgeois materialism,
had all to be sent back. The politically All Right
flat must have quivered in horror at the boxes
from Asprey's, Harrods, and the General Trad-
ing Company that piled up in corners of the tiny
space.

At first, I enjoyed playing house, even if it was
more a rathole than a house. I was, after all,
finally an independent housewife, trying not to
be bourgeois. But after a few months the thrill
wore off, and when I met my mother for the first
time after our marriage (under family pressure,
she had decided not to see me for a while to let
me 'settle down'), I was already constructing an
acceptable version of the depressing truth.

'We're living in the dearest little flat in Not-
ting Hill Gate,' I told her over lunch at the Ritz.

'That sounds wonderful, darling. When can I
come and see it? I'm sure we might have some
little pieces – one of those Directoire chairs in
my bedroom, perhaps – that would come in
useful.'

'Well, I'm not sure, Mummy. Alan's quite
spartan in his tastes, you know.'

'What about some kitchen equipment, then?

Heavens knows what that means, but I'm sure McCloud could come up with something.'

'It's only a tiny kitchen. There's not much room for equipment.'

My mother was relieved to hear it. 'I'm sure you wouldn't want to spend much time there anyway, darling. I never like to linger in our kitchen. I feel it's so distracting for McCloud.'

I allowed as how I wished I knew how to cook.

'Whatever for?' Mummy said, surprised. 'You can cook, anyway, Daphne. Remember how you always used to help me make that sardine savoury your father likes so much.'

She was referring to an odd little ritual, the one night a week McCloud was allowed to leave her post, when my mother opened a tin of sardines and spread it over some toast. I had always wondered whether it was the height of culinary art my mother always assured me it was.

'I'm not sure Alan like savouries, Mum. I don't think he knows what they are.'

That was a low blow to my spouse, and my mother was not one to let it pass. She squeezed my hand. 'My poor darling,' she said. 'But remember, your life is not yet over. I'm sure Daddy could get the whole awful thing annulled. He had lunch with the archbishop of York only the other day. He wants to get the dear old archbish on some Wildlife Fund. The archbish told your father that God did not like us mortals to spend so much time on dumb animals, instead of saving our own souls. Well, you can imagine what your father thought of that remark. He told him that Canterbury was already a founding member, wasn't that clever of him?'

My face must have failed to respond to my father's brilliance, as she went on hurriedly, 'Well, anyway, maybe I can find a little something for your bathroom.'

Once again I had to shake my head.

'Really, Daphne, don't tell me Alan won't let you have a bath either. This is too much. I'm sure we could get it annulled. By the way, let's have the smoked salmon. It's always safe here. Sometimes the Ritz soups fail one.'

'It's just that we have to share it.'

'Share the bathroom?' Several Ritz dowagers rustled in their chairs at my mother's shriek.

'With a family of Indians,' I bashed on. 'Well, I think there must be more than one family, actually. I can't believe one set of parents could have produced so many children.'

'Daphne, darling, this is terrible. What are we going to do?'

'Mummy, you're so bourgeois. It's fine, really. We all go at different times.'

Her voice faltered. 'When do Indians go, then?'

'Well, I suppose very early or very late.'

160

'I don't feel hungry any more,' my mother said faintly. 'Shall we go?'

I would have stayed for the smoked salmon, but my life seemed destined to be punctuated by incomplete meals. I almost suggested we go and have a curry, but I thought even my mother's sense of humour might fail at this attempt at wit. She kissed me goodbye as though I were re-entering the terminal wing of a hospital. 'If only you'd married Edmund Wales,' she murmured, pulling her hat more firmly on her Harvey Nichols hairdo, 'He's always being photographed in the newspapers, you know. They sound as though they are leading such an amusing life. And I'm sure he likes savouries.'

I may have put on a bold front for poor Mama, but things were not running altogether smoothly in Kilburn. For one thing, it was extremely cold since there was no central heating. Getting up in the morning was pure torture. One or the other of us had to leap out of bed, turn on the gas fire in ice-cold temperatures, then rush back into bed again and wait for the room to warm up. But it never did (no insulation, holes in the floorboards, etc.), so one had to dress practically with one's flesh scorching in the fire in order not to turn blue with frostbite. Of course I only had the class structure to blame for my softness; most of England endured the daily ordeal without flinching. I found, however, that neither the flames of love nor of political conviction could make me embrace the experience with enthusiasm.

To describe our kitchen as small was an exaggeration. It was a converted cupboard under the stairs, complete with slanted ceiling that practically sliced off the end of the stove. There was no window, and the sink regurgitated brown water at will. A refrigerator just big enough to store a yogurt in was slotted under the sink. Two small storage shelves were stocked with tins of mince, macaroni and cheese, ravioli, and the other staples of a noncook's diet, plus several spray cans of air freshener, a product I had always regarded as frightfully non-U, but which I was reduced to using to banish the lingering smells of politically All Right dinners and, yes, occasionally, the whiff of curry.

Nobody wanted to visit us in this luxurious palace, needless to say – not only because of its doubtful appointments but also because Alan and I were such poor company. Some people don't mind witnessing married couples argue all the time, and some couples like to argue in public, like Edmund and Louisa. We fitted into neither category, so nobody had a good time. I think Penny came once, pregnant, and fainted.

Louisa came twice, with Edmund. Edmund found Alan interesting and talked all evening about the Moss plan for revolution. Louisa told me she hated seeing me living in such squalor, and would I mind if she didn't come again. We used to meet for lunch occasionally instead. Alice was the most regular visitor, partly, I suspect, to witness our rapidly disintegrating marriage, and partly because I think, deep down, she fancied my working-class hero. I once actually saw her blush when he kissed her hand. She can't have realized he did it ironically.

Our dining area, as the design magazines called the prototype, was a space at the end of the tiny living room where a table had been set up with four rickety chairs bought by me at an 'antique' shop in Kilburn. (In Chelsea, it would have been called junk.) Alan watched like a lynx for any signs of upper-class taste seeping into his living quarters; all my wedding presents had gone except for a few he thought worth keeping, which were stored in the communal basement along with sacks of poppadoms. I'm sure the Indians picked out a few choice pieces of sterling along with their food supplies from time to time, but to suggest this would have been racist. (If Alan had suggested it, it would have been humour.) On the dinner table was a plastic cloth with geometric patterns on it, reminiscent of

163

working-class cafés. When I bought a flower, once, and stuck it in a soda bottle in the middle of this napery, Alan threw a fit, tossing the flower out of the room (he tried to throw it out of the window but the window was too warped to open), declaring that all flowers were green, all birds were brown, and Nature was a narcotic fostered by the ruling class to keep the masses subdued. Alice was present for that little scene. It was one of our better evenings, as I recall.

'Which Heinz Variety is this?' Alan asked as he slapped his spoon into the Chicken with Vegetables – or was it the Cream of Mushroom? 'I must have eaten all 57 by now. If I write to Heinz, do you think I'll get a medal? "All 57 Varieties, and still on his feet!"'

'Well, I can't help it they don't make any more,' I said.

Alan laughed. 'She's not bad, our Daphne,' he confided to Alice. 'You know, I never thought I'd feel homesick.'

'I suppose your mother's a fabulous cook,' Alice said.

'The best,' he said sentimentally, holding a hand over his heart.

'Well, why don't you do the cooking, then, if you care so much,' I said through my teeth.

'I haven't time, luv, as well you know. I'm far too busy with the Party.' He turned to Alice. 'I'm writing a manifesto for the Actors' Group of Catford. It's a key theoretical document.'

'They're a splinter group,' I explained. '"Theoretical document" means a play Alan is writing for them to do instead of *Separate Tables*. It's quite revolutionary.'

'By the way,' Alan said, 'I'll need a cheque from you for the rehearsal hall. We haven't paid last week's rent.'

I got up and wrote him a cheque.

'You see that?' Alan said to Alice. 'Did you see how fast she wrote that cheque?'

'I'm a fast writer,' I said proudly. 'Always have been. That's why I always did well in exams. Covered a lot of paper.'

'Bullshit,' Alan said. 'You write cheques fast because you are used to writing cheques fast. You write cheques fast because you don't have to think about what it means, I mean really means, this writing out a sum of money. You don't have to think about what it means, where it comes from, you are always writing cheques to pay off the poor, to pay off the downtrodden, to pay off the servant classes who do your dirty work, to pay off your miserable conscience.'

There was a stunned silence.

'I never thought about it like that before,' I muttered.

'Alan, that's tosh,' Alice said.

'I'm trying to politicize you,' he said, looking at her with his demonic gaze and grabbing her wrist. 'Don't you see, Alice, I must do this, this is what the revolution is all about. Don't you see that everything you do must bear this kind of investigation, otherwise you are acting in bad faith.'

'It's exhausting, anyway,' Alice said, staring at him in a strange sort of way until he loosened his grip.

Alan turned the TV on after that (some political broadcast), and Alice and I, trying to ignore his rudeness, made desultory conversation until she went home. Then came the part I dreaded. I could cope with the rhetoric, the temper, the selfishness; after all, I knew he was destined for greatness in his way, just as Edmund was in his. He was giving my life meaning.

But only in the daytime. At night, there was no politics, no historical materialism. At night, we were two bodies in the dark, fighting the cold, the hunger, and our own demons. Every time I took my clothes off, again huddled over that damn pathetic gas fire, my skin shrivelled and dried up like an old peapod. I would clutch myself to keep from shivering, then plunge into the icy sheets and bury my head under the eiderdown (Peter Jones, a last-minute Moss concession) and wait. Waiting for Alan would have made Godot seem punctual. He would go back into the living room and make himself another cup of coffee. He would smoke another cigarette, listen to a record. Anything, he said, to postpone the frigid experience of getting into bed. Ahah. I choose my words carefully here. Even the most amateur psychiatrist can see what I am driving at. You see, my dear Doktor, we had nothing to give each other in bed. Nothing. Not even comradely warmth. It's hard even now to say it. Was it the cold bedroom? Was it the Heinz 57 Varieties? Was it me?

At Oxford I had been innocent, a novice. If things weren't perfect, it could be put down to inexperience. But now, under the Peter Jones eiderdown, a thousand confessions of failure were enumerated to a lonely pair of chilblained feet. I was at heart a capitalist. That was the only possible explanation. Did Lenin ever have this problem with women? Did Lenin have women? Wasn't Trotsky supposed to be sexy? I didn't dare ask Alan. All I could do was wait.

11

ALICE

I was not particularly surprised when Daphne
rang up after her marriage had been limping
along for about a year and asked if she could
come and stay. 'I can't go home,' she said. 'It
would be too lowering. What I'd really like is a
bath.'

It turned out that Alan had become ena-
moured of a Greek girl who was working as a
stagehand for the Catford Actors' Group, and
who was very involved in Greek radical politics.
She was very different from Daphne in appearence, so he kindly told his wife – Melina was
dark, intense, with large, working-class bosoms.
'I am going to live with her in Mykonos,' the
Mighty Moss announced one night over Green
Pea or whichever it was. 'We will eat vine leaves
and moussaka and shish kebab and get back to
the origins of political thought by studying the
lessons of classical imperialism.' I told Daphne I
was glad he had added the part about the political thought. Otherwise it might have looked as

though Alan were simply thinking about his stomach.

Daphne took the announcement on the chin, realizing that politics would always have priority in Alan's life. If the Trotskyite spirit moved him, he would have to go. 'When are you going?' she asked him as a practical matter.

'Oh, in a month,' he said, rather as he had replied to Lord Fanthorpe over the famous marriage proposal.

This time, however, he did not keep his word. After five weeks, Alan was still there, listening to Greek music, talking about baklava, and spending the occasional night out with Melina. By now Daphne, quite rightly, had come to realize that his leaving was not such a bad idea, so from time to time she offered to get down his suitcase and help him pack. But our house revolutionary was apparently getting cold feet.

'He simply wouldn't go,' she told us. 'You know, deep down I think the poor darling was terrified of going off to some wog country with a Greek sex maniac. The working classes are really terribly conservative.' Gerald and I laughed. Daphne was definitely coming along. 'Anyway,' she continued, 'since he wouldn't leave I knew I had to. I mean, I never knew if he was going to be in to dinner. The adjustment to singlehood was surprisingly easy. To tell you the truth, I am the kind of person who is adversely affected by sharing a bathroom.' She sighed at her confession of imperfection. 'So here I am. I'll have to go and get my things. Will you come and help me?'

'My things' turned out to be something of a euphemism. When we split up the spoils of their Kilburn love nest, which was mostly the remains of the wedding presents from the Fanthorpe side, the take divided as follows: all books and records going to Alan; a black fur rug going to Alan; a small oak dining table covered in plastic and four rickety chairs going to Alan; bed, sheets, pillows, Peter Jones eiderdown, and electric blanket going to Alan; a gas fire going to Alan; sofa and two armchairs going to Alan; Fanthorpe-crested silver dinner canteen going to Alan; two Victorian watercolours going to Alan; four Fanthorpe candlesticks going to Alan; three glass decanters going to Alan; two silver toast racks going to Alan; a leather visitor's book going to Alan; a cheeseboard going to Alan; a Waterford vase going to Alan; two silver spoons going to Alan; record player going to Alan; radio going to Alan; one Savoy Hotel ashtray going to Alan; a jar of bathsalts going to Daphne.

'I didn't want to make a fuss,' Daphne explained. 'It would have seemed so materialistic.'

'It's not going to be easy getting all that stuff to Mykonos,' Gerald remarked.

'Oh, it's all for the Party,' Daphne said. 'He was very taken by the idea of the Fanthorpes ending up supporting the Cause in this way.'

I could see Alan's ironic, vulpine grin as he gathered up the crested silver. 'The beast,' I said, with perhaps an excess of heat, for I saw Daphne flash me a glance.

'Isn't he,' she said. 'Don't you love it, Alice?'

Poor Daphne. A broken marriage, bereft of possessions, no career. Not an auspicious beginning to Life after Oxford. She stayed with us for three months while Gerald experimented on her. He was deep into the subject of nutrition, an idea whose time had not nearly yet come. Nobody had heard about lecithin until ten years later, but Gerald was not only aware of calories, protein, and cholesterol, but believed our bodies were only as good as the stuff we put into them. Goodbye to cream, red meats, truffles, and *crème fraîche*. Hello to oatmeal, wheatgerm, nutcakes, and berries. I remember Daphne's permanently bemused expression at mealtimes as Gerald produced his strange dunglike patties, and then rushed off to write it all down for his column in *Herself Magazine*.

'Fibre, fertilized eggs, organic alfalfa, sea salt,' he would say. 'We must make you healthy, Daphne, after that miserable cuisine in Kilburn.'

People wondered at our sudden change of dietary habits, reckoning, with some truth, that our marriage to some extent hinged on, or was bound by, our mutual passion for stimulating the taste buds. Gerald's switch to the organic life therefore surely indicated some dissatisfaction on the home front. It was quite the reverse, as a matter of fact. Through food, we communicated with each other in a very comfortable sort of way.

Gerald and I, as I think I have already indicated, kept our emotional thoughts to ourselves, and thank goodness for it. More relationships have been wrecked by embarrassing outbursts of frankness, in my view, than any amount of sexual peccadilloes. People can only stand so much insight into other people's innermost hearts. Self-exposure is always the prelude to disaffection.

'One must preserve the fabric of life,' Gerald would say over a particularly offensive-looking nut pancake. 'It's a testimonial to civilization. Otherwise our lives are crippled by pain, incapacitated by despair. The Romantics have a lot to answer for.'

I so admired Gerald at those times that I would even endure a few mouthfuls of gritty bran for his sake. And I must confess that my waistline responded beautifully to our new regime. I began wearing a size ten for the first time since leaving Oxford.

Daphne failed to respond to our new routine. 'Give me Spaghetti-Os,' she would moan. She took to buying her own tins and hoarding them in her room, fearful of Gerald's condemnatory gaze. After she left, I found this little storehouse under her bed, rather like an alcoholic leaving behind a pile of empty bottles. Poor Daphne.

Poor Daphne. That's what her mother kept saying. Lady Fanthorpe phoned daily for a bulletin on her daughter, whispering into the receiver so Lord Fanthorpe would not hear.

'He actually said that Daphne should be sent underground like a badger for running out on the beast, Moss,' she confided to me one day, at full pitch since her spouse was at the House of Lords making a speech about silage. 'Really, sometimes his morality defeats me.'

I think Daphne must have communicated her food difficulties to her mother, because sometimes little packages from Fortnum's arrived, which Daphne whisked upstairs, no doubt to join the hoard of macaroni and cheese and corned-beef hash. But all this came to an end when Daphne met a new man and began a new life in America.

'America?' Gerald said. 'Rioting students, a stupid war, and a nation of overweights. Horror.'

'Do you know what they call chips? French fries.' As I said it, a shot of saliva rushed into my mouth. Naughty, naughty. How treacherous the body is.

I missed Daphne when she moved out, and I missed her exotic food supplies, the labels of which I would sometimes read when feeling low. Separation? Divorce? America? Who would have thought that Daphne would be the first one of us to break the rules?

DAPHNE

Herman Geist was my first real American. I didn't count the Rowed Scholars at Oxford, who were sort of embryonic Americans if you know what I mean – like huge puppies with outsized paws. Herman was at least fifty, and he was Jewish, which to someone like me was almost the same as being working-class. By which I mean madly exciting. Also, he was a screenwriter, which was a very American thing to me, and he hired me to type his screenplay. Of course I couldn't type, but luckily that didn't matter because he was a very slow writer, and dictated his lines at such a snail's pace that I was able to pick out the letters quite easily and keep up.

'Slow . . . fade . . .' he would say, puffing on his pipe and staring out of the window into Regent's Park. His flat was one of those huge furnished jobs that you see in the movies, with chandeliers and formal dining rooms and damask everywhere. My mother would have dismissed it at once as nouveau, but it made a nice change from Kilburn. 'Pan . . . to . . . open . . . window.' Puff. Puff. 'Ortrud . . . takes a strand of . . . hair . . . Make that . . . several . . . stands of hair . . .' Puff. Puff. 'And says . . .' He would pause and stare out of the window and I would stare at him, waiting for the muse to strike.

'How is your life today, Daphne?'

This was typical Herman. He would suddenly stop doing his screenplay and ask me about my private life. Well, I had to tell him I was separated, and sometimes I'm afraid I even cried a bit because he was so avuncular and kind and soothing, compared to Alan. He always relit his pipe when I cried and waited for me to stop and then said something incredibly mundane like, 'We all go through changes when we're young,'

175

and I would feel wonderfully restored. It was so courageous of him to say such idiotic things, when most of my friends tried to think up something clever and snappy and always made me feel worse.

'And when is Lady Fanthorpe taking you out to lunch again?'

That was the other thing, of course. He loved my parents having titles. Well, Americans do, so it was no big surprise, but I loved the way he rolled the word 'Lady' off his tongue. Sometimes, to tease me, he would call me 'the Honourable' before starting dictation. 'To think I have a typist who is an Honourable,' he would say, with his only smile – a small, reluctant grin like that of a small boy who can't help admitting he ate the last piece of chocolate cake.

Day after day, Herman dictated his great drama about Ortrud, and we both stared out of the window.

'Pan down . . . to her knees . . . which slowly cross with . . .' Puff. Puff. 'A rustle of . . . make that . . . a slither . . . of silk.' Puff. Puff. Puff.

I typed the words. 'Would you consider . . .?' Puff. Puff. I started to type. 'Who says that, Herman, Ortrud or Dagmar?'

Puff. Puff. I looked up, and there he was, right up beside me, gazing at me with a kind of gloomy elation.

'I suppose you are too honourable,' he said. 'But I would like to take you to California ... make that Hollywood.'

'Hollywood? Me?'

'Screenplays always have to be rewritten,' he said. 'That means, retyped. Revisions, you understand.' Puff. Puff. He went back to the window. 'The view is less ... agreeable there, however.'

'Gosh, I don't mind,' I said. 'I mean ... make that a yes.'

On a blustery day, on the roof of the Hilton Hotel, a place far enough from holes and burrows for Daddy not to sniff us out, I told my mother I was going to Hollywood.

'Who with?' she shrieked, holding on to her hat, a rather stylish straw boater of the sort worn at Oxford Eights Week.

'An American screenwriter called Herman Geist,' I shouted. 'But it's not like that. He's sort of my uncle.'

'Your uncle? Your uncle's in that terrible home for loonies, don't you remember? He kept trying to shoot the gardener.'

'Are you going to Eights Weeks, Mummy?' I asked as the boater wavered precariously in the wind.

'Of course not, darling. I hate boats. I'm opening a new wing at the Dorchester Hospital. My lady at Liberty's thought it was perfect with my beige linen. A little fun for all those poor invalids. Geist sounds German. I always knew you should have married Edmund Wales.'

'But he never asked me, Mummy. Besides he's married to Louisa.'

'And now you're going off to that ghastly place where they all wear polyester and the banks look like churches or the churches banks, I can't remember which. What on earth am I going to tell the family?'

'Your boater is going to fall off, Mummy. I'll get nice and suntanned and Mr Geist will give me a part in his film.'

'Your father will never get over it. He has had more than a few odd looks in the Lords, you know, since they found out that Red beast, Moss, is his son-in-law. I wish I hadn't put the whole thing in the *Times* and then no one need have known about it. I get a weight on my chest just thinking about it. And what about those wonderful candlesticks with the Fanthorpe crest?'

'Think of it as helping the underprivileged, Mummy. I'm sorry, I truly am.'

Well, I was, in a way. I was such a disappointing daughter. I should by rights have been happily installed in a Georgian house in Wiltshire, raising children and breeding horses and being photographed at the local point-to-point in

178

jodhpurs and a Liberty's headscarf. Instead of which I was on the roof of the Hilton Hotel wearing a miniskirt, watching Mummy's Liberty's boater, which at that point dipped and soared away over the roof, across Park Lane, and over towards Apsley House. Shrieking at the loss of this triumphant symbol of the leisured classes, we embraced and saluted the hat lady at Liberty's, each other, and the Society for the Preservation of the Vole. Darling Mummy. She was a sport, wasn't she?

In a fury of remorse (at least, I think it was remorse; he never gave me a present except after a particularly virulent quarrel), Alan sent me a farewell memento – one of the Victorian watercolours (another symbol of upper-class leisure, naturally) with a copy of his Catford manifesto wrapped around it. Alice, typically, said that he was probably using the watercolour as wrapping paper for the manifesto, but it didn't look like that to me. I had a little weep. It was such a final gesture. The manifesto somehow represented the end of my involvement with politics, and I knew I would never say 'historical materialism' again.

12

ALICE

With Daphne gone, and Penny mouldering away
in the country, Louisa and I were left in London
to represent the old Bardwell Road spirit. We
both had started what might loosely be called
careers, although that implies an intent entirely
lacking in our approach to the work force. My
job came about, as many women's did in those
days, completely by chance. I happened to meet
a man at a party who, after his fourth Pimms,
said he was leaving his job to become a full-time
poet and would I like to show up for work the
following day instead of him. I think I must have
been bemoaning my fate as a ward of society, a
welfare bum, etc., otherwise I surely would not
have felt impelled to accept his suggestion, thus
finding myself the next day in an advertising
agency in Berkeley Square. After a few vague
explanations, my Oxford degree persuaded the
departed poet's boss that I should stay. (That,
and also my physical charms, which for some
reason aroused the advertising executive to a

peak of desire I was able, on a monotonously regular basis, to frustrate.)

As the most junior of copywriters, I was given the dead-end accounts on which to polish my as-yet-unexplored talents as a wordsmith. My major task was to enthuse convincingly about Poona Brand Pickle (a thick yellow substance consisting of unmentionable vegetable leftovers marinated for years, like preseved foetuses) and Shini-Brite Bathroom Fixtures (sinks, basins, baths, bidets, and toilet bowls in a variety of decorator colours: Old Gold, Avocado, and Chiffon Pink). On very bad days, after a heavy night of champagne, I can assure you it was perfectly possible to confuse the two products, thus adding a level of mad original-ity to my copy.

Gerald rather surprisingly went overboard for Poona Brand Pickle, which I received by the case as a reward for my literary efforts. He regarded it as both medicinal and holistic and used it generously in the bean-sprout casseroles and fertilized-egg puddings that he was working on at the time. I did not object, relieved to be offered something to counteract the blandness of authentic nutrients. My advertising for the pickle was unabashedly imperial – sepia photo-graphs of the Indian Army, Sepoys, and the like, lined up in reverence behind their British mas-ters in those formal poses so beloved of Victorian photographers, with the tag line, 'A fine taste tradition passed on – the Pride of Poona Brand Pickle.' Since the reputation of our Empire was by then at an all-time low, this was taken to be a splendidly chic spoof, and Asian Imports Ltd were delighted with my efforts.

Inspiration juddered to a halt when it came to Shini-Brite bathroom fixtures. I was told to avoid anything frivolous, since the client thought his products the height of dignity. Such flourishes as 'flushing out the second-rate' were regarded as flippant. Nor did I receive any free sinks, basins, or bidets, although we could have put them to much better use than the Poona Brand Pickle in our crumbling North London pile. Under these restrictive conditions, 'Shini-Brite, a washing wonderland' was all I could come up with. (Dorothy Sayers couldn't have come up with anything better,' Gerald said kindly but untruthfully.)

These difficulties aside, I rather enjoyed becoming an advertising person, largely because everyone kept resigning, like my poet, to become a *real* something – a real painter, a real cartoonist, a real novelist – so that those left behind felt a nagging sense of *un*reality that could only be assuaged by constant visits to the pub. We would doodle helplessly at our desks, waiting for the local to open its doors at 11 A.M., at which happy hour we would rush downstairs and grab a booth and a drink and discuss the sex lives of our employers until lunchtime, at which happy hour we would have sausage and mash and more drinks until the pub closed, at which happy hour we would remove ourselves to some Soho drinking club until about 4:30, at which mournful hour we would return to our desks, think up some brilliant advertising lines, and retire, exhausted, to our domestic nests.

While I was destroying what was generously called my mind on these pursuits, Louisa was creeping about in the monolithic bureaucracy of the BBC, where she worked for a comedy quiz series called 'Push My Button.' In it a series of panellists (celebrities, mostly, like the Reverend Wales or the reigning Miss Croydon) were shown a photograph of a naked baby with its head blocked out. With this photograph and a few clues offered by the lovable and witty host, Ronnie McCloud (no relation to the Oxford coach or Lady Fanthorpe's cook), the guests made lovable and witty guesses as to the ownership of the infant torso. Louisa's job was to comb the photographic agencies, libraries, and newspaper morgues for suitable candidates as babies (they could be dead, but not murderers or sex offenders).

Ronnie McCloud was tickled pink to have such

a distinguished researcher as Louisa Wales on his staff. 'Frankly, this show is really a little off for someone with your education,' he would tell her over the nightly pint at the BBC Club at the Television Centre, where quiz researchers and light-entertainment presenters rubbed shoulders with drama producers or current-affairs directors in that icy, circumscribed harmony foreigners mistake for democracy. 'I know all those chaps' – nodding at the leather-patched tweed jackets which were the broadcasting uniform of the day – 'went to Oxford or Cambridge, unlike your truly who just managed to scrape through two years at Repton Tech, ha ha. And no doubt you would rather be over there letting them chat you up.' Louisa wisely kept silent. 'But let me tell you, me lass,' and here Ronnie's eyes would grow misty and his breath hot on her cheek, 'those posh buggers don't know nothing about what the British viewer wants, the grass-roots viewer. We do, you and I do. We have our finger on the pulse, right here with our show, and don't you forget it, Louisa.'

A few weeks later, 'Push My Button' was cancelled owing to lack of viewer support, and a new quiz called 'Take My Pulse' took its place. Ronnie kept his job as lovable and witty host, and Louisa kept her job as researcher, this time combing the photographic agencies, libraries, and newspaper morgues for celebrities *in extremis* (going into hospital, fainting in the street, falling off a horse, and so forth). Their heads were blocked out and the celebrities had to guess their identity (the subjects could be dead, but not murderers or sex offenders). A doctor then appeared on the screen to explain the medical aspects of the celebrity's condition. (This segment was insisted upon by the head of light entertainment to give the show a little more 'depth.')

'Why don't you leave?' I asked her, having wrenched myself away one lunchtime from the pub and taken Louisa to La Serafina in Shepherd's Bush, a restaurant whose only genuine Italian feature was the Chianti bottles used as candlesticks.

'Well, why don't you?' she asked. 'You just spend your time getting pissed in pubs with failed novelists.'

'We need the money,' I said. 'Gerald is getting so obscure that they are going to fold his column for arcanity – arcanity? I am not ready to join Daphne and the downtrodden in a miserable flat in Kilburn. We don't have the financial pulling power that you and Edmund do.'

'Thanks, but it's only Edmund who has pulling power. And I don't know how much he has of that, anyway.'

185

'I thought he was doing so well. We're always reading about him and his amazing magazine.'

After a lot of false starts in business, in real estate, in stockbroking, in newspapers, Edmund had founded a new magazine called the *London Gazette*. It published new writing, avant-garde poetry, stories by Russian émigrés, cartoons, all the rubbish that no one else would publish. It was getting noticed, largely because since Edmund was doing it, everyone thought it must be brilliant, and since it was avant-garde, people were scared to condemn it in case it produced a bona fide artist. Edmund was always being quoted saying things like, 'We are searching for a new kind of beatitude – pure experience, with reverberations that don't dissolve after the illusion has been broken. "For words divide and rend; But silence is most noble till the end."' Even if nobody knew he was quoting Swinburne (don't imagine I knew – Gerald tipped me off; Swinburne was a favourite, apparently, at Eton), and even if most of Edmund's remarks seemed to me a complete negation of the printed page and therefore his magazine, everyone knew the man was a genius.

'It's doing well enough,' Louisa said glumly. 'Edmund's so busy I never see him any more.'

'But you're always going to parties. I'm sick

and tired of seeing your mugs in all the gossip columns.'

'I hate the parties. Everyone's doped up on something so you can't talk to anyone, least of all Edmund. He's always surrounded by sycophants and would-be artists wanting to get published. It makes one sick to see it. Anyway, how would you like to be cooped up with Jean Shrimpton, Celia Hammond, Zandra Rhodes, and all those fabulous Chelsea types all night? I feel like a huge drab wallflower.'

'But Edmund would never look at anyone else. Surely you know that.'

Louisa sighed. 'That's the stupid part. I do know that.'

'Well, why are you so gloomy, then? You are bloody lucky, being married to someone who loves you, takes you to glamorous parties, and doesn't feed you tofu salad every day.'

Louisa sighed again. 'Well, at least you have something to talk about.'

'Good lord, Louisa. I've never met anyone who can talk about so many things as Edmund. He talks like an encyclopedia.'

'Exactly. I just can't keep up.'

'Heavens, do you want to get unmarried then? That would be our second. Do you want to join Daphne in the New World?'

'I wouldn't dare. Divorce the fabulous Edmund

Wales?' Louisa drained her glass of Italian red imported from Algeria. 'No, Alice. Forget it. It would be like renouncing citizenship.'

And with that, she drained my glass too.

'She says it would be like renouncing citizenship,' I told Gerald over supper (pine-nut stew with Poona Brand Pickle). 'She doesn't even like the parties.'

'Then she shouldn't go,' said my unsympathetic husband. 'Louisa's turning out to be a complainer. She's just spoiled rotten, that's all. Edmund treats her too well. She needs a good hard smack on the backside.'

'We're not all at prep school now, Gerald,' I said. 'She's really unhappy. I think you should talk to Edmund about it.'

'Talk to Edmund? About what?'

'About Louisa, silly.'

Gerald looked horrified. 'Christ, Alice,' he said, almost choking over his pickles. 'You must be joking. Edmund is my closest friend. I could no more interfere in a personal matter like that than eat pigshit.'

'But what are friends for, then? This is exactly when you should get involved.'

'And guarantee ruining the friendship forever? Edmund and I would never talk about that sort of thing. It's just not on.'

'You'd rather let him destroy his marriage?'

188

'There's no need to be so melodramatic. Really, you'd better stop seeing Louisa if she gets you into this kind of mood. Edmund is perfectly capable of handling his private affairs, and I have no intention of being so offensive as to imply otherwise. I think you need a new diet. Too many carbohydrates are making you over-emotional.'

Gerald was always so reasonable. The mysteries of male friendship deepened, but I knew I could not press the point. I picked up the fabric of life, wrapped it more firmly round me, and went to bed.

LOUISA

'At the recent opening of David Hockney's new show at Kasmin's, Lord Blueberry was seen talking to Edmund Wales, publisher of the hottest new magazine in town, the *London Gazette*. Copies disappear from the newsstands almost as soon as they arrive, and early issues are already being heralded as collectors' items. Wales, always surrounded by the beauties of the London scene, showed up later with his wife, George Better's daughter, Louisa, at a party at the Saddle Room after the premiere of Bunuel's new film, *Diary of a Chambermaid*, starring Jeanne Moreau. Jean Shrimpton and David Bailey made a brief appearance, then ran. Others in the PVC-clad crush were Françoise Hardy, Manfred Mann, Mary Quant, Vidal Sassoon, and Terence Stamp.'

Stories like that ran in William Hickey or the *Londoner's Diary* almost every week. The photograph always showed Edmund and some half-naked blonde. He always swore it wasn't his fault how they snapped him, and that if I would only stay closer to him at these public affairs they would photograph us together instead, which is what he wanted. Alice always laughed, saying it was good publicity for the mag.

How I loathed the *London Gazette*! I couldn't understand half the articles, the cartoons never made me laugh, and the layout made me think of some thirties trade journal rather than a sixties avant-garde rag. The worst thing of all was that when Edmund put it together he made me Associate Editor. Thank God Alice never knew about that. I lasted about three weeks. It was the worst three weeks of my life. I kept telling Edmund I couldn't do it. What did I know about publishing magazines, for Christ's sake? He kept telling me he knew I could do it, and that I would be so helpful, and that a woman's eye would contribute to the overall impact of it, and so forth. He talked me into believing all that stuff. How gullible can you get? So I agreed to go on the first masthead, just to make him

190

shut up really. Naturally all the rest of the staff hated me. They thought it was the most appalling case of nepotism, as indeed it was. I spent most of the time crying in my office, huge fat tears plopping down on to the mechanicals.

I realize now that Edmund was doing his usual trick. In putting me there, what he was really doing was humiliating me. He knew I couldn't do it. After three weeks I threw in the towel and he was shocked, really shocked. Took me out to dinner, bought me a necklace, apologized, said I was selling myself short, all that stuff. When I told my mother about it, she said I should trust him, and that if Edmund said I could do something, I should believe him. 'Making you Associate Editor with him? What a wonderful gesture,' she said. What she doesn't know is, this is a man whose life is made up of gestures.

That's actually what Markie said. Without Markie, I would never have had the courage to leave that awful place and go to the BBC. I didn't tell Alice about Markie either. Of course not. She would have had a field day with Markie.

Markie was an interior decorator. Mark Peloppides Design, Ltd. Edmund hired him to do our Chelsea house. I wanted to do it originally, but it was so difficult to make all the decisions, and Edmund said he wanted to make it easier for me, so he found Markie. Terry Stamp's hairdresser had recommended him or something. When he first came over to talk about the house, I couldn't believe my eyes. He was so incredibly beautiful. Dark, small, faunlike, with green upward-slanting eyes and a long, curly mouth. We got on at once. He told me I looked sad, and that I should never be sad because it spoiled the shape of my face. I knew what he meant. I had noticed it myself, actually.

We talked about sadness, and he told me his great sadness. He had once been married to a beautiful girl in Greece, a long time ago. Then he made a terrible mistake, and fell in love with the boy who delivered the olive oil to the village shop. They ran off to Mykonos together. It was a great scandal, even in Greece, home of homosexual love, because the olive-oil boy turned out to be a nephew of one of the colonels, and so Markie had to leave Greece and he came to London and became a famous decorator.

'It was one small mistake,' he said to me over retsina one night when Edmund was out at a party. (I took to retsina instantly – it was the drink I had always been looking for: dry, mysterious, with a kick to it.) 'When you are young, you make such mistakes. What you never realize then is that you have to pay for those mistakes for the rest of your life.'

192

Oh, I understood so well what he was saying. He could have been voicing my own thoughts When we made love that night, in the upstairs sitting room, on a sofa he had just had upholstered in a beautiful Colefax & Fowler chintz, it was as though his body spoke to mine. He was so gentle and smooth and flowing, like balalaika music. He knew I had not felt this way before.

'Your husband,' he said. 'Edmund Wales. So tall and handsome, yes?'

'Oh, yes,' I said, stroking Markie's soft, baby-like belly.

'Do you think he likes the way the house has turned out? Does he like chintz, I mean?'

There was a lot of chintz, to be sure. Markie had made a reputation for understanding the English country-house look. Being Greek was no handicap; indeed people felt it added to his perception of his adopted country's decorating style.

'Of course he likes it. He says he likes anything I like.'

'Really. He says all these things and yet he does not make you happy.'

'I know. It puzzles me too.'

'Yesterday he brought you home a beautiful bouquet of flowers. They would have looked wonderful in a bedroom I am doing in Hampstead. All pink and white, like an English nursery. He seems so often to show his love for you.'

'It's all show,' I said. 'He doesn't understand me, Markie. He sees people as objects, some to be collected, and some not. He puts people he likes on pedestals and then admires them. He did that with his housemaster at school and then his tutors at Oxford and now with me. I'm in a glass case. He turns me this way and that, nods approvingly, them turns the light off and goes away.'

'This is a man whose life is made up of gestures,' Markie said.

'You have said it perfectly,' I told him. He smiled and began to get dressed. 'I must go to a client in Mayfair,' he said. 'An American. She wants the English look for her penthouse. I want to do some swagged pelmets for her.'

Markie was always having to leave for other clients. I persuaded him to do some work on our dining-room curtains as well, so we could continue to meet. 'What about your husband?' Markie said again. 'Will he like my pelmet ideas?'

'Don't you remember,' I said, kissing him goodbye. 'He likes anything I like.'

'And that means me too?' Markie said, laughing. I thought nothing of that remark at the time, but I'll always remember how he laughed – eyes slanted up, mouth curling, body dancing a

little like a figure on a Greek vase. Mark Peloppides Design, Ltd. I can't stand chintz now.
Which is a little trying, since it's everywhere.

13

ALICE

It was July 1967, and I was in my office staring
at the cover of American *Vogue*, which had a
Richard Avedon photograph of Twiggy with a
blue flower painted round her right eye, when
the phone rang. It was Edmund, telling me that
Louisa was pregnant.

'How wonderful,' I managed. 'How is she?'

I had rather a severe hangover, having danced
till very late at the Saddle Room with a group of
advertising colleagues who were celebrating the
departure of yet another copywriter to the ranks
of the artistic unemployed. Why the Saddle
Room was one of the most popular haunts of the
time always puzzled me; nobody who went there
was remotely interested in horses, but it had
good space for what everyone wanted to do –
dance.

By that time, even I had got the idea about
dancing. Alan Moss's version, that had so distressed me, picked up from the working-class
dance halls in places like the Isle of Dogs, had

become middle-class. It was our revolution. In
our parents' day, you went to dancing classes
and then spent your evenings out stumbling
over men's shiny patent shoes muttering
furiously to yourself, slow, slow, quick quick,
slow. The early American rockers changed all
that, and then our own Beatles brought in their
own form of free-form jive, which anyone could
do, yeah, yeah, yeah. Discotheques suddenly
became the hottest real estate in town, where
Mylar walls, strobe lighting and a waxed floor
were sufficient interior decorating, and where
shopgirls rubbed shoulders with rock stars in a
frenzy of democratic debauchery.

'She's fine,' Edmund said. 'The trouble is, we
don't know who's the father. I rather thought
you might enlighten me.'

I stared at Twiggy's flower-painted eye. She
was also wearing a turquoise mink coat with
pink and lavender flowers. It looked as though
she were wearing it back-to-front.

'Oh, dear,' I said.

'She's furious that I am raising doubts, of
course,' he said. 'According to her, it's perfectly
obvious whose it is. But when I look at my diary,
it doesn't work out right, unless I have completely misunderstood the mechanics of human
fertilization.'

'Oh, dear,' I said again. My head was throbbing.

'I knew I could rely on you for an intelligent response,' he said with his usual impatience. 'I suggest you come over this evening and talk to her. She refuses to speak to me on the matter.'

'Do you know who the – er – other candidate is?' I asked, with a faint revival of energy.

'Of course. It's that pathetic decorator, the sleazy Greek.'

I put the phone down, head spinning. Markie? I could hardly credit it. Oh, I had heard about him all right. Louisa could never hide her romantic interests. Au contraire. When swept up in one of her passions, she looked completely transformed. I had guessed that Markie was holding her hand in between ruching the pelmets or zipping up the slipcovers, but actually to inseminate her? The notion failed to live.

When I arrived at Cheyne Row, Louisa was lying on one of the chintz chaise longues in her sitting room, eyes red with tears, a large glass of wine beside her, a sheaf of magazines strewn over the floor with their pages ripped out.

'What are you doing?' I asked. All the discarded pages were photographs of rooms by Mark Peloppides.

'What a pip-squeak,' she said furiously. 'What

a low pathetic, weak creature. How could I ever have trusted him?'

'Take it easy, Louisa,' I said. 'Remember, you are a hormonal kettle at the moment. Try to keep off the boil.'

'I suppose you are referring to my State,' she said, eyeing her still-flat belly. 'I am sick the whole time. The only thing that works is wine, which I expect is ruining the poor tadpole. I don't care. What do I want a baby for?'

'You are in a blessed condition,' I said sententiously. 'The one role a woman can fulfil in the scheme of things that is excluded to men – bearing children, continuing the human race. What an awesome responsibility.'

'Oh, shut up,' she said. 'Do we want a lot of little Edmunds?'

'Or Markies?' I suggested.

'I suppose Edmund's been talking to you,' she said. 'He's completely loony. He's got it into his head that it isn't his kid. I wish it wasn't, if you really want to know.'

'Well, are you sure it is?'

She glared at me. 'Do you think I don't know my own body?' she asked.

'Well, then, why are you so furious with poor Markie?'

'Poor Markie? Poor Markie? All poor Markie

wanted to do was to screw Edmund, that's all. Poor Markie indeed.'

Louisa began to cry. At this moment Edmund came in, looking distraught.

'She must be careful, Alice. She should be calm and relaxed, not this hopeless bundle of nerves. What can we do? Do you think I should send for my mother? She's so good at anything to do with reproduction.'

At this, Louisa's tears redoubled.

'Well, then, what about your mother?' he said hastily. 'Though what that bibulous poetaster could do in these circumstances is beyond me.'

'Go away, Edmund,' she sobbed. 'Just go away. You don't understand anything.'

Edmund looked at me despairingly, and I reluctantly nodded. 'You'd better go,' I told him. 'I'll stay here a bit. I'll see you later.'

He went out of the room, bowed down. I had never seen him so emotionally exercised.

'He's very emotionally exercised about all this,' I said to Louisa.

'Bollocks,' she said. 'He doesn't know the meaning of the word "emotion." He once asked me the difference between ballet and gymnastics. Now that question could only have been asked by someone who had no emotions. Am I right?' She did not give me time to answer. Louisa was on a roll. 'All he wants is his life to be in order. I'm rocking his boat, his damn blasted little yawl, which he'd much rather be in with Gerald and his housemaster, with no silly women getting in the way of the tiller.'

I stayed with Louisa about an hour, while she alternately cried, lambasted Markie and Edmund by turns, and bewailed her pregnancy as a fate wished on her by jealous gods. The chintz sofa was getting soaking wet with her tears.

'It won't run, will it?' I asked.

Louisa stopped for a minute. 'It's Colefax & Fowler,' she said. 'Perish the thought.'

I decided it was time to go and see Edmund. I told her I would come again in the morning, reluctantly forgoing my 11 A.M. meeting in the Bell and Thistle, currently our favourite drinking hole. I urged some Brand's Essence of Chicken on her, for sustenance, and said I would bring some Poona Brand Pickle in the morning.

Edmund was at his desk, reading a manuscript.

'What can I do?' he asked. 'I want her to be happy, but she won't let me help her. I told her she could go on seeing Markie if she wanted, if that would make her happy. But this seemed to upset her more. I don't understand it. You're the only person who understands her, Alice. What can be done?'

'Well, something obviously happened between her and Markie that we must get to the bottom of,' I said. 'But for now, I think the thing is to leave her alone and let everything sink in. She's just furious at everyone. She probably feels lousy, too. The first three months are often rough for pregnant women.'

The phone rang. It was some experimental poet, calling from America. Edmund immediately turned to his papers and started talking. I stood there for a minute, listening to his observations about a translation of Ovid. I think he had forgotten I was there. Finally, I waved my hand under his nose, he raised his eyes a fraction, then returned to Ovid. The distraught look had gone. A lock of hair fell, boylike, over his forehead. He was laughing into the telephone, a cigarette in his hand, the neck of his white shirt open, the cuffs undone, his slim wrists gesticulating over an ambiguous interpretation of the words *rudis indigestaque moles*. I thought how amused Freddy Weathering would have been at this exchange. Why were men so much better at the Classics than women? Why did I hate Latin so much when these fellows all adored it? Why were we so excluded from the club?

I realized I was beginning to sound like Louisa. Edmund obviously had the knack of lowering a woman's esteem. And yet, and yet . . .

'God, I'm sorry, Alice.' He was off the phone and at my feet. 'You mustn't go away. I depend on you completely. You're the only one whom I can talk to.'

'Well, what's all this fuss about Mark Peloppides, then?' I said, trying not to feel flattered.

'Christ,' he said pouring himself a scotch from a convenient decanter. 'I only thought it would help. It seemed to me that if Louisa were getting so much pleasure from her Apollo, my duty was to make it as easy as possible for her. I couldn't bear to lose her, and if I cut up a stink, she might run off with him.'

'So what did you do?'

'I took the greasy little chap out to dinner. To the White Tower, as a matter of fact. At least he'd be at home with the menu. And I told him, as gently as possible, that he was making my wife distressed and that we should be splendidly adult and decide what would make her happy.'

I began to laugh.

'Why are you laughing?' he said in injured tones. 'It was perfectly logical, after all. The problem was, this Peloppides chap kept asking me about my own life, and how he could make me happy. By the time we were into our baklava, I realized the little poufter was making a pass at me.'

He drank some scotch and began to laugh, too.

'Well, it was rather bizarre,' he admitted. 'I mean, imagine a five-foot-two-inch Greek interior decorator asking me in the middle of the White Tower about my favourite fags at Eton. He seemed very *au courant*, as a matter of fact. Chapter and verse, with some of the chaps.'

I saw why Louisa was ripping out Markie's creative contributions to the English country-house look. This revelation would have depressed a more level-headed individual than my poor friend.

'Well, so Louisa was betrayed on all fronts,' I said. Edmund looked surprised. 'What is wrong with trying to make her happy?' he asked. 'It's all I want, Alice. You know that. The irritating thing is that I treat her like an intelligent, sensitive, competent woman, give her a very high-level job at the magazine, and she turns round and thanks me with this.' He sighed. 'I must be patient, that's all. This Greek was obviously a passing thing. She could never have been serious about such a small person. I can't imagine how she considered him for a minute, but I suppose she was lonely. I think she needs a break. Why don't you take her away for a little holiday? The Lakes, maybe. It's so romantic there. I'll try and join you later. How about it?'

I said I would have to consult my husband,

who was deep in a series of articles about an unknown disease called Wet Mouth.

'I'll talk to Gerald,' he said. 'I want to talk to him anyway. He made some erroneous assumptions in a piece about the Irish potato famine. I actually thought he might do something for the *Gazete*.'

'By the way, Edmund,' I said. 'Did you really ask Louisa what the difference was between ballet and gymnastics?'

'Certainly I did,' he responded. 'And she could not come up with a satisfactory answer. Can you?'

'Well, er . . .' As I started stumbling into mental darkness, the phone rang. This time it was someone from the BBC wanting to interview him about the new sculpture show at the Institute of Contemporary Arts. He pulled out a diary, crammed with appointments, and started discussing dates. I waved to him in relief, blowing a kiss this time, and went to retrieve my coat.

'Wait, Alice,' he said, pursuing me into the hall. 'Have you found out the difference for me yet?'

'Well, er . . . The music, for instance.'

'Surely it is that in ballet the feet are very rarely positioned over the head.'

I had to laugh. 'Have you ever been to the ballet, Edmund?'

'Of course I have. *Giselle, Swan Lake*, and so on. I enjoyed them. So did Louisa. I must take her again.'

'Take me next time. I'll try to explain.' But I saw that I couldn't. It was impossible to explain that kind of thing to Edmund. How do you describe to a blind man the colour blue? It did make one, however, long to try. I kissed Edmund more fondly than I had kissed anyone for some time, and went home.

LOUISA

I lost the baby. Well, the poor mite never had a chance. Conceived in tribulation, as the Bible might say. It was the only thing I had ever done on my own – make a baby. I mean I know a man had to be involved at the beginning, but the creation of that little lump of tissue was mine alone. I felt for the first time that I was good for something. I knew then what Penny had felt all those years she carried babies in her belly. Powerful. Worth something. Competent. Supreme in an area where men could not touch me, not even Edmund, the fount of all wisdom.

206

For the first time, Edmund could not defeat me. I was transfigured for a few months.

And then, of course, it all gushed out like chunks of liver. Perfectly disgusting. A little life slithering out between your legs, piece by pathetic piece, in gusts of helplessness. Nothing to be done. No holding it in. No calling it back. I remember how surprised the doctor looked when I started crying in his office. 'But you'll have another,' he said in astonishment. 'Don't be upset. You'll have another.'

As if another mattered. How little he knew about his patient. Another? What could he mean? All I could think of was the delicately veined caskets of blood that I expelled, however hard I fought the tide, expelled from my faulty womb. The idea of another was repellent to me. I was faithful, and would always remain faithful, to my lost soul, my doomed firstborn. No usurper would take its place. She was a woman once, they would say. But she could not sustain it.

Markie went back to Greece after this little episode. Alice and I imagined he might run into Alan Moss and fall for him. What on earth would Alan make of that? Were homosexuals bourgeois? The fact that Markie had so deceived me ceased to bother me after a while. I was just annoyed that I had allowed him to bring so much chintz into the house. I asked Edmund if I could redecorate my rooms, which of course he was thrilled for me to do. 'Louisa's coming back to life,' he said to people over the phone. 'She's beginning to look her usual radiant self.'

Radiant self. It sounded so quaint, that expression. Markie had made me feel radiant, at least I give him that. But I had forgotten almost how it felt. 'La chair est triste, hélas, et j'ai lu tous les livres.' Professor Borianov used to like quoting that, in his wonderfully Russian voice, after more than the usual quota of sherry. Mallarmé. But of course Edmund would have known that. Edmund knew everything. Except what it felt like to be pregnant.

14

ALICE

'She'd better have an affair,' Gerald said, after I explained to him the surgical intricacies of a D and C. He was mixing a new salad dressing of sesame paste and crushed orange peel at the time and failed to see my expression of surprise.

'An affair? Really?

'It's perfectly logical. I was always given to understand that women felt more like women if they had an affair, or some such notion.'

'Don't tell me your housemaster told you that.'

'I think my father did, actually, when my mother bolted with the housepainter.'

'Is that what Edmund thinks?'

'Of course. I'm sure he would give his whole-hearted support to such a venture. He wants her to be happy, doesn't he?'

'But she just had an affair, and look what happened.'

'Well, she had such poor taste. I mean, that gnomelike moussaka-loving pansy. He was entirely unacceptable.'

'Well, your mother's taste doesn't sound so hot.'

'He did housepainting to make money for his wildlife photography,' Gerald said a trifle irritably. 'You know very little about my mother's taste.'

Gerald and I were not getting on particularly well at this point in our marriage. Diet probably had something to do with it. I was too busy at work and in the pub to analyse it too deeply. Personal discussions, anyway, were never Gerald's forte, being a chap who, trained from childhood like Edmund, preferred his psychological responses kept on the abstract plane.

'Well, funnily enough, Edmund has asked if I would take Louisa away for a while,' I remarked, increasingly attracted to the idea. 'I suppose that's what's on his mind. But the Lake District is just not the place.'

'The Lake District?' Gerald laughed. 'Venice is obviously the place.'

'But they went there on their honeymoon.'

'All the better. Happy memories, and all that.'

I found this reasoning odd, but allowed it to pass, considering I was about to get a free trip to Venice.

A week later we set off on our dubious voyage en douce. Penny, who had heard about the miscarriage, sent Louisa a book called *The Fertility*

Trap, and a diary with a Union Jack on it was enclosed by Freddy. My advertising friends, suspecting my sudden vacation might be a dry run for the ultimate artistic leap into the ranks of the unemployed, gave me *Writing Poetry for Fun and Profit*, by the Reverend Gossamer, chief writer for Hallmark Cards. Louisa snatched if from me and said it was precisely the book she had been looking for for her mother, whose poems were reaching a nadir of purpledom. I always thought she undervalued her mother, but perhaps if Mary Better had been my mother I might have turned out differently, too. Gerald gave me a bottle of diuretic medicine and asked me to note any unusual dishes we came across as he was interested in Mediterranean health ideas. Chekhov could hardly have expressed his devotion more opaquely, and I was duly moved. However, it was not my marriage we were fighting for, it was Louisa's.

Edmund, expansive as ever when it came to caring for his beloved, had decided that the Cipriani was the most suitable resting-place for Louisa and her companion. (I had already cast myself as a Henry James character in grey taffeta with pince-nez and bonnet, prepared to observe the minutest psychological turns of her friend – for, in all honesty, what else was there, if honesty was to be called forth during those

unremittingly mysterious days, for her to justify
this unexpected bounty except by throwing over
it – how could she have not resorted to such a
gesture – the silver tissue of decorum. I could go
on, but you get the gist.)

On our arrival in *La Serenissima*, we were
swept off in a water taxi with white lace curtains
and a polished pine cabin. I regretted that our
luggage was covered with the scratches of age
rather than the initials of status, but I was
proud of Louisa – she looked remote, pale, thin,
androgynous, full of hauteur, and *fine*, as the
Master would say. I knew that our arrival would
cause some speculation among the jaded habi-
tués of one of the world's most expensive hotels.

We were given two single rooms next to each
other with an adjoining door. ('To be used only
as a last resort,' I told her. 'I am prepared to
sacrifice even my body for your happiness.' To
which Louisa replied, 'No thanks. I like my
women strong and silent.')

The walls of our room, were covered in tinted
glass, huge windows overlooked the canal, and
creamy marble bathrooms were supplied with
designer soap in an intriguing shade of battle-
ship grey. The furniture was of the Venetian
variety, with desks and chairs and comfortable
sofas in velvet the colour of which decorators
would call taupe.

'Taupe,' I said. Louisa winced and I remembered Markie.

'Was he fond of the taupe?' I went on.

'Let's not think about it,' she said, shuddering. 'This is the colour of the Rolls Royces they chauffeur people around in at the Peninsula.'

'What's the Peninsula?'

'A hotel in Hong Kong. I went there once with my father.'

'I didn't know the Chinese played soccer.'

'It was an international sports conference. My mother had fallen into a ditch after a First Division play-off and broken her leg, so I went instead. I had a wonderful time.'

I began humming, 'My Heart Belongs to Daddy.' Louisa didn't notice.

On that happy note, we began our exploration of Venice. It was almost like being at Oxford again, partly because of the city's beauty, and partly because, without our spouses, we reverted to that blessed state of irresponsibility that governed our university days.

'I can leave the top of the toothpaste tube off without guilt,' Louisa said, as we sat down at Florian's in the Piazza San Marco and ordered Negronis.

'Marriage is an insidious process,' I observed. 'Like ageing. All the attempts to adapt take their toll. Animals couldn't do what we have to

213

do. I realize I have had indigestion for years.'

'I know what you mean. I think I'm permanently starved.'

We both ordered chocolate ice creams.

'At least now I know all the hairs on the comb are mine,' I mused.

'Bliss,' Louisa agreed.

I was roused from my reverie by the soulful looks of a lingering waiter. 'To business, Louisa. Do you have any class preference? Servants, employees, white collar workers, aristocrats? Must he have a beard? Hairy wrists? Be a Wagner-lover?'

Louisa groaned. 'Alice, you are so unromantic. It doesn't work like that.'

'Practical, that's all. It's no good hanging around the zoo if you don't like animals. After all, we only have a week.'

'I don't know why you think I have to fall into bed with someone. I don't feel like ever having sex again, if you really want to know.'

'Sometimes I feel just the same way. Do you think we should become nuns?'

'I could imagine giving my life to God,' Louisa said. 'It would be so wonderfully final. Married to God.' She looked at the glittering gold mosaics of St Mark's cathedral.

Wiser minds than mine have come to grief attempting to mate their friends. I decided to

drop the subject and concentrate on the pleas-
ures of Venice. Our first night we dined at the
Antico Martini on seafood bisque, osso buco, and
two bottles of Pino Grigio, at the end of which
we both decided to take Holy Orders. Back in
our taupe paradise, I fell into a bibulous, liberated sleep (no snoring or snuffling or sudden
wakings in the middle of the night to discover
Gerald taking his temperature or sipping a cup
of chamomile tea) with dreams that left me
restive in the morning.

Louisa and I met for breakfast on the terrace.
A buffet was laid out on a crisp white cloth –
juices, cereals, breads and rolls, eggs and bacon –
in silver dishes like an English stately home. I
noted for Gerald that our fresh-squeezed orange
juice was the soft red of a Tuscan wall, the colour
matching the bowl of pomegranates also set out
for one's delectation. The china out of which we
sipped our coffee was decorated in tiny Limoges
flowers; the bougainvillea and azaleas on the
terrace glistened with an early morning
watering.

'Do we need a man to complete all this?' I
asked dreamily. inhaling the various fragrances.

"Tis woman's whole existence,' murmured
Louisa.

'How wrong he was,' I said. 'But I can provide
one, if you want.'

'What do you mean?'

'Look over there.' I pointed at a man who was seated with his back to us, having breakfast. 'Isn't that Cliff?'

'Cliff?' Louisa looked vacant.

'You know, the American who took Daphne out at Oxford.'

'Really, Alice, you're regressing to the point of idiocy. You'll be seeing your old tutor next.'

'Honestly, I know it's him. I'd know that neck anywhere. One hundred per cent cartilage, from all that rowing.'

At that moment the man looked round. It was Clifford Honeywell all right, and he recognized us instantly.

'Why, if it isn't the Bardwell Road sirens,' he said, coming over to our table. 'What a swell surprise.' He shook our hands heartily. 'What are you doing here?'

'Well,' I began.

'Shopping,' Louisa said firmly. 'What about you?'

'I came because of Jeannie. That's my wife. She needed a break from New York. To be quite honest, I'm bored out of my skull here. No golf, no tennis, and the swimming pool is always crudded up with little old ladies in bathing hats. I'm sure glad to see you two. Where are the others? You always seemed to go around together, I recall. Daphne and Penny, wasn't it? Gee, that was a time, wasn't it? What about dinner tonight? I could use a little company. Jeannie's not feeling too good and I don't dare even go to the men's room alone around here.'

'What do you mean?' we asked.

'Well, Christ, you don't have to look very far. The hotel's full of 'em. The Thomas Mann set. Lovely fellas, too, medallions hanging down to their navels, black leather tights, the works. They shop all the time, just like you women. You should see the size of the shopping bags they bring back with them. You can hardly squeeze into the vaporetto when they're around.'

We laughed. Cliff had a set of splendidly even teeth. Excellent calcium absorption, evidently. 'Well, back to my post,' he said reluctantly. 'Jeannie always gives me hell if I stay away too long. She always has breakfast in bed. Thinks it's more ladylike or something. No, that can't be right. She gets mad if I call her a lady. Why someone wants to eat in bed and get all the crumbs into the sheets beats the hell out of me. Anyway, she's got ten museums to see before lunch. Thank Christ everything closes for the afternoon. Let's meet here in the bar at 7:30. Okay?'

He shook our hands again with the greatest

enthusiasm and shambled off in the loose-limbed
way of the natural athlete.

'If it had been me, I would definitely have
stayed for the Dover sole,' I said, looking after
him. 'How about it, Louisa? He's white, six feet
two inches tall, excellent calcium absorption,
the best neck since Ferdinand the Bull. And I
bet he doesn't just smell the flowers.'

'He looks like one of Dad's defencemen,'
Louisa said. 'Anyway, he's married.'

'I didn't think that would stop you,' She glared
at me.

'How can you say that?'

'Never mind.'

We spent the morning looking at churches,
discovering, needless to say, that while Louisa
swooned over the excesses of Titian and the
Rococo, I preferred the austerity of the Church
of Santa Maria Dei Miracoli and the later works
of Tintoretto.

'You're like Edmund,' she said. 'Those are the
things he liked, too.'

We were in the Scuola Grande di San Rocco,
trying to penetrate the gloom.

'Mahler versus Handel,' I said. 'And never the
twain shall meet.'

'Is that true? Edmund kept saying that he was
really much more romantic than I was, that he

believed in true devotion forever, fidelity, One Great Love of his Life, etc., etc . . .'

'Has he given you any reason to doubt that?' I gazed admiringly at what I could make out, in the darkness, of Tintoretto's cryptic, mystical Mary Magdalene.

'Not in any obvious way,' she said, sighing. 'That's what's so frustrating about the whole thing. He says all this poetic stuff, but he's not convincing. He doesn't ring true. Otherwise, why would I feel so unhappy all the time?'

'There's something perverse about it all,' I said. 'Do you want to love him?'

'Of course I do. He's brilliant, beautiful, and in love with me. We lead an interesting life. So what's wrong? It's me, of course, isn't it?'

'I think you'd better start trying to believe him,' I said.

There was a pause while I looked once more at the painting. How does one give advice like that to a friend, or to an enemy for that matter? I heard a snuffling noise. Looking around, I saw that Louisa was crying.

'I knew you'd say that,' she moaned. 'You're just like everyone else. You can't see he isn't perfect.'

'Come on out of here,' I said. 'The place is getting you down.'

We didn't say any more about Edmund after

that, but the disturbing part was that in my
heart I felt the deep stirrings of doubt. I *could*
see, more than Louisa knew.

LOUISA

I was so lonely. Alice and her blasted Tintoret-
tos. The beauties of Venice disgusted me. All I
wanted to do was go home to Surrey and watch
a football game on telly with my dad. And that
frightful Cliff showing up, reminding us, as if
we needed it, of all those wasted years at Oxford.
It was like a bad film. I half-expected Edmund
to appear, ready to direct the rest of the action
according to his brilliant script. If only we had
never come here. If only . . .

I think that all of life is made up of longing.

15

ALICE

Cliff's wife was Jeannie. Not with light brown hair, but a sort of reddish black colour, that I later learned was achieved with great expense at the hairdresser's. Her nose was also achieved with great expense – one of those strangely smooth, too-small, button noses that are instantly recognizable as man-made. I learned this later, too. Jeannie, in all respects, was what she would call a 'learning experience' for me.

Our first meeting was inauspicious. Cliff had obviously bored her with the exploits of the Bardwell Road Four. No woman likes tedious stories about the glamorous histories of other women, so her first greeting was sulky.

'So you were the belles of Oxford,' she said with an effort, lying back in a chair at the Cipriani bar.

'That was a long time ago,' Louisa said. 'As you can see.'

'We're just housewives now,' I added.

'You're putting me on,' Jeannie said.

'No,' we assured her.

'Perhaps *The Feminine Mystique* never got to England,' Cliff said. 'What'll you two housewives have to drink?'

'A Bellini,' we said.

'When I was here with Edmund we had to have Tizianos,' Louisa added.

'That was obviously when things began to go wrong,' I said.

'Go wrong?' Cliff asked.

'Wait a minute. Who's Edmund. What's a Tiziano?' Jeannie had taken a notebook out of her sequined bag and was detaching from it a tiny gold pencil.

'A drink made out of grape juice instead of peaches,' Louisa said.

'Edmund? I thought that was someone's name,' she said, her tiny, upward-slanting handwriting reminding me somehow of her tiny nose.

'Is that Edmund? The Edmund – Edmund Wales?' Cliff asked, downing a large brandy and soda.

'Who else?' Louisa said, downing her Bellini.

'You married that guy? Christ, he was the most brilliant undergraduate Oxford ever produced,' Cliff said, turning to Jeannie, who was writing furiously. 'He was a great athlete too, wasn't he? I heard him speak at the Union once. I swear to you, I couldn't understand a word he said. But it was something. What's he doing now?'

'Running an avant-garde magazine,' I told him.

'You're kidding. He should be running some corporation. In the States he'd probably be head of General Motors by now.'

'Ah, well, that's the difference between our two countries,' Louisa said. 'Edmund would never have thought of going into business.'

'Englishmen are weird,' Jeannie volunteered, pausing in her note-taking. 'I've heard they're all fags.'

'Jeannie's joined a women's group,' Cliff explained. 'She used to be a housewife, just like you, shopping at Saks and going to Chinese cooking classes. Now she just writes things down in endless little notebooks and stays home, talking on the phone and refusing even to go to the market for groceries. I have to eat out most of the time. She says she doesn't want to be a chattel any longer. I never said she was a chattel. I'm not too sure what a chattel is, but whatever it is, I swear I don't want it. I just want Jeannie to dress well and give me a nice egg foo yoong from time to time. But every time I say that, she gets madder than hell.'

Jeannie's tiny nose twitched and her lips

tightened. She flung her reddish black hair back, like Jennifer Jones.

'I'm just beginning to get in touch with my feelings,' she said to us, turning her back on her husband, who had ordered another round of drinks. 'I've never been able to handle my anger until now. I never had a proper education like you people. It's a learning experience for me. And a lot of pain.'

'I wouldn't say Oxford helped us get in touch with our feelings, would you, Louisa?' I enquired.

Louisa gazed deeply into her Bellini.

'Jeannie, cut it out,' Cliff said irritably. 'That's why I brought her here,' he said to me. 'To get away from all this women's stuff. New York is really getting to her. I wanted her to relax.'

'I am relaxed,' Jeannie said tensely. 'For Christ's sake, Cliff, stop getting into the act. This is an opportunity to open up a dialogue with others of the same oppressed class.'

'Wait a minute,' I said. 'You don't know a chap by the name of Alan Moss, do you, by an chance?'

'I remember him too,' Cliff said. 'Dark guy, great actor, what a Mercutio he did one year. Something about him though . . . too radical for my taste.'

'You see?' Jeannie said. 'Every time I start a

dialogue, he takes it away from me. It's pure MCP stuff. What a crapshoot.'

She began to write again. Cliff stood up, a vein sticking out of his magnificent neck, and walked through the French windows into the garden where, quite openly, he took a piss.

'Let's get the hell out of here and have something to eat,' he said, zipping up his fly with gusto. 'Sorry, girls,' he said, looking at our expressions. 'The old MCP jes' couldn't help himself.'

'Well, I'm sure the Cipriani garden has never been watered like that before,' I said cheerfully. 'Anyway, what on earth's an MCP?'

'I wouldn't want to shock you any more tonight,' Cliff said. 'Your friend here is looking quite alarmed.'

Louisa was looking a little pale. 'Actually, I think I'll go to bed,' she said. 'I don't feel too great. I'm sure it's all that rich food Alice has been making me eat.'

'Are you sure?' I was rather enjoying myself.

Louisa nodded and waved vaguely to Cliff. Jeannie made one last note and then put the little notebook back in her bag.

'Take care,' she said. 'We'll send you something up if you like.'

Louisa smiled at this kindness and shook her

head. 'I hope I see you again,' she said. 'I was interested in what you were saying.'

Cliff took my arm and propelled me towards the dining room. 'You don't want to let Jeannie loose on your friend,' he told me. 'She's ruined more marriages . . .'

We buried our heads in the menu, which was large and exciting. Cliff and I ordered lavishly. When the waiter came to take Jeannie's order, she handed him the menu and said, 'I don't want any of that. Just bring me three shrimps, raw, with a little mustard sauce on the side. And some endive.'

The waiter, appalled, wrote down her order. 'And some dressing?' he urged, describing a glittering list of herbs and oils.

'No dressing,' Jeannie said.

The waiter moved off, slumped in disappointment. I stared at her.

'Don't worry,' Cliff said. 'She never eats. She says eating is a woman's problem.'

'What a waste,' I ventured. 'This is supposed to be one of the finest restaurants in the world, and you eat three raw shrimps.'

'Women are brainwashed into thinking that food – and cooking – will make them lovable. So they get fat and then their men find them unlovable after all. It's a vicious cycle.'

'Circle,' I muttered.

'What?'

Jeannie fumbled about for her notebook.

'Never mind,' I said hastily. 'Jeannie'd better meet Gerald.'

'Who's Gerald?'

'My husband.'

'Was he at Oxford too, then?' She stifled an acid yawn.

'I'm afraid so, but he wasn't as famous as Edmund Wales. His main interest in life is the comings and goings of the intestinal tract.'

'I knew Englishmen were weird,' she said.

'I suppose so,' I said. 'I had never really thought about it.'

'That's why you should join a women's group,' Jeannie said. 'You need a support system and you won't get it from men, however hard you try. You need to raise your consciousness, Alice. I've learned so much from my group I feel I'm on the verge of a real breakthrough.'

Cliff ordered another brandy and soda.

'I'm not sure there are any women's groups in London,' I said.

'Where there are women, there are groups,' Jeannie declared confidently. 'And if you have any trouble, come to New York. There are groups starting up all over, even in Westchester, where my sister lives. Westchester!'

Cliff made a rude noise into his fettucine.

'Here,' Jeannie said, handing me a page from her notebook. 'It's my address. Be sure to call if you come to New York. And tell your friend. She looks as though she could use a support system too.'

'That's awfully kind of you,' I said, putting the paper into my pocket.

'I don't know about Alice, but Louisa's married to the most talented guy at Oxford, Jeannie,' Cliff interrupted. 'I haven't the foggiest why she would want to get involved in your fucking women's shit. You really do take the cake.'

'What do you mean?' she said, biting neatly into the tail of a shrimp. 'You are so out of it, Clifford Honeywell, you don't even know. Honestly, sometimes you are pathetic.'

I could see that vein starting to pop again, so I quickly moved on to more abstract matters, such as the price of gondolas. I didn't really want to see Cliff take another piss in the garden. The bougainvillea might not have taken kindly to a second dunking. When the meal was over, Jeannie walked quickly towards the exit, and Cliff took my arm again. 'Look,' he said, 'I'm really sorry about all this. There was no reason why we should sic our marital problems on you. Why don't we have another drink sometime, just you and me, okay?'

His brandy-flavoured breath wafted over me. A faint stubble of beard was beginning to show on his chin. His huge hand seemed to wrap twice around my arm. Our eyes locked for a fraction of a second. It was like turning a switch in my body. Dizziness swept over me. Pulling myself together, I said I would call him the next day and see how things were. He nodded and waved goodnight, following his wife with the slow, loping walk of a resigned Great Dane.

I had nearly fainted before. I remembered the occasion well enough. Well enough to make me nervous. What was my body doing? It was Louisa we were supposed to be animating, not the modest companion – even on the most unthinking of occasions, one would never think of as less than modest, for she herself so defined that word as to incorporate it into her whole being, her whole, that is to say, exposed self – who had been entrusted with such a magnificent, generous, and transforming task from one whose uncalculating hopes were there, as it were, laid out like newly pressed linens on a dining table . . . Shut up, Alice.

Guilty, I looked in on Louisa before going to bed. She was staring out of the window at the lights of the shimmering city.

'What do you think she was writing all those

229

things down for?' she asked me without turning round.

'Perhaps she's writing a novel.'

'Some novel. I don't think I could bear to read it. She certainly seemed unhappy.'

I inhaled the lemon-scented night air.

'Women always want something else,' I said slowly.

Louisa turned round and looked at me. There was a long silence, punctuated by the low hum of the vaporettos in the Grand Canal.

'Well,' I added finally. 'That's nothing new.'

'No,' said Louisa. There was another pause, then, 'Alice, are you all right?'

I said I was and went to bed. But of course I wasn't. How can you be all right if you nearly faint when someone takes you by the arm? I took my temperature and a large dose of epsom salts, which settled my stomach but not my mind. The night was long and filled with boringly predictable symbols of my overstimulated state.

My cure was very simple. The following day I got a note from Cliff saying they were unfortunately leaving for New York earlier than planned owing to a business emergency, but that he hoped to see me again sometime, preferably when Gerald was out of town. Louisa got a note from Jeannie's notebook, saying that negative

feelings had so infected her relationship with
Cliff that they were going right back to New
York for counselling and some group work. She
included a list of women's groups in New York
with their telephone numbers.

'I hope it wasn't anything we said,' Louisa
remarked as we took our morning swim.

'I'm sure not,' I said, wondering if Jeannie had
seen Cliff take my arm. I noticed a small bruise
on my upper arm when I got up in the morning,
an unusual memento, of which I was unreason-
ably proud.

We left Venice a day early. I think both of us
had had enough of its decadent offerings. The
tingling in my arm stopped. Louisa seemed
depressed, and nothing I could do shook her out
of her mood. She was clearly waiting, I now see
it, like a broody hen waiting for the egg to be
laid. And it happened in the most unlikely place
imaginable. Not in the Piazza San Marco, not in
the garden of the Cipriani, not on a gondola, not
sitting on the terrace of the Gritti Palace, not in
any of the places generally regarded as the most
conducive to romantic encounters. Oh, no, not
our Louisa. Contrary to the end, as perhaps I
should have foreseen.

The plane from Venice to London was jammed.
As Louisa and I began heaving our luggage

down the narrow aisle, ahead of us, waiting for the stream of passengers to push through, stood a smallish man with a black beard and green eyes. We continued to barge along, looking for seat numbers 23E and F, and in doing so were forced to squeeze past this green-eyed foreigner, who was blocking the aisle in the most infuriating way, instead of sitting down so that everyone could get by.

'Excuse me,' I said irritably. He smiled. His eyes, however, were not on me but on Louisa, who was huffing and puffing behind me, and the smile was suddenly transformed into a meaningful stare. I only noticed this with half my attention, since my eyes were raking the minuscule signs above the rows of seats, trying to ignore the strong smell of sweat and burning rubber that usually accompanies air travel. But when I finally found our row and looked back to tell Louisa, I saw she was suffused with a pink glow that was definitely not on account of our seating arrangements. I raised my eyebrows, but she began to push her hand luggage under the seat in front of her without a word of explanation. As we settled in, I saw that she occasionally looked back, but the glances were so rapid that I was not able to ascertain whether they had reached their target.

As the plane took off, I forgot this brief

encounter and started to read the inflight magazine (examining the advertisements, of course). Shortly after all the *don't* signs had been turned off, and my ears had returned to a semblance of normality, there appeared at Louisa's side this same gentleman who had blocked the corridor. He moved his head slightly, and without a word Louisa unbuckled her safety belt and left her seat. With some manoeuvring, I was able to see that they had returned to his row and she was squeezing into a vacant seat next to his.

I did not see her for the rest of the flight. I dozed, ate a lonely airline meal that would have horrified Gerald, and dozed again. As the *don't* signs came on again, Louisa reappeared, her lips plumped up like cushions.

'My neck is in a severe cramp,' I said. 'I'm not sure I can carry any luggage.'

'Don't worry about me,' Louisa said irrelevantly. 'I'm going with him.'

'What?'

'Never mind, Alice. You wouldn't understand. Just go home and get Gerald to massage your neck. I'll phone you later. Don't worry. You can say the mission was accomplished.'

'Accomplished? On an *aeroplane*?' Lady Bracknell could not have done it better. As my voice soared, I saw Green Eyes hovering behind us,

his smile anxious, as though I were going to
confiscate his trophy. I managed to paste a grin
on my face, which he irritatingly took to be
conspiratorial. 'I shall look after her,' he whispered to me as we left the plane. I muttered
something to them both and watched the happy
couple disappear into the depths of Heathrow
Airport.

So the mission was accomplished. Henry
James would surely have found it accomplished
in the most vulgar fashion imaginable. But then
Louisa was not exactly Milly Theale.

LOUISA

Let me think. It was his eyes, of course. They
were a really extraordinary green, as green as
the emerald stone in the middle of Penny's
mother's engagement ring. I always used to
stare at it when we were children. It didn't look
real, it was so green. Penny and I would pretend
it was magic, and create elaborate games in
which the magic stone was stolen by one or the
other, transforming us into fairy princesses or
romantic heroines of the spirit world. I used to
live in those worlds when I played with Penny.
She used to get rather bored and go off on her

234

own, or say she had to give the ring back to her mother. I suppose I had a starved imagination, what with all the soccer games I grew up with.

Carlos had these incredible emerald eyes, fringed by thick black lashes, and when he looked at me, it was as though he could see right through me. Carlos had been in psychoanalysis for ten years in Madrid, where he was married to a Swedish wife and had one daughter, whom he adored. Carlos was a handbag manufacturer, and the first thing he did when we got off the plane was give me a handbag. He had hundreds of them, in eight huge suitcases, to sell to English department stores. You can't imagine how long it took him to get through customs. They were all leather, in wonderful shades of brown. The one he gave me had a gold chain for a handle. I threw it out afterwards, needless to say. It went the way of the chintz.

But what he really did was make me understand why I was so depressed and lonely. It was because I was emotionally frustrated. Well, not that this was anything new, but he explained it so much better than anyone had before. His green eyes seemed to see into my soul. He told me that I really wanted to love – and love deeply – but that I was prevented by my perceptions of Edmund and by my perceptions of myself. He told me that I should love him, Carlos, because he understood me and knew how to release my repressed feelings.

Carlos was staying at the Grosvenor Hotel for a week and I stayed there with him. I didn't once leave the hotel room. It was magic, just like the emerald ring. I was immersed in this green-eyed man, who rushed out every morning with his handbags, then came back and took me in his arms and said how much he had missed me and wanted me and loved me. He told me I must talk about my feelings, and I learned to express my needs, and my fears. We made love the whole time, getting room service when we needed it, spending hours in the shower. It was bliss.

I only made one phone call, to Alice.

'So you're holed up in the Grosvenor Hotel with a Spanish handbag salesman,' she said with her usual delicacy.

'You can have one, if you like,' I offered.

'What, a handbag salesman? No thanks.'

'A handbag, silly. What colour would you like, beige or tan?'

'Louisa, pull yourself together. What am I going to tell Edmund?'

I remembered this was why I had phoned.

'Tell him I will be home in one week. That I miss him and feel better.' Carlos was nodding at me encouragingly. Then he took the phone from my hand.

'She is so much better now, you understand, Señora Alice,' he said. 'She is relaxed, warmed, instead of being encased in a shell.'

I wish I could have seen Alice's face.

On our last night, he caressed me and looked at me with his green eyes and told me I was the first woman he had loved since his Swedish wife. He said he wanted to have me close to him, to bring me to Madrid, to give me a little *apartamento* where he could visit me. I laughed, but it wasn't really funny. If only I had been born two centuries earlier, when I could have lived that kind of life, and no one would have chastised me for my weakness, my dependency, my lack of ambition, my lost opportunities. Once upon a time, this would have been a fine opportunity, the chance of a lifetime for a woman. I laughed and then cried, and thanked him for this invitation into a fairy-tale. But no, Carlos. No, and adios. I had to part from this little magician. The emerald ring had to be returned, as it always had been, to the realm of grown-ups.

16

ALICE

The first reunion of the Bardwell Road Four took place six years after we had all come down from Oxford – on the last day of the last month of the last year of the sixties, or less portentously, December 31, 1969. I endowed it with portentousness because to me, that reunion in London was the last time we were all still young enough to be, so to speak, *potential*. We were thirty, and counting. Some of us were already established in careers (Edmund, Gerald), others experimenting (Daphne, Freddy), or trying on responsibilities (Louisa and I). Time's winged chariot could not yet be spied over the horizon. Our faces had not made that first muscle-drop round the mouth, nor the crinkling round the eyes; our bodies still escaped the thickening of waist and thighs. Yes, we were still pasted together, the patina untarnished, the pieces well able to take the spotlight in the world's auction house.

And by the end of 1969, three of us were mothers. Penny had four children, Louisa had twins, and I had a boy. Louisa and I both got pregnant quite soon after the Venice episode. For Louisa, it was affirmation of her new attempt to make the marriage work. Inspired by Carlos the Handbag, who had apparently waxed lyrical on the joys of parenthood (perhaps I underestimated him), she had returned to Edmund full of good resolutions. The conception of what turned out to be a boy and a girl confirmed their new happiness, and the celebrations at Cheyne Row went on till dawn. As for me, I came home to a sad Gerald.

The magazine for which he had contributed his thoughts on modern nutrition had folded, the victim of late sixties paranoia, and he was, for the first time, out of work. He was quite well-known by this time, and I assured him that he would find a new column in no time. But Gerald seemed very put out by unemployment, and I had to exercise unusual ingenuity to shake him out of his depression.

'I suppose we could improve our sex life,' I said to him doubtfully one night after a bottle of Rioja. (Our financial position, needless to say, had been severely hampered by this turn of events.)

'What do you suggest?' he said, with a faint display of interest.

My relationship with Gerald was not built on

this level of intimate communication, nor, frankly, as the reader knows, was I the best-equipped person in the world to produce the innovative ideas the situation required. However, during one of my daily sessions in the Bell and Thistle, one of our more racy colleagues had produced some 'poppers,' which I had taken home out of medical curiosity but which I now saw might serve a different purpose.

They were an instant success. Gerald was transformed, and so, I believe, was I. The first night we experimented, Bert was conceived, and from then on, we only had to say 'angina' to each other to start the ball, so to speak, rolling again. ('Bert' was the kind of name most of our friends were giving their babies to show our support of the new classlessness represented by Harold Wilson, who kept on being Prime Minister at this period in our lives. It is only fair that we also included other names at the christening, such as Mark and Nicholas, in case the wind changed.)

My pregnancy was disappointingly normal, with little weight gain, no water retention, and a total lack of hormonal upheaval. For the first months after the confinement I found myself agreeing with Queen Victoria's observation that babies were extraordinarily unattractive in the 'frog' stage. But when the infant's legs stopped doing the Moro reflex and his arms actually wrapped round one's neck on purpose, he became inexpressibly lovable. As for Gerald, it was the saving of him. While I went to work, he played Nanny, inventing games, making Bert nap, generally acting totally soppy over his little offspring. But his real interest, needless to say, was dietary. When I came home I would find Gerald in the kitchen, poring over the blender, whipping up purées of all kinds for the poor little tyke. He found that all the baby-food jars on the market were full of salt and sugar, which he said was totally Wrong. He started plans to write a book about baby food. He was a new man. He would investigate Bert's nappies every day to see what difference the day's diet had made on the colour, texture, and so forth of the son and heir's turds. 'Good lord, Alice,' he would call triumphantly from the upstairs bathroom. 'It's completely orange today. Wasn't it yesterday I added the squash?'

The experience brought me closer to Penny, our model of motherhood, who sent hampers of clothes and, over the phone, lots of advice. She said that she was now thin for the first time since her marriage, and that Freddy had gone completely off her. 'He liked my fecundity,' she said cryptically. I said that my problem was that I never got to play with the baby. 'I'm out at work all day and when I come home, Gerald has already put him to bed, stuffed with new ingredients. All I do is wash the nappies.'

'You have a very unusual husband,' Penny told me. 'Just thank your lucky stars. After Christmas, I'm going to come down and get everyone together. It's been too long.'

So that is how it happened. We all assembled, at Penny's command, at her parents' London house. More of a contrast to the shabby if grand decor of the Weatherings' country house could hardly be imagined. The Coverdales had opted for Contemporary-Modern. The drawing room had a leopardskin wall-to-wall carpet, pink suede walls, and pink and orange taffeta curtains trimmed with white lace. Gilt mirrors with antiqued glass hung on the pink walls between school-of-Renoir portraits of Coverdale children. The dining room was mostly chrome, with blue plastic chairs studded with silver nails. An aquamarine Bakelite wall sculpture of abstract design decorated one wall. The dining table was smoked glass, thus allowing one to observe one's knees throughout the meal, an area of the anatomy, as Gerald remarked, least likely to inspire confidence. Its surface, rippled at the edges in imitation of a conch shell, played tricks of perspective, especially later in the evening when, after several rounds of generously supplied for-

tifier, guests found themselves crashing glasses
or spoons on to the undulating glass in an
injudicious estimate of its proximity.

While these rooms would have been useful as
a background to a TV commercial (I had more
than once recommended them myself), the
library was my personal favourite. It was lined
with handsome leather-bound volumes bought
by the yard, brown leatherette armchairs studded with gold nails, and a strange *faux-bois*
wallpaper. The fireplace contained the most
exact replica of a burning fire I had ever seen.
The trick was done by an intricate arrangement
of tiny gas vents, Mr Coverdale told me. He had
so admired it that his house in Weybridge apparently boasted one of these brilliant frauds in
every room. It was the kind of thing my father
would have appreciated.

It was to this mansion that we repaired at the
end of December. We were late, I remember,
because Bert had been playing up more than
usual, after Gerald had stuck a thermometer up
his backside to check for a suspected fever. ('The
boy didn't eat his mashed courgettes,' he said.
'That's a bad sign.') Penny opened the door,
looking stunning in a cream chiffon blouse and
yellow silk trousers. I realized I had forgotten
she had a figure.

'I'm finished with being a cow,' she said, ushering us into the library. 'My mind was turning to colostrum. I'm going to get a job.'

'What kind of a job?' I asked as we helped ourselves to drinks at a bar that was installed behind a fake panel of the *Collected Works of Smollett*.

'Something in art,' she said. 'The art world is where the action is.'

'I didn't know you knew anything about art,' I said.

'I'm taking a course.'

'So much for an Oxford education,' I said.

We all nodded knowingly and drank.

'So is everyone coming tonight?' Gerald said. 'The old troop?'

'Except Daphne, of course,' I said. 'She's still standing at Hollywood and Vine, waiting to be offered a part in the movies.'

Penny looked mysterious. 'Well, I'm not so sure,' she said. 'Louisa and Edmund will be here, that's for sure. Separately, of course. When they can each get away.'

Louisa had had the twins soon after I popped out Bert. This left her little room to manoeuvre, and nobody had seen her for some time. Edmund was reputed to be ecstatic about his little offspring, lavishing on them the love that he was not allowed to lavish on Louisa. He had also bought up several other magazines and was constantly being seen in various fashionable places talking to writers and publishers.

'I talked to Edmund the other day,' Gerald said. 'He was looking forward to this more than anything. We thought we might get a game of bridge up.'

'How boring,' I said.

At that point Louisa was ushered into the room by Loopy, brought up to London for butler-ing duties. He looked a little desiccated, but mixed Louisa a respectable martini. She had on a lot of eye makeup, white lipstick, and a black and white fringed silk kimono.

'I'm still so fat,' she wailed. 'Look at this, isn't it disgusting!' She picked up her dress to show the bulging belly beneath.

'Well, you just had twins,' Penny said. 'You can hardly expect otherwise. Motherhood is dif-ferent, you know.'

Louisa stared balefully at her. 'Not if I can help it,' she said. 'I'm determined to lose ten pounds by the New Year.'

'Well, that dress looks wonderful,' Gerald said in mollifying tones.

'Edmund bought it for me after the twins were born.'

'The only thing Gerald has ever bought for me was mixing bowls,' I said.

'Freddy buys me things, but they are always

mad, like gold lamé headbands and antique lace gloves,' Penny said.

'By the way, where is Freddy?' I asked.

'He's in the kitchen. It's his new thing, cooking. He went to Maxim's in Paris and trained. Unfortunately, I am trying to keep my weight down so it's all lost on me.'

'How interesting,' Gerald said. 'Do you think he'd mind if I went to see what he was doing?'

'Of course not,' Penny said. 'Go right ahead. Through there, on the left. But he's got a friend there with him. He's a bit weird, but don't be alarmed.'

Gerald rushed off to the kitchen, and we sat down, staring at each other curiously. Were there changes? No one was saying anything.

'Mr Edmund Wales,' Loopy said, an awed grin on his face.

Edmund swept in, smiling. 'Hello, Loopy,' he said. 'And how is that paragon of domestic bliss, Mrs Lupin? I'll never forget her raspberry pudding.'

Loopy practically expired from delight. 'Go and get Mr Wales a drink,' Penny said to him rather sharply. 'And then tell Mr Weathering that Mr Wales has arrived.'

Loopy, gazing with doglike devotion at Edmund, backed out of the room.

'Oh, Edmund, you're so famous,' I said.

Edmund laughed and kissed us all. He looked younger than ever, wearing a blazer and open-necked striped shirt, with a loosened Leander tie. 'Isn't it wonderful to be here together again. You look wonderful, Penny. You too, Alice. You're still the best-looking women in England. And as for Louisa . . .' He stood back to look at her. 'My wonderful Mummy, now,' he said. 'She has done it all. Would you like to see?'

He produced his wallet and took out a sheaf of photographs.

'Oh, for Christ's sake, Edmund,' Louisa said. 'They don't want to see those stupid pictures. There is nothing more boring than a proud father poring over baby pictures.'

'Oh, let him this once,' Penny said, laughing. 'If he can't do it with us, when can he do it?'

'That's Ben, and that's Nina,' Edmund said, pointing to two indistinguishable oranges in black wigs. 'Ben is just like his mother, beautiful, strong, independent. Nina is a little Wales, dreamy, sentimental, isn't that true, Louisa?'

'Well, if it isn't, you will certainly make it so,' she said, helping herself to more gin.

'She's a wonderful mother,' Edmund went on. 'Who would have thought Louisa had a maternal bone in her body.'

We murmured noncommittally.

'Do shut up, Edmund,' Louisa said.

'Is everyone here?' Freddy called through the doorway. 'Hello, Wales. How about some champers?'

There was something a little odd about Freddy's appearance. The pink silk blouse might possibly have been acceptable on its own, but the gold necklace was definitely disquieting. We all sat down again and Gerald began explaining to Freddy and Edmund how his exposure to baby food had changed his digestive philosophy. 'From birth, we are exposed to this artificial diet,' he said. 'It sets the pattern for the rest of our lives.'

'You could say that about all sorts of things,' Louisa said. 'I just had a letter from Jeannie explaining that it was the fact that she was dressed in pink from birth that ruined her life.'

'Who is Jeannie?' Penny said.

'We met her in Venice. She married that Rhodes scholar, Cliff Honeywell, remember?'

'The one with the neck,' I added, trying to suppress a faint hot flush.

'Jeannie says that Emmeline Pankhurst was the last role model England ever produced and surely it's time that Englishwomen moved to the forefront of the movement and radicalized their passive sisters.'

'Hear, hear,' Edmund said, looking at his baby photographs.

'But pink is such a flattering colour,' Freddy
said. 'It's absurd to condemn it because it has
political overtones.'

'Alan Moss probably liked it a lot,' I said. The
Coverdale door chimes suddenly rang out. 'How
perfectly timed,' Penny said, smiling broadly.

A few minutes later she was back – with
Daphne. Our shrieks were muffled by the *faux-
bois* and leatherette, but the noise was still
considerable. Loopy came rushing in, holding a
fire extinguisher.

Daphne looked completely different. Her hair
was very long and pale silver. Her skin was
brown and she had put on a little weight, which
suited her. Her eyes were ringed in kohl. She
was wearing what looked like a beaded curtain
from an Indian restaurant, held together by
scarves, with a quilted shawl round her shoulders, and open-toed sandals. Round her neck she
wore a yellowing tooth, and round her wrist
several others, though whether from the same
set of molars it was impossible to determine.
Two large pigeon feathers hung from her ears.
She carried an enormous macramé bag, hung
with tassels and beads, and decorated with buttons that said Flower Power, and Kiss Me, I'm
Irish.

'Gosh, Daphne.' We crowded round her, fingering her garments as though in the fabric depart-

ment of John Lewis. Loopy retired, his back bent from the weight of the fire extinguisher.

'What is this made of?'

'Are they shark's teeth?'

'Aren't your feet cold?'

'When did you get here?'

She smiled at us serenely. 'I just came back to say goodbye,' she said. Her voice was tinged with American. 'I'm going back to LA to get married.'

'Who to?'

'Aren't you still married to Alan Moss?'

'Oh, I divorced Alan. At least, Mummy divorced him. I just signed a paper she got for me. She was thrilled, of course.'

'And did Lord Fanthorpe approve?'

'Mummy told him Alan was a Communist. I think she told him he was working on a play about battered babies, crippled earls, and the Welfare State, for the unemployed car workers at Dagenham. That did it. Daddy was a lamb after that. He now makes speeches in the Lords about our Red sons-in-law.'

'Who are you going to marry?'

'An artist. A sculptor. A musician. He writes, too.'

'A Renaissance man,' Gerald commented.

'Everyone is an artist in LA. In fact, everyone is an artist, period. I am an artist. You, Penny, are an artist. You, Edmund, are an artist.'

'Well, it certainly saves a lot of explanations,' Edmund said. 'Artists get away with everything. You never have to show your work. Yet society grants you a kind of respect for your creative talent. People take much more interest in you if you say you are an artist, rather than an accountant, for instance. It's a splendid profession, Daphne. I congratulate you.'

'Well,' said Penny, 'let's let poor Daphne sit down and relax. What about a drink, Daphne?'

'No, thanks,' she said, digging into her macramé bag and bringing out a small tin box. She opened it carefully and withdrew a thin, mangled-looking cigarette.

'I rolled these before I came,' she said. 'So we could all trip together.'

She put the cigarette delicately in her mouth and lit it. Then she inhaled deeply and went on inhaling until finally she started choking as though she were having a seizure. Gerald jumped up to help her, but suddenly Daphne expelled all the breath in a great gasp and smiled seraphically.

'Acapulco gold,' she said. 'Great stuff.'

A sweetish smell invaded the room. Loopy appeared at the door with the fire extinguisher.

'What on earth is Freddy cooking?' Gerald asked, sniffing.

Daphne giggled. 'It's the pot, lovey.'

'Pot. Au feu?'

She must have thought we were pathetic.

'Feu,' Loopy said, waving the fire extinguisher. 'Excuse me, but Mr Wales is wanted on the phone. New York.'

Edmund got up, putting his baby pictures back in his wallet.

'For God's sake put that fire extinguisher down,' Penny said. 'And let's have dinner.'

We quickly refilled our drinks to show that alcohol still had some standing among discerning people. Daphne smoked some more, and the smell filled our nostrils. I inhaled, wondering if I might get a little high.

'You can have some if you want,' she said, offering the mangled cigarette. But Penny called us in to dinner, and Daphne squeezed the tip of the cigarette, snuffing it out. She put the remains back in the tin and seemed to glide into the dining room. All that aquamarine and chrome must have looked particularly aqueous under a mindexpanding substance.

That, actually, was the last intelligent thought I remember having that night.

DAPHNE

Wow, I felt out of it. Everything seemed so
middle-class, so parochial, so straight, so dull.
They didn't even talk about Vietnam. What had
I come back for? To see these old roommates who
no longer knew anything about me, or spoke the
same language even? I felt totally alien. It was
a horrible disappointment. I got higher than I
usually did simply to escape their dreary comments about artists and stuff. What a put-down.
And these were the people who were going to
run the world? The great hopes of our generation, the voices of the future? Forget it. Frankly,
I couldn't wait to get out of there.

PENNY

I could have killed her. Slopping in like some
drugged-up Flower Child, showing off, irresponsible, giving in to whatever fad was around at
the time. How could Daphne have so lost her
bearings? Committing herself to a country
racked with political and social upheavals, to a

253

city where everyone seemed spaced-out on some kind of hallucinogenic drug, escaping reality. But then Daphne always escaped reality. Becoming a Trotskyite one minute, a Hollywood movie star the next. And now a junkie. It seemed she had gone too far for help.

The worst thing was, she got everybody else going. She handed that damn weed around, murmuring about how fabulous it was to get high, and how we had to go with the flow, and how it was an open-ended trip to the soul, or some other meaningless jargon. And they all took it, I mean they took the joint and the jargon, fell for it. The dinner was a disaster.

Only Edmund saw clearly what was happening. He refused to smoke the stuff, and everyone turned on him and said he was a coward, threatened by alternative states of consciousness, hidebound by convention, etc.

'Escapist claptrap,' he said impatiently. 'Intellectual sterility, masquerading as a new reality. Distortions of reality are for the genuinely mad, not for ordinary people purporting to be divine. Attempting to blend the traditions of Western thought with Eastern religious mysticism smacks of the kind of Band-Aid mentality that is undermining our culture. Naïveté is regarded as purity, confusion as creativity. Ignorance is replacing learning as the message to our children. We are being confronted by barrenness, a litany of fallacies, spiritual casualties, impotence.'

There were groans around the table.

'Don't you see,' Edmund went on, his anger spilling over. 'This is our lifetime, our generation, we are condemned to this. *There is no other choice.*'

But Louisa laughed, and Gerald ate, and Freddy and his friend, Mario, held hands. Even Alice had been affected. She sat in silence, immobile, gazing at Edmund as though listening to every word, and then finally, she muttered,

'All cartilage. Here's to Cliff, and life in Venice.'

At which point everybody burst out laughing, and went on laughing as though she had said something wildly funny. Edmund looked at me across the table, and he shrugged, his face in a kind of despairing grimace.

'And this is only marijuana,' he said. 'Scrambled minds, exhaled in a puff of smoke. It's only the beginning. In the old days, the cream of a nation's youth were sent off to die in the trenches. Now, they die at home, in private, of self-inflicted chemicals, wasted to death.'

I remember this is when Daphne stood up, swaying slightly.

'Excuse me,' she said. 'This is becoming a drag. I'm getting out of here.'

That quieted everyone for a moment. We watched her slowly glide out of the room, smiling to herself. This was Daphne, our glorious Daphne, gliding out of our lives.

'Eheu, fugaces, Postume, Postume, labuntur anni,' Freddy intoned, emerging from the kitchen with a Baked Alaska. Everybody fell about giggling again.

And these were my friends. These were the people who had known me longest, known me most intimately, known me at the most impressionable period of my life, when we were all young. I would never be known so well again. Yet at that moment they meant nothing to me. Less than nothing. It was as though I were looking at a pile of worn-out clothes – things that had an ancient familiarity, but that no longer counted in my life.

It was a terrible feeling. I felt alone, as though I had just left home for the first time. Ten years lost. Freddy lost. Alice, Louisa, lost. Daphne lost. Edmund, I think, saw my panic and understood. Gerald, enigmatic as always, remained aloof. What remained were my children, my four darlings, already crippled by a nonfather, a single mother, an unjust entrée into life. That was where my loyalty lay, my duty lay. I would work. Just like Masha in *The Three Sisters*, I would work to make a place for us in the world, regardless of handicaps, despite them. I would work and I would succeed.

LOUISA

We had to go to America. I saw that at once, that night of Penny's party. America was the place where everything was happening. Freddy's reactionary decadence, Alice and Gerald's cynicism, Penny's maternal frustration, all suddenly seemed so provincial. Daphne shook us all to our roots. Even Edmund had his back to the wall. I told him later that we must go at once to New York.

He was appalled, of course. He had that typical snobbish English view about America, a view nourished by Oxbridge in particular. I remember Professor Borianov once laughing about a book some American had written with more footnotes than text. I laughed too, but I felt differently after seeing Daphne. She had the right idea, I knew. My only hope was to get out of the awful claustrophobia of English morals, English attitudes, English complacency. It

might even change Edmund. He could make pots
more money over there, anyway.

When I told Alice, she laughed. 'You don't
give up, do you, Louisa,' she said, and then she
added, 'Poor Edmund.'

I could have got furious with her for that, but
what with packing and arranging for the twins'
new Nanny, by that time I didn't even care.

Part Two

LOUISA

Dear Alice,

America is wonderful. We have been inundated
with invitations to amazing parties in apartments
that look like palaces, and everyone seems to want to
know us and befriend us. Of course it's mostly
Edmund they want. He is being wooed by all sorts of
publishers and magazine owners to become consult-
ant of this or editor of that. Why they think he is so
desirable I can't imagine. One can only assume that
the local talent is unbelievably weedy. Also one can't
understand how there can be so many job vacancies
that he is being asked to fill. (Or do they just remove
people at will?) It certainly makes one feel wanted,
which no one at home ever made one feel. They are
also very different towards women from at home. I
can't put my finger on it yet, but let's just say they
absolutely faint at the idea of women leaving the
table after dinner. Of course, the men don't drink port
which may have something to do with it.

The hotel is very grand, all marble and plush, with
a piano bar where trendies meet and listen to a black
piano player, who sings Oldies but Goldies in a kind
of noncommittal talky way that Americans think is

the last word in sophistication. I'd rather have Elvis myself, but I know I'm retarded. We are supposedly looking for an apartment (flat to you) that will house us, plus twins, Nanny, and secretary, but all I do is lie in our room and watch the soap operas on TV (absolute heaven, Alice, you'd adore them), while Edmund rushes about having lunch and being written up in the social columns.

The twins seem slightly bemused about it all and think Central Park is fabulous. It stinks something terrible of dog poo. All New Yorkers have dogs, and there is only one park, where of course they all have to do their business. It's barbaric. Do come over soon, you'd be amazed at it all. But don't bring your miniskirts. They haven't reached here yet, and everyone thinks I'm a tart.

Write soon. Love, Louisa.

1085 Fifth Avenue, July 12, 1971

Dear Alice,

I know I haven't written but neither have you. The thing is, I've got this job. I'm working on a kind of interior decorating magazine called *Living Interiors*. Don't laugh. They think because I'm English, and because I had this apparently famous house in Cheyne Row, I therefore am the fount of all interior design knowledge. Who am I to disabuse them? All I say is that in England we like chintz, and unlined curtains, and faded Persian rugs, and they think I'm a genius. And as soon as I let drop that Hockney, Twiggy, Kasmin, Terry Stamp, and Michael Caine all came to our parties, they think I'm a social lioness. I tell you, it's easy.

The Last Romantics

I know what you're thinking. You're thinking I got the job because someone tipped them off about that greasy Greek decorator I had the misfortune to fall for. I suppose we did get written up a bit, didn't we? Only the *Daily Mail*, if I recall. Anyway, Markie's standing over here is far less important than what they regard as my impressive social contacts. By the way, *take no notice* of those silly William Hickey stories that have recently been leaking out about my new 'interest'. The *Daily Express* stringer here is a fat old pig who had his best days in the early sixties and now just hangs about and says he's going to get my name in the paper – as though I hadn't been in it often enough, God know. It just shows how desperate those ex-Fleet Street hacks are to fill their gossip columns. It is true that Edmund is at home at the moment while I go to the office (a fabulous place on Madison Avenue all done in grey and gold). But he is always having lunch with people at the Russian Tea Room, a restaurant where you eat pancakes with sour cream and worry about getting fat while you check out all the other famous people there to see if they are also eating pancakes and sour cream and getting fat. We have a great Nanny from Belize now (the English one got homesick, silly thing, and went home to Mum in Cardiff), I bet you've never heard of it, neither had I.

I must say, I am finding America really a very jolly place. People keep complimenting me on my accent as though I'd worked very hard on it. I try to explain that it comes naturally, but they go on about longing to speak like me until I want to scream. They also drink a lot more – the average gin and tonic here would put you under the table after one swig. I'm always half-

plastered. The women wear much more makeup and
go to the hairdresser practically every day – at least it
looks like it, all the streaked curls neatly in place. I
always feel terribly scruffy, but because they think
anything English is the ultimate in chic, I sort of get
away with my old Biba dresses. They are also agog
with excitement when they hear I went to Oxford.
'Oxford,' they murmur, gazing at me as though I were
some wonderful freak. 'It was nothing,' I say casually,
only adding to the mystique.

I hope your mutterings about coming over here are
real. It would be a great relief to have you here. I
don't seem to have any women friends – American
women are frostily correct (like their hair) but they
are brought up to believe in sexual competitiveness,
and I know they think I am going to run off with
their husbands or boyfriends. They are also very
pushy and always ask me where I bought my shoes
or necklace or whatever (complete strangers do this
at bus stops; most unnerving), as though they want
to co-opt me or copy me and therefore make me less
of a threat. Not the kind of atmosphere for a nice cup
of tea and a chat. You can imagine what it's like at
the office – this English upstart being given all the
plum assignments! No wonder Jeannie Honeywell is
like she is. In this context, she's really quite normal.
Women here really have it rough.

As for the English contingent – well, you can
imagine, the worst kind of chinless wonders with
their twin-set-and-pearls wives, over here for a stint
at Kleinwort's or Lazard's, sending their children
Back Home to Eton and complaining all the time
because they can't get any decent hunting. Or, if you
prefer, there are the cold, calculating hustlers, using

their English charm and elegant manners and a few
unauthorized titles to get them into rich Americans'
houses, whereupon they batten upon the silly innocent wives and get 'taken up' in the most embarrassing way.

It's the money here, though, Alice. I met a fellow
about our age who's a lawyer, and he's earning
$50,000 a year! When I fainted, he said he saved
quite a lot! *Saved!* I fainted again and he said everyone in America saves. It's part of the culture, and
salaries reflect that expectation. I said it was
regarded as very poor form in England if one did *not*
have an overdraft. That made *him* faint!

Penny sent me a note saying Freddy had taken a
villa in Ibiza and was gone for the year. What does
that mean? I had a phone call from Daphne sounding
very spaced-out, I imagined her shooting up in some
bus-station loo, but she said she was working things
out and would call again. Of course she never did. I
saw a reprint of one of Gerald's articles in *US Health
Today* (about diets, about which everyone is completely obsessed here), and thought he would get a
job incredibly easily here. Like me. And Edmund if
he'd only commit himself. You can come and stay
with us as long as you like. Our apartment is so vast
I spend most of my time trying to find everybody.
Must go and check some photographs of a house in
Southampton we might do in the magazine. Love,
Louisa.

Salzburg, Austria, September 14, 1971 postcard to
Alice Glynn

Blissful place, blissful weather, blissfully happy.

Austria is so romantic. You might ask Gerald to phone Edmund in New York, it was his birthday yesterday and you know what he is about anniversaries and stuff like that. I wasn't there (obviously) and he might be feeling a bit low. Kisses, Louisa.

1085 Fifth Avenue, February 20, 1972

Dear Alice,

You were so sweet to send Ben and Nina those adorable Paddington Bears, and as for the Yardley soaps, they are quite divine. Christmas was unutterably ghastly, as you can imagine. I don't know how I got through it. At leats I was allowed to take a leave of absence from work. They all knew what I had been through. Edmund, needless to say, was the worst – being noble and generous and kind to me and making it all much more unbearable, when all I wanted was Heinrich. At least I feel I can write about it now, which I could not have done a month ago.

The *Daily Express* man had it right, for a change. I wish it wasn't so obvious to everyone when I fall in love. It's always written all over my stupid face. Anyway, Heinrich von Berg is one of our best photographers – I've never seen anyone make a room come alive the way he does. I'd been working for some time with him on various interiors, and then, well, need I say more? Those silly New York columnists thought I was having it off with the art director, who's one of those AC/DC types who go to all the best parties because they get on with Everyone, my dear. Perish the thought I should have got within a mile of him. Anyway, with Heinrich it was the real thing, Alice. We shared interests, he liked my ideas, for the first

266

time in my life I felt like a real person, not an embalmed corpse. We went to do a story in Salzburg together (didn't I send you a postcard from there?), and after that Edmund began asking questions. He hadn't noticed any change in me, naturally enough, until I had actually fled the nest. Then, o ho ho, all the old machinery started grinding into action.

First, my dearly beloved husband and monster took Heinrich out to lunch. (Yes, Alice. The Markie Technique, all over again). At the Russian Tea Room, of course. There, he turned on his famous Christ Church charm and told him that he, Edmund, knew what was best for me and that I occasionally went off the rails a bit but that was all it was, and that I would be much happier if he, Heinrich, didn't hang around any more. You know Edmund's inexorable logic – 'Now we both want Louisa's happiness, don't we, Heinrich, old man. So piss off.' The worst part, though, absolutely the worst part, was that Heinrich thought Edmund was a 'first-rate chap,' and ended up by inviting him to a boar hunt at his father's estate in Austria. It turned out they had known the same people at school or something. In fact, they are going to have a reunion at the Knickerbocker in the spring. Imagine it, Alice, when Heinrich came to pick up some camera equipment he had left at the apartment, all he could talk about was how wonderfully understanding Edmund was and how lucky I was to be married to such a clever fellow! As for Edmund, he goes on about how much he still loves me and he couldn't bear for me to leave him and that he would do anything to prevent it. I could kill them both.

Jeannie is my only consolation. She says I'm an Uncle Tom and a disgrace to the Movement and that

I should leave and that I should not confuse falling in love with fucking and then she makes a lot of notes in that notebook. I tell her I have no money and anyway I like living at 1085 Fifth, it's a fabulous apartment (when are you coming to stay?), and what's the point of rushing off into the void? She meanwhile is having her own problems with Cliff and they are going to five different shrinks (a different one every day) which is costing them fifty times more than their mortgage.

Edmund thinks I am getting mercenary. But money is somehow different in America. Like blondes, it's more fun. Heinrich used to say that money is a great aphrodisiac. Oh God, I miss him. I wish you were here to cheer me up. Love, Louisa.

17

ALICE

It was Gerald's unhappiness with his immune
system that took us to America, not, as was the
case with the more fortunate, tax evasion, nor, I
regret to say, my concern over Louisa. (It was as
hard for me to take Heinrich the photographer
seriously as Carlos the handbag man; her resili-
ence in the first case led me to have confidence
in her survival from the second.) Gerald had
been noticing signs of physical degeneration – a
tendency to dyspepsia, plus laxative resistance,
aggravated, needless to say, by his continued
unemployment – and after serious discussion,
we agreed that the time had come to leave the
Motherland and seek our fortunes in the New
World.

Like most representatives of the English
middle class, by the beginning of the 1970s we
were starting to feel the effects of economic ruin.
Loyal as we were to the principles of democratic
rule, it was clear that all that was left of the
silly sixties was a lot of tatty silver foil and

bleak visions of Harold Wilson and the Trade Unions. Only people like Lord Weathering, who owned acres of English countryside, and Penny's father, who made something that people still needed (such as tractors to plough Lord Weathering's acres of English countryside), were doing anything except washing down macaroni and cheese with revolting Algerian plonk.

Our house was in such a dilapidated state that we could not even make money on the spiralling real-estate values. Poor Bert, our five-year-old son and heir, was sleeping in a room whose ceiling reminded one of a teenage complexion; when we started to pack, I found in the attic, as well as dry rot, the chain-mail minidress I had worn to Edmund's Marshall McLuhan party. It looked as tarnished and antiquated as the pennies we had surrendered to the decimal revolution. Vidal Sassoon, Michael Caine, and John Lennon had gone to America. Jean Shrimpton had wrinkles. Terry Stamp was a recluse. It was definitely time to go.

It was 1973, and Watergate was in mid-flood as we stepped off the plane in New York.

'Think of it, we are in the homeland of Ehrlichman and Haldeman,' I said to Bert as we trudged through customs.

'What your mother means,' said Gerald, pale

from pressure changes in flight, 'is never trust an ex-advertising person.'

Fortunately, I was not an ex-advertising person at that point. I had wangled an interview with the American arm of the advertising agency I had served so faithfully in between sessions at the pub, and after a brief encounter with a granite-faced creative director landed a copywriter's spot in an admittedly junior position (English advertising being one of the few aspects of our country that Americans correctly regarded as inferior to the point of infantilism) with the Eez-i-Phit Support Bra account.

Gerald was equally lucky. Since his reputation as a nutritional expert was well-established, he soon secured a job on the magazine *Health in America*, a new publication geared to cash in on the fledgling physical health craze. There was to be a postage-stamp photograph of our hero at the top of a column. At the thought of this, Gerald's pulse rate rose thrillingly, his body restored to biorhythmic harmony.

These instant scores confirmed Louisa's sanguine view about America's generosity. However, our salaries did not yet measure up to our distinguished status, and for the first few months we stayed at the George Washington Hotel on Lexington Avenue, a place not conducive to grand notions of worldly success.

'Auden stayed here,' Gerald said when we moved in.

'It probably didn't look like this then,' I said.

'It probably did,' Gerald said. 'Auden liked this kind of thing. Perhaps it reminded him of home.'

I telephoned Louisa shortly after we arrived.

'Thank goodness you're here,' she said. 'What's it like at your hotel?' I told her Bert was very pleased with the cockroaches.

'Well, come on over,' she said. 'I'll give you a nice cup of tea. I don't have to work today.'

The Wales's apartment was two apartments, actually, one on top of the other with the ceilings knocked out. This gave the impression of immense height, as though one was entering a cathedral. The place had formerly belonged to a famous art collector called Florence Van Zuylen, who preferred to remain vague as to the precise origins of her husband's fortune. (Articles of feminine hygiene, we assumed.) Mr Van Zuylen died young, leaving his bride to use his wealth on dwelling places (she owned mansions in Florida, Barbados, and Cannes, as well as the New York *pied-à-terre*), and on possessions. Impressionists and Islamic art, Ming and Chippendale, Savonnerie and Kilim, Phidias and Fabergé all jostled for space in room upon room of aesthetic excess. Mrs Van Zuylen's girth reflected her

272

taste. The doorways were made especially wide to allow her to move freely; the double-width bathtubs, showers and WCs were also legacies of the lady's penchant for ample proportion in human as well as material terms. The impression was of having happened upon the home of the Jolly Green Giant.

By the time Edmund and Louisa came upon the scene, Mrs Van Zuylen had departed for the great auction house in the sky, but the collections remained earthbound, subject, apparently, to some gargantuan lawsuit involving some Van Zuylen offspring, that, like Jarndyce and Jarndyce, threatened to cost more than the disputed treasures themselves by the time it was wound up to everybody's satisfaction. Meanwhile, some influential executors of the estate, falling for the charm of these young English émigrés, allowed the Wales family to rent the elephantine museum for an indefinite period.

'Well, it's a change from Chelsea,' I said as we sat down on a huge sofa with our cups of tea.

'That's what Edmund said,' Louisa sighed. 'He thought this would amuse me.'

'And doesn't it?'

I searched for a smile on Louisa's face. She looked well, actually. Her eyes seemed darker, and her skin fairer, than I had remembered. Her skinniness was exaggerated by the extremely well-cut suit she wore. She looked, in a word, groomed.

'You look very – groomed,' I said. 'Manicures, hairdresser, all that?'

'Well, you simply can't go about wearing the kind of layered stuff we used to wear in London,' Louisa explained. 'Everyone here thought I was pregnant all the time. It got so boring that I decided I must chuck everything out and begin again. I must say, they are very keen on figures here.' She gave herself a self-satisfied preen. I looked at my own Rubens-like form and sighed.

'That was what was so wonderful about smocks,' I said. 'They concealed a multitude of sins. You mean I can't wear them any more?'

'Not unless you don't mind endlessly explaining that the baby is not due any minute.'

'Speaking of babies, where are yours?'

'Edmund's taken them to the park.'

'Edmund? Why is he at home?'

'Christ knows. He won't take any of the offers people have made him. It's idiotic. He's completely round the bend. He hangs about the apartment all day, reading books, making phone calls, listening to Mozart. And every night he has this bridge game. You remember how all those school friends of his wanted to play bridge all the time? He's got a group of English types here, and they come over every night and play bridge till dawn. He refuses to be alone. It's driving me mad.' She rattled her teacup angrily.

'Well, I expect you're still feeling upset about this Heinrich person,' I said, unwilling to think about the implications of this news about Edmund. 'What was he like, anyway?'

Louisa's face softened.

'He used to cup my face in his hand and kiss my eyes and call me Mein Liebchen. I felt as though I were awakening from a hundred-year sleep. He was such a brilliant photographer. I loved working with him. Of course we can't ever work together again. It's such a waste. He's gone to Europe for a while. I work with this idiot now, he just has no idea about dimension or space. All his interiors look so boring. He's the kind of photographer who turns on all the lamps in a room before taking the picture. Imagine!'

'Is that so terrible?'

Louisa groaned.

'Well,' I went on, 'I was never a very visual person. I never thought you were, either.'

'Of course not. No one thought I was anything, including Edmund. He can't take the fact that I am doing so well at the magazine.'

'Is that why he's in this slump?'

Louisa shrugged. 'Don't ask me what goes on in Edmund's mind. All he says is he wants to be with the children since I am out so much. We have a perfectly good Nanny, but that's not enough for Edmund. Admittedly, she can't speak a word of English, and the only thing she likes doing is watching TV. But everyone we know in New York has someone like that, and you don't hear them complaining.'

'I suppose I'll have to find someone for Bert.'

'He can go to school all day, can't he? There are lots of day-care places. It's only Edmund who won't use them.'

'Yes, well,' I said. 'Meanwhile, I'd better get back to our little one, stuck there in poet's corner. Gerald is not the best babysitter. He's always hovering over the stove, cooking. Cockroach mousse, probably.'

'Do move in here,' Louisa said. 'The place is much too big for us. You can have the Empire suite. It has an original Boucher wall panel.'

'More flesh,' I said, sighing again.

Gerald did not take kindly to the idea of the Van Zuylen apartment. 'I don't want to sponge off our better-placed chums,' he said. 'If we move in there, we'll get seduced by it all and never move out.'

'And you'll have to play bridge every night,' I said, secretly pleased by Gerald's stand.

So we found a little duplex apartment in a West-Side brownstone, with a day-care centre next door and a fire escape for Gerald to grow herbs, or 'erbs as we discovered it was pronounced in America. 'I never thought I'd have to learn to drop my aitches,' I said. 'Most people pay a fortune to get them picked up.'

'I wonder what happened to Alan Moss,' Gerald said, following my own train of thought in the way that old married couples do.

'I heard he's just written a new play about crippled earls, battered babies, and the Welfare State and that it's going to be performed in the West End.'

'The West End?' Gerald exclaimed. 'Surely not.'

'It's an idea whose time has come,' I explained. 'He's going to be a huge success. The West End. Broadway. Hollywood. Daphne should have stuck with him.'

'I don't know,' Gerald said. 'She made a very poor Leftie.'

'Is she a better hippie?'

'Let's wait and see,' said Gerald.

Once we'd moved in, we got telephone calls regularly from Edmund asking Gerald to play bridge. He went over from time to time but seemed not to enjoy it.

'He plays with such twits,' he told me. 'I don't know where he picks them up from. Hustlers, tax-evaders, drunks, you name it. They don't even play a good hand.'

I didn't like the sound of it. When Edmund came over to dinner with us (alone of course; Louisa was away on a photographic trip), he seemed tired and grey, the bloom off his boyish good looks. He was horrified when he heard we lived on the West Side.

'It's all right, Edmund,' I reassured him. 'You can see the East Side from our window. I'll point it out to you.'

He arrived, late, by taxi. There was a slight delay while he tried to get into the house, unaccustomed as he was to buildings without doormen. Logic finally triumphed.

He drank a scotch very quickly. I refilled his glass.

'All right, Edmund,' I said. 'What's up?'

'What do you mean?'

'Why aren't you accepting any of these fabulous offers? Why do you play bridge all night with beasts? What is going on?'

Gerald, embarrassed by these personal questions, left the room, mumbling about making dinner.

'America's so appalling,' Edmund said, gazing into his drink. 'It represents everything one despises about the twentieth century. Quick money, instant fame, and a packaged world, in which you market your product, whether it be face cream, the President, or your own personality. Look at Watergate. It degrades the human spirit.'

'You don't have to be involved with it,' I said. 'I rather like working here. Everyone is so enthusiastic and keen. The rewards are good. There's so much energy.'

'You have just demonstrated your own subjection,' Edmund said. I felt my usual sense of inadequacy when faced with Edmund's style of debate.

'It's no good arguing with you,' I said.

Edmund laughed bitterly. 'You never make any attempt to argue with me,' he said. 'You're just like Louisa. You retreat behind emotional outbursts. I thought you might help me.'

'Help you with what?'

'Louisa is going away from me. She's got involved in this most trivial of careers, photographing rooms, of all things. "Rooms express the personality," she says. "That does not say much for the personality," I suggest. At which she slams the door in my face and rushes off in her usual rage. She has no maternal feeling for the children. She has infatuations for Krauts. She spends hours rubbing scented unguents into her skeletal body. She is furious that I spend time with my friends playing bridge, the most innocuous, I would have thought, of activities,

279

and a game which at least requires a modicum of intellectual skills.'

'But you've always encouraged her to work.'

'Of course I have. It would be a criminal waste if she didn't.'

'Then why do you run down her interior design activities?'

'Because the job is not worthy of her, Alice. She's far too intelligent to be moving flowers around on coffee tables. She didn't go to Oxford for that.' He paused, and drained his glass. 'I wish we had never come to this bloody country.'

'Why don't you go home?' I asked.

'Louisa'd never agree. She loves it here. And Louisa is the only person in the world, apart from Nina and Ben, who means anything to me. She is the only thing that counts. I love her, Alice. Even when things look grim, like now. There are moments, when something has gone well and we are alone together, that we can relive old times and feel happy again. Sometimes she shows me that deep down, she loves me too. Sometimes she comes to me for advice about work, or some office problem. Often she likes to tell me how she is getting on. Those are the moments worth waiting for. And they come, from time to time. For the rest, I know I must be patient. In the end, I believe we will be all right together. I must believe that. Surely you understand, Alice?'

The appeal was so touching I did not have the heart to say no. But of course I did not. I had never understood. Edmund was surely loony. All I could do was to urge Gerald to go on playing bridge with him whenever possible. It seemed the only helpful thing to suggest, for the moment.

LOUISA

1085 Fifth Avenue, January 15, 1974

Darling Penny,

How are you? We hear you are doing exciting things in the art business. I think we should get together, we're sort of in the same field. Which is really why I am writing – apart, of course, from inviting you to come and stay whenever you want in our amazing museum of an apartment. Enough art here to keep you busy for years! I remember you used to go and stay in all sorts of fabulous houses when you were at Oxford. We used to tease you about staying for those ghastly shooting weekends etc. Well, now things are different and I am actually very interested in knowing some of those houses for the magazine. Is there any chance you could give me the names of some of the places, or, even better, arrange with the owners for me to come and visit? We are planning a British issue, and I have been put in charge of it, the editors misguidedly thinking that I am connected to every aristocrat in the country. So I am desperate for contacts, and thought you might be able to come up with some. Sorry to bother you when you are so busy, but I hope to hear from you. How are your kids? Ben and Nina are in school here and speak with splendid American accents. I don't see Alice as much as I'd like, we are all so busy. Edmund is now working for some obscure environmental organization, I can't think why. He could have had all sorts of wonderful jobs. Lots of love, Louisa.

1085 Fifth Avenue, New York, January 23, 1974

Darling Daphne,

I bet you aren't at this address any more, but I thought I'd give it a try. I hope you are surviving in that mad California. The reason I am writing, apart from wanting you to come to New York and stay with us – any time, really, we have space for thousands – is to ask you a favour. When you were growing up you must have gone to lots of fabulous country houses for weekends etc. Your parents must know a lot too. Well, I am planning a British issue of *Living Interiors* and I am supposed to find a lot of English houses to photograph, and of course I don't know any. I wonder if you could drop me a line with a list, or even better, write to the people for me asking if I could come and visit? I know it's a bore, and you are probably much too busy freaking out somewhere, but you are just the sort of person who can help me.

Life is very busy, I never see Alice because we are always rushing off in different directions. Gerald and

Edmund play bridge all the time – some things never change – but I am really loving New York and think you would too. Much love, Louisa.

PENNY

How wonderfully selfish Louisa was! 'Those fabulous houses' indeed! As if, after all these years, I had stayed in touch with those people whose reluctant hospitality I was forced to accept as Freddy Weathering's bluestocking and nouveau-riche wife? Louisa's request brought back the most miserable memories of sitting alone, clutching a glass of sherry, leafing through the pages of *Country Life* as though riveted by their contents, while the rest of the house party prattled merrily about Ascot, shooting, school friends, and their beloved dogs. Was it likely I would want to renew acquaintance with them? Was it likely they would want to renew acquaintance with me, no longer on sufferance as the odd paramour of dear old Freddy?

I did, however, take up her offer about coming to stay. All the children were at boarding school, and I had been anxious to get to New York for some time. I wanted to call on a few art dealers I had done business with over the years, without ever having met them face to face. Also, if New York was not becoming the centre of the art world, then I was very much mistaken.

I was shocked by Edmund. Not his appearance, although his face seemed to have melted somehow, like Francis Bacon portrait, and his movements, once so lithe and energetic, seemed listless. It was his work that was so distressing. Our brilliant boy, our double first, our intellectual paragon, had already, in his mid-thirties, begun a spiral to nowhere. Not that he hadn't had offers. Au contraire. Americans thought him marvellous, brilliant, inspiring, a new talent on the scene. His conversational powers remained compelling, particularly for those unfamiliar with his technique. And for many Americans, his verbal skills alone, laced as they were with literature, philosophy, and poetry, guaranteed him a welcome in almost any institution or corporation in the country. Add to that his physical impact, his style of dress, his innocent sexuality, and you have an Englishman all Americans would like to call their own.

But he refused them all, preferring to take a small, uninfluential, untesting post where his skills were mostly useless. Was it fear? Panic? Boredom? Had he lost his nerve? Had Louisa somehow undermined him? The question gnawed at me as I stayed at their extraordinary mausoleum on Fifth Avenue, and watched the marriage grind on, endlessly stinging itself like the death dance of the tarantula attacked by fire.

So much in New York was interesting. The art business was exploding, and I found many ways to increase my own business. In England I had a small gallery, specializing in nineteenth-century English paintings, which I sold to small, discerning collectors. America wanted art on quite a different scale. The corporations were hungry for art as a thirsty man craves water, and as far as I could see, very few people had begun to fulfil this need. I was a specialist, I knew English art, and there was not a corporate executive in New York who did not feel safe buying some of my products.

It was marketing, to be sure, as Edmund was the first to point out, declaring that I, like everyone else, had sold out to the values of a Moroccan souk. But he could afford his luxurious morality. I, like everyone else, had to pay for mine. I was alone. Freddy had disappeared into his own morality, for which I felt no censure, and little sorrow. Only sadness for my children, on whom this burden would take its toll in their own adult lives.

America was enlightening in this respect, too. Though in many ways deeply reactionary and

conservative to a fault in social behaviour, New
York at least was beginning to become a city of
women. Gloria Steinem was New York's god-
dess, a glamorous ex-sex bomb with curtains of
long blonde hair and aviator glasses, looking
like Miss America while relentlessly delivering
vicious attacks on men. No one else seemed
amused or puzzled by this paradox. Ambiguity
reigned supreme on the sexual front.

This is perhaps best illustrated by the extraordinary debate going on when I arrived about the
precise origin of the orgasm. Was it inside,
outside, upstairs, downstairs, or in my lady's
chamber? asked the media people, the psycholo-
gists, the sex therapists, even the women themselves. They seek it here, they seek it there, the
ladies seek it everywhere, Edmund murmured
one night at dinner, causing Louisa to throw her
napkin down in fury saying if he understood one
thing about it, he might have known what the
trouble was between them. This brand of Louisa-
candour (or was it sadism?) brought a blush
even to my cheeks, but Edmund seemed, as
always, immune to her taunts or the meaning
between them.

'Really, Louisa,' he said scathingly, 'you seem
to have descended to the American level of
ascribing all interpersonal ills to sex. It's too
depressing. I don't see why I have to act like a

caveman to prove I love you. What has happened
to your sensibilities? I have always treated you
as an equal, which is precisely what you deserve.
These brutish times have affected your common
sense.'

'Equality is so unsatisfactory,' Louisa muttered, getting up from the rather delicious
orange mousse provided by her fashionable
caterer. 'Everyone is so anxious to see the other
person's point of view that nothing ever gets
done.'

With that, she glared at us and stomped out of
the room.

Edmund looked at me, and shrugged, and we
both laughed.

Which brings me to the crux of this, my first
trip to the States, a trip so successful profession-
ally, and so distressing in other ways. Edmund
took me out to dinner one night towards the end
of my visit. Louisa had gone off to Virginia to
photograph some State-Department flunky's
country estate, and as Edmund and I found
ourselves both without appointments, we agreed
to dine at a small French bistro off Second
Avenue that Edmund found faintly less preten-
tious than most of the Parisian pastiches available on the Upper East Side.

Edmund drank two champagne cocktails without even noticing. For myself, by the end of one

I was feeling that strange feeling in the back of my head that spelled danger. I ignored it, and we had two bottles of wine over a good, simple dinner that neither of us took the slightest notice of. He spent the evening talking about Louisa. How he had met her, what we had all said at that idiotic Bardwell Road tea, what she had looked like, every single exchange practically that had taken place during those Oxford years. His memory was phenomenal. It was as though he remembered nothing else but his times with Louisa. They say the memory is selective, but this was surely pathological. I remembered Freud's definition of neurosis as an abnormal attachment to the past.

Obsessions tend to grip the imagination, and I was transfixed by this strange outpouring, delivered with his usual mixture of scholasticism and expressiveness. I was both touched and repulsed by his frankness. It was as though I were listening to a paraplegic describe in the minutest detail the circumstances which had left him crippled.

At the end of the meal we returned to Mrs Van Zuylen's museum, I hardly remember how. We sat in his study, where photographs of Oxford, his rowing crew at Eton, cricket in some pastoral setting, and other nostalgic emblems covered the Chinese-tea-papered walls. It was

288

there that he knelt at my knee, like an acolyte, looking up with a smile that resembled a grimace, and said that if it hadn't been Louisa it was me that he would have chosen.

'If only,' he said. 'If only ... How different everything would have been.'

'Please, Edmund,' I remember pleading. 'Please don't.' I felt the overwhelming urge to lift him up and embrace him, just as I had all those public-school boys at Oxford so many years ago. He seemed so young, so innocent. But all I could see was Louisa, looming behind him like the Wicked Witch of the West, ready to pounce on me for my treachery.

'I can't, Edmund,' I said. 'I just can't. I'm so terribly sorry.'

I didn't dare look at him again, but the picture of his hunched body, as I left him kneeling on Mrs Van Zuylen's richly patterned Persian rug, will never leave me.

The following day he had left the apartment before I appeared for breakfast. Greeted with enthusiasm by the twins, I tried to ignore my throbbing brain and behave like the mother I really was.

'Do you like living in America?' I asked.

'I like the chewing gum,' said Ben.

'I don't like it,' Nina said.

'Why not?'

'She can't blow bubbles,' Ben volunteered. 'She always tries to swallow it.'

'I don't,' Nina retorted. 'I'd hate to eat it. Yuk. I just don't like this place, that's all.' She looked round the apartment. 'I miss our house in London. I miss Mummy.'

'But she's here, isn't she?'

'Only sometimes. She was here much more in England.'

Later a small bouquet of roses arrived for me, with no note. I did not see Edmund or Louisa again. I spent a rather useless day with Alice at the Met, and then almost immediately left for Chicago and London, my portfolio full of commissions, contacts, and promises of lucrative art deals to come.

I thought of writing a letter, simply to thank him for the flowers. But when I started to put pen to paper, somehow it seemed incriminating. I would rather leave no trace.

18

ALICE

Penny had become the complete business-woman. When she rang me up to arrange a lunch, she sounded like somebody's executive secretary, rather than one of my oldest friends. I suppose I was a little irritated that she decided to stay with Louisa. Well, naturally she would, as Gerald pointed out. If she had stayed with us we would have had to move Bert into the living room and she would have had to sleep in an environment entirely dominated by posters of football players – American football players, that is, those strange-looking people with padded shoulders and plastic-encased elbows and thighs, for whom Bert had developed the most astonishing devotion. I found this assimilation into foreign culture quite alarming, although Gerald was very pleased, and said it showed Bert had a sense of the world that would stand him in good stead. For what, he did not explain. Anyway, flesh for flesh, Boucher clearly was the winner over Joe Namath (though in my weaker moments I might have forced a toss).

Penny and I met on the steps of the Met among the dope smokers, bag ladies and cruising sex maniacs. Penny was very brisk and businesslike, and we kissed perfunctorily, during which time she established that I still looked very English in my smocks and florals, which, in spite of Louisa's scorn, I still found helped conceal the occasional flaw in my contours. (Not helped, I told Penny, by the huge portions provided in America – not only in restaurants, where the ludicrous idea of doggy-bags had had to be invented, but in supermarkets, where even yogurts, the dieter's saviour, were the size of beer barrels.) While she sized me up (Gerald would have appreciated that pun), I took in that she was incredibly thin and stylish looking, in clinging silk jersey with a fur collar. It was difficult to imagine she had borne four children.

'How are the children?' I asked as we climbed the steps to the museum. She slowed, and her face softened.

'Wonderful,' she said. 'The only one I worry about is Caspar. He minded most about his Daddy going away. And he minded by being the most cheerful, trying to look after me and his sisters and brother, never letting on how miserable he was. That, my dear Alice, is a bad sign.'

'Are you actually divorced?'

Penny laughed. 'Lord, no. Why on earth should we do that?'

'Oh, I don't know. I thought that's what happened when people separated.'

'You are old-fashioned, Alice.'

'Mmm,' I agreed.

'Neither of us has the slightest interest in breaking it up,' Penny went on. 'He runs the finances and the farm; he visits the children when he can. They go and stay with him in Italy. I keep the household going. We live in London most of the time now, since I am very busy with my company, and the children are at boarding school. It's a very efficient arrangement for both of us. Why go through all sorts of dramas when you don't have to?'

'Oh, quite,' I said. 'But what if you fell in love with someone else?'

'I'm not like Louisa, you know,' Penny.

'Perish the thought,' I said.

We were walking through the galleries, without looking at the paintings. Penny wanted to look at something in particular, and was not about to dally among the Rembrandts. Finally we walked through a room that had one painting, all by itself, at the end, roped off and specially lit.

'This is Velázquez's portrait of Juan de Pareja,' Penny said. 'This is the one everyone made all that fuss about. You have to admit it wasn't worth it. They've done a cosmetic job on him too.'

We peered at the Spaniard's haughty face. The canvas looked oily enough to fry an egg on.

'What was the fuss about?' I asked.

'The Met bought it in 1971 for five million dollars,' Penny said. 'It was the highest price ever paid for a painting.'

'I remember reading about it. It was before we came here. Wasn't everyone appalled?'

'Yes, but excited too. Though it's by no means Velázquez's best.'

'I don't know why they didn't just put five million dollars in a frame and let everyone come and look at that instead,' I suggested.

Penny laughed. 'You've got something there. It's the classic confusion here between Money and Art. The key question any collector asks a dealer is, How much does it cost? The more pricey, the better the art. We don't look at this poor Spaniard any more, we look at the price tag.'

'That's what Edmund is always on about,' I said as we began to walk back down the gallery.

'Oh, Edmund.' Penny was silent.

'Did you see him? By the way, let's look at the Turners.'

'Whatever for?'

'I like them.'

'Typical,' she said. 'You come here to the biggest collection of art in the world, full of masterpieces you could never have come close to before, and all you want to see are the Turners. How parochial can you get? Really, Alice.'

In this way she deflected me from the subject of Edmund, though I was too annoyed to notice it at the time. I followed her sulkily past various paintings I had never heard of and then suggested lunch at the Stanhope.

'It's a perfect day and we can sit outside.'

'Just a drink,' she said. 'I have a lot of dealers to call on today. And then I have to catch a plane to Chicago. Don't you have to go back to work?'

'Oh, yes, but people in advertising here have very long lunches. Rather like London. And since the drinks are so huge they don't bother about things in the afternoon.'

'You really are a lazy cow, aren't you.'

I couldn't argue with that, and we drank our Camparis under the canopy at the Stanhope in silence.

'Are you going to come back?' I asked. 'It's funny that we are all over here now.'

'Business is very good,' Penny admitted. 'I would really love to spend some time here. But I can't transplant four children. You three were lucky. You did not have so many dependants.

You could get out when the going was good.'

'I miss England, though,' I mused.

'I wouldn't bother,' Penny said. 'It's an old, tired country, and nothing that should be changed is being changed.'

'Edmund misses it too. I think he hates it here.'

'Oh, Edmund,' Penny said again.

'Did you think Louisa was all right?'

'I didn't see her much. She seemed her usual angry self. Looking for love is awfully hard work. And as far as I can see, that's all she does.'

'Looking for love,' I murmured. 'It sounds so splendid, somehow.'

'It's pathetic.'

'I wonder how many women, not counting nuns, have never had an orgasm.'

Penny snorted into her drink. 'Don't tell me you've started,' she exclaimed. 'It's like water on the brain over here. I never met a more hysterical bunch of navel gazers.'

'But Penny, you don't understand. It's one of those divisions in the world, like the one between women who have had children and women who haven't. You are in one group and cannot see how the question can possibly be interesting to the other. Why else do you think such reams of magazine and newsprint have been written on the subject? Anyway,' I added, 'it's a little further down than the navel.'

'I suppose you and Louisa have been getting together,' Penny said. 'She certainly gave Edmund a cosy little aside about it in my presence.'

'It's all your fault,' I said. 'You should have been straighter with us at Oxford. We never had the proper education.'

Penny laughed. 'That's rich, that is. Your wretched sex lives are entirely the responsibility of yours truly, Penelope Coverdale.'

'Have you reverted to your maiden name, then?' I asked.

'Yes, I have, if you must know.'

'Gosh, Penny, you are advanced,' I said admiringly.

'Well, it got a bit uncomfortable being called Weathering, if you really want to know,' she said. 'I mean, when Freddy first hit the headlines with his new, um, live-in. People kept eyeing me curiously. And all the men I met felt sure I was totally sex-starved and leaped on me quite unmercifully.'

'Did Freddy ever talk to you about it? I mean, afterwards?'

'You know him. Lovely lines of Latin poetry, some jewellery winkled out of his mother in compensation, a few silent, rueful laughs. It wasn't his fault. If it was anyone's, it was mine.'

She shook herself and picked up the bill.

'This is on me,' she said. 'Expenses.'

It felt odd being taken out by one of one's oldest friends. I felt quite like a schoolgirl again.

'What shall we do about Louisa?' I asked, as we said goodbye.

'Oh, find her a new man, I suppose,' Penny said, with a parting kiss, adding hurriedly, 'and by the way, look after Edmund.'

Some task, I thought. Finding a new man in New York, and looking after Edmund, were about as easy as climbing Mount Everest in plimsolls.

LOUISA

Jeannie Honeywell is my only friend. Penny disapproves of me, Alice is bored with me, Gerald hates me because I am not nice to his best friend, Edmund, and Daphne, well, Daphne is lost, presumed drowned. She never even answered my letter. But at least Jeannie understands what I am going through, because she is going through it too, and she says that all women are going through it.

'But what precisely are we going through?' I asked her yesterday at lunch. We usually meet at a small, crowded salad bar where every other working woman has lunch, because the salads are all dressing-free, and there is nothing to drink except fruit juice. Sometimes I yearn for a bottle of Chablis, just to unwind a little bit, but Jeannie would faint with horror. Drinking is not a feminist pursuit, in her view. It's like music to a Marxist.

'We need to be in touch with our feelings,' she told me, turning over pale iceberg lettuce shavings with a restless fork. 'You need to reach out and touch somebody. Yourself.'

'But what about the Fabric of Life?'

'Fabric of life, what's that, some kind of polyester?' she demanded impatiently. 'You Oxford types are always trying to intellectualize things. You are like all the English, not in touch with your own sexuality.'

'But surely you don't want me to walk about with my hand up my skirt all the time.'

'Baby, you are so naïve,' Jeannie said. 'You should really see my shrink, he's fabulous about things like that. You are trying to desex yourself, Louisa. Think of those London parties you used to give. Weren't they the most sexless gatherings in the world?'

I tried to remember them, but all that came to mind were images of people throwing up into flowerpots or passing out under strobe lights.

'I see what you mean,' I conceded. 'But we all wore topless things and miniskirts. You never even got round to that here.'

'That was all a red herring,' Jeannie explained. 'My therapist explained it to me. Miniskirts were like bra-burning, provocative in quite the wrong way, and played into the hands of the male chauvinist pigs. Even after five years of therapy, I'm still afraid to think of myself as a sexual person.'

'In Cyril Connolly's last year at Eton, he was eighteen and a half and he'd never had sexual intercourse and never masturbated,' I informed her.

'There you are,' Jeannie exclaimed triumphantly. 'You see what we're up against? I bet your Edmund wasn't much different. Is he a friend of this Connolly's, or what? I'd love to get them both to see my therapist. Talk about changing their lives!'

'Forget it, Jeannie. Neither of them would go for it.'

'And you are prepared to remain in this crazy relationship? I tell you, Louisa, you have to do something. What happened about this Heinrich guy?'

I groaned. I had told Jeannie how I had changed when I was with Heinrich. I had told her everything. The way I felt a new person, pulsing with fire, my skin as fresh as Nina's cheek, my eyes bright, my energy level inexhaustible. Oh God, Jeannie, that was when I was alive, when everything had meaning, when the colours of the sky were radiating rainbows, when I could have taken on the world. What is the point of any other state than that? Why look for anything else? Why not choose that ultimate in sensation, that ultimate in excitement, that ultimate in being alive?

'Ah, Heinrich, the shitface Kraut,' I said, biting on a shrivelled radish. 'He has gone forever. Will Edmund ever let me find my happiness?'

Then Jeannie creased her much-lotioned brow (only for a second so the marks would not linger), and wrinkled her man-made nose (which, since her devotion to the Cause, she now deeply regretted).

'You mean a man, don't you, Louisa? she said evenly.

'I know, I know,' I said, fending off the expected argument. 'It's absurd to expect anything in New York, I know what the statistics are.'

Jeannie sighed and shook her head.

'We still have much work to do,' she said, pushing away a limp piece of tofu. 'You see, it's not through a man that you will find what you want. Remember that, Louisa. It's not through a man. Men are like Edmund. They do not know, in the end.'

'But what about Heinrich?' I pleaded. 'I want those wonderful feelings again. I'm sorry, I do.'

An overweight waitress removed our picked-over salad bowls, her face a picture of disgust at this travesty of a meal.

'You are still in a bad way, Louisa,' my friend said in deepest gloom. 'Remember what I say. You must be your own best friend. Work on it. My therapist has Thursday afternoons free from four to five. Think about it. No coffee,' she added to the resigned waitress. 'Unless you have caffeine-free.'

My mouth flooded with sudden longing for a maximum-strength espresso. I swallowed hastily. 'Thanks, Jeannie,' I said.

She put her clawlike hand on my arm and gripped it. 'We must always be close to each other,' she said urgently. 'We are friends, aren't we – aren't we?'

At times like this her raw openness, her vulnerability, made me expire with embarrassment. Mumbling endearments, sweating buckets, I would push her off. Yet I longed to break out of my stupid ingrained reticence and respond, for deep down, I felt sure her approach was right. Where would I have been without Jeannie?

302

19

ALICE

I got a message in my office in early spring that a Daphne Fanthorpe had called from Southampton, Long Island, and that she wanted me to see her pool. I told Gerald I thought Daphne was in a serious state of expanded consciousness, but he assured me the phone number was authentic. So one Saturday morning in late June I found myself on the Long Island Railroad to Southampton. Gerald was giving an exhibition of vegetarian timbale-making to the Citizens for a Smaller New York benefit committee in the Brooklyn Botanic Garden, an event I felt lacked pulling power. On such occasions, Gerald would wow his audience with his laconic wit and nutritional expertise (a pale shadow of an orator compared to Edmund, but those public-school charms never failed to impress), while excitable women wearing lime-green scarves and fuchsia lip-gloss would accost me and tell me how wonderful the Queen was, and that their ancestors were Scottish, did I know them?

Little Bert was going to stay with his Daddy, which pleased them both well enough. Bert was not interested in cooking, but he always got to eat the results of his father's labours, and this satisfied his ever-ready palate. A chip off the old block, my mother would say. Since she had never had a boy, she did not know that it was simply a matter of permanent hunger on her grandson's part.

The train to the Hamptons shook and bounced its passengers, a posse of suntanned bank tellers and dentists, all the way to unmentionable delights in Singles Heaven. The Gin-Lane set had long since completed the trip in comfort and were already at work on some tall ones beside the pool. Unfortunately most of my companions fled the train at their various group-house destinations, and therefore did not see Daphne, standing by a brown Rolls Royce, rush to meet me as I stepped off the bone-cracker, bruised and weary, at Southampton.

'I don't usually drive this,' she said. 'But Parker is playing in a tennis tournament and said I could take it.'

Daphne's new appearence was interesting. Her hair was now short and tightly curled like Shirley Temple's. She was wearing a pair of pink shorts (tiny) and a scarlet halter top (tiny) that confirmed the staying power of her figure. I was running a poor fourth in the Bardwell Road weight stakes.

'You look remarkably healthy for someone who's been shooting up in bus-station loos,' I said, settling into the plush interior of the Rolls. 'I wonder if Louisa would call this taupe.'

'What?'

'Never mind,' I said as the car swerved alarmingly.

'I was never really druggy, you know,' she said. 'You always loved to think the worst about me.'

'Well, you were a bit peculiar when we saw you in London. And then Louisa said she had these spacy telephone calls.'

'Louisa's such a dramatizer. I was probably on LSD, that's all. Poor old Kumar spent most of his time on acid so I felt I had to keep him company. Unfortunately, he seemed bent on destruction, hanging off the roof of our apartment in LA, trying to cut all the TV aerials down with nail-scissors. That's when I thought I'd better push on.'

'Where did you push on to?'

'It's a long story,' she said, aiming the car into a pillar-lined driveway. 'I'll tell you later.'

She waved at an old retainer shaving a topiary moose's ears. The house, when we finally arrived, was Chenonceaux in miniature – water, trees, turrets, shutters, and all.

'The architect had a fixation about the Loire,' Daphne explained unnecessarily. 'He even imported Loire water so it would be right. That's the rather odd smell.'

'Goodness,' I said.

'Fun, don't you think? I've chosen you a nice bedroom, done in Liberty's to remind you of home. View of the ocean thrown in. Round marble bath with gold taps . . .'

'Stop,' I said. 'I think I'm going to be sick.'

We entered the château. The hall was filled with vases of bougainvillea, azaleas, hibiscus.

'Don't tell me these all grow in the garden.'

'Parker lets me order what I want. I have a thing for these waxy ones. They fly them in from Lord knows where. Let me show you to your room.'

'I never knew you harboured a passion for flowers.'

'It's recent,' Daphne conceded.

We went up a gracefully curved staircase to the first floor, which was like a large piazza with lots of doors leading off it, a perfect set for a French farce.

'A lot of changing partners, then?' I asked.

'I only play with Parker,' she said, surprised.

'Never mind,' I said.

My bedroom was roughly the size of Centre
Court at Wimbledon. Liberty print armchairs, a
desk, and silk-fringed lamps, were arranged
round a four-poster bed wrapped in shimmering
blue and gold draperies. The window overlooked
the garden, and past that, the sea, also shimmering blue and gold, Life imitating Art. Beside the
bed was a Cartier clock, a telephone, and four
books: *The Inner Game of Tennis*, by Timothy
Gallwey, *How to Play Mixed Doubles without
Raising Your Blood Pressure*, by John Lob, *So
You're Going to Take Tennis Seriously*, by Jack
Roberto, and *Montgomery of Alamein* by Brian
Scoles. Daphne opened a trompe l'oeil door (the
trompe was a Directoire mirror) at the far end of
the room, to reveal a forget-me-not blue and
white striped bathroom, reflected in mirrors
placed against the door, around the bath, and on
the ceiling. The taps on the bath, which was
smoky blue marble and round as a lollipop, were
gold, as were the tumblers, shower curtains, and
mat fringes. Piles of blue towels, folded in perfect symmetry, with scarlet edges and the monogram PCF picked out in gold, were, displayed
in a mirrored shelf against one wall.

'I don't like this one,' I said. 'What else have
you got?'

'If you need anything use the telephone,'
Daphne said. 'Dial 211 to make a long-distance

call, 5 for the kitchen, 4 for the bar, 3 for me,
and 001 for a private line to Parker. Actually, I
don't recommend dialling for Parker. He's not
very good on the phone. Anyway, they are all
unplugged now as the staff is on vacation.'

'I was hoping I could ring for you to run my
bath,' I complained.

'Ha ha. Let's go and have a swim.'

The pool was a bright blue kidney, with a
pavilion at the far end like a Greek temple, covered in mosaic. At each side of the pavilion were
changing cubicles, and in the centre a large play-
room with Ping-Pong table, television, an artist's
easel, and dumbbells. On one wall were photographs of a fierce-looking man with various
famous people. Eisenhower, the Duke of Windsor
(the number of Americans I had seen pictured
with the Duke of Windsor made me wonder sometimes if poor David did anything else except pose
for photographers), Claudette Colbert, and Frank
Sinatra were the only ones I recognized. On the
opposite wall there were pictures of the same
fierce-looking man in various poses on the tennis
court – doing a high smash, holding a silver cup,
shaking hands over the net, with his arm round
Vic Seixas.

'I've always loved Vic Seixas,' I said, peering
at his wiry form.

'You're supposed to be admiring Parker, not

Vic Seixas,' Daphne said. 'But I see what you mean.'

'Parker's the fierce-looking one, then?'

'He's not really fierce. He's a sweetie. You'll see.'

'Mmm,' I said, looking at the pictures again. 'You could have fooled me.'

'Do you want a drink?'

Mr Gimlet-Eyes glared down at us as Daphne pressed a button to reveal American's most significant contribution to interior decorating – the bar. This one was a particularly good example, the bottles lined up in little gold stands, the glasses all backlit to look like Lalique masterpieces, the walls lined in a soft taupe (definitely, this time) ultrasuede.

'Mint juleps, I think,' Daphne said opening a small icebox with containers of mint, juniper berries, maraschino cherries, orange and lemon slices – the fruit of a drinker's loom. I watched as she expertly mixed the drinks.

'I think I'm the one who's hallucinating,' I said.

'What?'

'Never mind.'

We found two blue and white striped deck chairs with little side arms attached with niches for one's accessories – drink, book, suntan lotion, etc. – and as we settled down in the hot afternoon sun, Daphne told me what had happened to her since her last-ever appearance six years earlier in London.

'I met a man at a party in Malibu,' she told me. 'I was on my own because Kumar was on the roof snipping away as usual. This man looked like an Oriental wrestler, with a shaved head and deep growling voice, and he told me he could give me unlimited orgasms, so I decided to take him up on it. Life with Kumar had been on the austere side, owing to all the chemical substances.'

Orgasms, I thought. I sipped my mint julep and waited.

'He was an advance man for the Playboy Club,' she went on. 'He travelled around the country buying real estate for Hugh Hefner to build on, and also screwing girls – an advance man for them too, really. When I went to his hotel room on Sunset Boulevard, a girl was just leaving, and when I left a girl was waiting outside. He was a service industry.'

A sudden sharp noise interrupted us.

I jumped. 'What was that?'

It came again, a searing, sizzling sound like frying fat.

'Oh, don't worry, that's the mosquito zapper. It doesn't usually work until after dark. It was probably some errant fly.'

She pointed up to the ceiling of the pavilion, where a flat metal rectangle with six bars, like the grill of an electric fire, was hanging from two wires. A blue light glowed along the top. As I watched it, tiny sparks suddenly flew from the bars and the sizzling sound came again.

'It's new,' Daphne explained. 'We only just installed it. Marvellous little invention. The mosquitoes are attracted by the ultraviolet light, come flying towards it full tilt, and crash into the electric rods, which fry them to Kingdom Come.'

'My father should have come up with something like that,' I said. 'It would have been much more successful than the barking machine.'

'What was that?'

'You put in a field to frighten the birds away – like a scarecrow.'

'Sounds ingenious enough.'

'Well, it was in theory, like all my father's ideas. The trouble was that it was either too sensitive, and would bark whenever an ant started to crawl about, or, when you adjusted it, would only operate when a herd of elephants charged through. Poor Daddy.'

'Aren't parents funny,' Daphne mused. 'I like mine much better now. I've forgiven them everything.'

311

'I bet you didn't tell them about the Oriental wrestler.'

'Well, no. They wouldn't have got the point.'

'And you did?'

'What?'

'Did he live up to his word?'

'Christ, yes,' Daphne said, gazing dreamily into the sky. 'He most certainly did.'

'Can you describe it for me?' I said, lying back and gazing into the sky with her.

'Alice,' Daphne sounded shocked.

'Well, remember I'm an old married woman. We just don't know these things.'

'All right.' Daphne lay back in her chair, with one hand under her head, the other holding her glass.

'First of all,' she said, 'he ordered me to take off my clothes. Then he carried me to the bed, which was one of those enormous double beds that American hotels always have. It had a frightful orange and yellow brocade bedspread and the frame was stained walnut.'

'Never mind that. You were hardly in a position to criticize the decor.'

'So he laid me flat on my back – '

'Hurled you on to the bed, swollen with passion.'

'Okay. Then he started to suck my nipples till they stuck out like pink lollipops.'

312

'E M Forster was right. Nothing is more obdurate to artistic treatment than the carnal. Do go on.'

'Actually I remember gazing down at his shiny bald head and wondering how often he had to shave it. But then he moved down my body, licking everywhere, until he got to you-know-where.'

'You mean your forest of desire?'

'Mossy, I believe it is often described, Alice. He licked and licked like a huge dog – '

'Make that a Dobermann pinscher.'

'Alsatian, perhaps. Until my – '

'Your delicate pink bud?'

'Burst into flower, overflowing with nectar . . .'

'And you screamed nameless words into his ear – '

'My nails digging into his heaving back. Then finally when I thought my body had turned forever into a molten furnace . . .'

'Good.'

'He thrust his organ into me.'

'Organ? Manhood, Daphne, manhood.'

'He thrust his manhood into me. Are you sure that's right, Alice?'

'All right, how about rod?'

'And then the, let me see, the deep rhythms of the earth overpowered me.'

313

'Fine. And rendered you senseless. Now what about the waves?'

'The waves. Well, wave after wave sucked me into its profound depths. There was a roaring in my ears, and I thought I would be engulfed in the cosmic ocean. His secret was, of course,' she added in a normal voice, 'that he never came.'

'Never came?'

'Not that I can remember. He just slammed away and I just kept being engulfed in cosmic oceans and then by golly he'd be there slamming again and I just went on and on until I said I had to go because I was too exhausted to continue. So he gave me a couple more slams just to be on the safe side, pulled me up, gave me my clothes, and that was that. I went out with bow legs and a silly grin on my face, past the next client who looked pale with excitement, and went home to my freaked-out acidhead and his nail-scissors. Well, he just didn't look the same. So I went back to the hotel a couple of times, just to make sure I hadn't been dreaming, and then he went off to Minneapolis and that was that. He told me some girls followed him wherever he went, but I couldn't afford a plane ticket to Minneapolis.'

We fell silent in contemplation.

'Think of him,' I said finally, 'like the Flying Dutchman, travelling from city to city, unable to come, only to go, bestowing his compulsive gift on the hungry residents, leaving emotional and physical devastation in his wake. I wonder where he is now.'

'Aha, Alice, I can see you are ready to take off this minute.'

'Well, I must say it sounds interesting. Ever since my thirtieth birthday, I've planned to drink life to the dregs.'

'But what about Gerald?'

'Let's face it, he's no Flying Dutchman.'

'No, I can see that. But you wouldn't want it all the time, Alice, I can assure you. Parker is no Flying Dutchman either.'

'He's a tennis player, I take it,' I said.

'How did you guess? Don't underestimate him. You should see him on the court. For someone of his age, he's really amazing. People half his age stagger off the court after a match with Parker. He's really making me understand the game. I want to be his mixed-doubles partner one day.'

'So you're planning to stay a while?'

'Oh, yes. I've been playing quite regularly since I met Parker. He's given me loads of lessons. It's a fascinating game, Alice. Really psychological. I'm entering some of the women's tournaments myself next month.'

This was hard to take, harder than the Flying

Dutchman. Was this to be Daphne's latest role – the new Little Mo?

'And what does Lady Fanthorpe say to this transformation?'

'She's absolutely thrilled. She said she always saw me as a summer person, whatever that means. She's coming to stay here later this year. After Wimbledon, of course. She's going to bring some Teddy Tinling dresses for me. Parker's terribly excited about her coming. He loves titles.'

'Not just tennis titles?'

Daphne glared. 'I'm not going to have you mocking me again, Alice. If you're not going to behave properly, you can leave. I can see Parker coming down the lawn now.'

Parker Canute Ferris was a tall, bony, grey-haired man with a razor-sharp beak for a nose, a slit for a mouth, and tiny bright blue eyes that fixed like limpets upon one's weakest attribute – in my case, the lower torso.

'Please to meet you,' he rapped out. 'Great game today, Daffers. I'll tell you all later. Must take a shower now. See you for dinner later, er, Alice, was it? So nice for Daphne to have a friend here. Gets a bit lonely when I'm on the court all day. Cheers.'

With whirlwind speed, the tennis player vanished back into the house.

'He showers a lot,' Daphne explained, as we slowly followed him indoors. 'That's because he plays so much tennis. All Americans shower, you know.'

At dinner I was able to study my friend's new amour more carefully. He was an exponent of the monogram. There were monograms on his blue silk shirt, on his cuffs, on his blazer pocket, on his handkerchief, on his tie, and on his blue velvet slippers. I noticed that the monograms were not limited to his person; the living-room upholstery was a design of PCFs, as was the carpet. His cigarette lighter was monogrammed, so were the backgammon dice – very discreetly, in a corner. The only items not so marked were emblazoned with frogs. The glasses, the dinner service, the mats, the napkins, the lampshades, and Parker Ferris's trousers had green frogs on them in various formations – climbing frogs, dancing frogs, squatting frogs, sleeping frogs, hand-in-hand frogs, leaping frogs.

As we sat down to dinner, Parker looked at the frog-covered soup plates and barked to Daphne, 'I'm sick of these. Take them away.'

Daphne dutifully collected up the plates and replaced them with another set, monogrammed in green. The following day we rushed off to the local store to buy some more. Daphne picked out a set with embracing frogs.

317

'But these are frogs again?' I objected.

'Of course, silly. He has to have frogs. He just didn't like the old ones.'

Parker Ferris was a man of the monogram, and a man of impulse, but he was also a man of property, most of it accumulating handily in the stock market. Unlike poor Freddy Weathering, this comfortable way of life did not require Parker to look for projects. Apart from his affection for his stock portfolio, Parker's main interests in life were tennis and the late Field Marshal Montgomery, the one who wore a beret all through the Second World War and irritated all the American generals by wanting to be everywhere first. Parker mentioned his fondness for the field marshal to me over dinner, and asked me if I had noticed Montgomery's military insignia painted on the doors of his Rolls Royce. He then showed me his basement room, which was devoted to Montgomery memorabilia – an army stick, two gold buttons, a Sam Browne Belt, a rather grey handkerchief, and some old maps. Parker also possessed a Montgomery-type beret, which he put on proudly, giving me the opportunity to comment on the uncanny resemblance. I refrained from quoting to him Churchill's comment about Monty: 'In defeat invincible, in victory insufferable.' Gerald used to quote it when he played bridge with Edmund.

Perhaps Parker was like that on the tennis
court.

'How about some tennis tomorrow, eh, Alice?'
he asked me after dinner, an invitation that
Daphne told me later was the highest compliment he could bestow. Reluctant as I was to
refuse a game, I felt it my duty to return to my
family, sweltering away in our modest city
home. Daphne drove me to the station, having
said goodbye to Parker as he set off on yet
another day of the serve and volley.

'You know what it is,' she said as we waited
for the train. 'It is the ultimate test of the
personality.'

'Tennis?' I said incredulously.

'Look,' Daphne explained. 'I play here with a
friend, whom I don't really like. When I face her
across the tennis net, all these feelings surge to
the surface, and I really want to beat her. But at
the same time I can feel a message in my head
saying, 'You're no good, Daphne, she's going to
beat you hollow, because you really ought to like
her and you feel guilty and so you are going to
let her win . . .' I mean it goes on like that, like
some bloody tape in my head, and I can't shake
it off and of course I play horribly and the cow
wins!'

She looked at me in triumph.

'Daphne,' I said. 'You've been in America too

long. I expect you have been working on self-actualization through the backhand.'

'The trouble with you, Alice,' she said as the train pulled in, 'is that you never get involved in anything. You're living your life at one stage removed. That's for the birds.'

'And the answer is, take up tennis,' I said, laughing. 'Thanks, Daphne, I really loved the visit. I mean that. I hope I can come back.'

'Bring party clothes next time,' she said. 'I'll invite you when my mother comes, and you can bring Gerald and Bert. I'd love to see them.'

I nodded and waved and settled back for the bumpy ride back to New York. The train was empty this Sunday morning – the bank tellers and dentist all nursing hangovers and satiated desire, no doubt. I thought about the Flying Dutchman. Daphne had certainly actualized herself more than the rest of us. It was time, I decided, for me to catch up.

DAPHNE

I did get into sex in California, of course. In the middle sixties, in the home of drugs and flower power, how could it be otherwise? But most of the time it was inexpressibly dreary. I used to pair up with some girl I had picked up in a bar, and we would cruise about the place, and finally latch on to some Hollywood type with a suntan and a line about the movies, and off we'd go to his El Dorado up Laurel Canyon where we'd all get high and take our clothes off and wait for – well, something.

I don't remember much about it, actually, since my mind had usually been cooked by various weeds to a thick white sauce like the ones dear old McCloud used to serve up to me at home. Looking back, I can see this was fortunate, since the few memories that do, like a lump of cauliflower, penetrate the grey fog are of the most depressing nature. I remember, for instance, being taken to the house of a once-famous television star called Joe Webster, who had played a tough old cop in a serial about the Chicago Police Department. He was a bit before my time, but our pimp (for that's really what he was) insisted to my current girlfriend and me that this chap was incredibly famous and we should count ourselves lucky to have fallen into his glamorous clutches.

So we arrived at his large pad above the Hollywood Hills, vaguely anticipating an amusing evening. (Amusing? I soon learned to erase the word from my vocabulary. Evenings were many things, but never, ever, amusing.) The place was classic movie-fan fodder. The theme seemed to be horses – the main A-frame room was done like a stable, with beams and iron bars, and saddles hanging over the fireplace like trophies. Frightful oil paintings of horses covered the walls (modern copies of Stubbs, only lacking his understanding of the anatomy of the animal), hunting scenes, and a few bridles decorated the raw stone walls. The bar, which was contained within a central island that dominated the room, was lined in studded leather, with stirrup cups lining the shelves along with huge highball glasses decorated with horses' heads. I also spotted a rack of hunting whips, which gave me the idea that this horse business was just a front for unspeakable practices. But that was par for the course, too, in Hollywood.

We drank hugely, unnerved by this equestrian setting, and even more unnerved by the arrival of Joe Webster, who took one look at us and obviously decided we were not his type.

'Jesus, Mack,' I heard him mutter in the famous flat voice that had put the fear of God into a thousand criminals and thrilled a million viewers, 'what dumb-shit have you brought me this time?'

Looking round at the equipment on the walls, I had the feeling that our experience was not quite up to what was expected by our hero. I whispered to my girlfriend, whose name I have now forgotten (I don't think I ever saw her again), that I thought we were in the wrong stable.

'But this is Joe Webster,' she whined. 'I'd really like to go to bed with him.' (Look, I'd pair up with anyone in those days. You simply couldn't get around alone.)

I took Mack aside and told him my problem. 'This isn't my scene, but you can keep her,' I said. 'Just get me on the road and I'll thumb a lift back to town.'

Mack looked furious, but knew that a sulky date could put a damper on the most promising of evenings. I shook hands with Joe Webster, explaining I had remembered another appointment, but indicating with enthusiasm the presence of my complaisant friend. The actor looked confused by my exit, it was not something he could relate to, I suppose. Not written into the script. Being a washed-up star must be pretty confusing, too, come to think of it.

I hitchhiked back to Hollywood with a guy who was going to acting school with Jeff Corey, where I had planned to start classes. I moved in with him for a few weeks, so the evening was not entirely wasted. I never got to the classes because after that I decided to shack up with Kumar, who had an adorable apartment with a

garden that I could plant tomatoes in. Kumar
wanted me to take up painting, so I did that
instead. I thought I might have a talent for
watercolours, but looking at them later I saw
they were quite embarrassing (a bad watercolour is sort of nauseating, all that blurry stuff
suggesting nothing so much as the need for
prescription glasses), so they went the way of all
my artistic endeavours.

It's depressing, isn't it? All that wasted energy.
But I suppose for someone like Alice, it sounds
intriguing. She's obviously missing out somewhere. I've never seen anyone so interested in all
the lurid details of my sex life. Not that I told her
the whole truth, of course. Do any of us tell the
whole truth about our sex lives? Even to our
nearest and dearest? Will my mother ever tell
me? Does she care? Do mothers ever tell daughters? Mummy was brought up in the country-
house tradition, where as far as I can make out
adultery was not only par for the course but
positively encouraged by lascivious hostesses,
who probably wanted to get in on the act themselves. I hope for her sake she availed herself of
the opportunities, since now, country-house
weekends being more or less brought up-to-date
and therefore entirely moral (unless specifically
requested otherwise), the chances are pretty minimal of a nice bit on the side. (How ironic that in

our new, sexually liberated world, the house-party life has gone completely conventional). I wonder if this is what Louisa was really interested in when she sent me that note about wanting to know all the owners. If so, she is a few decades too late.

I'm not going to let Louisa meet Parker. He's just the type she'd fall for. He's older, and he's got lots of confidence, and he's disciplined. It's a real lesson for me. I'll never be as decisive as he is, of course, but as long as I'm with him I feel that my life has meaning, has shape, has a sense of direction. Mainly, it's to improve my game, but with the lessons I'm taking at the Meadow Club, I'm really coming along. The pro says so, and so does Parker. That's what counts in the end.

I had a Nanny once who was so keen on discipline that she broke a plate over my head because I wouldn't eat my carrots. That's going a bit far, but I think deep down all the English (at least all the ones who share my background) respond to discipline in a strange sort of way. I think that's what's so fabulous about Parker. He's made me feel completely at home for the first time since I was a child, and I *love* it.

20

ALICE

The Glynn family returned to Southampton one
sweltering hot night in early August, the weekend Lady Fanthorpe was due to make her
appearance. Gerald did not enjoy the train ride,
staring gloomily at the suntanned and muscular
examples of his sex who jogged up and down the
crowded corridors of the Friday night special.
While they were high with anticipation of physical joys to come, poor Gerald's spirits were
plummeting at the thought of spending the
weekend by a swimming pool, whose chlorine-
filled contours he compared to the water holes
used by primitive jungle people for their bodily
wastes.

'Sewers,' he muttered. 'Sewers painted blue
and surrounded by peeling pink flesh.'

Put like that, even Daphne's Southampton
paradise took on a faintly depressing hue, but
Bert soon cheered us up.

'I love swimming, Daddy,' he said. 'It makes
my head feel so light. I don't see why swimming

pools are sewers. I've only done wee-wee in one once.'

'Ssh, Bert,' I said. 'You must promise not to do that in Daphne's pool. It's very bad manners.'

'It's better than crapping into it,' he said, his innocent little face looking up into mine.

I had had doubts about bringing Bert with us on this weekend, but the alternative was either a visit to his best friend, Adam, a latent juvenile delinquent who lived behind the Church of the Heavenly Rest on East Ninetieth Street, and whose favourite pastime was to lob gum balls into the throngs of designer-clad parishioners and their angelic WASP children after matins on Sunday, and from whom Bert learned his frightful language; or a trip to the Bronx where our cleaning lady, Annunziata Lopez, lived with her six illegitimate children in a dilapidated brownstone, full of plants, cats, and cockroaches.

'Read your book,' I told him, handing him his comic-strip version of *The Night of the Living Dead*. Gerald sighed and opened his book, too, *Micronutrition or How to Fill Your Body with Less and Still Lead an Active Life*. I would have looked out at the increasingly seaside-looking view if any of the so-called windows had been clean enough to look out of. As it was, I painted my nails a dashing plum colour in between bumps and hoped I had packed enough clothes.

We were met by Daphne in the Rolls. Gerald
brightened.

'Parker playing tennis?' I asked.

'A big tournament at the Meadow Club. He
won't be back until late so we have to get our
own supper.'

Gerald brightened again. 'I imagine you have
a pretty good kitchen,' he said hopefully.

'I want a double order of french fries,' Bert
said.

'You are awful, just like my Fanthorpe cousins,' Daphne said in a friendly fashion. 'You
can have loads of ketchup, too, if you like.'

Bert looked pleased.

'I hope you aren't including us in that kind
offer,' Gerald said, as we settled back for the
drive to the mansion.

'Parker isn't very interested in food,' Daphne
explained. 'In fact, his favourite meal is Mrs
Paul's Crab Cakes and Bird's Eye Tiny Green
Peas, followed by jelly – or Jell-O, as he calls it.
So that's all there is in the fridge.'

Gerald's face fell.

'You could always rush out and get something,' Daphne went on helpfully. 'Perhaps
there's something in the freezer.'

'Never mind,' I said. 'Just this once Gerald
will eat an ordinary, down-to-earth people's
meal. It'll make a good column.'

'You may be right,' he said. 'I may be getting too rarefied. Do you know, I don't think I've had a frozen meal since we came to the States.'

'How scandalous,' Daphne said. 'You're as bad as my mother, taking her own Fortnum & Mason tea bags to China.'

'When is Her Ladyship coming?' we asked.

'Tomorrow, on the morning train. Thank goodness you're here too. She's becoming a bit much in her old age. I'm dreading her meeting with Parker.'

'Don't worry,' Gerald said. 'I'm very good with mothers. Except my own, of course.'

'I'm very good with mothers, too,' Bert said, squeezing my arm affectionately. Daphne looked longingly at us as mother and son cheerfully embraced.

'He's just showing off,' I said. 'His mother-phase is due to come to an end round about now. Then I'm in the doghouse for a few years and Gerald takes over. That's what the books say, anyway.'

'Don't apologize,' Daphne said. 'I think it's nice to see tough old Alice becoming soft over her little boy. I am beginning to think along those lines myself.'

'You're not pregnant?' I asked nervously.

'Are you joking? I have three tournaments to

prepare for this summer. Anyway, we're not married.'

'Have you become conventional again, Daphne?' Gerald asked in amusement.

She looked at him irritably, raced the car into the garage, and leaped out.

'I have to go and practise my forehand,' she said. 'We have a little backboard with lights so we can do it at night. See you later.'

We found Bert a wonderful single room with a telescope in it so he could spend the night gazing at the neighbours. I took Gerald to my former suite, with which he was suitably impressed, and then we foraged in the kitchen and made a good salad and crab-cakes supper, which everyone ate with enthusiasm. Gerald was amorous that night in our huge four-poster. 'Reminds me of old times at home,' he said. 'Country weekends, dances, scrambled eggs and champagne at midnight.'

'When did you ever do that,' I asked, 'except those few Commems at Oxford?'

'Perhaps never,' he said. 'But living here brings those memories back as if they were true. Is that what expatriates always have to do, I wonder? Remember a world we never actually knew, but which we recreate for our newly adopted countrymen?'

'What do you mean?' I said.

'We, as foreigners, represent something. We represent our country. We must answer the questions of those who want to know about things English, about English habits, about English life. But as time goes on we cannot continue to report the truth, because we do not live there any more and therefore do not any longer know the truth. So we start instead reporting on our memories, filtered through distance, time, historical knowledge, a changed perspective. The impressions, in short, of a grown-up who recalls the scenes of his childhood, scenes filled with inchoate emotions, confusions, and nostalgia.'

'That doesn't sound much fun,' I murmured.

'No, it isn't. It also creates a self-perpetuating fallacy about the meaning of "home".'

'Do you want to go home? Is that really what you are saying?'

'Edmund and I talked about this all last night,' he said. 'Edmund wants to go home, but he doesn't mind that the home he means no longer exists. For him, home is in his mind and therefore inviolate. For me, everything has changed there and I don't think I like the changes. I like it here, Alice. But I think Edmund should go home. I think you should talk to Louisa.'

'Do you know, Gerald, my love, I think you

are becoming quite American,' I said.

He laughed. 'Because I think you should talk to Louisa?'

'And because you talked to Edmund. I mean, really talked.' He laughed again.

'It was only in between bridge rubbers,' he said defensively. 'And I don't think he knew I was discussing anything more than the question of expatriatism. In general, you understand.'

'Oh, I understand,' I said, 'only too well.' And we went to sleep.

At breakfast the next morning we watched in silence as Daphne laid several slices of bacon in a narrow drawer that was attached to a small machine. She then pushed the drawer in and for several minutes we listened to a sizzling noise, somewhat similar, only more regular in tone, to the famous mosquito-roaster in Parker's pool pavilion. She finally pulled out the tray and there it was – flattened bacon, its fat ironed out until the texture was that of dry toast.

'Gosh,' Bert said, entranced.

'Parker likes it like this,' Daphne explained. 'Crisp, without fat, and wrinkle-free.'

'Just like me,' Gerald said.

'It would be a great form of torture,' Bert said, eyes glinting.

'What do you mean?' I asked, rumpling his dear hair.

'Well, picture it, Mummy. You could put bodies on it and then push them in and pull them out and they'd come out like . . .'

I rumpled his dear hair a little less enthusiastically.

'Aren't children wonderful,' Daphne said soppily. Bert gave her an adoring smile.

Parker appeared at this point, dressed in a white towelling bathrobe, with initials on the pocket.

'Met you before, right?' he said, staring at me with his gimlet-eyes. 'Play tennis, any of you?'

'I do,' piped up Bert.

'I don't think Mr Ferris means you, darling,' I said. 'You haven't yet perfected your overhead smash.'

'How did the match go yesterday?' Gerald asked politely.

'Not bad, not bad. I had a second-round with Pete Pape. You know, some years ago I could beat the hell out of Pete Pape, but he's lost a lot of weight and he's been practising his backhand and now he's tough to beat. My third round was a cinch – Jim Barrett, who really should be off the courts after the morning matches, he runs out of steam so quickly. Fourth round was old Larry Bond, you met him at the Beach Club a few weeks ago. Young fella, very trim, but he's just started using one of those oversized rackets

and his serve was way off. So now we come to
the semifinals and I'm up against last year's
winner, a ranked player. Jeez, what a game. Of
course, my reflexes aren't what they were, and
Harry Van Pelt has one of the best topspin
backhands in the business – I saw him take two
sets off Lew Hoad in the US Open some years
back – so I just had to give way in the end to
some superior stroking. 6–4, 4–6, 2–6. You can
tell from that score how the old legs gave up.
Hell, what a match. Everyone stopped playing
when they heard about the score. If it hadn't
gone to three sets, I might have outfitnessed
him. Christ, what a topspin that guy has. If he
had a few more years on me, though, I could
have damn near reversed that score.'

I made a mental note not to ask Parker Ferris
how his matches went. Daphne, however, looked
as though he had just been reading her Shakespeare's love sonnets. Bert had gone to sleep.

After breakfast there was a choice of tennis,
the pool, shopping for frogware, or playing backgammon in the living room until it was time to
meet Lady Fanthorpe's train. The living room
had a hunting theme, largely consisting of
stuffed versions of all the animals Lord Fanthorpe spent his time protecting.

'Thank goodness he's not coming too,' I murmured to Gerald.

'Did you shoot them?' Bert asked, having woken up.

Parker had changed into tennis clothes.

'Hell, no, young fella,' he said. 'Bought them in some shop in New York.'

He looked at our disapproving faces.

'Daphne,' he barked. 'Get them out of here.'

Bert started to cry.

'He didn't mean us,' I explained, 'he meant the stuffed heads.'

'I know,' Bert moaned. 'I love them.'

Daphne kissed Parker goodbye and telephoned for a handyman to wrench all the moose, bison, and deer off the walls, while we piled into the car to replace them at the store. Since even the frogware stockist clearly drew the line at stuffed frogs, we were reduced to choosing a series of etchings of frogs to fill the holes in the wall made by the offending taxidermy.

'Just the ticket,' we agreed.

'Where do you put all the stuff he gets sick of?' Gerald asked.

'In the garage,' she said. 'A van comes to take it away. Once they forgot to call and before we knew it all the locals had come in thinking it was a garage sale. Parker was furious.'

When we got back, Bert disappeared into the garage to play with the stuffed animals and we reassembled to meet Lady Fanthorpe.

335

She stepped off the train wearing pink chiffon pyjamas and a mink fur cape.

'Hello, Mummy,' Daphne said weakly.

'I know I've brought all the wrong clothes,' she shrieked to us. 'Daphne kept telling me it was warm but I've been suffering terrible stiffness in my shoulders from this dreadful air-conditioning one encounters everywhere. It's like living in a morgue, so damp and cold. Americans are odd, aren't they? Without my mink, I don't think I could move my head at all.'

'You wait till you come here in the winter,' Gerald said, enlivened by the turn the conversation was taking. 'The rooms are so hot that one is permanently in a muck sweat, Lady Fanthorpe, I assure you. Not only that, but most windows in the newer apartments, and in all hotels, are made not to open. *You cannot open a window.* This seems to me more barbaric than putting jam on Yorkshire pudding, another local custom.'

Lady Fanthorpe laughed. 'Well, we must be forbearing, mustn't we? After all, it was no doubt our frightful influence that got them going in the first place, wasn't it? Like the convicts in Australia. All the worst elements being shipped off to pastures new.'

'I wouldn't talk too much about it around here, if I were you, Mummy,' Daphne said, lurching through Southampton at a fast clip. 'They might not get your subtle humour.'

'So this is Long Island,' her mother said, grasping her mink more firmly round her. 'What splendid houses, just like European ones. They do seem to lack originality, don't they? Haven't you noticed that, Alice? I think it's so odd the way they have all these places with English names, like Dedham, and Worcester, and Cambridge, and so forth. I can't think why they couldn't come up with a few names of their own instead of copying ours all the time.'

'Perhaps they were homesick,' Gerald offered. 'They wanted to remind themselves of home.'

'Mmm,' said Lady Fanthorpe doubtfully. 'Well, New England could hardly look less like Old England, what little I've seen of it. All those trees.'

Daphne veered into the driveway and up to the house.

'Isn't this just like Villandry, darling?' Lady Fanthorpe exclaimed.

She stepped from the Rolls with the expertise of much practice. 'Except there aren't the wonderful gardens.'

'You wait, Lady Fanthorpe,' we said. 'There's a swimming pool and pavilion instead.'

'I don't remember Villandry having a swimming pool. I'm sure those French aristos didn't swim in those days.'

'Do stop talking about Villandry, Mummy. It's Chenonceaux, anyway. I'll show you your room. You have the Corot suite.'

'I've always loved Corot,' she said. 'Not very fashionable now, unfortunately. Your father thinks he's very wet, but then he only like those frightfully bloody pictures by that man who always does hounds tearing horses apart, what's his name?'

'Daddy like those? I'd have thought he'd hate them, with his soft heart about animals.'

'Men are brutes really, darling, under all that Old Etonian polish.'

Gerald gave a brutish laugh, which did not convince.

'And then we'll have lunch,' Daphne said. 'I've ordered a little something by the pool. Why don't you and Gerald go down there now, Alice, and I'll get Mummy settled in.'

'I'd better check on Bert,' I said with a mother's prescience. 'He's been in the garage with the bison.'

'What?' Lady Fanthorpe looked alarmed.

'Stuffed, Mummy, just like at home.' Lady Fanthorpe nodded, reassured.

I was wrong. Bert had found the mosquito-burner at the pool, and had taken it down from

338

its perch. By the time we got there, the thing was surrounded by tiny corpses, hand-picked by my little son and carried carefully to their electrical funeral pyre. As we arrived, he was nursing what looked like a small mouse in preparation for death.

'Bert,' I said, trying not to faint. 'Take that poor animal away and get washed. It's lunchtime.'

'But we all have to die, Mummy. You told me so yourself. I just thought I'd make it easier for them. It's a fabulous invention. Like the Baconizer.'

'The what?'

We swept up the pathetic ashes and I combed Bert's hair. He looked like a perfectly normal eight-year-old. 'Just be good at lunch,' I suggested. 'Daphne's mother is here and I want you to behave.'

'Trust me,' he said, with a polished smile. But would he ever be an Old Etonian? Did we want him to be? Did I want Bert to be like Edmund and Gerald? Perish the thought. But then what did I want Bert to be like? What do mothers want their sons to be like – apart from lovers, of course? I wanted my son to remain the cuddly, affectionate, bloodthirsty brute of a boy I saw before me. I shunned the idea of acne, shaved chins, hairy ears, and receding hairlines, at which point I knew Bert would be lost to me forever. Children open up attic loads of emotional treasures in a grown-up's padlocked mind, treasures that, once unfolded and exposed to the light, can never quite be put away again. Whatever I felt about Gerald, my feelings for Bert both substituted and surpassed, allowing me, at moments like this, a feeling of fulfilment that justified, honestly, my life.

And there was no one I could tell. Mummy's little secret. Gerald would, rightly, have minded, even if only a little bit. Louisa seemed to have no trace of the old maternal flame that beat so strongly in my bosom. Daphne had no offspring to ignite said flame. Penny would have understood, perhaps. But Penny seemed so determined to shuffle off her maternal coil (by inserting one of the non-Shakespearean variety, no doubt), that the subject had never come up on her brief visit here.

'Come and sit on my lap, Bert,' I said.

So he sat on my lap as we watched two servants appear from the house and begin walking towards us. They set up two tables, put tablecloths on, opened unbrellas, and began to set out a banquet. By the time the others joined us, they were just putting the finishing touches to plates of cold salmon, shrimp, lobster, mussels in vinaigrette sauce, guacamole, and toasted muffins and rolls, all beautifully displayed on the finest Ferris frogware. Hock glasses and several bottles of Chablis on ice were lined up on the bar.

'Daphne, you are clever, I always knew you were a summer person,' said Lady Fanthorpe, dressed in fuchsia satin and her mink.

Gerald looked enthusiastically at the spread.

'Well, it's better than the 57 Varieties she used to produce for poor Alan Moss,' he said. 'I bet this would have saved that marriage.'

'Shut up, Gerald,' Daphne said. 'Parker might hear you.'

'Doesn't he know about your interesting past?'

'Oh, don't let's talk about it,' Lady Fanthorpe said. 'I shall never forgive that awful man for marrying my daughter.'

'Well, it was your idea, Mummy. I was quite happy to go and live in sin with him.'

'What does live in sin mean?' Bert asked, having escaped from my lap.

'Who is this?' Lady Fanthorpe asked with hardly more enthusiasm in her voice than when talking about Alan Moss.

'This is our son, Lady Fanthorpe. Bert, say hello.'

'How nice,' Lady Fanthorpe murmured. 'Bert. Bert. I suppose it's quite a normal name in America.'

'Burt Lancaster,' Daphne suggested encouragingly.

'Of course,' Lady Fanthorpe relaxed. 'How sweet.'

Bert bridled, and looked yearningly at Daphne, who giggled.

'Have some lunch, Mummy.'

'But shouldn't we wait for, er . . .'

'He's coming now, I see him.'

Parker Ferris sprang into view, tennis whites gleaming.

'Mummy, this is Parker Ferris.'

'I'm honoured to meet you,' Parker said feverishly, gripping her hand like a tennis racket. 'Your countrymen make the finest generals in the world.' Lady Fanthorpe's arm swung out for a backhand. 'Without Montgomery and Churchill and Alexander of course' – he relinquished the racket – 'the war would never have been won.'

'What a charming thing to say, Mr Parker,' Lady Fanthorpe said, discreetly testing for broken fingers. 'You know, we always found you Americans just a teeny bit difficult during the war. Of course we would never have said a word then, but I think it's safe now to speak frankly, don't you? It was because you were all so young and keen. And so big. It was all that milk you got fed as babies.'

'I got fed milk as a baby,' Bert said, in between munches of lettuce. 'Am I very big?'

'Not for a grown-up,' Lady Fanthorpe said, looking him up and down.

'I'm eight,' Bert explained.

'You must excuse my appearance, Lady Fanthorpe,' Parker went on. 'But I hope Daphne explained that I am playing in a tennis tournament at the Meadow Club. We get ranked players there, you know.'

'Why, I think you look just as you should on a sunny weekend like this,' Lady Fanthorpe gushed. 'We used to play tennis as girls. Vicarage tennis, of course. Though I don't know why vicars always seemed to play tennis. A good Christian game, I suppose. Of course we never looked so smart as you. Isn't that a little frog embroidered on your pocket?'

'No, as a matter of fact it's my initials, Lady Fanthorpe. PCF. Parker Canute Ferris. You see? P, then C in the middle, and F. It happens to be embroidered in green. Green and white are often used together around here.'

Lady Fanthorpe peered at Parker's chest. 'Of course, how silly of me. PCF. For a moment it looked just like a frog, Mr Parker.' She laughed heartily, downing a large draught of Chablis.

'Ferris, Mummy,' Daphne said. 'His name is Parker Ferris.'

343

'Oh, sorry, darling, I thought Parker was his surname. In England, it would be. You know,' she smiled sweetly at the tennis player, 'in England we don't usually have surnames as Christian names. It's too confusing. And how amusing of me to have taken your initials for a frog. Frogs are the most unappealing little creatures, don't you think?'

Several pairs of eyes swivelled to the table and then to the sky.

'Daddy likes them,' Daphne said desperately.

'Well, your father likes everything that has bulging little eyes and scrabbly little feet. Except your first husband, of course.' She laughed delightedly. 'Oh, I am naughty. It must be the air. *No*, seriously, my husband takes a great interest in beavers, otters, stoats, you know the sort of thing, Mr Ferret – er – Ferris?'

Parker looked at her a shade doubtfully.

'How about some lobster salad, Lady Fanthorpe,' he said, proffering her a plate. Daphne seized it and began covering all the offending decoration with lettuce leaves.

'What are you doing that for?' Bert asked.

'To look pretty,' I said.

'Will you do it to mine, too?'

Daphne glared but had to obey. Soon all our plates were ready to be photographed for *Gourmet*'s studios.

344

We ate in exhausted silence for a while. Then I suggested to Bert, who was beginning to focus again on the mosquito-machine, that he go into the house for a rest.

'That's my cue, too,' Parker said, jumping up. 'I really must get back to the courts.'

'How's it going, Parker?' Daphne asked. Gerald and I held our breath.

'Well, the first round doubles was an easy one. The Fenison-Dent team has been a disaster and we weren't even stretched. Probably would have been better if we had – I was hardly warmed up for the next match, which was a real doozie. Dooley O'Brien and Sandy McQueen. Well, I hate these Irishmen, they play a really tricky game – short crosscourt returns, then lobs from the baseline. If they hadn't lost their timing in the final set, I wouldn't be going back this afternoon. The last game we were 30–40, I was serving, first one into the net (trying for too much topspin), then I thought, to hell with it, hit a long hard deep one for the second to make Dooley hit a backhand long. That was it. They couldn't pull it out.'

'Goodness.' Lady Fanthorpe looked bemused.

'Perhaps you'd like to come and watch this afternoon, Lady Fanthorpe. I can promise you some good tennis, although my partner, Joe Ivanhoe, is not really on his best form. His wife

is taking him to the cleaners in their divorce
case and his mind is not really on the ball, I'm
sorry to say. But I'm in fairly steady form and
there should be some lively points.'

'Well, it's very kind of you, Mr Ferris, but I
really think I should put my feet up this afternoon. Didn't Daphne say we were all going to a
party tonight?'

'That's right. Joe's brother, Wally. It'll be
Greek. I'll get back in time for a shower,
Daphne, honey.'

With that, Ferris picked up his racket, waved
cheerfully, and sprinted up towards the house.

'Aren't Americans energetic?' Daphne's
mother said admiringly. 'You know, I never
knew there was so much one could say about
tennis. Our vicarage games were totally devoid
of drama. Just a few sets, and then a rest and
some wonderful Pimms. Though how a vicar
would have thought of Pimms, the Lord only
knows. By the way, darling, what did Mr Ferris
mean by "Greek"? I don't think I have a thing
that could be called Greek in my wardrobe, not
even that robe I bought in Athens when your
father and I did a Swann's Tour. So interesting
it was, all the people were so clever, I hardly
understood a word but I learned an enormous
amount. I wonder if one day we ought to give
those Elgin Marbles back. They aren't ours,

really, you know. What do you think, Gerald?'

'If we give them back, we might as well give back the whole of the British Museum, the National Gallery, and everywhere else, Lady Fanthorpe.'

'Oh, well, I see what you mean. But you shouldn't let that stop you going to Greece.'

'We're not that keen on Greek food, actually, Lady Fanthorpe,' I said. 'They've a bit of a heavy hand with the olive oil.'

'Wouldn't it be funny if all the museums were empty,' Bert said.

'No proof of the past any more. No history. A tabula rasa. Most fascinating,' Gerald said. 'No opportunity for nostalgia.'

'We would all behave quite differently, I expect,' Lady Fanthorpe said. 'And now I must get my rest before this party. He couldn't really have been called Ivanhoe, could he?'

'I think it would be great,' Bert said as we moved towards the house. 'Museums are deadly dull anyway, and I wouldn't have to go round them any more.'

'That's enough, Bert,' I said. 'You're too young to appreciate them.'

'How old must I be?' he asked.

For the moment, no one could come up with an answer.

DAPHNE

It seemed strange having Alice and Gerald to
stay. I had never had anyone to stay before.
With Alan, no one wanted to stay to dinner, let
alone stay a night, owing to our frightful rows.
Anyway, if someone wanted to stay the night
they would have had to have slept on the sofa in
the sitting room, which was the size of most
people's downstairs cloakroom, so it would have
been like the French song Mummy used to sing
me as a child, 'avec les pieds contre la muraille,
et la tête sous le robinet,' only there would not
have been any wine flowing. As for my time
with Kumar, the only people who came to stay
were hippies too stoned to leave, hardly guests
so much as barnacles, and the only hospitable
gesture I ever gave them was to point to the
door.

Mostly, I would not have wanted guests
anyway. I was a guest myself. I've always been
a guest really. It's more fun – less responsibilities, less work, and you can *always leave*. I
always loved Mummy's story of some friend of

hers who had given a dinner party, and the
guests just would not leave, until finally the
hostess looked at her watch and said, 'Good
heavens, it's one o'clock. Time to go!' At which
everyone jumped up and left.

I suppose you could say I was a guest in
Parker's house, but he never made me feel like
it. He always wanted my friends to come and
stay, and he put me in total charge of the
running of the house. I'd never had that experience before, and I must confess it had its charms.
Parker was the first person who did not make
me feel trapped at being put in charge. That's
why my mother had come to America. She
wanted to see for herself.

My mother, you see, had never been put in
charge of anything. Englishwomen of her class
never were. That's probably what bothered Alan
so terribly when we got married. He was used to
his efficient, all-powerful mother doing everything, as working-class mothers do. For me, it
was entirely a man's world. The man owned
everything because he inherited everything, or
vice versa. Primogeniture saw to that. Wives
were grateful guests in the stately home, seeing
to flowers, backstairs, and menus. They frequently never even did the placements at dinner
parties. At country-house weekends with the
Westminsters at Eaton in the thirties, my

mother told me the old duke used to put next to him the two people who interested him most and just dump the rest of the cards in any old order – and that had to remain as the seating for the whole weekend! Luckily he had a feisty wife who changed all that, but you had to be feisty to shift all those centuries of tradition, and most women weren't up to it, even if they wanted to try. Mummy never really wanted to try. Her upbringing had ingrained in her that this was how it was, and so she took everything for granted. She was quite typical. That's what made the class system so secure, really. I remember she was quite shocked when the duchess of Devonshire complained that living at Chatsworth meant she lived in someone else's furnished rooms, that nothing at Chatsworth would ever belong to her, and that if she was widowed she'd have to move out at once, like a temporary typist being sacked on the arrival of the permanent secretary. 'Well, and why not?' said my mother indignantly. 'That's how it is, and that's the price you pay for marrying so grandly. Why should she complain?'

Well, some people did complain, and still do, but nothing has changed, and the system has certainly kept houses in families for aeons, unlike America, where I had hardly heard of a single house lived in by more than one genera-

tion – except perhaps in Texas or in Maine.
Parker's father had built Chenonceaux, to be
sure, but Parker couldn't care less about possessions, as must have been obvious to Alice and
Gerald when he casually dismissed his frog
dinner service and the old moose heads. I
thought that was so wonderfully American,
wanting something new and different all the
time, instead of hanging on to dreary old objects
that belonged to one's great grandmother.

Mind you, I was beginning to wonder whether
Parker might not one day feel the same way
about me – I mean want something new and
different. Frankly, the idea of marriage was
beginning to loom larger and larger in the old
grey cells. I knew everyone would laugh at the
idea of my marrying Parker, but they'd laughed
at all the others and it hadn't made the slightest
difference. Why shouldn't I marry Parker
Ferris? No other member of our famous four
seemed to have come up with a more brilliant
choice in the marital stakes. One divorce (tech-
nically, if not literally), one marriage totally on
the rocks, and the other? Well, Alice and Gerald
seemed the most harmonious, but it was the
harmony of bread and milk, suitable for invalids
rather than people in their prime. It was Bert
who kept them together, I felt sure of that. I
thought that little boy was adorable, and they

were jolly lucky to have had him. Frankly, it
strained the imagination to think about Alice
and Gerald doing whatever had to be done to
conceive him. Almost as difficult as imagining
one's parents . . .

I was just jealous, I suppose. I had noticed I
was beginning to look moonily in prams. Broody,
you see. Definitely a bad sign. How on earth
could I fit pregnancy into my tennis schedule?
And let's face it, how would Parker take Canadian doubles? These were the questions that
swirled through my head as I practised my
strokes on the backboard. Parker was no longer
in the first bloom of youth (fifty-five, to be
honest), though his physique was that of a much
younger man. His doctor apparently had to redo
some tests, because the results were so remarkable. As for myself, well, I was what you might
call a well-used thirty-three, just moving into
the tricky side of fertility. Eheu, fugaces,
Daphne, Daphne, anni labuntur. That bloody
phrase of Freddy's – now, more than ever, it
would not go away.

21

ALICE

Wally Ivanhoe was a Long Island playboy and former professional golfer who got so drunk during a championship game that he stunned a small white poodle with a five-iron under the impression that the tiny pet was relieving itself over the fourteenth hole. Since 'Pookie' belonged to the wife of the sponsor of the golf tournament, Ivanhoe was invited to retire from the game. After some uncharacteristically speedy mental calculations, the former golfer took into matrimony a Greek shipping heiress called Iphigenia Spetsipoulos, a handsome woman in her very late forties whose main ambition was to join the East Hampton set but who had been finding it heavy going owing to the doubt aroused amongst some local members over the Semitic cast to her features. The marriage instantly cleared up any physiological confusion, and *Women's Wear Daily* was there to record the happy event; Ivanhoe, glass in hand, declaring undying devotion, and Iphigenia, a lily above her ear, declaring two hitherto-unannounced marriages. The union was celebrated at a grand party at the River Club.

During the following week, four men of various unspecified nationalities, including one garage mechanic and one massage-parlour owner, telephoned the newspapers in high dudgeon, to inform them that they, too, had once been the husbands of Iphigenia Spetsipoulos, and why were they not good enough to be mentioned in her wedding speech? Ivanhoe, glass in hand and subdued of demeanour, made a statement to the press to the effect that even had he known that his bride had already enjoyed six marriages, it would in no way have dimmed his ardour. Iphigenia, a gladiolus above her ear, announced that she had been under the impression that most of her husbands were deceased, and that anyway Greeks always had trouble with their relations.

Every year after this auspicious beginning, the Ivanhoes threw a Greek-inspired party at their vast house overlooking the ocean in East Hampton, paid for by Iphigenia's oil tankers. When our party arrived, some three hundred people had already assembled and were wandering about the Greek-colonnaded patio, drinking ouzo, retsina, and other ethnic potions. Lady Fanthorpe had selected for the evening an orange pleated sarong, with a black shawl fringed in orange silk draped over her suffering shoulders. Parker wore a citrus shirt monogrammed in pink, fuchsia and green patterned trousers that looked as though they had been given a rinse in food colouring, and black velvet bedroom slippers monogrammed in green. On first sighting, I had mistakenly thought these two members of our party might be slightly overdoing it in their colour choices. Au contraire. The general tenor of the evening made our team paragons of discretion. Technicolour yawns – I adapt this crude but vivid expression from our Australian cousins – exploded on every side. The only cool corner was ours; Gerald in white shirt and jeans, myself in the usual faded smock, Daphne in a skin-coloured halter top and miniskirt that made her look entirely naked.

Bert had agreed to stay home under the inducement of watching one of Ferris's war movies (*The Young Lions*, I think it was), to the accompaniment of a triple order of french fries, all set up in the screening room in the basement.

'Are you sure he'll be all right?' Daphne asked with concern. 'Isn't he sweet, Parker, and he loves all your war stuff.'

Parker, making an effort to respond to this unexpected appeal, grunted something to the effect that Montgomery had been a very independent kid too. 'That's what made him master of the battlefield,' he added.

'Shsh, it's starting,' said Bert as the credits started to roll.

The party was as noisy as one of the field marshal's skirmishes, what with Greek musicians strolling about, drinks being carried hither and thither, and the loud, braying cries of the Long Island campaigner at play. At the far end of the patio, about a dozen dinner tables were set up, and at the side of each was a large pile of crockery stacked on the flagstones.

'What a lot of courses we must be going to have,' Gerald said, licking his lips in anticipation.

'You break them,' Daphne explained.

Before we could examine this concept further, Gerald was swept off by Madame Ivanhoe to discuss the powers of tofu with her best friend, a Mexican health-farmer whose dietary methods were garnering her great acclaim amongst the rich, bored population of Manhattan. Daphne and I began to sidle round the patio, looking for prospective conversations. 'Not quite like an Oxford party,' I murmured to her. 'But we were so spoiled then,' she said. 'With that ratio of women to men, anyone in a skirt was to be encouraged. It's quite the reverse in New York, you know. Lots of hungry women and no men.'

I looked at Gerald with a sudden rush of fondness. He looked positively Byronic with his white shirt, pale face, and soulful eyes. The fact that he was discussing the nutritional qualities of some new Japanese root rather than going a-roving by the light of the moon seemed not to matter to the two ladies who stood gazing raptly at him.

'I have an incipient headache,' he said to me shortly afterwards. 'These women are like terminal patients looking for everlasting life. It's like everything here – analysed so much that any pleasure pertaining to it is squeezed out of existence. Freud has a lot to answer for.'

We sat down to a dinner of moussaka, shish kebab, and other menu selections found in Charlotte Street restaurants, the difference being that a low-fat polyunsaturated oil had been substituted for the olive variety. It tasted infinitely worse. Iphigenia, at the head table, with green vine leaves entwined above her ear, sprang up and brandished a plate she had lifted from the pile at her side.

'I will go first,' she cried. 'Please, everyone have fun!'

With that, she hurled the plate into the centre of the dance floor, narrowly missing the ankles of a few misguided couples enjoying a quiet smooch. The plate smashed into smithereens, everyone shrieked, either from joy or terror, and the attack commenced.

Parker, with Montgomery-like eagerness, was the first at our table to enter the fray. Picking up a plate from the stack allotted to him, he tossed it on to the dance floor, now empty of terpsichoreans. The plate broke into fragments, joining others already thrown by enlivened guests.

Parker gazed discontentedly at his efforts. 'It's the same every year,' he complained. 'There's no strategic finesse to it. You try it, Daphne.'

Daphne picked up a plate and tentatively manoeuvred it into a throwing position. It missed the floor completely and skidded up someone's unheeding skirt.

'Not like that,' Gerald exclaimed, jumping up. He picked up a plate and sent it crashing to the ground, where it broke in a thousand pieces. He smiled ecstatically and picked up another.

People from every table were doing the same thing. Chips of broken china were flying everywhere. The noise was deafening. The piles of plates were rapidly diminishing. I quickly grabbed one and threw it, watching it break into tiny fragments.

'It reminds me of Nanny!' Daphne shouted across to me. She was in fits of giggles, pointing

to Gerald, who had gone completely haywire
with excitement, and was pitching plates right,
left, and centre with bestial energy.

Suddenly, it was over. The music started up
again, the guests sat down and demurely picked
up napkins, forks, and conversation as though
nothing had happened. Meanwhile a small black
boy appeared with a broom and started to sweep
up the pieces.

After the main course was over, it began
again. Fresh piles of plates had miraculously
appeared beside each table, only to be savagely
destroyed in a matter of minutes. Again the
black servant patiently swept up the mess made
by Whitey at play, while the guests, aggressions
satisfactorily appeased, ate and drank themselves serenely into oblivion.

'Primal therapy for the Suzy crowd,' a voice
murmured in my ear. Swivelling round in my
seat, I saw the familiar, tense face of Jeannie
Honeywell. She was wearing what looked like a
gauze bandage. Behind her, equally original in
a pink and white striped leisure suit and aviator
glasses, was Cliff. He was clapping Gerald on
the shoulder as though they were long-lost
friends.

'So you actually know someone here,' Daphne
said, gazing curiously at the couple. 'Who on
earth is that hunk of Blackpool rock? I can't

stand these types who wear pinstripes all week on Wall Street and then let their hair down and dress like Roman candles at the weekend. They always look as if their wives have just been sick all over them.'

'Jeannie probably has,' I said. 'Right, Jeannie?'

Jeannie laughed mirthlessly as she sucked on a cigarette. 'You better believe it,' she said. 'Can you believe this scene? I mean, talk about anal.'

'Gerald is beside himself,' I told her. 'I never saw a man so happy.'

'But of course,' Jeannie exclaimed. 'That's what I mean. Is his friend Edmund here? I'd love to see that one relating to the experience.'

Daphne had been eyeing her with distaste.

'How do you know all our friends?' she asked, with a trace of the old Fanthorpe hauteur.

'Daphne, this is Jeannie Honeywell. And that hunk of Blackpool rock is Cliff Honeywell. *Cliff*. Remember? Oxford? Dover soles?'

I saw no sign of recognition in Daphne's eyes as Cliff came over to us.

'Well, well, well,' he said. 'First Venice with Louisa, and now East Hampton with Daphne. You sure get around, Alice.'

He gave me a large kiss full on the mouth in front of everybody.

'Hello, Cliff,' I said when my mouth was free.

'How clever of you to remember Daphne.'

'Remember her? How could I forget her? She was the little Miss Goody Two Shoes of all time, if I'm not mistaken.'

'We were all young then,' Daphne said stiffly. 'I expect I behaved rather badly.'

'Badly? If only you had!' He started laughing, and pulled a bottle of champagne towards us. 'I think we should celebrate being older and wiser, and more badly behaved, eh, Alice?'

I felt the usual uncomfortable physical symptoms that Cliff always seemed to produce in me. How could I feel this way for a hunk of Blackpool rock, as Daphne had so brilliantly put it?

'I suppose you liked throwing a few plates, didn't you, Cliff?' I said sarcastically.

'I don't get a lot out of that sort of stuff,' he said. 'It's you uptight types who find it amusing.'

Out of the corner of my eyes, I saw Gerald making off with a whole raft of crockery, a mad grin on his face.

'Freud has a lot to answer for,' I mimicked.

'That's what my therapist says,' Jeannie chimed in.

'What are you doing here anyway?' Cliff asked, pouring us all drinks. 'I thought you moved in higher circles.'

'We're with Parker Ferris,' I said, looking

round to point him out. 'Good Lord, Daphne, look!'

Parker was on the far side of the dance floor, without a stitch of clothes on, dancing with Wally Ivanhoe. Parker's expression was one of trancelike solemnity; Ivanhoe was looking round agonizedly for help.

'Never mind,' I said hastily to Cliff and Jeannie. 'I won't bother to introduce him now.' I caught sight of Iphigenia spiriting Parker off the floor, wrapping a Greek toga round his private parts. She gave a look worthy of the Eumenides at her husband as, glass in hand, he shambled after her.

'Did you see that?' I whispered to Daphne.

'Oh, don't worry,' she said calmly. 'He sometimes does that after a particularly strenuous tennis tournament. It's the strain. Never remembers a thing about it afterwards.'

'What are you two girls chatting about?' Cliff said, staring at my nonexistent chest. 'Do you want to dance, Alice?'

It would have been rude to say no.

When I got back, Daphne and Jeannie were talking about Louisa.

'Her eating habits are terrible,' Jeannie was saying. 'She won't come with me to the health bars. It's crazy. And she needs a good diet for her mind as well as her body. I'm really worried about her.'

'She's so undisciplined,' Daphne said.

'I wish she'd come to my group. It would really help.'

'She would have been here,' I said. 'Look how much better Gerald is.'

We looked at Gerald, who was flushed and smiling as he joined us. 'I've just been throwing up in one of the bougainvillea bushes,' he said. 'I've not felt so well since I tried out for the school boat in '55. There's something really therapeutic about that plate business. Rather like throwing bread rolls, only more satisfying. I wonder if it would have made a difference if the plates had been Royal Doulton.'

'You see?' Jeannie snorted triumphantly. 'You just can't help it, can you? You just have to cerebralize everything.'

'Cerebralize?' Gerald mulled over the word. 'Cerebrate, maybe?'

'Sure, let's celebrate,' said Cliff. 'Jeannie's just sold her first book.'

'Really?' Daphne and I stared at her, impressed, recalling all those tiny notes in that little black notebook.

'It's not my book, asshole,' Jeannie said. 'I just got together with some of my friends and we decided to work out our anger in a more profitable way than simply sicking it all up for our analysts to use. Those guys then turn round and make a million dollars from a book made up out of our case histories, right? I simply package the material, we get it mostly in group. Let's see, we've put together *The Orgasm-less Sleep, A Womb with a View* (though I'm not sure that title's not already been used), and the one that I'm into right now is tentatively entitled *The Barbie Trap*.'

'Gosh, Jeannie, that's wonderful,' we said. Cliff made a face.

'As long as they allow me to retire, that's okay with me,' he said. 'I hope when Alice writes a book, it'll be a little more – romantic.'

'*Gone with the Wind*, you mean?' I enquired.

'Ah, Leslie Howard as Ashley Wilkes, the archetypical Englishman,' Jeannie said scornfully.

'This is getting rather embarrassing,' Gerald said. 'I think we'd better go home. Anyway, they've run out of plates.'

We said goodbye to the Honeywells. Cliff gripped me by the shoulder as I left, so hard that it hurt. I looked firmly at the ground.

Daphne explained that Parker had gone home separately (driven by Iphigenia herself, no doubt), so we gathered up Lady Fanthorpe, who had been deep in conversation for most of the evening with a young voice coach called Ronnie Mailorder. 'He told me the voice is a reflection of the personality,' she said as we weaved our way back to the Ferris estate. 'A thin, high-pitched voice means . . .'

'Quite,' we agreed in deep, husky tones.

'He has given me the most wonderful breathing exercises to do,' Lady Fanthorpe went on. 'He said that if I really worked on it, I would have more success at opening fetes. People so often chat and clatter teacups when I'm making my speech. Frightfully tiresome. Ronnie is going to come tomorrow and start working with me. I do hope Mr Ferris won't mind, Daphne darling.'

'I'm sure he won't, Mummy.'

'That's what I like about America. Everyone's so relaxed. I suppose it comes from having plate-throwing sessions from time to time, though I can't imagine how it would go down in England. Mind you, I did worry a teeny bit about that poor little sweeper-upper. It can't help the colour problem over here.'

'There isn't a colour problem over here,' Gerald told her. 'It's called racism.'

Arriving at Chenonceaux, we found Parker at the door, like Cinderella, fully dressed again in complete Montgomery regalia, including beret.

'You remind me of someone, Mr Ferris,' said Lady Fanthorpe said vaguely, departing for bed. 'Let me see.'

We all held our breath.

'Is it Maurice Chevalier?'

Humming a little tune to herself, she threw her shawl around her and swept upstairs.

'Don't mind Mummy,' Daphne said, putting a comforting hand through Parker's arm. 'Her eyes are never very good, particularly at night. Let's all go and have a nightcap.'

We sat under the frog picture in the trophy room and drank Stingers. Gerald was looking transfigured, like Gandhi after stopping some trains. Parker, in contrast, was on edge, fidgeting, darting looks at Daphne. Was there some tennis problem afoot?

'Daphne,' he suddenly barked out. 'Do you want children?'

Daphne looked surprised. 'Well,' she said carefully, 'it's one of life's opportunities I haven't enjoyed yet.'

'Here's the way I see it,' said the tennis player. 'If I'm to have someone to leave my portfolio to, I must start working on it now. I have no intention of leaving it to charity, and I have no relations alive who are capable of signing their names, let alone playing a reasonable game of singles with. I need an heir, someone like Bert, who appreciates *The Young Lions*.'

'You can have Bert, if you like,' Gerald said,

coming out of his trance. 'For a reasonable sum, of course.'

Daphne was looking deeply into her Stinger. I could see she was moved.

'Perhaps Gerald and I should leave the room at this delicate juncture in negotiations,' I suggested.

'Hell, no,' Parker said. 'I need witnesses. There's nothing private about this. I'll marry Daphne any time she wants, the sooner the better – that is, if she is willing – and able.'

'And able?' I looked at my friend for signs of senility.

'To conceive, of course. I don't want to waste time and energy otherwise. I shall also require a prenuptial agreement.'

'A what?'

'Prenuptial agreement,' Parker said briskly. 'Surely you girls have run across those before?'

'We do not see much of them in England, actually, sir,' Gerald explained. 'Probably because most rich people's money is so efficiently tied up for generations to come that no fortune hunter could get her hands on it. It means you have to agree not to take hubby for every penny if you divorce, Daphne.'

'More than a million, that's as far as I'll go,' Parker said, taking off his beret and lighting a cigar. He had obviously thought this through.

'Well, Daphne, I think that's a very fair offer,' I said.

'Shut up, Alice. Nobody's ever proposed to me like this before. Come to think of it, nobody's ever proposed to me at all before.'

'Well, what do you say, old girl? Want to make it mixed doubles?'

'I'll have to think about it,' Daphne murmured.

'Of course. I'll turn in now and let you hash things over with your friends. I've an interesting little one-day tournament tomorrow to be thinking about.'

He gave us a military-style salute and retired to his tent.

'Well, what a perfect end to a perfect evening,' Gerald said. 'Come on, Alice, I think we should leave our Daphne – '

'Alone with her thoughts,' I went on, 'and the maiden blush still on her cheeks.'

'Do shut up,' she said. 'Actually, I've made up my mind. Shall I go and tell him now?'

'Why not?' we said, snapping our fingers. 'You don't want to waste a minute getting at those millions.'

'Shut up.' She scampered upstairs, and we followed more slowly, as befitted the wise and mature people we were.

'Daphne's pregnant,' Gerald reflected. 'A difficult concept, somehow.'

'I don't see why.' I could feel twinges of arthritis attacking my shoulder.

Gerald began giggling.

'What is it?' I said. His giggles always irritated me, as they usually preceded some particularly creaky joke.

'There's a great Orson Welles story,' he said, putting on his pyjamas, striped, with a cotton drawstring, such as he had worn since prep school. 'He was at a party, and a female guest approached him and patted his stomach, saying, "If that were on a woman, we'd know what to think." And Orson replied, "It was on a woman, only an hour ago."'

I sighed. The pain was creeping down my arm. I realized it was the arm that Cliff had squeezed. I examined it. Sure enough, there was a bruise. I stared at the blowsy pink peonies decorating the curtains of our bedroom. Cliff Honeywell, with the neck and the teeth and the athletic body, who gave me bruises. I bet he never wore pyjamas. I remembered how Gerald had worn his, back to front, that first night at Oxford. I felt myself cracking, like one of those plates. The decision was made. My body had decided for me. I knew, then and there, as I looked at Gerald asleep in those pyjamas, that I would be unfaithful. Yes, Alice, yes, yes, I'll say yes. I told my inflamed limbs. This was my time, at last. Yes, The peonies rustled and shook as I finally smiled myself to sleep (a relaxed jaw does it every time).

In my dreams, a thousand Royal Doulton plates crashed into the sea.

DAPHNE

That was quite a night. Mummy was thrilled – well, thrilled is perhaps not quite the right word. Relieved I think would describe it better. She could now tell all her friends that Daphne was no longer a dropout spinster, but was about to be a properly married woman just as all her friends' daughters were. Nobody went into the precise nature of these marriages, most of which were probably marriages in name only, with love and sex either stuffed into an old pillowcase like the organ described by Beckett in some book I read, or worked out in sophisticated arrangements that somehow spared everybody's feelings. Nobody had any other expectations, of course. It was the institution that counted, not the relationship.

'I think I'll wear my blue,' Mummy said, when I told her of my impending nuptials. 'And I must

get a new hat.' I could see she was already
envisioning the event as the wedding of the year
in *Jennifer's Diary*. To be honest, I didn't mind.
I felt it was a relief too, to be back in the fold, so
to speak. It's such an effort being anti-every-
thing, and as time went on I only seemed to
remember the nice things about my upbringing.
I know this sounds like unbelievable weakness
of character, and Alan would have put me up
against the wall and shot me for it. But most
people get more reactionary in their old age,
even Alan, I shouldn't wonder.

I worried more about marrying without love, I
mean love in the true, romantic sense of the
word. I knew how Louisa railed against her fate,
and yet found it impossible to escape it, as
though Edmund were her keeper in some way.
Maybe he was. I didn't see Parker in the same
way. He was too busy with his exterior life to
put barbed wire round mine, and anyway we
had lived together long enough to understand
each other's quirks and habits. But love had
awfully little to do with it, when I really faced
facts. I had never loved anyone properly since
Alan. As for the others – well, at least I never
confused love and sex.

But Parker was different. Parker made me
feel as if I belonged somewhere, and as if I were
contributing to the fabric of life. That may not

be love, but it's a very nice feeling, particularly when you have spent most of your grown-up life tearing the fabric up into little strips, as I felt I had been doing. I just hoped my ovarian organs were up to the challenge of producing a little Ferris, especially given the potential father's punishing work schedule. I had never thought I would have difficulty in having children if I'd wanted them. It did give a rather different cast to one's sex life, however. What a turn-up for the books! Promiscuity, dear Daffers, for the first time in your life, was *out*.

22

ALICE

And so we found ourselves in 1976, the year of
the Bicentennial. Cities all over America were
frantically trying to come up with ideas to celebrate what to the English residents was a sin-
gularly uninspiring year. Towns and villages
across the country painted signs, put up mark-
ers, built models, and made gardens to mark
two-hundred-year-old events of hitherto-unme-
morable local interest. History, after all its years
of disrepute, was finally becoming relevant
again. Although New York as usual had no
money to pay for grand Bicentennial schemes,
the city's trump card was the notion of the Tall
Ships – antique-rigged ships from all over the
world collecting in New York Harbor on July
Fourth and sailing in splendour around
Manhattan.

Every building on both side of the island was
requisitioned for prime viewing of the river
festival. Rooftops unused for years were suddenly reactivated; unpopular people who hap-

pened to live on Riverside Drive and East End
Avenue were suddenly showered with love and
attention. Gerald and I racked our brains for
someone with the right address to cultivate, but
it was Edmund, needless to say, who finally
arranged everything.

The Tall Ships was, of course, a typical
Edmund thing. It was your perfect Boy's Own
event, redolent of male camaraderie, swashbuc-
kling feats, captains courageous, and Kiss Me,
Hardy. Edmund was as excited as a twelve-year-
old, studying form, describing the intricacies of
the old rigs, learning the ships' colours and
lineups, finding the perfect spot from which to
watch the spectacle.

Several people had plumped for a front-row
view on the water at the Battery, where selected
boat owners could anchor their vessels close to
the course of the big ships. Edmund wanted
more comfort, more space. He found a penthouse
on Riverside Drive, its terraces wrapping round
two sides of the apartment, facing both west and
south over the river. One could see in the distance the George Washington Bridge to the
north, and down past the forest of midtown
skyscrapers, the river curling in towards Battery Park to the south. The terraces were decorated with ficus trees, azaleas, and geraniums;

white wrought-iron tables and chairs, with pale pink cushions, were placed at convenient viewing angles; white-coated youths with trays slid discreetly about, their necks permanently bent like swans to catch the faintest whisper of a request. I never found out whose apartment it was; nobody cared. That day, it was as though the whole city were being offered up to its inhabitants.

That Fourth of July was like no other. The city was silent. The crashing, whirring, honking sounds of New York were stilled. The quiet was like the muffled hush that becalmed the city after a snowfall. People walked, without rushing, through the streets. Taxi drivers were relaxed, even jovial. Passersby smiled without fear at each other. Even I, who would rather undergo Chinese torture than speak to a stranger, nodded amiably. We were all thinking of the ships, the peacefulness, the suspended world.

It was a white day. In my memory of it all the images have a bleached cast, like a slightly overexposed film. The sky was not blue, but whitish grey (later it rained), and the beautiful old riggings, some with red sails, some blue, but mostly white, added soft colour as they shook and trembled in the tiny breeze like children's handkerchiefs. One or two of the ships had black

375

sails. These appeared like shadows cast across the sun, utering ghostly warnings. I thought of the Flying Dutchman, and smiled.

Louisa and I were both wearing floaty white cotton dresses with white, wide-brimmed hats. Daphne looked like a flapper in a lemon-yellow crepe de Chine pleated tunic, with a green cloche hat. Penny, in town for the occasion, wore black and white stripes, with a red velvet choker. Yes, we were all together, for the first time since Penny's dinner party in London seven years before. And yes, it was like Oxford, the hazy light, the skyscrapers gleaming like spires, the Tall Ships, the champagne, the flags, the river.

The party itself sustained the illusion. It was full of the British types Louisa had once summarized for me – Old Etonians in cricket-club ties, referring to old friends at The House, bemoaning the fact that there was no Pimms to drink, and murmuring that the real sailing was still to be done at Cowes, while their Laura Ashley-dressed wives complained about the heat, the air-conditioning, the bad schools, and the lack of reliable help. Then there were the hustlers, razor-thin aristocrats, who looked down snooty noses and tossed out sarcastic remarks that made the natives quiver with excitement, or youthful charmers who spoke very fast in high-pitched, clipped voices, their conversation laced with brilliant literary references and many 'darling's, waving jet-black cigarette holders to hypnotize their colonial listeners.

And there was the talk about England. There were discussions of the IRA bombings back home, with people complaining that they did not dare to go to their favourite Knightsbridge restaurants any more. People wondered about the strange goings-on in the Church of England, with new-style archbishops and TV vicars like the Reverend Wales, dragging the institution by its heels into a mostly unwelcome modernity. There was talk about the decline in the quality of British beer.

But most of all it was like Oxford because of Edmund. He wore a white open-necked shirt, and white flannels, with a striped blazer thrown over his shoulders. The ensemble lacked only a boater to have been perfectly put together for those wonderful June days of Eights Week, when Oxford took to the boats and even the most antirowing types dropped everything and flocked to the river to watch the races. Perhaps I should have taken warning from his face, which, on first greeting, looked crunched and dry like an old biscuit. But after the first glass of champagne, it eased into its old boyish lines and our icon was restored.

'Isn't this wonderful, Alice?' he said, putting
his arm around me. 'Bardwell Road Redivivus.
My laughing fellow rovers.'

'What?'

'"I must down to the seas again, to the lonely
sea and the sky, And all I ask is a tall ship and
a star to steer her by."'

'Edmund, why do you always have the perfect
quote for everything? It's so unfair.'

'Unfair?' Edmund laughed. 'We have been
blessed with the greatest poetry in the world.
How foolish not to make use of it. Poets on the
whole express things rather better than us mere
mortals, don't you agree?' He drank some champagne and looked at a beautiful three-rigged
ship glide past.

'Magnificent,' he went on. 'But I can assure
you, I would rather look at you and Penny and
Daphne and Louisa.'

'Oh, Edmund,' I groaned.

'Do you remember that party at Worcester for
Bodger McCloud, when someone managed to
bring a punt on to the lawn and we all danced in
it?'

'Or threw up in it,' I said.

'Alice, how can you be so prosaic?' he
protested.

'Do you remember everything that happened
to you at school, Edmund? And at Oxford?'

'Yes, of course,' he said, eyes glittering. 'Don't you?'

The only thing I could remember with any clarity about St Dunstan's School for Girls was our devotion to a game called Stables in which one took turns to be the horse.

'What I remember I prefer to forget,' I said.

'Looking back, those places seem like "humming fortified paradises" to me . . . days of grace. The present lacks dignity or style. People's lives are trite, mediocre, bogged down by petty narcissism and meanness of spirit. There are no grand gestures any more.' His face had gone dry again. It was quite alarming.

He patted my cheek. 'Don't worry, Alice,' he said, laughing. 'I don't feel the slightest bit tragic. Not on a day like this. And just look at my wife. If I didn't know better, I would have said she'd been with a lover!'

Louisa did indeed look triumphant. Her face had that inner glow I had come to recognize.

'Don't be silly, Edmund,' I said.

'Well, go and talk to her,' he said. 'She never talks to me at parties. Believes it's a waste of time, since she can talk to me enough at home. Not that she does, of course. I'm allowed a few moments after breakfast, before she dashes off to some mansion or other to take pictures of people's linen cupboards. And we had a wonder-

ful afternoon with the children at Shea Stadium.
But of course she doesn't really try to understand baseball. Not surprising, with that soccer
background, of course.' His voice had an edge
that I had not heard before.

A young woman came up to us and began to
fumble with a notebook.

'Excuse me,' she said, 'I'm doing a story on the
Bicentennial for *New York Magazine* and someone told me you were a very famous Brit.'

Edmund glanced at her scornfully. 'It
depends,' he said. 'Fame in New York is not
what it is in Europe.'

'But weren't you one of the people voted most
likely to be prime minister of England?' she
went on.

'Heaven forbid,' he said. 'English politics is
hardly worthy of anyone's time.'

'But, Mr Wales,' she persisted, 'isn't it true
that . . .?'

'Excuse me,' Edmund interrupted. 'But I
really find this kind of interview extremely
boring. I would rather talk to my wife if you
don't mind.'

'Your wife?' The journalist looked round, as
Louisa joined us.

'I want a private talk with Alice, please,
Edmund,' she said brusquely, without looking at
him.

The journalist looked at them both with interest.

'Yes, of course,' Edmund said smoothly. 'I'll go and check the progress of the ships.' He smiled at her and moved away. The journalist followed him, looking back keenly at Louisa. I felt a flush on my cheeks.

'That was a journalist, Louisa,' I said. 'You weren't very nice to Edmund in front of her.'

She looked surprised.

'What do you mean? I was perfectly normal.'

'Normal?' I made a face.

'I don't know what you're talking about. Listen, Alice, I want to borrow your apartment.'

I groaned. 'Who is it this time?'

'How did you know?' she said.

'Come on, Louisa,' I said. 'Even your husband couldn't miss the telltale signs. Let me guess. We've had Spanish and German, so how about a Frog, they're supposed to be very romantic.'

'If you really want to know, he's a hundred per cent American.'

'There's no such thing, but it's a nice thought this Bicentennial year. Tell me more.'

'Well, he's tall, blond, athletic, and works for Merrill Lynch.'

'Sounds thrilling. And married?'

'Yes. Four children.'

I groaned. 'And of course he loves them.'

'Of course.'

'Where's the wife?'

'Where are most wives? In Greenwich, Connecticut.'

'How's it going?'

She sighed. 'Wonderfully. It's the real thing this time, Alice. The others were just –'

'Foreplay?'

A rather smart woman in a hat gave me a curious stare as she moved towards the terrace for a better view.

'Don't be crude. Anyway, we're supposed to be watching ships.' She made it sound a fearful ordeal.

'How can you go on doing this, Louisa?'

'Charlie, you mean? He's changed my life, Alice. You don't understand. I have a problem with my self-esteem. There's been a lot of pain in my life. I am beginning to get in touch with –'

'Don't tell me. You've been seeing Jeannie's shrink.'

'Well, yes, as a matter of fact. Charlie thinks it's a good idea too. It's really helping me.'

'What is the conclusion?'

'There are no conclusions, silly. But the therapist did suggest I, er, wash Edmund's feet.' She began to giggle.

'What?'

'Well, Edmund was supposed to wash my feet, too.'

'Sounds like your shrink has a Mary Magdalene complex.'

'It's supposed to generate tender feelings between husband and wife. That was the idea behind it, I mean.'

'Did you?'

She looked at me and we both shrieked with laughter.

'Louisa, you are truly crazy, but your shrink should be in Bellevue.'

'He is,' she said, waving to someone. 'I must go. Thanks loads for the flat.'

Feet-washing? Gerald's toes were rather an odd shape, and sometimes black at the top as though afflicted with frostbite. The idea of applying soap and flannel to them filled me less with tender feelings than a distinct sense of nausea. Is that what they call aversion therapy?

Gerald and Penny were deep in conversation over a large plate of guacamole. Gerald had that peculiarly intent look on his face that appeared whenever his intestinal tract was under pressure. As I watched, Penny whispered something in his ear, and he doubled up in an impression of pain – Gerald at his flirtatious best.

'Break it up,' I said. 'We are supposed to be grieving on this day, not larking about.'

'It's Americans who grieve,' Gerald said. 'Their Anglophilia merely proves that like a child sent out into the world on its own, Americans still yearn for the umbilical cord of the motherland. It's most curious.'

'I felt sure after all the disasters back home that their feelings would diminish,' agreed Penny. 'Bankruptcies of the great names like Rolls Royce, the invasion of the Arabs, bombs all over the place, the corruption of quality in workmanship, and so on. But it is as though their view of England stopped at the end of the last century, and all the odd values still exist somehow.'

'And we expatriates reinforce this by romanticizing our own past. Emotion against reason. It shouldn't be allowed.'

'Up with logic again,' I sighed. 'Can we never escape the public-school mentality? I'm going to talk to Daphne. She at least has moved out of its stranglehold.'

I moved away, to another corner of the terrace, where Daphne was sitting under a small palm tree, discussing her diamond engagement ring with a distinguished-looking man who had a loupe stuck in his eye like a monocle. As I watched, she slipped it off her finger and gave it to her companion, who nodded as he examined it.

'Well,' I said, going over to her. 'And how much is it worth?'

'Oh, dear,' Daphne said guiltily, taking back the ring. 'Do you think I am totally corrupted?'

'Just tuck it away somewhere, can you?' I said. 'It's blinding me so I can't see the ships.'

'It was just that this kind man noticed it and said it was rather a good one and could he look at it,' she went on. 'Parker went mad when we went to Tiffany's. Honestly, I would have been quite happy with a smaller one.'

'Well, Daphne, you are the only one of us who is actually marrying a millionaire,' I said. 'Congratulations. At least Oxford did something for someone.'

'Oxford?' she laughed. 'It never trained me for this. It even makes Parker nervous when he remembers I have this degree. I have to assure him it doesn't mean anything, and that I'd much rather be good at tennis.'

I remembered not to ask how her game was.

'Tennis?' The man with the loupe bestirred himself. 'You play tennis? Not at the Midtown Tennis Club, by any chance?'

I hastily excused myself and looked round the terrace. Louisa was standing in one corner, talking to a suntanned man with aviator glasses and a shirt open to the navel, his chest sporting a heavy gold medallion. Suddenly I realized who

he was – one Dr Heller, a famous plastic surgeon, much favoured by the gossip columns for
his exotic love life and flamboyant parties, and
famous up and down Park Avenue for his
botched mastectomies. His hand was hovering
over Louisa's concave bosom like a bird of prey.

'All alone, Alice?' It was Edmund, carrying a
bottle of champagne. 'You look so beautiful
today.'

'Oh, Edmund. Did you get rid of that awful
journalist?'

He kissed me on the cheek. I could tell he had
been drinking.

'I've always wanted you, you know,' he said.
'I've often thought that if I hadn't met Louisa, it
was you I really would have loved.'

A huge ship with black sails floated past my
consciousness. The wind suddenly became
stronger, fluttering people's skirts and rustling
the leaves. I felt I was being sucked into the
bleached white sky.

I looked at his face, now deeply creased, his
skin aged before its time like all those with
light, fair, child's complexions.

I had never thought of Edmund.

He'd always belonged to Louisa. To think that
all these years we had never spoken of it.

'It's too late, Edmund,' I stammered. 'You
know I love you, but . . .'

He had his arm round my shoulder, gently, lightly, making no bruise. I could so easily have melted into the crook of his sloping arm.

'I wish you had gone off ages ago,' I burst out. 'Not with me, but with someone. Anyone. We all seem to do things too late.'

Edmund stared at me.

'Anyone? Anyone, Alice? Is that all it means to you? Some anonymous body, groping in the dark?'

'Sometimes that way is good,' I said defensively. 'You and Gerald are so alike, so remote from ... the core of things. You don't seem to have any impulses or instincts.'

He drew away from me. 'How can you say that, Alice? You sound like a prostitute.' He gave a short laugh. 'You know what Flaubert found out in Egypt? He found out that *almeh*, the word for "bluestocking," had gradually lost its original meaning and come to mean "whore."'

'All right,' I said angrily. 'Mock if you like. But you're making a silly mistake over some idiotic rationalization, and it's destroying you. How can you go without sex? Girls are always throwing themselves at you, begging you, adoring you. Why do you always turn them away? What's wrong with you?'

'Wrong with me?' He laughed again, scornfully. 'Wrong with *me*? Who are these girls who

387

"throw themselves at me," Alice? Why on earth
would I want them? I do not love them, I do not
even like most of them. I like you, and Penny,
and Daphne, and I love Louisa. What more do
you want? "Impulses and instincts." Really,
Alice, I should have thought you knew better.'

His ironic tone was infuriating. I suddenly
saw these English as truly a breed apart –
desexed by housemasters and hypocrisy, taught
to believe that impulses and instincts were disgusting, ungentlemanly. These marmoreal
faces, bloodless lips, chilled bodies, flippant com-
mentators on a passionless life.

'Why go on, Edmund,' I asked wearily. 'Why
struggle with this hopeless relationship? She
doesn't love you. She won't ever love you. You're
hitting your head against a wall. Forget her.
Start again, before it's too late. You're nearly
forty and you're shrivelling away, a forgotten
man.'

'You sound like a B movie, Alice. One doesn't
change love like a shirt. You lack a sense of
poetry, my dear. Let me give you a definition of
the romantic imagination – "the suction of the
infinite." Isn't that a splendid expression? Why
shouldn't one pursue such an honourable goal? I
don't feel tragic. I have done more than most
people. I have my wife. I have my children. I
couldn't desert them now. I never leave a per-

formance before the end. I consider that the
height of self-indulgence. I thought you, of all
people, would understand.'

That reproach again. Did I understand? I
watched Daphne slide her diamond ring up and
down her finger as she talked to her jeweller. I
watched Gerald put his ear to Penny's chest as
though to check for lung congestion. I watched
Louisa rapt, as the plastic surgeon sculpted
melons for her out of the air. So much for poetry.
Was this what Edmund despised so much?

'Do you remember that May afternoon in our
second year,' he was saying, 'when we all went
out on the river and Penny brought a picnic and
then afterwards we listened to the Christ
Church choir rehearsing Britten's *Nunc
Dimittis*?'

'It wasn't the *Nunc Dimittis*,' I said automati-
cally. 'It was the *Missa Brevis*.'

That was it, though. That was what was
wrong. The memory was not quite accurate any
more. The past was not the truth, in Edmund's
telling of it. Perhaps it never had been. I remembered Gerald's description of the falsehoods
indulged in by the expatriate mind. Edmund
was guilty of falsehoods, and I hated him for it.

'You're like a disease,' I wanted to say to him.
'You keep us in your thrall with your tales and
your nostalgia and your memories and your

past, and you drag us down with you in an orgy of regret. But it's not true, any of it. It was never quite like that.'

I turned to him, but at that moment a voice interrupted me. It was one of those bright, nasal voices that American women use in department stores.

'Excuse me,' she said, and I turned round to see the woman who had brushed past me earlier.

'I didn't want to interrupt you,' she said. 'But I just can't stand it a moment longer.'

I braced myself.

'Where did you get your boots?'

'My boots?' I looked down at the white Courrèges boots I had kept since the sixties.

'Oh, dear,' I said, starting to laugh. 'I really couldn't tell you. You'd have to go back in time about a decade, and even then it would be difficult to know where to look.'

She frowned, looking at me a little oddly, and moved on. When I turned back, Edmund had vanished.

So I never said the last part that thrummed in my head. When I think of that day, I think of Edmund, frozen in time, with the four of us, Daphne, Louisa, Penny, and I, on the roof of a New York apartment, looking at ships.

DAPHNE

It was the oddest thing. After the Tall Ships party, I was planning to go straight back to Long Island, where Parker was preparing for a golf tournament with his old friend Wally Ivanhoe. (A touch of tennis elbow was keeping him off the court.) On the way out Edmund came up to me, three sheets to the wind, I thought, and asked if I wanted some dinner. I looked round for Penny or Alice, but couldn't see them. Edmund said Louisa was having a business dinner, which I had the tact not to question.

We went to a little French place that Edmund seemed very fond of, and he drank several champagne cocktails, and then he started telling me about our days at Oxford and the parties and so on. He even brought out a photograph he had once taken of us all at a cricket match. I laughed when I saw it, we all looked so different somehow, so . . . young. Edmund shushed me, telling me how wonderful it was that we had not changed at all and how I was always the most beautiful one, etc. etc. and that if he had not fallen for Louisa, I was the one who would have really made him happy. Well, I am not one to argue with a compliment, but this seemed so absurd that I had to laugh.

'I wasn't really interested in people like you in those days,' I said. 'I was after something more exotic, like a boy from South London.' I went on in this vein for a while, but he kept looking at me with the most desperate expression, and I finally twigged that he was making at pass at me.

Edmund Wales! So he wasn't so different, after all. There was something like a little boy in his attitude, looking hopefully for success. And this the same person who pulverized people with his scathing talk and impatient wit! I was flattered, needless to say. And I am not saying that on another occasion I might not have pursued the whole thing further. You never know when you are going to run into another Flying Dutchman (though the odds in this case were pretty long).

Women perhaps will understand when I say that I just did not feel up to it, what with Parker and pregnancy and getting married. Was I just getting more and more conventional? After all, presumably there were ways to get round the difficulty, what with modern science and all. But it just seemed wrong to me.

I left him in the restaurant because I had to catch a train. He didn't appear to have to go anywhere. I seem often to leave people in restaurants, but at least this time I managed to finish the meal. Was this a sign of maturity? I put my coat on and waved to him, but he didn't look up. When I got home, I realized I still had the photograph. The awful thing is, when I finally got round to sending it back, it was too late.

23

ALICE

That autumn I was given a new account –
Goodboy High-Speed Radial Tires. On my
enquiring whether it was wise to assign such an
unalluring product to someone of my talents, the
creative director answered that they were looking for something new in car advertising and
besides, they were an equal opportunity
employer. (A female employee was bringing a
class-action suit on sex discrimination against
the agency because she claimed she was always
made to work on the Milady Feminine Napkins
account instead of Red-Hot Rototiller.)

One morning, as I was immersed in the technology of 'tread,' 'traction,' and 'cornering
power,' the telephone rang. It was Cliff
Honeywell.

'I'm inviting you to the Princeton-Yale game,'
he said. 'It's next Saturday. You and Gerald and
Bert. And Daphne, if she can escape from that
tennis nut.'

'What about Edmund?' I asked. 'He's the one who'd really like that sort of thing.'

'He's apparently gone to England. I've left messages everywhere. Louisa is in Paris photographing bathrooms, and the babysitter doesn't speak English, so I'm not getting anywhere.'

I had not seen or talked to Edmund since July, but the fact that he had gone to England made me faintly uneasy.

'Why did he go?' I asked Gerald. 'Did you know?'

Gerald shrugged. His magazine had just been taken over by an oil company one of whose subsidiaries was a chain of fast-food outlets called Cap'n Jack Tartan. Gerald suspected that his health column might be axed in favour of restaurant reviews. He was therefore not in a mood for discussion about his friend's travel plans.

'He probably went to find a better bridge game,' he said.

'You're not helping,' I said. 'I feel there's something wrong.'

'Can't you see I have other things on my mind than what you may or may not feel,' he snapped. 'Everyone here is obsessed with *feelings*. I want to talk about *things*.'

He did agree to come with us to the football game, however. Daphne showed up for it wearing a thrift-shop fur to show she was not completely corrupted. The diamond ring kept catching in it and pulling out tufts of fur. 'I really want to immerse myself in American culture,' she told us, explaining her absence from the current Maidstone tennis tournament circuit. 'After all, this is to be my home. I don't want to be one of those snotty expatriates who keep using English words and talk about Ascot all the time.'

'Like "snotty,"' I said, pulling some thrift-shop fur out of my mouth. We were jammed together in the back of Cliff's car. Bert was torn between the opportunity of cuddling up to Daphne and the chance of getting carsick, but decided on the latter and was sitting in comfort in the front.

'It takes practice,' Daphne said loftily. 'I bet you still say things like that.'

'Bollocks,' I said, removing some more fur. 'Why isn't Jeannie with us?'

'She's at a pro-abortion rally in Madison Square Garden,' Cliff said. 'Gloria's supposed to speak. Jeannie's doing publicity for her new book, *Fetushood: The Shadow Knows.*'

I gazed at the back of Cliff's neck.

'Is that an adventure story?' asked Bert.

'Sure,' said Cliff. 'It's like this, see . . .'

'What about explaining the football,' I said hurriedly.

'The thing to do is go to the freshman game first and watch them at close quarters,' Cliff obliged. 'Then you can really see what kind of physical skills are involved.'

'You really get up close?' asked Bert.

'Sure. You can hear the thuds and grunts as they barrel into each other.'

'You don't get that on the telly,' Bert said.

'Sounds positively sadistic,' Gerald said. 'I think I may break out in hives.'

'It's good clean fun,' Cliff said. 'Those guys are pretty tough, you know. Weigh in at something over two hundred pounds, some of them.'

'Gosh,' Bert breathed.

'You know, physical fitness is so psychological,' Daphne observed. 'Parker's game has really picked up since he went to this therapist. He had a little tendinitis last month so we flew him to a specialist in Rio de Janeiro who said he was too tense, and that he should express his anger by breaking rackets if he felt like it. His serve's okay, just the backhands and topspin lobs have been off. But the last few tournaments were really interesting. He won a tournament in Tuxedo Park that he couldn't have won a year ago. The score was, let me see, 6–4, 3–6, 7–5, and that doesn't really show the true quality of the game. If it had gone to five sets we would have had a world war on our hands. He broke six rackets in one game. That was the turning point, I think. The other tournament he played in he only broke three, and he won 6–3, 4–6, 6–3.'

And she wasn't even married yet.

When we reached the outskirts of Princeton everyone remarked on the pretty clapboard houses with pastel shutters that lined the streets. The weather was perfect – one of those crystal-bright, sunny days that the Eastern seaboard came up with in the autumn, when the trees were flaming orange and yellow and the sky was so blue that you had to shield your eyes.

'This makes me think of my mother,' Daphne said. 'Her wardrobe, you know.'

'How is Lady Fanthorpe?' Gerald asked.

'Her voice is much deeper now, thanks to Ronnie Mailorder. When she answers the phone, people think she's a man.'

'Ronnie Mailorder once put his hand up my – ' Bert piped up.

'Shut up, Bert,' I said.

Cliff drove slowly down a street of large houses and turned into a small driveway leading to a grim red brick mock-Tudor mansion with a green slate roof and mullioned windows.

'Ooh, good, a witch must live here,' Bert said.

'This is the Ivy Club,' Cliff said proudly.

An ancient retainer bowed and called, 'Good

day, Mr Honeywell,' as he waved us through.

'He looked rather like Loopy,' I murmured. 'Remember him?'

'He's in a home,' Gerald said. 'Penny told me. One night he went berserk and rushed about with the fire extinguisher, saying that His Lordship was being attacked, until he finally knocked himself out with it and was never the same again. Mrs Lupin's gone too – she ran off with the plumber as soon as Loopy was removed.'

'Où sont les neiges . . .' I sighed.

'What is the Ivy Club anyway?' Daphne asked as we drove past the forbidding edifice towards the car park.

'Princeton is made up of private clubs,' Cliff explained. 'In my day everyone belonged to one. In fact, if you were not picked for one, you were a complete outcast and didn't have anywhere to eat.'

'What do you mean, "picked"?' asked Gerald. 'Didn't you simply sign up for the one you wanted?'

'Do you just sign up for the Carlton Club or Brooks's, or Boodle's?' Cliff asked. 'Hell, no. The club picked you – if you were suitable, that is.'

'How perfectly dreadful,' I said.

'And I thought America was democratic,' Daphne said.

'Just copying your English system, old girl,' Cliff said. 'We had a great model.'

Who could argue with that? We climbed out of the car to see large groups of other Ivy Club members and their families, clustered round their cars unpacking picnics.

'It's rather like a point-to-point,' Daphne said, 'only no shooting sticks.'

'We call it tailgating,' Cliff said, as we followed him to the back of his car. 'People eat their picnics by the trunks of their automobiles. Look. It's quite a sight.'

And it was. Most of the people were standing round the rear ends of the station wagons, tucking into picnics of the most lavish proportions. Tiffany cocktail shakers filled with Bloody Marys and martinis; porcelain plates laden with shrimp salad and pâté; one family was barbecuing spareribs on a portable grill. One table was spread with a white linen cloth, and candlesticks.

'That would never play at York races,' Daphne murmured.

'Give me a pork pie and a bottle of Watneys,' I muttered to Gerald as we watched the gourmet feasting. But Gerald was in ecstasy. 'Oh, look,' he said. 'Isn't that steak tartare being spread on to a croissant? What invention!' Off he went, stalking the picnics with greedy eyes, a notebook and pencil in hand.

'Mummy always used to dish up some dried-up old pheasant pie when we went to the races,' Daphne said. 'She always said she wanted her picnics to be different. So we had dried-up pheasant pie, Scotch eggs of course, and sardines for Daddy. We had to eat off cheap paper plates that always went soggy in the middle, and as it was always raining you were lucky if you got anything in your stomach at all except wads of damp papier-mâché. The drinks were worse. Mummy disapproved of alcohol at race-meetings – said it meant bad luck with the horses and anyway you wanted a clear head to read the form – so she had McCloud cook up some disgusting lemonade spiked with bitters that we had to drink out of the one thermos top that wasn't cracked, which always tasted of plastic and burnt coffee. That is why,' she added, accepting Cliff's Baccarat glass of Veuve Clicquot with enthusiasm, 'I'd rather be in America.'

'How materialistic,' I said, also welcoming Cliff's champagne.

'What is so wonderful about unnecessary slumming?' Daphne asked. 'Is it so good for the soul, or something?'

'It's a perverse puritanical hangover,' I suggested. 'That sort of pleasure is considered sinful. Alan Moss is the one to ask.'

'Don't,' Daphne moaned. 'I am beginning to feel class-conscious.'

'Well, while you two girls discuss the intellectual justifications for enjoying my champagne, I'm going to take Bert to where the real action is – the freshman game.' Bert looked up at Cliff with adoration. 'If you want to stay around the car, that's fine by me. But you're missing the real flavour of the day.'

Daphne and I reluctantly met this challenge and followed the chaps to the mud-soaked freshman football field, where proud parents watched and cheered as their sons tore ligaments, lost teeth, and twisted ankles in the cause of a Princeton victory. Daphne began to giggle.

'Actually it's rather fun, isn't it?' she said over the grunts of pain and carnage.

Cliff was explaining to Bert the finer points of the defensive line. I found myself watching him rather than the poor animals on the field. His physique put theirs to shame.

'Did you play this game, Cliff?' I asked him.

'Sure,' he said. 'I was one of Princeton's greatest pass rushers. Me and Danny Sachs . . .'

'They look so sweet and innocent to behave so roughly,' Daphne said, gazing at the bulging necks, heaving chests, and tousled hair as the

402

exhausted players took off their helmets and sank down on the bench.

'Don't believe it,' Cliff said. 'Sweet and innocent?' He laughed and put his arm round my shoulders. 'What do you think about sweet and innocent, Alice?'

I felt myself blushing, and my shoulders tingled where the heavy weight of his arm rested. Right on the old bruise. He laughed again and I could see his white, shining teeth. American dentists were so much better than British ones.

'You're looking very sexy today,' he whispered into my ear.

'I look the same as I always look,' I managed to say.

'That's what I mean,' he said. 'That cold English manner can drive a man crazy.'

I laughed and tried to push his arm away but it wouldn't budge.

'Hadn't we better go back?' I asked. 'Bert, don't you think you've had enough?'

A stupid question, and deserved the glance I received in response.

'We should start making our way back soon,' Cliff said, finally removing his arm. 'We don't want to miss the kickoff and it gets kind of crowded up there. Come on, kid, you'll want to see the big boys now.'

He took Bert's hand, and Daphne took his

other one. The boy was in paradise. As we threaded our way through the cars, Cliff was greeted by a large number of people who spoke to him in what seemed to be a sort of code.

'Well, it's Honeywell, class of '59, how are you, boy?'

'There's Winty, class of '60, wasn't he?'

'Sixty-one, I think. His father was '38.'

'You know what happened to Butch, he was in your father's class, wasn't he?'

'No, '40. Didn't he run off with some bimbo?'

'Bimbo? It was Bud's wife, class of '55.'

'Where's Chaz, class of '58? I thought I saw him over there.'

'His brother was a sophomore when I was a freshman. Some tight end.'

'Wasn't Benjie in your class, or was it '61?'

'Remember Wally, class of '58, that great back?'

'Touchdown in the last five seconds, '57, remember that?'

'You weren't such a bad rusher yourself, Cliff, huh?'

Interspersed with these remarks are comments for our benefit on the nature of Cliff's character, which we received with solemn attention. I must have smiled politely at a hundred Chipp jackets. I suddenly thought of Edmund, who would have so loved this scene, and a wave

404

of anxiety swept over me. A fellow with round glasses and chubby cheeks distracted me. He was from Yale, he told me, and therefore an outsider, as I was. 'Don't take any notice of these Princeton types,' he told me. 'They're such terrible snobs. I only come for the booze and smoked salmon. Yale always wins anyway.' He laughed uproariously and shook my hand. 'Bailey Simple at your service,' he said. 'Let me tell you, Yalies have more fun. You can come and sit with us if you like.'

Cliff overheard this and grabbed me by the neck.

'Not on your life,' he said. 'This one is mine.' He held up his finger to forbid argument. Bailey Simple shrugged.

'Princeton snob,' he said. 'Don't listen to him, if you value your sanity.' I felt about twenty-one years old. It was lovely.

By the time we reached Cliff's car the visitors were beginning to make their way through the park to the stadium, whose crenellated walls gave the impression of some medieval fortification.

'Hurry now,' Cliff said. 'It's nearly kickoff time.'

'There's Gerald,' I said, waving to him. He was deep in conversation with a man in a fishing hat, gnawing a large lobster claw.

'Come on, Gerald,' I said, attempting my loyal wife voice.

'I was just about to get an invitation to Maine,' he whispered furiously to me as I dragged him off. 'That fellow makes lobster boats and sells them for huge sums of money to slumming aristocrats.'

People shouting, 'Tigers, hurrah!' rushed past us, waving orange and black flags and pompoms that matched the orange and black scarves we saw everywhere. Our seats were high up in the stadium ('The best place,' Cliff assured us as we struggled up the narrow steps). I saw Bailey Simple in the distance. He waved and gave me a mock yawn.

'Who was that?' Daphne said.

'A Yalie,' I said.

'What's a Yalie?' she asked.

'I saw a Yalie being carried off with a concussion,' Bert announced. 'I could see blood squirting from his eye. It looked really squishy.'

'I think Bert is going to be a doctor,' Daphne observed.

'Or a mortician,' Gerald said.

We were exhorted to rise for 'The Star-Spangled Banner,' which everyone sang with gusto, the crowd being largely of the conservative persuasion. The ball was then kicked off to the accompaniment of a loud roar, and everyone sat down. I was sitting between Cliff and Bert, which turned out to resemble the position of a tennis net.

'I think Yale has a weak offensive line,' Bert would say to Cliff over my head.

'With luck, the Tigers can break through with a couple of running plays,' Cliff would call back. 'But watch Number Seventy-three, Yale's best defensive end.'

Cliff was right about one thing. Being too far away to hear the moans and crunches of the assaulted players undoubtedly lessened whatever involvement one might feel about the sport. I was not devoid of sporting enthusiasm. I had enjoyed my few occasions at the Fulham football ground. But soccer was a game of permanent movement. This Princeton-Yale battle seemed to consist entirely of a series of collisions in the mud. I grew increasingly conscious of Cliff's hand on my knee, providing a warm spot on my otherwise rapidly chilling body.

'Princeton should go to the air,' Bert declared.

'One of our best receivers is hurt,' Cliff responded.

'I'm getting cold,' I said. 'Gerald, can I have something to warm me up?'

Gerald's hands were clasped affectionately round a thermos of reduced Madeira sauce masquerading as soup. 'You wouldn't like it,' he assured me. 'It's a concoction I made up for my sciatic nerve.'

'Poor Alice,' Cliff said, laughing and moving his hand up a little. 'English husbands are not worth a damn. We'll go into the clubhouse at halftime and get you warmed up.' He gave me a look that temporarily sent my body temperature shooting up.

'Thank you,' I said breathlessly.'

I did not have to wait long. As the whistle blew, Gerald and Daphne agreed to forage for hot dogs and hot chocolate, with Bert trailing behind, looking adoringly at Daphne. His crush was evidently reaching fever pitch. Cliff and I walked through the Ivy Club car park and up to the clubhouse, which looked dark and gloomy as the late shadows of the afternoon started to creep over it. It reminded me of winter evenings in Bardwell Road, and I wondered what I was doing in the company of someone rejected all those years ago by Daphne.

The house was deserted, as it was not customary for these keen fans to go very far from the stadium at halftime, and any student not watching the game was out of the club for the afternoon. Cliff showed me the dining room, where white-coated servants were setting out cups and plates for snacks after the game.

'Not as big as an Oxford Hall,' he explained,

'but on the same lines.' He indicated the panelling, oak tables, and leather armchairs. In one of the chairs was a white-haired old gentleman, his newspaper fallen to the floor, his mouth open as he snored slightly.

'Class of '35,' Cliff said. 'Great running back. Gave us one of our best wins ever against Harvard.'

I laughed. 'You're so sentimental.'

'You are so uptight,' he returned. 'But underneath all that composure, you're a wild animal, right?'

I couldn't think what to say. Cliff laughed and took my arm. 'I'll find you something to drink,' he said. 'English people need artificial means to loosen them up, I have noticed. What drinkers you people are!'

'What about the game?' I asked. I was beginning to feel feverish.

'Yale is slicing up the Princeton secondary. There's nothing to go back for.'

'Oh.'

Cliff took me into the billiard room, a large room off the porch, the two billiard tables empty except for a few scattered balls. The walls were panelled and at the far end was a large leather window seat. We looked at it at the same time.

'Stay here,' he said. 'I'll get some booze.'

I watched him walk out of the room, with his

easy, loping gait. I felt suddenly scared as I sat and looked at those two silent billiard tables, the green baize smooth and cool, as though hardly ever used. Don't think, I told myself. The English think too much. Jeannie's right. Jeannie. Don't think of her either, you clown.

Cliff came back with two glasses of brandy, and handed me one. I took a large swig. He held out his hand, and I took it. His was warm and dry, unlike mine. The heat went through me like an electric current. We sat back on the old leather window seat. He pulled me to him.

'Are you ready?' he asked.

'Ready?' I was petrified.

'Say *fuck*, Alice.'

I stared at his mouth, which was within an inch of mine. He was smiling, and I could see little cracks in his lips.

'I can't.'

'Say *fuck*. Fuck. Say it.' He leaned closer.

'I *can't*.'

'Christ, you're priceless. Say *fuck*. Come on now. It rhymes with *Chuck*. *Fuck*. *Fuck Chuck*.'

'F-f-fuck . . . Chuck.' As I put my lips together to form the words, I could feel them trembling, but whether it was laughter or fear, I did not know. 'Fuck,' I said again. 'Fuck. Fuck Chuck!' We both began to giggle.

410

'Good, Alice, alpha plus. Now say it again. Doesn't it feel good?'

'Fuck,' I said, 'fuck, fuck, fuck . . .' My voice grew stronger with every one. 'Fuck,' I shouted. 'Fuck Chuck!'

A wheezing noise halted my progress. We turned round to see an old servant tottering into the room. He evidently had respiratory difficulties.

'Are you looking for some balls?' the old man asked. 'You know people don't generally play a lot of pool on a football weekend, but I'm sure I could . . .'

'That's all right, Jimmy,' Cliff said. 'We're not going to play right now.'

'What did you say, sir?' The old servant cupped his ear. 'I'm afraid I can't hear like I used to. But I'd be happy to get the balls for you. I remember in '45, just after the war it was . . .'

'Never mind,' Cliff said loudly, getting up and shepherding the old man from the room. 'We're busy right now, thanks very much. Why don't you come back later?'

Grinning, Cliff came back to our seat and took me in his arms.

'One more time, Alice,' he said. 'It rhymes with Chuck, remember?'

On the wall over his shoulder I could see a photograph of a football team. Through the door at the end I could hear the faint plink-plink of someone strumming on a piano. The window seat was soft and wide, made of faded red leather did not slip or creak. My toes began to curl.

Well, as Esther Summerson says in *Bleak House*, sometimes the narrator has to take centre stage. I had certainly waited long enough. Cliff was not the Flying Dutchman perhaps, but he pulled out all the stops and I was gone. Wave upon wave, just as Daphne had described it. The ludicrous part was that those idiotic words were true – oceans, waves, roarings, the lot. Roarings certainly. As I began to return to myself, the roarings seemed to increase. Suddenly I realized that Cliff was cheering madly. I smiled with modest satisfaction as he leaped off me.

'Princeton touchdown!' he exclaimed. 'This has the makings of an upset!'

'What?'

The cheering from the stadium echoed round the billiard room. I slowly lifted up my head.

'Listen to that crowd,' Cliff said. 'The Tigers are on the move!'

'But what about . . .?'

My voice trailed away.

'Let's go back and see their victory,' Cliff urged. 'Are you ready?'

'I think I must go to the Ladies Room,' I murmured.

The Last Romantics

'Oh, sure, Alice. It's up two flights of stairs. I'll wait for you here.' He gave me a kiss on the mouth. 'You're a real sport, you know that?'

On the way out I saw the photograph on the wall commemorated the Centennial game between Princeton Ivy Club and Rutgers Delta Phi in 1969. Score two-nothing Princeton. A colourful stained-glass window threw its gothic rays on me as I climbed slowly up the stairs. The window had an inscription. It read, 'In memory of Algergon Brooke Roberts, 1896.' At the top of the second flight of stairs a dignified-looking lady in a fox-fur cape and hat was sitting in an armchair knitting as she listened to the game on the radio.

'I never go to the stadium, it's always too cold,' she volunteered as I sidled past her.

'What's the score?' I asked.

'Princeton's losing. Don't be fooled by that touchdown,' she informed me. 'On days like this I wish I'd never left Philadelphia.' Her knitting was orange and black. It looked like a tea cosy.

Why should I be fooled by the touchdown? I asked myself as I descended the stairs. I was sure Algernon Brooke Roberts would not have been fooled. His name alone inspired confidence, gleaming in the evening light. Were things better in 1896? Surely not. After all, Alice had got what she wanted. A good fuck. Fuck Chuck.

413

Why should she expect anything else? A bouquet of flowers for her courage? For her betrayal of Gerald – and Jeannie? For her achievement of the Big O after all these years? I hugged myself as I passed Mr Roberts's name on the stairs.

Fuck Chuck. My lips kept forming the words as I made my way with Cliff back to our seats. He was solicitous, arm on my shoulder again, patting my back. 'Too little, too late,' he said. I would have agreed, but he was speaking about the Princeton touchdown.

Gerald and Daphne were huddled together in our seats, sharing the last of Gerald's sciatic-nerve medicine. Bert was looking depressed, as were the orange-and-black supporters surrounding us. It grew colder by the minute, and when the final whistle blew I felt as though I were one of Michelangelo's torsos trapped forever in the imprisoning stone. Only Bailey Simple still looked cheerful. 'What did I tell you?' he called to me. 'All these guys are fit for is putting holes in doughnuts.'

As we struggled to our feet, I noticed people beginning to sing another song, with as much intensity as they had sung the national anthem. 'In praise of Old Nassau,' they intoned raptly, 'in praise of Old Nassau.' Cliff too, head high, inched out a baritone rumble with the others. And as they sang, they began beating their breasts with their right hands. Misty-eyed boys, grown men, and grandfathers in their dotage all smiting their breasts in unison; then, with one more gorilla-like roar, it was over.

We made our way back to the car park in silence. Even Bert had been subdued by this last expression of tribal feeling. Fuck Chuck, I thought to myself, beginning to feel better. Everything was going to be all right.

'What I don't understand is why you were all singing about the Bahamas,' Gerald said as we got into the car.

'Old Nassau is a name for Princeton,' Cliff explained.

'Oxford never had a song, did it?' I said. Gerald laughed.

'Who would have sung it?' he asked rhetorically.

I don't know. But if there had been a song, judging from the way I felt then, I might have sung it.

Part Three

LOUISA

It was the *Daily Express* who got on to me first.
To have one's life measured out, not with coffee
spoons, but with column inches. The modern way.
I was in New York, just back from a trip. Edmund
had been coming and going a lot recently,
explaining that he had some new projects in
England that required his presence there. That
was fine by me, but the twins hated their father
being away so much so I tried to curtail my work
for a while, particularly after Christmas, when
family morale was at an all-time low.

It was March 29, 1977. The phone rang about
noon. I had been out buying a present at Bloom-
ingdale's for a colleague at the office who'd just
had her fourth baby, poor benighted idiot. Catholic, of course. I wanted to get something for her,
not for the baby. Something to pamper the poor
mother. Actually, now I come to think of it, it
was odd her being Catholic under the circumstances. Well, the point is that the *Daily Express*
was on the phone from London. 'Have you

heard?' they said in that insidious lip-licking voice I had come to know so well.

'Heard what?' I said as coldly as possible. For the moment, I could not think of any reason for them to be on to me. The last time Charlie and I had been seen together was at the Henry Street Settlement benefit, and as his wife was on the board I had only been able to exchange a few words with him. We were planning a trip to Bermuda together, but nobody knew about that except us, and it was difficult enough getting that off the ground what with Merrill Lynch and Greenwich. Married men were getting more difficult all the time, it seemed. But Charlie was worth the wait.

'A boat exploded this morning. Off the coast of Ireland.'

'What has that to do with me?'

'There was a man in the boat. Alone. Preliminary identification indicates it was Edmund Wales.'

'What?'

'Your husband, Mrs Wales. It seems he's just been blown up.'

'By the IRA?' I couldn't take it in.

'No one is saying that yet.'

'I – ' I stopped myself from saying anything further.

'Thank you,' I said. As they began asking for

my comments, I put the phone down.

The children were at school. My babysitter was out. I had the Van Zuylen palace to myself. I sat down in the kitchen and stared at the fridge, which was covered with children's paintings and little notes about piano lessons and school closings, pinioned to the door with magenta plastic magnets in the shape of strawberries and watermelons and tomatoes.

Edmund. What was he doing in a boat? That was a silly question, of course. But in March? Even for one so hardy, this scarcely seemed the time of year for a sail. And why would the IRA want to blow him up? What had he been doing with the Irish? I realized I had not the vaguest idea of what Edmund had been doing in London all these months. The first time he went was right after that July Fourth party when everyone got so embarrassingly sentimental. Such a mistake. It put Edmund into a completely weird mood and off he went – 'home' as he still called it. But had he gone into politics? Was he working for the Prots somehow? I couldn't remember him ever saying he was going to Ireland.

Edmund. Dead. Husbandless. Widow. I suddenly remembered a story I'd read about an invalid woman who is kept at home, protected from life, imprisoned in effect, by her overpossessive, suffocating husband. One day she learns that he has been killed in a car accident. Slowly, inexorably, her strength comes back to her, and against the wishes of her family, she begins to get up, walk about, think about going out, embrace the life of the world outside, from which she had been so long excluded. One day she decides to go out for the very first time. As she walks down the stairs and moves towards the front door and freedom, breathless with anticipation and excitement, she is told that the husband is not dead at all, but alive, and about to return to her. His miraculous return to life is, of course, the end of hers.

A frightening story. I was frightened now. Not by Edmund's life, but by his death. I sensed a feeling of closing in. What did it mean? Charlie – I must tell Charlie. Wouldn't that help? Thoughts crowded my mind – Charlie's face, the children crying, Edmund in a boat . . .

Then the phone began to ring.

PENNY

I was in London, getting dressed to go to a party at the Tate Gallery, when Freddy telephoned. We often talked, because there was nearly always some children's arrangement to be made.

I had given up worrying about the toll Freddy's what Americans would call 'lifestyle' would take on my darling ones. They seemed to have such fun with him, and he took his paternal role so seriously, that I found no cause to complain. At least I had no difficulty having to cope with a second wife or girlfriend, as some of my friends were forced to do. Undoing the damage done by stepmothers was a seemingly endless task. Freddy taught our four Latin and Greek stories and poems, which they found amusing, and he took them to operas, ballets, and concerts, which they loved. No football games or hiking trips however. I was convinced that at least one of them would become a wrestler or carpenter, to counteract this rarefied upbringing. But from what I had seen of other families, children would always choose their own singular path, whatever the pressure from parents.

On this occasion, however, Freddy was not phoning for a family chat. I remember vividly how I had just put on my green silk dress and was wondering whether to wear the pearls or the rubies (one of the few Weathering heirlooms I had retained) when the phone rang. I picked it up, looking at myself in the mirror while I continued thinking about the jewellery. As I listened, I saw my body in the mirror stiffen as though someone had put a wooden board down my back. It was an extraordinary sensation, staring at myself as though it were not me out there, but a complete stranger who had turned as white as the bedspread.

'A boat exploded,' Freddy was saying. 'Edmund. They think Edmund was on it.'

Exploded? We had become so used to the word. Bombs exploded all the time, it seems. Harrods, Oxford Street, sandbags everywhere. Like an Arab country we had become. I remembered once seeing a huge black limousine draw up outside Harvey Nichols in Knightsbridge, and four women get out, all shrouded from head to foot in black and gold veils, with narrow slits for their eyes. While shabby London housewives stopped and stared, clutching their string shopping bags, these exotic apparitions were escorted hurriedly into the huge department store. What to buy, we asked ourselves as we shook our heads and went about our business. Chanel Number 5? A Gucci handbag? Pink tights?

'I must go to New York,' I said to Freddy. 'Be with Louisa. Can you – ?'

'I'll take the children,' he said at once. 'Poor Edmund. "Fuimus Troes, fuit Ilium et ingens Gloria Teucrorum."'

'But is it certain, Freddy?' I rushed on. 'How can they be sure?'

'"The great glory of the Trojans is departed,"'

he intoned. I stopped, feeling a twinge of the old mixture of frustration and admiration. Freddy was an anachronism, his mind rooted in antiquity, in dead languages and dead worlds, and yet his words somehow rang with a vividness and force that belied their archaism. Who else could have quoted Virgil on Hector's death and make it sound so poignant, so right?

'Edmund would have liked that,' I said, beginning to cry.

'Yes,' said Freddy, sighing. 'My dear, we are the losers.'

After I put the phone down, I remember crying some more as I took the green dress off and put the pearls and rubies away. I would not be needing them for a while.

DAPHNE

Penny phoned me from London to tell me. Louisa was too proud to tell us herself. Let them come to me, she said. Well, we did. I couldn't believe it at first, even after I read it in the papers – *FAMOUS PARSON'S SON DEAD IN BOAT EXPLOSION; IRA SUSPECTED*, the *Daily Express* said, with a lot of guff about Edmund's Oxford career and his life in London and his reclusive recent years in America and how this promising career had been cut short, etc. etc. Edmund had never been involved in Irish politics, had he? No one in his right mind would want to be, surely. I remember my father once saying that if the Irish had only decided to belong to America, everything would have been all right. Americans seem to love the Irish, if St Patrick's Day is anything to go on. Never have I seen such hysteria; all the 'wearing of the green' that day is enough to turn a leprechaun pink in shame. I steer a wide birth of the city on that day, while they all get drunk and throw things and make a terrible mess that the poor city has to clean up the next day. That's the only time an English accent is less than welcome in this country.

Parker was sweet about it. He said I must go at once to Louisa and stay as long as necessary. He said that there was a very good tennis court at the River Club, of which he was a member, and he would come in and play with me whenever I felt like a game. What a brick. I felt completely adrift at the awful news.

Edmund was the first person I knew well who had died; the first of our generation to go. I remembered hearing of a distant Oxford acquaintance who had committed suicide, but that was not like losing a limb, as I now felt on losing Edmund. He was part of us; he kept us together. How could he be so thoughtless as to leave us? We were lucky, of course, spoiled, you might say, to have had so little exposure to death. I thought of my grandmother's generation, all those young men snuffed out in the Great War. And my mother's brothers, cousins, and friends wiped out all over again twenty years later. Imagine all the people you had grown up with – gone. Gone like Edmund.

And I had never sent him back the photograph. I thought back to that strange evening after the July the Fourth party. What did he want? Why was he making a pass at me after all these years? Why was he carrying around that idiotic photograph? What did we mean to him? It didn't make sense. Perhaps if I had stayed, and talked to him . . . But I could never talk to him. I could never talk to Alan Moss, either. I never had to talk to Kumar. I don't believe we addressed more than six sentences to each other throughout our thrilling relationship. And now, Parker. What a relief. Game, set, and match to Parker Ferris.

But then, I never said I was the brainy one.

24

When Gerald heard the news about Edmund's
death, he became quite unhinged. Desperate,
drunk, raging, he roared around the house
shouting, 'Reports of his death are greatly exaggerated,' as though by repeating this old joke he
could somehow bring Edmund back to life. It
was a terrible sight to witness, and even Bert's
attempts at comfort could not relieve Gerald of
his grief.

Very late that night, after I had talked to
Louisa and arranged to go to her in the morning,
he came to himself and sat on the bed, and
talked to me in stone cold sober terms about
school, England, and Edmund.

'When Matthew Arnold decided that an aris-
tocratic education required Latin and Greek, as
opposed to the sciences, he set British education
on a course from which it never recovered,' he
said, drinking red wine and eating processed
cheese. (The processed cheese had been for Bert's
hamburger; it was proof of the extent to which

428

Gerald had become deranged that my great gourmet could eat it neat – and in its plastic wrap too, until I noticed and unpeeled it).

'I don't know what you mean,' I said, wondering if he would eat the Hershey's Kisses Bert had been given at a birthday party in their wrappers too.

'We were all trained to think logically – that was the goal to which our minds aspired. All our reading, writing, exercises, debates, were focused on that classical mode of thought invented by Aristotle and canonized by the Oxford School. Edmund was the star proponent of this method, the ideal pupil, the unblemished product. He was everyone's shining example, for he so perfectly epitomized the life of the mind considered essential for an English gentleman.

'Edmund, my dear Alice, was so skilled at rationalizing, at that glorious technology called logic, that he could always see – and argue – why *not* to do anything. Thus, as for all of Arnold's heirs, completely stifling the creative, risk-taking element in intellectual life.

'It left him, ultimately, with nowhere to go – except to devote his energies on an empty relationship, and when that wasn't enough, to blow himself up.'

'But did he blow himself up?'

'What else?'

'But surely nobody has said . . . Louisa didn't say . . .'

'Ah, Louisa,' Gerald said viciously. 'We must protect Louisa, the grieving widow.'

He made love to me that night with a kind of furious passion that I had never known in him before. In the morning we were very quiet, and then, without talking any more about it, I left to go to Louisa.

Daphne and Penny had already arrived at the Fifth Avenue apartment when I got there. Louisa was leaving for London with the children the following morning, so this was our chance to hold a wake, if that is what it was going to be, and show the old Bardwell Road flag for her and each other. Black dress it was, for all of us. There seemed something strange about our uniform, as though we were a modern-dance group preparing to perform some obscure piece of choreography. Louisa had poured on the hospitality, providing delicious foods and champagne from her latest caterer, and we all moved rather self-consciously to the bar.

Edmund had wanted to be cremated, which the Reverend Wales undertook to honour as a gesture of respect towards his dead son. (It also showed the Reverend's remarkably ecumenical and modern outlook on life, as he was careful to point out in his BBC TV interview in the following Sunday's God spot.) Our favourite man of the cloth did, however, also promise a large memorial service to be held in London at a future date, when all the proper spiritual and temporal messages could be imparted to his mourning flock about the greatness of the departed, and the departed's family, in particular his father, from whom Edmund had inherited etc. etc.

We sympathized with Louisa's inevitable encounters with her in-laws.

'I never understood how Edmund emerged from that background,' Penny said.

'Well, all our parents were a little bit screwy,' Daphne pointed out.

'Would you rather have a mad parson or a mad inventor as a father?' I said, helping myself to some smoked salmon.

'The less religion the better,' Penny said.

'Particularly,' Louisa said, 'when it's a question of suicide.'

'What do you mean?' Daphne said, pouring more champagne. We were hitting the bubbly quite enthusiastically, for reasons which will not escape anyone familiar with the kind of occasion we were celebrating.

'How do you think Edmund died?'

We all paused in our filling of glasses and nibbling of canapés.

431

'Must we talk about it? I mean, specifically?' wailed Daphne.

'Yes,' said Louisa.

'All right, tell us,' said Penny firmly, evidently thinking this the right psychological approach.

'Yes, tell us,' I agreed. We had all lived long enough in America by this time to know that 'talking about it' could, on occasion, be therapeutic.

'Don't threat me like an idiot,' Louisa said, sitting down in a huge armchair embroidered with what looked like parts of the Bayeux tapestry. 'All I'm saying is that you shouldn't believe everything you read in the papers.'

'But the IRA – the explosion – what do you mean?' Daphne stammered.

'Clever old Gerald,' I murmured.

'It seems everyone jumped to conclusions,' Louisa said in a bored voice. 'The police can't find any evidence of a bomb on the boat. They can't find any evidence of what they call foul play. They have told me, in confidence of course, that they believe he did himself in.'

We were silent. Outside, a police siren shrieked down Fifth Avenue.

'Oh, God.'

'He couldn't.'

'Why not?' Louisa stared at each one of us in

432

turn. She gripped the sides of the armchair, as though to spring at us.

'It's what Gerald thought,' I volunteered.

'Gerald knew him, but you didn't?' Louisa demanded, with a sarcastic laugh. She faced us, her eyes with red streaks in them. She must have been crying.

'You – you all thought you knew him so well. You knew what was "like him." You knew him, you admired him, you followed his career, you examined his marriage, you knew everything, didn't you? Don't think I didn't know how you lusted after him, and hated me for being in the way.'

She got up and moved towards us, glaring at each one of us as we stood, frozen in place, hands gripping forgotten champagne glasses, half-eaten olives.

'Of course you all knew him,' she went on, her voice rising sharply. 'After all, *you all slept with him, didn't you?*'

This time the silence was glacial. As the words embedded themselves in the heavily brocaded walls, Daphne, Penny, and I stared at each other and then at Louisa. We were like Kay in *The Snow Queen*, whose vision is suddenly distorted by an evil sliver of glass. What could we see in each other's face? Who was guilty? All of us?

Fuck Chuck, I thought. I felt my cheeks go pink.

'Do you want us all to go?' I asked feebly.

'Is that what you have imagined all this time, Louisa?' Penny said.

'Perhaps it would have been better if we had,' Daphne said. Penny and I looked at her and then at each other. Louisa sank back into the chair, exhausted.

'It doesn't matter now anyway,' she said. 'He's dead, and I should never have married him.'

'And you thought we should have liked to have been in your place?' Penny asked. 'Perish the thought.' But her voice wavered and she looked down as she said it, and I wondered what she was thinking. Has she perhaps, in the early days at Oxford, when we were all such beginners – had Penny and Edmund . . .?

'I think I could have helped him more,' said Daphne, walking towards the window. 'I know it sounds silly, but I think he once . . .' Her voice too trailed off, and she twitched the curtains absentmindedly.

'It wasn't like him to commit suicide, though,' I mused. 'It is not the act of a rational man. I still think it may have been an accident.'

'Suicide is profoundly rational,' Penny argued. 'Suicide is the ultimate act of control over one's life – and death.'

434

'Edmund always lived entirely in the conscious mind,' Louisa said. 'It seems so obvious, when you think about it.' She began to cry.

'Why did you never leave him?' Daphne asked. 'I could never understand that.'

'I couldn't. I had nowhere to go, nowhere to live, no money to look after the children with. How could I have lived? Besides,' she added, 'I kept hoping for a miracle. Everyone else saw nothing but good in him. I kept hoping one day I would wake up and look at him and be madly in love. I kept trying to stick to the rules. Silly me.'

We were all silent. Another siren whined in the distance.

'We won't, of course, spread this around,' Daphne said. 'After all, there is a reasonable doubt.'

'No,' agreed Penny. 'There's no point in opening up speculation, is there, Louisa?'

Louisa looked at the three of us with a small smile.

'Wouldn't he have been amused at us discussing so reasonably his death and its repercussions? So unlike us, he would have said, usually so hopelessly emotional.'

'Perhaps we have changed,' Penny said. 'After all, we have lived nearly half our lives.'

At that moment, we heard the children being brought home from the park by their babysitter.

435

We changed the subject with the skill of those trained to handle all social situations, and shortly afterwards, said our goodbyes. To our credit, the casual observer would never have known what had just gone on in that room. Perhaps there is something to be said for an English upbringing after all.

LOUISA

So calm, my friends. I admired their moderation. It made things easier. But of course they were guilty. They lied about sleeping with him. Even if it had not happened in fact, they were guilty in their minds. I didn't blame them, really. We had all slept with each other, in a way, thanks to Edmund. It was he who kept us together, insisting on seeing us all in the same way. Daphne ran away. Alice hid behind Gerald. Penny turned to a career. But we were all afflicted by Edmund's persistent image of the four of us, locked together in some idiotic, nostalgic dance.

That is why Alice, Daphne, and Penny did not walk out on me. They could not. Too much had become known between us. We belonged to each other. We belonged to each other as we did not belong to our husbands.

A week after Edmund died, I got a letter from him. It had been posted from Ireland the day before the accident. All it contained was part of a poem. I felt he was watching me when I opened it.

'My darling Louisa,' he wrote, in that elegant old-fashioned calligraphy of his, 'I wanted to send you this poem by Yeats. I would have read it to you, but you never gave me time.

> We were the last romantics – chosen for there
> Traditional sanctity and loveliness;
> Whatever's written in what poets name
> The book of the people; whatever most can bless
> The mind of man or elevate a rhyme;
> But all is changed, that high horse riderless,
> Though mounted in that saddle Homer rode
> Where the swan drifts upon a darkening flood.

All my love, Edmund.'

I didn't know what it meant. I rarely knew what Edmund meant. But if he meant me to be haunted by its elegiac beauty, he succeeded.

DAPHNE

Arrangements for my wedding helped put the endless thoughts about poor Edmund into the background. Parker and I had decided we must go ahead, in spite of the tragedy, and so we set the wedding date for October 1977. This was the year of the Queen's Silver Jubilee, our country's riposte to the Bicentennial, or so it seemed to me. By the time I arrived from New York the shops were selling off all the commemorative flags and mugs and plates and ashtrays at bargain prices. It was reminiscent of the sixties, when Freddy's Union Jacks filled the souvenir shops. In fact, the whole procedure surrounding my wedding contained a strong element of déjà vu.

For one thing, it was my second go at it, and I was feeling decidedly edgy about having this gargantuan show at the House of Lords. It was my mother and Parker who were responsible for it all. Parker was delighted that he would be allowed to have a party in the House of Lords, and had no intention of passing it up. Nor had my mother. Since all her friends and relations had been deprived of a party the first time round, thanks to the political stripe of my former fiancé, she was determined to give them a hundred-percenter this time to make up for it. We went to tea at the Lords to discuss it all with Daddy.

'Parker has a taupe Rolls, darling, like the ones at the Peninsula,' my mother told him in conciliatory tones. 'I'm sure I told you. And he has a French château in Little Hampton.'

'Jolly good,' said my father. 'There's a very interesting beaver colony near Littlehampton. I might go and stay with him and visit it.'

'It's not Littlehampton, Daddy, it's Southampton. And anyway, it's in America.'

'You mean this chappie's American?'

I looked round desperately. We were sitting in the House of Lords dining room, an august space faintly reminiscent of a railway-station refreshments lounge, with high ceilings, walls papered in the red rose emblem of Lancaster, maroon leather chairs with gold crests, and large portraits of unrecognizable Peers of the Realm framed in ornate gilt frames. The tablecloths and napkins were paper, and Their Lordships received their meal bills on the kind of receipt form used in fast-food establishments – showing democracy at work even in the highest chamber in the land, one supposed. Lord Fanthorpe's tone of horror at the news of the origins of his future son-in-law rang round the dining room, rattling the ancient teeth of the lords temporal and spiritual, some of whom looked up momentarily from their maroon and gold teacups or paused in the act of biting into the toasted tea cake with strawberry jam that was obviously a speciality de la maison.

'He's awfully sweet, darling,' my mother said soothingly, in her new deep voice. 'Loves everything English. And he's madly keen on Monty.'

'You mean he's a gambler?'

This time no one, spiritual or temporal, raised an eyebrow, assuming that Fanthorpe was yet another wigged-out member entering his dotage. Those hallowed halls had witnessed enough archbishops and earls, dukes and baronesses over the centuries keel over happily after finishing their tea cake and cup of Earl Grey, knowing they were breathing their last among their peers.

'Daddy, he's a businessman.'

'And Mr Ferris is a keen tennis player. Daphne's really playing wonderfully now.'

'Ferrets? He has ferrets?'

'I don't think so, darling. I never saw any. Of course he might have kept them in the garage. Did Daphne tell you he had ferrets?'

I sighed. My parents seemed even more dotty to me after my stay in America. My mother winked at me sympathetically.

'They have good teas here still, don't they, Daphne? I expect it's the result of a select committee. Old Charlie Herring-Bone always insisted on a special brand of Lapsang and Orange Pekoe when he came to stay with us, and he no doubt persuaded the Lords to do the same. No, I certainly don't remember ferrets. He did seem strangely drawn to frogs, now I come to think of it.'

'It's Earl Grey, Mummy,' I murmured.

'Is it? Do you know, ever since Mr Mailorder worked his magic on my vocal cords, something seems to have happened to my taste buds. Do you think there's a connection?'

'Splendid, splendid,' my father was exclaiming. 'Far too few frog experts around these days. Perhaps I can get him to join my Council on Water-Based Animal Relations. We're shockingly over-subscribed with otter chaps at the moment.'

'Anyway, darling,' my mother said to my father in the way she talked to infants, 'I want you to line up Marchbanks and Miss Teazle for the wedding reception here in the Cholmondeley Room.'

'What, again? Haven't we just had some frightful bash here?'

'It was not a frightful bash. It was our Golden Wedding, and everyone adored it. We want the tent and the food. Of course we'll have to find a church first.'

She looked round vaguely, as though hoping to see a friendly bishop having tea, who would jump to offer his services for the Fanthorpe nuptials.

'Must get back to the Chamber,' Daddy said, mopping his mouth with a paper napkin. 'Damn good, those tea cakes. There's a debate on the Shops Bill, do you want the shops open on Sunday, that's the question?'

No wonder people talk of revolution, I thought to myself as we said goodbye. A full-scale debate on Sunday shop opening – it was the kind of thing Alan Moss would have relished.

My mother and I went to the outer hall where we had left our coats. It was no common cloak-room, needless to say, except that it was self-service. Rows of hooks, each individually named, were provided for lordly coats. I had been going to hang mine on the one designated for the Duke of Edinburgh, until my mother, with an unusual spark of humour, had pointed out a better one. This was set off all by itself at the end of the rack, much more ornately carved than the others. It said The Prince of Wales.

'Do we have to have a church, Mummy?' I complained as I wrested my shabby mackintosh from the Prince's hook.

'You didn't have a church wedding with that frightful Moss,' she said. 'You deserve to have one now.'

I put on my mac, smiling again at the thought of Alan. Two doddery lords passed us on their way to the Chamber. 'Shops open on Sunday?' one of them said. 'Who on earth would want to shop on Sunday? That's when McCloud comes up to the house with the week's game.' The other shook his head in a bewildered fashion. 'It's those Labour chappies,' he said ruefully. 'They're ruining the country.'

Alan would have relished that too. Then and there, I decided to get in touch with him after all these years, just to tell him I was getting married again, and to find out how he was doing. Wasn't it ironic? My parents would have expired at the thought that it was going to the House of Lords that had made me want the frightful Moss once more.

PENNY

Guilt is a terrible thing. I don't know if I've ever been free of it. I had such beautiful things as a child. Too beautiful. I remember being asked to

a friend's birthday party, to which we were all
told to bring our favourite doll. My doll had a
beautiful fur coat with a hood and satin lining,
and since it was snowing, it seemed obvious that
she should wear it. But despite my mother's
urgings, I refused to put it on the doll. 'Too
fancy,' I muttered in explanation. (Too embarrassed, the symptom of guilt.) Though I cried
having to take my poor doll out in the snow
wearing only a cotton smock.

And now I must look at my own children and
bear the guilt – a different guilt. I brought it
upon myself, because of my own arrogance. I
thought I could make the marriage work. I
thought I was strong enough. I was proving the
power of my sex. It is true that today's world is
very different, and soon we shall have lesbian
marriages and artificially inseminated mothers
and test-tube babies. But I fear for those children as much as I fear for my own. Who do they
think they are, these self-indulgent would-be
parents, to twist nature to their whim? You
might as well bring into the world a child with
one leg as a child who has never known – and
will never know – his father. And I don't mean
those fathers killed in wars or by disease. Those
are real people, with faces, names, alive in
memory. I mean the others, the pods, the sub-

stances, the frozen liquids, substitutes for flesh and blood.

'Yes, dear, your father was simply a seed in a turkey baster, but never mind.' Never mind? A permanent cripple – that is what you have produced, you consumer of emotional fulfilment.

A turkey baster? I read it in a book. I'd rather laugh at that, than cry over Edmund. For Louisa was right, ultimately. I did want to sleep with him, that night in New York. I am guilty of that, and guilty of failing to do so; thus, perhaps, accelerating his desperation. I don't know. I'm not sure it was me he wanted. It was my part in the friendship, my connection to the past, that he was trying to keep alive. He had lost Louisa, and he knew it. All that was left was the three of us. And we, in the end, could not pull him through.

LOUISA

I saw Charlie last night. He wanted to meet me at our usual pub, but I reminded him it was Irish, and he saw the point. We finally made it to the Oak Room of the Plaza. I wanted somewhere big, dark, and anonymous, for I was very much afraid of what he was going to tell me.

445

I had phoned him about Edmund's death and
he had been wonderful. Came over to the apartment and brought me flowers, held me, consoled
me. With everything else going on, it was a
small moment of pure happiness for me. We
looked at the obituaries together. Not surprisingly, there was a gossipy piece in the *New York
Post* about it, because Rupert Murdoch had
brought in lots of Fleet Street journalists when
he bought the rag and they still thought
Edmund was newsworthy. I was gratified,
though, that even the *New York Times* had a
tiny paragraph about 'this promising English
scholar felled by Irish terrorism.'

Charlie understood at once how confused I
felt. I had told him then that I didn't want to see
him for a while, and he understood that too. He
knew I wanted a little space, to sort out my
feelings about Edmund, and how I was going to
go on alone, and how best to look after the
children. I should have felt wrong somehow,
learning how to be a correct and honourable
widow, while at the same time seeing the man
who meant most to me in the world. I felt how
Jackie Kennedy must have felt, having lived in
a marriage that had come to mean so little, on
her husband's death becoming once again the
wife.

But after a few weeks, when I had returned

446

from England and the memorial service and
dealt with all the Waleses and generally finished
the public appearances necessary on such occasions, I found that I wanted to see Charlie again.
Just for reassurance, really. To feel a woman
again. To make sure nothing had changed. He
couldn't meet me at once, because he said his
wife was sick and he had to stay in Greenwich
to look after the children. Was I right to be
suspicious? Since when did a senior officer at
Merrill Lynch become a house husband, unless
he was prepared to lose his job? Or was it that
Charlie, so open and honest, could not think up
a more convincing lie? I didn't dare to speculate.

The Oak Room was crowded, as usual, with
elegant young men and thin young women
looking round the room in case somebody
famous was lurking in the shadows. I chose a
table where I could sit with my back to the
window. I had once read in a novel of an ageing
woman who always chose this spot because it
was kind to her wrinkled complexion. I had
never forgotten the tip and now followed it
myself. The face is a funny thing. For years,
from about twenty-five to thirty-three, I hardly
saw any change in its appearance, and people
would comment about how young I looked.
Then suddenly, overnight it seemed, the skin
'fell.' Furrows appeared round my mouth, the

crinkles under my eyes became dry and harshly etched, my cheeks began to look hollow. People no longer commented on how young I looked, but instead remarked that I must have lost weight. It was not that. The soft, cushiony skin that I touch so enviously on my children had simply become worn out, and was now hanging on my face like a piece of threadbare fabric, exposing the bones.

Charlie sat down, bringing my usual vodka and tonic. He smiled and kissed my hand, but he was nervous and it showed.

'I've missed you,' I said.

'So have I,' he said heartily. 'You look wonderful, Louisa.'

I smiled. 'What shall we do tonight?' I asked.

Charlie took a large gulp of his scotch.

'There's a problem,' he said, looking at the ice in his glass and shaking it, like a child with a rattle. 'Uh, I have to go home early.'

I could feel my heart skid.

'Your wife still ill, then?'

'My wife? Oh, yes, she's . . .'

'Yes?' I said.

'The thing is, Louisa . . .' He shook the glass again, until I wondered if it was his hand that was shaking.

'Go on,' I said.

'I think we must stop seeing each other.' He

took a swig of his drink and looked away.

'We?' I said. '*We?*'

'Well, you and I . . .'

'Oh, I see,' I said. 'You have kindly made the decision for me as well. How thoughtful.'

'Louisa,' he pleaded.

'Do you know what I might feel about that? Have you ever wondered what I feel? In your lovely house in Greenwich, has it ever occurred to you to ask what I think? Of course not. That's too much to ask. Poor Louisa, down there in the city. I think we must stop seeing each other. Ha!'

'Don't,' he said. 'Please don't. I know it's awful. But . . .' He opened his hands in a helpless way. This was a man not used to such scenes, that at least was obvious.

'It's because of Edmund, isn't it?' I said helpfully. 'It was all fine and dandy as long as I was married to Edmund. It was safe then, I was under control, I had a husband, everything was just neatly tied up in a bundle. And then the fellow had to go and get himself killed, and at once everything changed.'

'My feelings for you haven't changed,' stammered the poor fool. 'I still love you, Louisa.'

'Phooey,' I said. 'You never had any feelings for me, so how could they change? What you liked was the situation. Here you had a nice married woman, who loved you and gave you pleasure and was always there when you wanted her. Every man's dream, what? It wasn't me you loved, it was the circumstance. And when the circumstance changed, goodbye Charlie.' I started to laugh. 'How about that? Goodbye Charlie!'

Charlie looked round, his face red with embarrassment. I noticed beads of sweat at the side of his vein-swelled temples. How disgusting he looked, swilling down his drink, chewing on the ice, an animal in a corner.

'Bloody Edmund,' I said, half to myself. 'He's done it again. Even from the grave!'

'Louisa,' he muttered. 'Please, don't.'

'Why not? *De mortuis*, you mean? Oh, but I suppose you don't understand Latin. Only English people know Latin. It's so useful. Gets you out of a hole in no time.'

I started to laugh.

'Louisa. Please. Shall I take you home?'

'Home? I'm just beginning to enjoy myself. It's my moment, isn't it? The woman's rejection. Can't I play it any way I want to? At least you should allow me that satisfaction. Not only am I a widow, but the one man in the world I loved has deserted me. That's great, that's just hunky-dory. Why shouldn't I say Goodbye Charlie?'

He sat there, frozen. I suddenly got bored.

'You don't take a hint, do you?' I said, getting

up. 'Well, if you can't leave, I'll do it for you. Thanks for the drink. This time it really is Goodbye Charlie.'

I walked as slowly as I could out of the bar. Perhaps all over the city little dramas like mine were taking place. I sometimes took comfort in thinking that. At that very moment, in some dark corner, another woman was being told that her affair was over. I could feel for her, for all of us. Sometimes I would look at couples in bars or walking along the street, trying to spot from their expressions whether they might be going through a similar scene. Morbid, you might say. Harmless, though. Jeannie would approve, regarding it as a form of networking. I sighed, wondering whether I was ready to rejoin her group. Its materialism was sometimes a little too honest, particularly coming from a crowd of rejected women. Once Jeannie and I were both asked why we did not leave our respective spouses. 'Are you crazy?' Jeannie said sharply. 'Marriage and divorce in this town comes down to who owns the co-op.'

And now I didn't even have that. I would have to move out. I had nothing. After all these years, I had nothing. And with time's winged chariot hurrying near, I knew it might already be too late to try again. I remembered Daphne once telling me that almost without exception, any man she had gone out with made a pass at her sooner or later. If only I could have had that knowledge, what a difference it would have made.

DAPHNE

Alan had a new car, a Porsche, and he made me get in it.

'Where are we going?' I asked.

'Don't ask.'

He looked so much the same that I almost laughed. His hair was thinner, and there was a little grey at the ears and back, but the craggy face and mobile expressions were completely unchanged, and the eyes seemed darker and more volatile than ever.

'Men are so lucky,' I said, fingering my laugh lines.

'Aren't we just,' he said, in mock-cockney. 'It's a man's world, luv, and don't you forget it.'

He revved up the engine and we zoomed through London. It was like an old movie: down Park Lane, past the Hilton Hotel, on whose roof I had told my mother of the end of my marriage and of my departure for Hollywood; through

Hyde Park Corner, past all the clubs where we had danced ourselves silly to the Beatles and the Rolling Stones, past the House of Lords, within waving distance of the Savoy Hotel where our wonderfully romantic honeymoon had taken place, and over Westminster Bridge. He was taking me south, to Peckham. I suddenly realized that. He was taking me home.

He stopped outside 4 North Villas, one of those ugly Edwardian semi-detached brick houses built to contain an urban working class. I had been there with Alan only once or twice in my married life, on account of his belief that his parents needed protection from my class superiority, which of course I would manifest in all its arrogance by criticizing the ducks on the wall or plastic-covered upholstery or whatever else he regarded as vulnerable to my snobbish eye. That I found his parents warm and friendly and decidedly easier to talk to than my own he always interpreted as an insult, a condescending pose from Lady Bountiful.

On this occasion there was no warning about ill-advised remarks, only a brief and edgy explanation that his mother was very ill.

'But Alan, how awful. I didn't know. I should have brought her some flowers or something,' I whispered as he propelled me through the front door.

He glared at me. 'And been like the Hospital Visitor in her fur coat, dispensing charity? No thank you.'

He hadn't changed.

He took me into the parlour, as they called it, which had been turned into a sickroom. Mrs Moss lay in a hospital bed by the window, with bottles, cotton wool balls, and a rubber tube on a nearby table. She was breathing in short, raspy gasps.

'Hello, Mum,' he said, bending down to kiss her. 'Look who's here.'

I stepped forward nervously.

'Hello, Mrs Moss,' I said. 'It's wonderful to see you.'

Her face lit up with such genuine pleasure that she suddenly looked like a little girl. Alan grinned and nodded at me.

'It's the old woman, Mum. Come back to see us. She's getting married again, to a rich Yank. Much more suitable than poor old Moss 'ere, who couldn't afford to buy his old girl so much as a bracelet from Woolworth's.'

'Oh, shut up, Alan,' I said, laughing.

'He hasn't changed, has he?' Mrs Moss whispered, looking with pride at her son. 'Just the same old terror. But he's doing well now, you know, Alice.' She stopped for a moment, to take some breaths. 'He's having things done on the telly all the time. We never get to go out, Dad and I, in case we miss something.'

I looked at Alan, who shrugged self-deprecatingly.

'Well, I got a few jobs, is all,' he conceded. 'I do a lot of TV documentaries now. It's more lucrative than the stage. And a lot easier on the digestive system.' He patted his belly, which looked a little more generously rounded than in my day. Not surprising, when you consider the cuisine.

'And you're getting married again, then?' Mrs Moss held out her hand to me. 'I hope you'll be happy, luv.' Her hand dropped on the bed and she closed her eyes for a minute.

'We'll be going, then, Mum,' Alan said quickly. 'Is Dad around?'

'He went to get some cigarettes,' Mrs Moss said, breathing with difficulty. 'Isn't that ridiculous? Mr Moss with his cough, fit as a fiddle at seventy-five, and me like this. Well, you have to laugh.'

And she did, a cheerful, strangled sound that brought tears to my eyes. Alan was as moved as I was. He kissed her and held her hand and kissed her again. I tiptoed out of the room and waited for him by the car. I remembered how he had hated sickness and the smell of hospitals.

We drove back in silence for a while.

'Thank you,' I said. 'You paid me a great compliment in bringing me there.'

'She always liked you,' he said. 'I can't think why.'

He looked me over and we laughed. I felt utterly relaxed with him, as I never had when we were married. I felt I knew him, I knew how to deal with him, I knew how to live with him. I had grown up.

'So what do you want to marry this old money-bags for then?' he asked, as we raced round Elephant and Castle. 'It sounds the death to me.'

'Parker's a good man,' I said. 'I need what he can give me.'

'A million dollars, you mean.'

'If you like,' I said. 'Now I can produce all your plays for you.'

'No handouts, thank you, luv,' he said. We crossed the Thames, which looked misty and beautiful in the late afternoon light.

'Shall we go to bed then?' he asked. 'Just for old times' sake?'

So we did. Not at the Savoy, nor in Kilburn, but in my parents' bed in Cadogan Gardens. It was hilarious. I was pleased to show Alan how much I had learned since my pathetic efforts all those years ago (not my fault, as I was careful to point out to him), and he was delighted at the

456

strange mixture of old and new that our bodies were to each other.

'I can feel the beady eyes of Lord Fanthorpe looking down on us from a great height,' he said afterwards, lighting a cigarette and looking mock-nervously round the chintz-and-Chippendale room.

'Oh, Daddy wouldn't mind. It's a natural function after all. We could say we were just doing what otters do.'

'Otters? Your Dad should be put in a glass case and exhibited. "You should study the peerage, Gerald – it's the best thing in fiction the English have ever done." By the way, how is Gerald? Did he fall apart after Edmund's death? Or wasn't that "good form"?'

'Well, it wasn't "good form" to explode in a boat. Not the code at all, don't you know. He was pretty shaken up, yes. But Alice was marvellous. She's becoming much mellower recently, I don't know why. I like her a lot more than I used to.'

'Well, we're all mellow now, luv,' Alan said, rubbing his hair with a rueful gesture. 'It's like politics. After a bit you have to face the fact that politics is fantasy disguised as reality. That's why I'm out of it. All the people you thought were doing good things turn out to be as corrupt as the institutions you're trying to overturn. The arsehole who ran my drama section turned out to be cooking the books. Christ, what a turn-up, eh?'

'Do you need money, Alan?' I asked suddenly.

He chuckled. 'Not from you, darlin',' he said, kissing my nose. 'No charity from ex-wives, thank you very much. You can do something else for me, though.'

'What?'

He whispered lengthily in my ear, and at the end I had to laugh.

'All right,' I said. 'Why not? It seems just the right thing, somehow.'

We dressed and worked our way through the huge flat. 'Scenes of former glory,' Alan said, picking up a silver ashtray and tossing it up and down. 'Your mother didn't trust us then, so why should she trust us now?'

I remembered Mick and Fred drinking Chivas Regal and looking as though they wanted to overturn the furniture.

'Wasn't it awful,' I said.

'Awful.'

We looked at each other and groaned. As I put my arms round him to kiss him goodbye, I could feel something hard in his pocket. He hadn't changed. It was the ashtray.

25

ALICE

Everyone turned up in force for Daphne's *secondes noces*. Nobody wanted to miss this 'wedding of the year,' as Lady Fanthorpe had instructed *Jennifer's Diary* to pronounce it. There had been a few stumbling blocks along the way. One was the business of the church. Lady Fanthorpe had been forced to reconsider her position when the archbishop of Canterbury, backed into a corner after a fete-opening ceremony, reluctantly refused her plea to officiate at the momentous event, citing Church of England regulations concerning second marriages. The Church of American Saints in Earl's Court, unusually dilapidated for a piece of American real estate, was the only House of God that would accept Daphne in her soiled condition, Americans being in this, as in so many cases, more flexible when it came to the separation of Church and State. The Reverend Jerry Madeira, a former dentist from Tenafly, New Jersey, assured Her Ladyship, in the shadow of his

peeling chancel, that his service was just as good
as the English one, its only drawback being that
the marriage would unfortunately have absolutely no legal standing in the eyes of British
law.

This indeed was something to chew on; the
upshot being that Daphne was once again forced
to pay a call at the Chelsea Registry Office with a
pliant but bewildered Ferris, while Gerald and I
again took up our familiar roles as witnesses. The
military adviser to small South American dictatorships remained at her post as registrar, her
face unmarked by all these years of coupling. We
examined her expression closely for signs of recognition, but her mind was presumably closed to
optimistic recidivists.

Afterwards, we once more repaired to the
Markham Arms, filled now with youths in
leather jackets and studs rather than androgynous Terry Stamp look-alikes.

'I don't know which I'd rather have,' Gerald
mused.

'What a great English pub,' Parker said,
downing his warm beer with enthusiasm.

'It's funny to be here again,' Daphne said.

Funny did not seem quite the appropriate
word, but Daphne seemed serene enough in this
place so filled with memories. Of course almost

any place is filled with memories if you live long enough.

At least the second part of the day was an improvement on that earlier go-round of marital celebration. The Church of American Saints had been decorated with flowers, and its pock-marked walls were less obvious in the subtle candlelighting of the interior. All Parker's friends, needless to say, had flocked into town in chartered jets. Moss Bros must have been quite cleaned out of tails (or cutaways, as the colonials called them), and grey toppers. Correct to the last platinum cuff link, some of the visitors looked so ill at ease that the casual observer might have thought them candidates for a train-ing course for maître d's. Others, lean and sun-tanned, looked as though they still carried their tennis rackets in their hands. Parker's best man was Wally Ivanhoe, who stood up near the altar, red-faced and obviously suffering a terrible thirst. His wife, Iphigenia, was sitting in the front row, recognizable by her enormous gar-denia-covered hat, from which trailed a lavender veil. The only Americans there we knew well were Cliff and Jeannie. Cliff was wearing a pink-striped shirt and yellow and green plaid trousers; Jeannie wore a black dinner jacket and black bow tie.

'Surely they got dressed in each other's

461

clothes?' Gerald said in mock bewilderment. Gerald was in good form, having been awarded a prize by the Hotels Association of Great Britain for writing an article in his new restaurant column in praise of the English breakfast. In it, he extemporized on the nuances of English bacon, as compared to that produced by unmentionable machines, his preference heavily in favour of the thick-sliced, flabby, fatty version found on home shores.

'You are very old-fashioned,' I whispered back.

The Oxford contingent was well-represented. Four of our children were taking part in the ceremony: Camilla, the Weatherings' youngest daughter, with Nina Wales, and our Bert with Ben Wales as pages. The Wales children looked pale, I thought, and apprehensive, but who could blame them? Speaking objectively, I have to admit that Bert, in spite of the fact that he insisted on wearing his American football shoulder pads under the ruffled shirt ordained by Lady Fanthorpe, held up much the best during the service. He told me later he was going through all the players in the NFL in his mind to pick what he considered the best all-round team to play in an international super bowl. He said this took his mind off the fact that Daphne was marrying someone else.

On the bride's side of the aisle Penny looked

chic in a green silk dress with some stunning
rubies at her throat, while Freddy, hair dyed
pale yellow, wore a blue suede suit, a wide pink-
striped tie, grey tails, and one jet earring. Their
children also wore blue suede suits designed, it
turned out, by their father. In the pew behind
the Weathering family were three young men of
foreign cast, who from time to time attended to
the children, offering them handkerchiefs when
they sneezed, showing them the place in the
prayer book, tying a recalcitrant bow. As I
watched, one of them began to give Freddy a
neck massage.

'Isn't that going a bit far?' I murmured to
Gerald.

'Who's old-fashioned now?' he retorted.

Also in their row was a person of feminine
appearance and demeanour, but well over six
feet in height, with false eyelashes and what
looked like a wig. This character seemed to
belong quite comfortably in that particular pew,
but something bothered me about her. She
looked vaguely familiar. My attention was distracted by the arrival of Louisa, looking magnificent in white moiré, with a small white hat
decorated with an aigrette. I then noticed something else about her.

'Am I wrong, or has Louisa done something
about her bustline?' I whispered to Gerald, who

was making violent hand signals to Bert outside the church door. Gerald's eyes fixed on the subject in question.

'Va-va-voom,' he said, adding, 'but so old-fashioned.'

Suddenly some very large lights were turned on, brilliantly illuminating the audience. The lights were like those one sees on film sets, and I could not imagine what they were doing in a church. Handel's *Water Music* carilloned out, and we all craned vulgarly to see our Daphne in her moment of glory. I had wanted her to buy a dress from a shop in New York which had a sign in the window saying, Number One in Bridal Illusion, but she said crossly she did not see what her marriage had to do with illusion. Instead she had another off-white dress from Liberty's. Perhaps Lady Fanthorpe got a teeny commission.

Daphne walked down the aisle on the arm of her father, whose tails were fluffy with what looked like animal fur. Parker stepped out stiffly, like Montgomery before his men, while Wally Ivanhoe, his hand groping uselessly for a drink, drooped beside him. Iphigenia had changed her headgear and was now wearing a crown.

The lights were making us all sweat rather heavily, and several people began complaining.

464

But the service went on as it had for centuries, until the Reverend Madeira came to the part where one always tended to hold one's breath. 'If any of you can show just cause why they may not lawfully be married, speak now; or else forever hold your peace.' There was a small hush, and then Madeira gasped, his face turning the colour of a rare steak.

Someone was walking up the aisle. The pews twittered with excitement. A piece of peeling stucco fell on the floor with a splat. Somebody on the American side popped a piece of bubble gum.

'CUT!' said a voice. Suddenly all the lights went out and the church was plunged into cooling darkness. Alan Moss appeared at the bride's side and shook the parson's hand.

'Alan Moss!' we gasped. The rest looked stunned. He looked wonderful, in beige chamois and white trousers. He talked to Daphne intently for a few minutes and then kissed her. He shook hands with Parker, whose bewildered expression was becoming a habit, then waved to some invisible henchmen, turned on his heel and walked back down the aisle. As he passed me, he thrust into my hand a crumpled brown paper bag. 'Give it to Daphne,' he said gruffly. 'It's for her.' And with that, he was gone. I clutched the bag and put it in my coat pocket. It felt small and hard – a grenade, perhaps.

Madeira picked up the prayer book and continued the service, his voice hoarse with excitement. The guests rustled and fluttered, and Lady
Fanthorpe could be heard booming in her new
resonant baritone, 'The beast. Still the same
socks!' Another piece of the church fell into the
aisle.

The service was completed without more ado,
but Alan's diversion had somehow distracted us
from further serious religious contemplation.
Parker, the picture of bravery in the face of
confusion, led his bride down the aisle at a
military clip. Daphne looked as though she were
trying not to giggle. I was dying to know what
Moss had been doing. Had it something to do
with sabotaging her current pursuit of bourgeois
respectability?

We milled about outside the church, practical
matters for the moment displacing our curiosity
about the Moss episode. To get from Earl's Court
to the House of Lords on Saturday afternoon was
a problem to which the best minds in the country
were inadequate. To our great relief, we saw
that the Americans, practical as always, had
solved it by lining up the most impressive array
of limousines we had ever seen. Shrieking like a
rookery, we dived into the cars, hats, handbags,
and children flapping behind. Our American
friends, bemused at this scavengerlike charge

by the cream of English gentry, could only nod and smile and wave the drivers on to their impressive destination, while remaining behind, stalwart to the end, wondering what other customs of the country they had somehow failed to assimilate.

The Cholmondeley Room at the House of Lords had little to recommend it except its pronunciation, which was 'Chumley.' It bore no relation to the handsome exterior of the House, boasting no fine furniture or decoration, only a stiff portrait of lots of lords in the Chamber hanging on one wall, and a view through the gothic French windows leading out to the terrace and the Thames.

Daphne and Parker stood in the receiving line kissing people, with Lady Fanthorpe at their side. Lord Fanthorpe was already at the bar, pinned in place by Iphigenia Ivanhoe, who had evidently determined to make contact with British titles. Her crown was attracting His Lordship as headlights do a rabbit.

'What on earth did Alan want?' I whispered as I gave the bride the obligatory peck on the cheek.

'I'll tell you later,' Daphne said. 'Wasn't it hysterical?'

'Well, not for us,' I said. 'Those lights were damn hot. And where are the consent forms?'

Pressure from guests in the queue cut short
this conversation, and I moved with Gerald to
the champagne department and the outside. The
terrace, partially covered by a striped awning,
looked its best with flowers and sunshine. Tables
were laden with food, which Gerald started in
on with his usual zest. 'This reminds me of a
pâté I had in Boston in '74,' he said, 'or was it
Philadelphia in '75?' My husband had reached
the age where experiences were labelled by date,
a habit only necessary to those whose memories
would otherwise be confused. His gustatory
memory, however, remained undimmed by time,
an attribute I found very appealing. We had
been eating well together recently.

'Still the same old Gerald, I see.' It was
Freddy, earring swinging, surrounded by the
young men we had seen in church.

'This is Gianni, and Plon-Plon, and Kendo,'
Freddy said, waving a hand. 'Aren't they too
perfect. They are Nannies, dress designers, and
musicians, all three. One simply has to be ver-
satile these days. My United Nations, I call
them, Italian, French, and Japanese, you see.
They are going to play a little Mozart to send off
our Daphnis and Chloe later today, aren't you,
darlings?'

Gerald and I showed enthusiasm for the musical departure. 'Had any good projects lately, Freddy?' I asked.

'My dear, Fugate, I have no time for projects any more. Since my Penelope has become such a success with her gallery, I must be on permanent duty as father to our large brood. And that includes the United Nations, of course. Caspar, Chloe, Camilla, and Crispin adore them, thank goodness. I want to introduce them to Lady Fanthorpe. I so adore her new voice, she'd make a fabulous Amneris.'

Like the Pied Piper, Freddy drifted away, followed by the many children in his charge. As we watched, the six-footer in the wig who had sat in church with them came up to me and gave me a big smile.

'Hello, Alice,' the person said. 'It's been ages. I don't expect you'll remember me actually, but I was at Oxford with you.' There was a pause. 'I was Charles then. Now I'm Clarissa.'

'Aha.' This seemed the appropriate response.

'Isn't this fun, Daphne getting married to that extraordinary man.'

'He's a very good tennis player,' I said stoutly.

'It was so awful about Edmund, wasn't it? I could hardly believe it. An Enemy of Promise all right.'

I couldn't bring myself to answer. Luckily, I didn't have to.

'And Alan Moss stopping the show. I remember being terrified of him at Oxford. He was so – left-wing. What does it all mean?'

'I wish I knew,' I said. I remembered him now. He invited me out to coffee once when I fell off my bicycle outside St John's. Weakened by the accident (my gown had got caught in the spokes), I was unusually nice to this amiable giant, and this led him to think we were embarking on an affair. I soon disabused him of his error, and for a few weeks after that he sent me haiku, or at least I assumed they were haiku, that being the customary euphemism at Oxford for very short unrhymed notes that made absolutely no sense.

'Do you still write haiku, er, Clarissa?'

Hearing a child's cry of fury, and knowing whence it came, I did not wait for an answer, but tore myself away from this nostalgic encounter and rushed to the eye of the hurricane, where I found Bert pulling Camilla's headdress off, while Nina and Ben urged him on.

'Don't interfere,' Penny said in my ear. 'I want her to fight her own battles.' I was about to protest, when another scene caught my eye. It was Cliff and Jeannie, surrounded by admiring guests.

'Isn't that something?' they were saying. 'What an extraordinary idea,' and other such exclamations of wonder, accompanied by crude

470

guffaws. On moving closer, I saw that the focus of their attention was Cliff's belt, a large leather affair with an ornate buckle that seemed innocuous enough, but on closer inspection turned out to represent a couple fornicating, the male organ neatly slotted into the female to form the aptly named, on this occasion, clasp. The metal figures were sculpted in the style of Giacometti, thus further elongating their already exaggerated anatomies.

'How revolting,' I said, as Cliff affably clasped and unclasped it to demonstrate its finer points of workmanship. Jeannie greeted me warmly, causing a small flicker of guilt to lick through my bones.

'Are you still married then?' I said lamely.

'Well, it's what's called an open marriage. We're sharing a whole lifestyle,' Jeannie explained. 'We're living with another couple. He's a ski instructor, and she's an air hostess.'

'Aha,' I said, for the second time that day.

Jeannie laughed. 'I know it's not your personal reality, Alice,' she said. 'I just love it here in England, Now I know where all your shit is coming from. I just wish Edmund could be here to tie up the package.'

'Oh, Jeannie,' I said sadly.

Cliff disentangled himself from the clasp fans and gave me a hug. 'Here's my girl,' he said.

471

'She brought Princeton its only touchdown of the day, right, Alice?'

'Right,' I said, cheering up.

'We ought to try it again sometime, what do you say, Alice?' he went on, grinning at me.

'There's Daphne,' I said hastily. 'Do let's see what on earth Alan Moss was doing.'

Daphne announced, amidst waves to guests, that Alan Moss was making a documentary for American television about crippled earls, battered babies, and the Welfare State. He had asked her if she would allow him to shoot some footage of her wedding to show the decline of the British upper classes. The guests loved it, particularly the British upper classes. 'In a film, what?' I heard Daphne's aunt shriek to her deaf husband. 'I say, what fun!' We learned later that the Reverend Madeira had agreed to let cameras into his church, partly because it was a well-known American custom, and partly because he had been assured that a generous gift would be forthcoming to refurbish the interior of the Church of American Saints, whose congregation currently consisted of a few secular American widows and the occasional pissed Australian who had fallen in after a typical Down Under night in the Earl's Court Road. As an additional sweetener, Madeira, who had let drop the information that he had an as-yet-unpublished manuscript available, was promised that the opus would be read and critiqued by a professional agent or editor provided by Alan Moss.

'But why does your wedding have anything to do with the decline of the British upper classes?' wondered a few doubters.

'Alan's point is that in times of crisis the British aristocracy will traditionally start taking in new blood to revive the line – generally in the form of rich Americans such as Consuelo Vanderbilt or Mary Leiter – my circumstances being simply a gender reversal, as is natural in a period of great change in contemporary sex roles.'

Jeannie had her notebook out and was filling it rapidly. 'Wow, I never thought of it like that,' she murmured.

'The reason why the aristocracy has lasted so long is in part its skill in adapting when necessary to new conditions, thus inhibiting the revolutionary momentum and defusing the proletarian opposition.'

'A skill of which Daphne herself is the perfect exponent,' Gerald said to whoever wanted to listen to him. 'In terms of adaptation, the woman is a miracle of modern science.'

'But wait a minute, Daphne,' I said, trying to catch her attention. 'You're playing the wrong tape. This is your second marriage, remember? The old mixed doubles game?'

'Oh, I know. Don't worry, Alice darling. Parker and I are leaving in a minute. I just wanted everyone to get the picture.'

'It'll make a great book,' Jeannie exclaimed to Cliff. 'How about it? *Fermentation or Feminism – An Adaptive Approach.* I'll get the group on to it right away.'

At that moment Lady Fanthorpe began beckoning people towards the entrance to the Cholmondeley Room, where Lord Fanthorpe was being jockeyed into position, with Daphne and Parker squeezing in beside him.

'Ladies and Gentlemen,' His Lordship began in ringing tones. 'Friends and animal-lovers, we are here today to celebrate the opening of the first wildlife centre devoted to the domesticated variety of the European polecat, that is, the hunting ferret.'

'Order! Order!' cried a few guests familiar with Parliamentary procedure. 'Would the Noble Lord care to . . .'

'Daphne and Parker, darling. They just got married,' came the contralto tones of his wife.

'Ladies and Gentlemen, my fellow Americans,' Lord Fanthorpe began again, without missing a beat, 'let us salute this transatlantic mating between two fine specimens of Homo sapiens.

This union thus postpones, we hope, the appearance of our species on the endangered list, what?' Roars of hearty laughter greeted this more seasonal introduction, and the bride's father, flushed with this success, raised his glass in the toast, 'The Bride and Groom.'

We all intoned the words, raised our glasses, and then drank, noisy slurpings eching round the room. Always an odd ritual, it seemed particularly tribal that day. If there had been a song, we would have sang it.

Expectant glances awaited the traditional reply from the groom, who looked like Ethelred the Unready.

'Nobody told me,' he whispered to Daphne furiously. 'I had no idea I had to make a speech. I have no game plan.' Looking around sternly, he picked up his arm as though to serve, and said: 'Field Marshal Montgomery was a first-class general. His strategy and tactics were invariably right. I only hope I can make as good a husband. Thank you.'

Who could not be disarmed by such a speech? Daphne gave him a warm kiss and we all had a few more toasts to him, her, them, and ourselves. After that, the party disintegrated. Parker and Daphne left, amidst cries of farewell, to their honeymoon at a tennis camp in Arizona. The United Nations played Mozart with fiendish enthusiasm, unheard by anyone over the din of departing guests. Cliff took his belt off and donated it to Wally Ivanhoe, while Iphigenia looked furiously on, attempting to adjust her tilted crown.

Louisa, Penny, and I came together, as we collected children and coats.

'Well, off and running,' Penny said, nodding at the departing Daphne.

'I wonder if we'll ever meet at this sort of occasion again,' I said.

'Have you written me off then?' Louisa said.

'Not with those,' I said, indicating her new, improved figure. 'Did that awful Dr Heller do it?'

Louisa glared at me. 'How can I get married again? Nobody will let me. Edmund is irreplaceable so why bother? He might as well still be alive for all the difference it's made.'

'Louisa!'

'That's all right,' I said. 'If she can't say it to us, who can she say it to? She's said everything else after all.'

Louisa looked at us and shrugged.

'We belong to each other,' she said. 'That's the thing about England I miss. No one has friends anywhere like they have in England.'

'As Guy Burgess said to Stephen Spender,' I said.

The Last Romantics

'Edmund certainly believed that,' Penny said.

'He would have loved this,' I said. 'An Oxford Reunion.'

'We were the last romantics . . .' Louisa murmured.

'Speak for yourself,' I told her.

'Sentimental claptrap,' Penny added.

We all laughed.

'Come on,' Penny said. 'Aren't there some people out there who are waiting for us?'

'At last,' I said, 'I've got a song. "We'll meet again, don't know where, don't know when . . ."'

They groaned. As I was putting my coat on I felt something in my pocket. It was the crumpled paper bag Alan Moss had given me.

'Wait a minute,' I said. 'I forgot to give this to Daphne. It's from Alan.' They watched as I opened the bag. It was a silver ashtray.

I picked up my song, and soon the others joined in, and, in our best Vera Lynn voices, that is how we walked into the courtyard outside the West Gate of the House of Lords and left Daphne's wedding.

'"But I know we'll meet again some sunny day . . ."'

Outstanding fiction in paperback from Grafton
Books

Barbara Pym

Quartet in Autumn	£2.50 ☐
The Sweet Dove Died	£2.50 ☐
Less Than Angels	£1.95 ☐
Some Tame Gazelle	£1.95 ☐
A Few Green Leaves	£1.95 ☐
No Fond Return of Love	£1.95 ☐
Jane and Prudence	£2.50 ☐
An Unsuitable Attachment	£2.50 ☐
Crampton Hodnet	£2.50 ☐
A Very Private Eye (non-fiction)	£2.95 ☐

Elizabeth Smart

By Grand Central Station I Sat Down and Wept	£2.50 ☐

Maggie Gee

Dying, in Other Words	£1.50 ☐

Ruth Prawer Jhabvala

A Stronger Climate	£2.50 ☐
A New Dominion	£1.95 ☐
Like Birds, Like Fishes	£2.50 ☐

Clare Nonhebel

Cold Showers	£2.50 ☐

To order direct from the publisher just tick the titles you want
and fill in the order form.   GF1281

All these books are available at your local bookshop or newsagent, or can be ordered direct from the publisher.

To order direct from the publishers just tick the titles you want and fill in the form below.

Name _____

Address _____

_____

Send to:
Grafton Cash Sales
PO Box 11, Falmouth, Cornwall TR10 9EN.

Please enclose remittance to the value of the cover price plus:

UK 60p for the first book, 25p for the second book plus 15p per copy for each additional book ordered to a maximum charge of £1.90.

BFPO 60p for the first book, 25p for the second book plus 15p per copy for the next 7 books, thereafter 9p per book.

Overseas including Eire £1.25 for the first book, 75p for second book and 28p for each additional book.